PRAISE FOR *A YEAR IN THE WILD*

'There's family conflict, romance, funny anecdotes, poaching and all kinds of intrigue – in other words, something for everyone.'
– KAYANN VAN ROOYEN, *GO!*

'I laughed, cried and basically didn't want the book to end.'
– NICI DE WET, *You*

'Brilliantly written, sharply witty and excruciatingly funny – a must for anyone who knows the private lodge industry and those who enjoy a good laugh!'
– HUGH MARSHALL, involved in guiding and lodge operations for over 25 years

'*A Year in the Wild* is more than an amusing and entertaining account of game lodge goings on; it is also a coming-of-age tale of two brothers who explore life, love, lust and loss.'
– CHRIS ROCHE, Wilderness Safaris

To the memory and legacy of Johnson Mkansi.

A YEAR IN THE WILD

A Novel

JAMES HENDRY

MACMILLAN

First published in 2011 and republished in 2013

This edition published in 2022 by Pan Macmillan South Africa
Private Bag X19
Northlands
Johannesburg
2116
www.panmacmillan.co.za

ISBN 978-1-77010-827-1
e-ISBN 978-1-77010-828-8

Editing by Sharon Dell
Proofreading by Tracey Hawthorne
Cover design by publicide
Cover photograph by James Hendry

BACKGROUND

Angus MacNaughton (26 years) and Hugh MacNaughton (22 years) are brothers.

They dislike each other.

A lot.

From the moment that Hugh bit Angus at a family picnic in the summer of his second year, the brothers have been locked in a feud. They have competed for their parents' approval, for scholastic achievements and sporting accolades and, later, over girls. Instead of growing out of their rivalry, age has deepened the brothers' mutual disdain.

The family has finally had enough. As a last-ditch attempt to forge a brotherly bond between the two, Mr and Mrs MacNaughton secure them each a job at an exclusive, five-star game lodge – Sasekile Private Game Reserve. They manage to convince (bribe, in the case of Angus) them to work there for a year ... together. Hugh agrees to the idea because he has just finished hotel school and is keen to apply his training at a five-star establishment. Angus acquiesces begrudgingly because he is thoroughly bored working in a corporate environmental consultancy.

DRAMATIS PERSONAE

THE MACNAUGHTONS

Angus

Angus is 26. He is a biologist by training but has never really fixed on one thing. He is a talented but introverted musician. Angus has dark hair, angry blue eyes and is shorter than average. He has never come to terms with the fact that his younger brother is the taller sibling. He is intelligent but incredibly cynical and sarcastic – he easily puts people's noses out of joint and has a vicious temper. Angus's job at the lodge is that of ranger. He starts off as a trainee ranger, the lowest form of lodge staff.

Hugh (String Bean or SB to his brother)

Hugh is 22. He is a recent graduate (cum laude) of a distinguished hotel school in Cape Town. There has never been any doubt that Hugh would make a career in hospitality. He is tall, blond, extroverted and jovial – the polar opposite of his brother. He loves to act and entertain people. Although not as openly sarcastic and cynical as Angus, if one were to observe them carefully one would see that they share a similar sense of humour. Hugh joins the lodge as an assistant camp manager, which initially makes him senior to his elder brother.

Julia

Julia is the beloved sister. She is 24, pretty, independent and clever. Born between the two brothers, she means different things to each of them. To Angus, she has always been a friend and confidante because she understands him. Their closeness in age meant that they moved in the same circles at school (although Julia was considerably more popular than her sarky brother).

To Hugh, Julia is something of a mentor. She is his source in the unfathomable world of women. Hugh tells her everything and she, in turn, dotes on her little brother the way Angus never has.

SASEKILE LODGE STAFF

Heads of department

PJ Woodstock (42) – General Manager. Calm, collected, unfazed by much and highly competent.

Anton Muller (32) – Head Ranger. Large man (six-foot-five), grew up in Pretoria. Played provincial age-group rugby. Limited intelligence.

Jacob 'Spear of the Lowveld' Mkhonto (41) – Conservation Manager. Mighty Shangane of immense strength. The 'go to guy' whenever there is trouble (bush fires, elephants in camp, etc.).

Arno van der Vyfer (35) – Maintenance Manager. Hates everything and everybody. Chain smoker.

Hilda Botha (38) – Head of Finance. 120 kg. Unmarried.

Simone Robertson (21) – Children Minder. Looks after young guests. Pretty, happy, no-nonsense and full of fun.

Camp management

Anna Trescott (32) – Rhino Camp Manager. Dark-haired, striking. Quiet, mysterious and very self-assured.

Jenny Sutherland (23) – Main Camp Assistant Manager. Attractive, blonde and competent young woman with a good sense of humour. From Johannesburg on a two-year stint in the bush.

September Mathebula (45) – Tamboti Camp Manager. A Shangane of great character. Prone to a heavy whisky before dinner. Immensely loveable man.

Melissa Mandelay (25) – Kingfisher Camp Manager. Ditsy with a severe lisp. Very few social graces. Massive cringe factor.

Rangers

A team of 16 including:

Jeff Rhodes (22) – the other trainee ranger. Angus's neighbour. A likeable yet gormless creature.

Alistair 'Jonesy The Legend' Jones (27) – One of the senior rangers. Good-looking, clever, arrogant. A man's man and a woman-slayer.

Carrie Bartlett (30) – Only female ranger. Quiet, butch, excellent bush skills.

Sipho (23), Jamie (33), Duncan (28), Richard (24), Mango (22), Jabu (25), Brandon (26) – and various others.

Trackers

A team of 16, the most important being:

Elvis Sithole (40) – 120 kg. Highly experienced, silent, Shangane tracker.

Johnson (54), Vuvuzela (45), Zub-Zub (34) and One-eyed Joe (28).

Other lodge staff

Candice Anderson (25) – Receptionist. Answers the phones. Very inefficient. Elastic morals.

Efficient Mathebula (54) – Security Guard. Unenthused with his job.

Ashleigh and Natasha (both 20) – Trainee Chefs. Attractive girls from Cape Town, doing a year's practical training at the lodge.

Outside of the lodge

The Major (85) – Angus and Hugh's senile grandfather.

Trubshaw (35 dog years) – The MacNaughton family hound – a profoundly stupid Staffordshire Bull Terrier.

PLACES

Sasekile Private Game Reserve – 'the lodge'
Sasekile is a five-star establishment situated on a private game reserve in the north-eastern Lowveld of South Africa. It adjoins the Kruger National Park and as such is a game-viewing paradise. The nearest town is the dubious settlement of Hoedspruit.

The lodge consists of four camps: Main – twenty-four beds; Tamboti – twelve beds; Kingfisher – eighteen beds; and Rhino – six beds. They are all beautifully appointed. The camps are situated adjacent to each other on the banks of the annual Tsessebe River.

All operations of the lodge are run centrally (finance, maintenance, laundry, rangers, trackers, kitchen, etc.).

The staff are housed in a widely spread staff village and there are just over 150 people employed at the lodge, most of them are local, rural Shangane people.

Avusheni Eatery
The staff canteen.

Twin Palms and the Staff Shop
Staff entertainment venues separate from the lodge.

The Office
A number of rooms where the administration staff of the lodge work (general manager, finance, switchboard, maintenance, etc.).

The Rangers' Room
A large room next to the office where the rangers and trackers gather before and after game drives to shoot the breeze, share heroic stories, sort out issues and use the Internet, etc.

The Maintenance Shed
A dingy storeroom close to the Twin Palms.

DEFINITIONS AND TERMS

Boet – Afrikaans word for brother. Used as one might use 'buddy' or 'mate'.

Boma – Acronym for British-Officers-Mess-Area. Place where soldiers used to surround a central fire with their wagons and a thorn fence in order to keep predators and the enemy at bay. In the lodge, the boma is an outside eating area surrounded by a split-pole fence. It has a central fireplace, cooking area and bar.

Bru – Afrikaans word for brother. Also used as 'buddy' or 'mate'.

Doos – Afrikaans word for box. Used as an insult.

Koppie – Rocky outcrop or hill.

Lowveld – North-eastern, low-lying (approximately 400 metres above sea level) part of South Africa. The Kruger National Park and the country's other premier game-viewing destinations are in the Lowveld.

Mfo – Shortened form of the Zulu word mfowethu, meaning brother and used more literally as 'friend'. Also used in Shangane.

Moer – Afrikaans word for kill.

Pap – Afrikaans word for porridge.

Pax – A word for guests or passengers used normally by airline and hotel staff and preferably not by personable lodge staff.

Shangane – A group of people who settled in the Lowveld at the turn of the 19th century. They are mainly a combination of the Tsonga people of Mozambique and an Nguni clan called the Ndwandwe and were named after a man called SoShangane.

Skinder – Afrikaans word for gossip.

JULIA MACNAUGHTON - EMAIL FOLDER

The following pages contain a series of weekly emails from Angus and Hugh to their sister Julia. They trace the brothers' lives over the course of a year at Sasekile Private Game Reserve. Also included are a few notable responses from Julia, the MacNaughton parents and others.

From: 'Hugh MacNaughton'
Sent: 09 January, 17h58
To: 'Jules'
Subject: Arrival!!

Hey Jules,

We have arrived and it's so exciting to be here!

Obviously, Angus insisted on driving the whole way because of his greater age. In light of my genuine commitment to make this bush experience as bonding as possible, I didn't mention his 2 auto accidents – both within the last 6 months. Despite his somewhat terrifying skills behind the wheel, the trip was not too arduous and we made good time into the Lowveld.

Scenically, the drive was stunning. As we descended the escarpment, the landscape changed completely and the last 2 hours from the Strydom Tunnel were breathtaking. The views out east into the Kruger National Park were spectacular, bathed in the endless green shades of summer. There was such a sense of space. My enjoyment of the Lowveld vistas was briefly interrupted by an 18-wheeler with which we almost collided because of Angus's vile temper.

In spite of this near-death experience, we have both arrived in 1 piece and I have settled in adequately.

Of course, I can't speak for Angus when I say "adequately". My accommodation, although not luxurious by any stretch of the imagination, is far superior to his little den of filth. Good god, I laughed when I saw his poor excuse for a room. It makes our Standard 6 boarding school dormitory look like something out of a *Leading Hotels of the World* catalogue. Angus, naturally, demanded to swap when he laid eyes on my small but cosy cottage, complete with en suite bathroom and air conditioner, but I was having none of it.

Unfortunately for my beastly sibling, he is but a lowly Trainee Ranger and I am going into an Assistant Camp Manager position. This means that although the organisational structure out here is pretty flat, I am actually more senior until he qualifies. The Ranger training here takes anything between 3 and 6 months so I am rather enjoying my start to the year. This situation is not helping to create a brotherly bond, but I suppose that is Angus's problem for the moment.

The people here are really fantastic – everybody has been extremely welcoming and PJ, the General Manager, seems like a great guy. He has been working in the bush for over 10 years and although very laid-back on the surface, he seems to be incredibly competent. I think this year in the middle of nowhere will provide me with some useful skills and experience for the future.

PJ has already set out my induction week during which I spend a short time in every Lodge department so that I get to know everybody and learn how the Lodge works from soup to nuts. It seems like a great idea. The programme starts tomorrow at the Morning Meeting. Apparently, all frontline staff have to attend this daily gathering. It is here that the guest arrivals, special requests and general Lodge logistics for the day are discussed.

On a slightly embarrassing note, I must add that I've spotted a girl who has already made a big impression on me. Although I have not yet introduced myself, she seems really nice. Of course, given my track record, she has probably been dating the Head Ranger for years and is less available than Gisele Bündchen. Time will tell, I suppose.

Please send my best to The Major when you go through to see him over the weekend.

I will write soon.

Lots of love,

Hugh

From: 'Angus MacNaughton'
Sent: 09 January, 18h30
To: 'Julia MacNaughton'
Subject: Hades

Dear Julia,

We've arrived.

Alive.

That's the sum total of what's good.

I've no idea how Mum and Dad managed to convince me that this was a good idea. Some brothers just never like each other. Hugh and I have nothing in common and never will as far as I'm concerned. I will try to remain open-minded about the whole thing but it was a bad idea from the outset.

Hugh thinks I'm a rubbish driver and had the bloody temerity to try and drive us here. I may be shorter than String Bean but he supposes that my 26 years to his 22 mean nothing. What a git. I obviously told him to get stuffed and then conveyed us safely to this place – a place that the Good Lord clearly forsook decades ago. Allow me to tell you a bit about my home for the next year.

The brochure describes the place as a 'paradise'. Well, it might be set in a natural paradise but that's where it ends. The collection of creatures they have masquerading as five-star staff here would make the thieving macaques of Gibraltar recoil in horror. The general manager is about as awake and effective as a corpse. He, however, is like General Patton when compared with the moron employed as the head ranger.

This cretin is my immediate superior and thus in charge of my training for the next four months. Train? He could no more train a person in the art of breathing than teach me anything. His name is Anton and he is, of course, about eight-foot-three, has biceps the size of Namibia, calves that look like my thighs and the ego of Alexander the Great. These vast characteristics are offset by two things. Firstly, a pair of shorts that look like he's owned them since he was in Grade 1 and, secondly, an incredibly small brain. His employment here is as mystifying as the construction of the pyramids.

The room they have given me to live in is smaller than the bath at home and I can touch opposite walls when I lie on the bed. There are bats living in the roof. This means that it looks like someone has been throwing custard pies at the ceiling and the whole place smells like that vile guano mother puts on the roses every year. The bathroom I must share with the other trainee, Jeff, who seems quite friendly but is utterly gormless and manages to souse the place every time he goes in. Perhaps he was once intelligent and has been rendered a twit by Anton's 'training'.

Bloody Hugh is in a veritable palace. For some reason his hospitality degree has made him some sort of manager – imagine my delight when I heard that. It would seem that management holds learning to open wine bottles in higher esteem than a science thesis.

I start my induction programme tomorrow. String Bean was handed a neatly bound file with his orientation all laid out for him. I was handed a piece of paper that looked as if a rhino had sneezed on it. I think Anton had written my induction on it but I couldn't tell. Induction means that I'll be spending time in all the Lodge departments.

Sorry I cannot be more positive but I must be honest about things. At least I'm back in the bush. I'll console myself with the sunset.

Hope you're fine.

Your pissed-off brother,

Angus

From: 'Mum'
Sent: 10 January, 08h03
To: 'Angus'; 'Hugh'
Subject: Safety

Dear Boys,

I am very glad to hear that you have arrived safely. I did worry about the long drive together but it seems you managed not to kill each other on the way. Angus, please be very careful in the bush; don't do anything silly just to spite anyone.

Hugh, please don't put too much pressure on yourself to achieve too much too quickly. Take your time to learn about the lodge thoroughly.

Dad and I wish you both all the very best of luck for the year and hope that you will come to appreciate each other's many wonderful attributes.

All our love,

Mum and Dad

From: 'Hugh MacNaughton'
Sent: 16 January, 18h05
To: 'Jules'
Subject: Induction

Hey Jules,

It's been a frantic first week out here. This whole induction programme is constantly being re-prioritised behind endless pressing issues.

Yesterday, while in the middle of an ironing demonstration with Fortunate and Aletta, who work in the laundry, I was pulled out to fold welcome cards for a big group that will be taking over the whole camp later today. The day before that, I joined the Bush Banqueting team (they are responsible for meals which happen in the middle of the bush – if you can believe it). I helped clear a breakfast which had been prepared for the Main Camp Guests somewhere on the banks of the Tsessebe River. The breakfast site had to be abandoned halfway through the meal as what I'm sure was 80% of the reserve's bee population invaded. The strawberry jam and orange juice were covered in thick layers of drowning or drowned bees. Hell's delight, it was unpleasant – I was stung twice!

When not working in the Lodge departments (mostly at night), I shadow the Manager of Rhino Camp. Her name is Anna and I think she is about 10 years older than me. She is a very warm and helpful person, and pretty stunning to look at in a dark, intimidating sort of way. I am learning a huge amount from her.

Of course, these rather unglamorous jobs pale into insignificance when compared to what has quickly become part of Angus's daily routine. He is, in his lowly position as a Trainee Ranger, now responsible for cleaning up the staff bar every morning. This place normally resembles Tiger Tiger in Cape Town after a first-year Pig Night party. To be honest, I don't know if he is going to last here. He utterly detests everyone and, understandably, most of the staff are not particularly crazy about him either. I guess time will tell.

Excitingly, I had my first interaction with the fair Simone (the girl I mentioned in my previous email). The good news is that she is not the better half of Anton the psychotic Head Ranger, but unfortunately she "sort of" has a boyfriend in Johannesburg. What the hell is wrong with all the women I meet? "Sort of" – what is that supposed to mean? On the bright side, I suppose "sort of" is better than simply "having" a boyfriend. I am still optimistic that I might actually get my act together with this 1. She turns 21 this year, so is only a year younger than me. Simone is quiet, reserved, very attractive and really interesting.

I wonder if The Major still has contacts with any Lebanese gangs in Joburg who might help me with eliminating the "sort of" hurdle in my quest for love and passion.

Induction, which is not even nearly on track, is supposed to end in 4 days, at which point I am to begin working in 1 of the camps. At this rate I'll still be on induction by the time we are supposed to leave in December, but hopefully that will not be the case.

Good to hear from your last email that The Major is feeling upbeat and that his racial slurs towards Ivy have diminished slightly. Quite amazing that she continues to work for him. I suppose they have grown old together but she'd probably have a real case at the labour court. One thing is for sure, he would not last long out here.

Chat soon and lots of love,

Hugh

From: 'Angus MacNaughton'
Sent: 16 January, 18h32
To: 'Julia MacNaughton'
Subject: Dogsbody

Dear Julia,

Well, I've made it through week one.

Fifty-one to go. Joy and rapture.

This week I came to understand the role of 'trainee ranger' – my present exalted designation.

Dogsbody.

I am basically the camp skivvy. I have no status, and hardly anyone has bothered to remember my name. Anton, my immediate 'superior', has taken to calling me Shark Crap (because apparently shark faeces reside at the very bottom of the ocean).

I have one standing duty during my training and that is to clean the staff bar each morning. This is what my sorry existence has come to – cleaning up after a bunch of drunken peons. Please ask Mum and Dad if this is what they intended when they paid for my private schooling and university education.

During my 'induction' I finally managed to see the whole lodge. I say finally because, but for menial tasks, I am not allowed to leave my bat cave where I'm supposed to be studying. Obviously, I can't adhere to this because I'd die of ammonia inhalation on account of the bat excrement. I've taken to going on short, illegal, exploratory walks outside the camp with a book or two. The lodge sleeps about 60 people in four different camps that are closely joined to each other. Each camp overlooks the meandering Tsessebe River which dries up in the deep winter.

My first day of induction was spent out on the Main Camp deck, supposedly helping the butlers serve meals. They did not want to be helped as they thought I would want to share their tips. The camp manager is a smooth guy, about my age, I think – Andrew Jackson. As far as I can tell, his job is to talk to the guests and check them in and out – tasks of such daunting intellectualism that it's no wonder he's paid more than twice the sum I am.

Other enthralling induction tasks have included ironing in the laundry, cleaning the rubbish bins at the recycling centre (a task, I note, that is not in Hugh's induction), helping fix Land Rovers, cutting garlic in the kitchen and going out into the bush with Anton for a conservation induction. It was during this last section, to which I was actually quite looking forward, that my initial impressions of Anton were confirmed.

He is a human (?) with the brain of a dung beetle.

We drove around the reserve while he regaled me with stories of the guests he has bedded and how well he can shoot. When I asked him if any of his conquests were women he looked angry. When I asked him if he'd ever fired a weapon at anything other than a box, he looked like he might kill me, so I pointed at a bird and said, 'Ooh, what's that?' to change the subject. It was a brown snake-eagle but he called it a Wahlberg's eagle. I decided against pointing out this obvious mistake.

But the highlight of my week was meeting Hilda Botha, the head of finance. This hippo-esque woman must weigh in excess of 120 kg. (I watched her eat half a cake on the Main Camp deck when the guests had gone on game drive the other day.) She has a personality to match her looks and is clearly still bitter about the Boer War.

Although she could barely be arsed to tell me the time of day, she did manage to mumble what my salary is going to be. I nearly puked when this little gem spewed from her gargoylous head. R1 750 a month. Yes, that is correct. The princely sum of R1 750. I bet Hugh is earning three times that.

I feel I should also update you on my 'room' situation. The bats seem to be multiplying at a terrific rate. Well, why wouldn't they? The insects in the vicinity of my cave outnumber the grains of sand in the Sahara. While I appreciate the bats catching these for me, the custard-coloured ceiling boards are starting to bow under the weight of their evil-smelling droppings. It's a matter of time before it all comes crashing down on my head as I sleep.

I asked my gormless neighbour, Jeff, why he has the bathroom habits of an ill-educated ape and he looked hurt.

So that's it for this week. As you can see I'm still having a marvellous time out here and I cannot thank Mum and Dad enough for organising this for me. Please send my regards to The Major. If he were here he'd have killed at least one of the idiots I have to deal with by now. Please also give Trubshaw my best. Must run, I have to go and clean some vomit off the staff bar floor.

Your still-pissed-off brother,

Angus

From: 'Hugh MacNaughton'
Sent: 23 January, 17h57
To: 'Jules'
Subject: Elephant!

Hey Jules,

Good grief, it has been an interesting week!

Just as this whole induction thing was coming to an end, I had the misfortune of joining Angus's new boss on 1 of his big 5 jaunts into the bush. This formed the final component of my induction programme – learning about the primary reason Guests from around the world spend such brutal amounts of money to come here. After my horrendous experience with Anton, I am convinced that if it is "wild animals" drawing such flocks of wealthy, nature-seeking humans to this area, then the majority of them would be more than satisfied simply meeting the Head Ranger. The guy is an absolute lunatic and if it were not for the amusing reality that he is Angus's superior, I would wish him a painful demise.

Having assumed that Angus was simply being his pessimistic and sarcastic self, I was upbeat about joining the Head Ranger for a day out in the field. After all, I have become rather enthusiastic about the bush lately and I was interested to see what separates this piece of wilderness from the mass of competitors located in the same reserve – it really is amazing how many other lodges there are down here.

Anyway, we drove around in Anton's (and only Anton's) V8 game drive vehicle, while he mumbled a few seemingly inaccurate details about the history of the area. (Surely it cannot be possible for the original inhabitants of this land to have copulated with female lions before skinning them for their coats and then eating their meat?) At 1 point, I stupidly enquired what Anton believed made him a top-class Game Ranger. There was a pause. Then, without even looking at me, he accelerated, moving from third to fourth and then to fifth gear.

"I'm not gonna tell you why I's so bloody good, but I am gonna show you!" he shouted above the roar of the V8.

11

Instantly realising my mistake and reluctant to ask further questions on account of the velocity at which we were moving, I asked,

"Where exactly are we going?"

I couldn't really hear his reply because of the sheer speed at which we were moving. But I think he muttered something along the lines of,

"Deep south, *boet*. Elephant graveyard!"

After driving fast for about half an hour, Anton relented and pulled his vehicle over to the side of the dirt track. He explained that just ahead of the thick bush in front of us was what is known in poaching circles as *"Tifile tindlopfu* – The Elephant Graveyard". Apparently, almost a century ago, just after the Kruger National Park was proclaimed, a bunch of disgruntled Boer hunters demonstrated their outrage with an act so heinous that it rocked the fledgeling world of conservation. In the dead of night a group of elite poachers surrounded a large breeding herd and forced them into a circle with flaming torches and rifles. They then burned a ring of fire around the helpless beasts.

"Over a hundred elephants were burned to death that night," he said, "and even today they has never forgotten."

At this point I thought it was most certainly necessary to float my third and final question,

"Um ... well, what the hell are we doing here then, Anton?"

"*Boet*, you want to see why I's so good – follow me." He picked up his .458 rifle. "We're walking in!"

I have no idea why I followed him. I privately questioned this brute's sanity as I wandered behind him through the thick bush. And then, not unexpectedly, all hell broke loose.

Barahhh rahhhrahh rah!

An old cow elephant, who was probably still mourning the demise of her great grandparents, came hurtling out of the bush. All I could see was grey and green and dust and branches everywhere. Anton let off a warning shot to no avail and then shouted,

"Fok, boet, this puppy's coming – run for the car!"

I don't know how we came away alive from the ordeal but I can only think that the good Lord himself must have intervened. I was sure it was over when I saw the cow in full charge. I just remember turning, running and not stopping until I reached the vehicle.

On the way back to the Lodge, Anton said that he was 1 of only a handful of Rangers who were "brave" enough to walk into the elephant graveyard. That, he explained, is what makes him such a dynamic, cutting-edge Ranger. It will disturb me for the rest of my days that he chose the word "brave" to describe his behaviour. Words such as "stupid", "arrogant", "dim-witted" or, my favourite, "braindead" would have been far more appropriate, in my opinion.

I am sorry that my email this week has been so concentrated on this incident, but the whole situation shook me up quite a bit and I am sure you will hear from Angus as to the trials (his experience, not mine) of our welcome drinks at a recent staff party.

Lots of love,

Your (happy-to-still-be-alive) brother,

Hugh

From: 'Angus MacNaughton'
Sent: 24 January, 18h27
To: 'Julia MacNaughton'
Subject: Welcome vomit

Dear Julia,

Three weeks down, 49 to go. Gee, how time flies by when you're ecstatic.

I was still being inducted this week and, as such, was helping Portia and Queenie (housekeepers) with general duties. My incompetence at bed-making quickly became apparent so I was banished to cleaning loos.

There was a real positive to the week, however.

Hugh was almost savaged by an elephant.

He has yet to recover from the shock and when I'm feeling miserable (a lot of the time) I think of him running for his life from the enraged animal and chuckle merrily. Mum and Dad's plan to tighten our brotherly bond is going for the ball of chalk that I predicted. Anyway, I'm sure he'll give you details (with some exaggeration about how close it was, no doubt). My only comment, and this is strangely on his side, is that the incident was undoubtedly caused by the gargantuan ego of that utter knobthorn, Anton.

Enough of String Bean's woes.

This week, there was what the troop (metaphor for less-evolved primates intended) here call a Twin Palms. This is both a place and a staff party.

The Twin Palms (place) is the large, dark staff bar (which I mentioned last week) with a buggered sound system. The place smells like the bowels of Satan and I would not venture in there without shoes and a valid tetanus shot.

A Twin Palms (staff party) is when people go to this vile den, drink all manner of booze and then behave like creatures that would make *Australopithecines* embarrassed. Trainees, like me, are usually not allowed to attend a Twin Palms but I was invited to this one in order to receive my 'welcome drink'. SB and I were stood up on boxes and handed glasses of some evil concoction. PJ – the general manager, no less — made a speech welcoming us. We were then called upon to down the abominable liquid to screamed drinking songs. Naturally, Hugh was the big hero because he is able to 'down' things. I just gag and splutter. It ended with everyone patting Hugh on the back and telling him how great he is, while I fell off my box and retched in the corner. Just my scene.

I left soon after but was treated to tales of who had done what to whom at the next morning meeting. Apparently, a drunken Anton followed Jenny (Main Camp assistant camp manager) home. He tried to 'lunge' (local parlance for 'kiss') her at her door, she side-stepped and he hit his barren skull on the door frame. To my delight, he is sporting a cut above his left eye.

On the subject of Jenny, I had an altercation with her this week. She is not fond of me. I was playing my guitar quietly in my room — a good way to forget about my predicament. I left the door open because of the appalling guano stink. She walked past on her way from the staff village to the camp and stopped on hearing the sweet notes I was producing. She asked what I was doing.

'I appear to be playing the guitar,' I replied in a tone that implied, 'piss-off immediately'.

She ignored my sarcasm and continued.

'You should come and play in the camp for our British guests tonight. They're a young crowd and I think they'd like it.'

Andrew, the permanent Main Camp manager, is on leave so perhaps Jenny was trying to introduce entertainment innovations.

Julia, you know how I hate to play for people, so I said,

'I believe I'd rather take the strings on this instrument and hang myself from the roof beams of this bat-infested cave.' There was a silence.

'You're going to carry on being miserable if that's how you're going to treat people,' she said evenly.

'Thank you,' I replied. 'That is a profound piece of wisdom. Are such pearls free or do I need to pay you?'

She shook her head and glared at me. 'Fuck you,' she replied quietly and stalked off.

That's it for this week. I'll try and keep SB from being ironed by some animal until next time – only for Mum and Dad's sake, though.

Your 'unable-to-down-things' brother,

Angus

From: 'Hugh MacNaughton'
Sent: 30 January, 17h45
To: 'Jules'
Subject: Angus trying to ruin my life – again

Hey Jules,

Just to let you know, I hate Angus.

Just when I felt that there may have been a chance for our relationship to reach a stage where we could actually tolerate 1 another, he had to go and do something like this! It is quite clear to me now that he has no intention of even trying to build our non-existent brotherly bond. I have really been making an effort – even defending him when other staff have asked me,

"What's up with your brother? He's always so angry with life." But now, I care no longer.

After watching him meet with the fair Simone in the half-light of the maintenance shed on Monday night, I am convinced that he is purposefully trying to undermine me and take what is currently most important to me. Stupidly, I told him that I thought she was cute and that I actually quite like her. Knowing him, he probably distorted my innocent confession of affection and told her that I had soiled my pants during the recent elephant charge in order to give himself a chance with her.

Although dim, the scene before my eyes in the maintenance shed was all too reminiscent of my Matric dance after-party. As I'm sure you remember, Angus arrived home late after some heavy drinking at a local bar. He seduced my partner and enticed her down to the tool shed at the bottom of the garden. Who could forget my anguish at finding them spooning atop a bag of Natal Agri fertiliser?

Although it is no lie that I had to change my underwear after nearly dying last week, I really don't think he needed to bring it up with Simone, who is now bound to hate me. I am terrified to even see her. I mean, what sort of self-respecting woman in her right mind wants to go out with somebody who has a reputation for soiling himself every time he sees an elephant? Everybody around here is right: Angus really is an arsehole!

Apart from that, however, things are going well. I have now started working in camps – something I have been looking forward to for some time. PJ has posted me to Tamboti Camp as the Assistant Camp Manager. It is the oldest camp here and has an ambiance of history which makes it special. The camp has 6 suites (12 Guests at capacity), a pool, a boma and what seems like a nice team of staff.

September (a name not a month) is the Camp Manager and he has worked here for over 20 years. He started in the Main Camp as a gardener at about the same time I arrived at the Sandton Clinic back in '87, and he has systematically worked his way up over the years. Over and above weeding, his credentials include security, tractor driving, butlering and my position. He has a wonderful manner about him and Guests take to the 45-year-old Shangane very well.

To be honest, though, there are very few procedures and systems in place and the camp is a bit of a free-for-all for both Guests and staff, so I am excited at the prospect of adding some value from my experience in the Cape Hotels last year. I have been working at the camp for 3 days now and I'm really enjoying it.

That said, I'm still in an absolute state about what must surely be the end of my chances with Simone.

I can't believe Angus. This act will not go unpunished. I am already plotting my revenge for him ruining my first real chance with a reasonable girl in 22 years. Melissa, 1 of the less intellectual female members of the staff team, is about to receive a note – from him.

Hah, hah, hah. Things are about to get drastically worse for my elder brother and if you think you're going to warn him, I would have already sent the offending letter by the time I click send. It is unfortunate that it has come to this, but revenge is the only way to make this situation right.

Lots of love,

Hugh

P.S. Hereunder, I have attached a copy of the note for Melissa – I have just returned from slipping it under her door. Welcome to the house of pain, Angus!

Dear Melissa,

I have wanted to write you this note for some time, but have not had the courage until now. Nevertheless, I have noticed you around a lot recently and am beginning to fall for you. I become all tongue-tied every time I see you and have consequently decided to confess my affection for you in written form. I do hope you feel the same way and that our relationship may 1 day materialise into something more than me simply having to visualise our 2 bodies entwined.

Huggies and kissies,

Angus

From: 'Angus MacNaughton'
Sent: 30 January, 18h35
To: 'Julia MacNaughton'
Subject: Ridiculous

Dear Julia,

This is the fourth email of my trials in the wilderness. I shall perhaps publish these one day as a warning to parents who insist on interfering in the natural hate that some siblings have for each other. Black eagles engage in siblicide and so do hyenas. Their parents don't complain.

Speaking of death, I have just heard one of the most ridiculous things. Ranger training in this utter madhouse includes two weeks of solo, unarmed walking around the reserve. This is done in order to learn the roads and, in the words of Anton, '... decide if you are man enough for this job'.

In case you think this sounds reasonable, consider that it has to be done armed with nothing but a radio and a first aid kit. The 'first aid kit' pre-dates the Anglo-Zulu war, and is so empty that I believe it to have been used to dress the wounded British at Isandlwana. What sort of self-administered 'first aid' do you think would be most effective when I have a buffalo inflicted, pawpaw-sized hole in my midriff and a first aid box containing a band-aid, a condom and a safety pin?

The imminent physical trauma I face is made worse by the fact that the vast Hilda hasn't managed to sort out my medical aid yet. Naturally, Hugh's is all fine despite the fact that the most dangerous part of his job is laying out toothpicks.

In preparation for these walks, Anton is going to take me into the bush with one of the trackers. His name is Elvis. Elvis is a giant of a man and, unlike most of the people here, does not feel the need to talk incessantly. In fact, he does not talk at all so I think we'll get on fine. The idea behind this experience is to (again in Anton-speak) '... check out some *gonnies* [lions] on foot. Check if you man enough to stand down a fokken charge.'

Bloody fool idea, if you ask me. If you don't get a mail next week, you'll know I've been consumed by Africa's largest cat.

I had to spend a day this week helping Simone – the child minder – with a large group of small and disgusting children. She quickly banned me from talking to them after I spanked one for spitting on his sister. I think SB is quite keen on the girl – imagine if he managed to succeed in snaring a girlfriend. She, astoundingly, doesn't seem averse. She asked me a few questions about him while we were packing away the equipment in the dingy maintenance shed that evening. She's obviously myopic.

After my little, shall we say, awkward, exchange with Jenny last week, PJ ordered me to play my guitar in the Main Camp boma for a large Swiss family. I was not amused and put together a playlist that, coupled with the guests' dull sense of humour, should ensure that I'm never asked to perform again. I opened with the Metallica classic, 'Enter Sandman', and followed this with Guns 'n Roses, 'Welcome to the Jungle'. When I announced that the next song was going to be my own composition, 'Eat the Baby', Jenny asked me to leave.

'Angus, what the hell … what are you doing?' she asked as I packed away my guitar outside the boma.

'What?' I asked mildly.

'You know what!' she shouted, '"Eat the Baby"? Are you mad? They'll never come back here!'

'Oh, really?' I feigned concern. 'What a dreadful thought. Pity, 'cause they're such fun.'

'You're a real ...,' she snarled, searching for the appropriate description.

'Rock star?' I offered.

'Oh, piss off,' she hissed, turned on her heel and walked back to the boma. So ended our second meeting. I think I've successfully cured everyone here of any desire to see or hear me play again.

Until next week, I'll be trying to forge a relationship with the enormous Elvis so that when the time comes to view lions on foot, he'll allow me to hide behind him.

Your ever-popular brother,

Angus

From: 'Julia MacNaughton'
Sent: 03 February, 18h00
To: 'Brother A'
Subject: Mum all aflutter

Hey Angus,

It was the usual post-dinner scene in the MacNaughton household last night. All of us in the family room: Mum doing her embroidery, Dad engrossed with the contents of the paper and me trying to follow the nuances of this week's episode of *The Wire* – a difficult task over the less-than-subtle snoring emanating from Trubshaw's form resplendent on the sofa next to me.

During one of the ad breaks, I remembered that you were about to set off on your unarmed walk thing and mentioned it to the assembled company. As you might expect, Mum completely flipped out.

'Oh, my poor boy!' she cried, spilling several embroidery silks onto the floor. 'Douglas, you must do something about this!'

'I'm sure the people in charge know what they're doing down there,' replied Dad from behind his paper. 'I'm sure he won't be the first person to do these walks.'

'How can you be so callous? Just thinking of our precious first-born wandering defenceless and all alone in the wilderness is enough to drive me demented! You'll have to phone the general manager ...,' she continued.

'Mmm,' replied Dad, turning the page.

'Oh, Douglas, you're so impossible sometimes!'

You will no doubt be reassured by the fact that Trubshaw's gentle, Hummer-like breathing remained unchanged throughout.

Be careful out there, see?

Love,

Jules

From: 'Hugh MacNaughton'
Sent: 06 February, 18h12
To: 'Jules'
Subject: Sweet revenge

Hey Jules,

Life is peachy.

I have thoroughly enjoyed working at Tamboti Camp this week; 2 different Guests generously handed me US$100 worth of gratuities, and Angus hasn't said a word to me. Revenge is sweet and my plan to make his life more miserable than it already is has worked better than I could possibly have imagined. The entire Lodge is now convinced that he is having a steamy affair with Melissa (the rather dim-witted young girl who runs the camp next door to Tamboti). Her incessant and often incoherent babble on the radio had been irritating me throughout the course of last week so I thought I would kill 2 birds with 1 stone, so to speak. She is the secondary victim in my cunning plan to get even with my beastly sibling.

Melissa, not surprisingly, sucked up the whole thing and some heated banter ensued when she confronted Angus late on Thursday evening. Amazingly, and quite fortunately for me, she was suppressing feelings for Angus – it truly couldn't have worked out better. Apparently Angus's only friend, Jeff, who lives next door to him, couldn't keep his mouth shut when he overheard the goings on. I really don't feel bad about it. It's the least our brother deserves for meddling in my quest for romance. I doubt he'll be trying anything in the maintenance shed after this!

As far as life at Tamboti Camp goes, September has given me a lot of responsibility. I close the camp on most evenings; I open up with the Butlers at 06:00, while September arrives for breakfast at 09:30 when the Guests return from game drive. I now check in all Guests for the day, while he joins them for drinks (quite a few) before dinner. While I am working far harder than the actual Manager, I marvel at his ability to tell stories to the Guests – he keeps them totally enthralled round the fire before dinner and sometimes long after they have eaten. So while

September's camp leaves a lot to be desired on the efficiency front, the Guests have a wonderful time at Tamboti.

In some respects I feel as though I have been thrown in the deep end a bit, but with so much responsibility, I am learning fast. I am also meeting a lot of fantastic Guests and because I only go to bed once they do, I am learning about different nationalities, countries and cultures from around the world. It's like travelling the globe by staying in the same place.

As I mentioned earlier, I have made a few extra tips which add to my salary. As many of the Guests who come through the camp go on to Cape Town after leaving the bush, I have created a list of all the good restaurants and wine estates for them to visit. Often, I offer to book these restaurants for them ahead of time so that they don't have to worry about it once they arrive in the Mother City. This is doing wonders for my secondary income.

I have also enjoyed working with the 4 Butlers at Tamboti Camp. They are all Shangane people and their names are Redman, Mattress, Nora and Incredible. "Incredible" sadly only refers to his name and certainly not his performance. The other 3 are all brilliant, though, and have been here for well over 5 years.

Incredible has recently been promoted from Security Guard and, although quite a jovial sort, is unspeakably incompetent. Yesterday, an elderly American lady named Alma asked him if he would be so kind as to pour her a Bloody Mary. I was talking to her at the time, so when Incredible failed to ask how spicy she would like it, I prompted him.

She replied, "Oh, yes, I like it just a little spicy." With that, Incredible disappeared and returned a few moments later looking very pleased with the red concoction he had prepared. Alma thanked him for it and took a sip. She coughed slightly and said, "I'm sorry to be difficult, but this is probably just a bit too spicy for me."

I reacted quickly and offered to take the glass and make her another, which she accepted. However, before doing so I thought that I would just pop into the kitchen to taste the 1 that Incredible had mixed.

When I say that it felt like I had just ingested a neat shot of lava, I am not joking. I had to douse my burning palate with some leftover tzatziki which, thank god, was in the fridge close by. I don't know how that old duck survived her sip without going into cardiac arrest. Incredible had used half a bottle of Tabasco sauce in her cocktail. He obviously thought that a "little" spicy meant 125 ml of the hottest pepper sauce in the world. Utter lunatic. To make him understand the consequences of such an unfathomably hot drink, I attempted to make him taste his creation. I was unsuccessful, though, as he claimed his religion forbade the consumption of alcohol. He's lucky it wasn't a Virgin Mary that she'd asked for.

Anyway, treasured sister, that's it for this week. Please send news about The Major and send him my best regards. I hope his Tourette's hasn't got him into too much trouble recently.

Lots of love,

The King of Revenge – Hugh

From: 'Angus MacNaughton'
Sent: 07 February, 18h40
To: 'Julia MacNaughton'
Subject: Charging lion, spitting woman

Dear Julia,

You will not bloody believe the goings on at this funny farm. This week's update is so outrageously implausible that I couldn't have fabricated it even if I'd been tripping on acid (which, by the way, I think half of the staff here are doing regularly).

I began my unarmed walks this week, and if that is not bad enough, the entire lodge thinks I'm having a raging affair with Melissa. I've not mentioned her before. She is the manager of Kingfisher Camp. Allow me to digress for a brief description of this creature.

Melissa has a lisp so severe that she could wash a car by standing in front of it and saying 'sausage' a few times. She has violently red hair. You remember those model airplanes Hugh and I used to build – the ones that came with all the pieces in a box, the plane useless before assembly? I liken Melitha's brain case to a box of model pieces. All the bits are there, but so malfunctioning is this organ of hers that you can almost hear the pieces rattle as she walks.

Five nights ago I was preparing for my first unarmed walk. I packed my binoculars, some bananas and a can of condensed milk. I also wrote a rudimentary will, leaving all my worldly belongings (about three) to various people (except String Bean, of course). Jeff, who had just finished his nightly flooding of the bathroom, came in to wish me luck. (I've decided my incoherent neighbour is best likened to a South African version of Spike from that film *Notting Hill.*) Once I'd chased him out, I climbed into bed and just as I had turned out the light there was a knock on the door.

'Go away, Jeff,' I said, irritated. There was a silence and then another knock. 'Piss off!' I yelled. There was a pause and then the most terrifying sound grated my ears. It made my stomach turn and my toes curl until they began to cramp.

'Itth not Jeff, baby, itth me … Melitha!' she whithpered – yes, that is what she did, because she's unable to whisper. I lay there in silence, confounded as to what she could possibly want. Before I had time to consider what to say, the door swung open. There she stood, silhouetted by the light from our bathroom. She recoiled when the smell of the guano hit her, but recovered quickly. The creature was dressed in a loose-fitting pink negligee with fur trimming. The colour disagreed viciously with her hair. I stared, speechless, as she executed what I assume she thought was a sexy slink towards my bed, allowing a strap to fall terrifyingly off her shoulder.

'Stop ... right ... there,' I snarled at her.

'Oh, Anguth, I retheived your methage! I jutht had no idea you were tho into me!'

'Into you? Are you out of your mind?' I stammered, realising the completely rhetorical nature of my question. 'What meth ... message?!'

'Thith methage,' she said huskily, holding up a scrap of paper. She 'slinked' a bit closer and then tripped on my bag. This sent her flying towards me. I reacted like a startled impala and shot sideways out of the bed. She missed me and careened into the wall behind. Luckily for her, she hit her thick skull.

There was a rattle.

She lay there a bit dazed. I grabbed the offending message from her and flicked on the light. You'll never believe what I saw.

The message extolled the 'virtues' of Melitha in words so cheesy and so vile in sweetness that I nearly brought up. It was signed,

'Huggies and kissies,' wait for it ... 'Angus'.

Yes, my name appended to the words huggies and kissies! The writing on the message was easily identifiable. It was written in our brother's own hand. Hugh, that utter wanghead, set the whole thing up. I swore loudly which brought Jeff out of his room and into mine. He appeared at the door and went silent as he took in the scene before him. (I should state at this juncture that he was dressed in long flannel pyjamas that were stuck to his body because he'd forgotten to dry himself.) He giggled inanely, clapped his hand over his mouth and ran out. Shortly thereafter, I bundled a dazed and protesting Melitha out of my room.

Naturally, Jeff went and told everyone he could find that he'd seen Melitha on my bed in a negligee (although there's no way he used the word 'negligee'). Everyone thinks this is very amusing. None more so than Jenny who just falls about laughing every time she sees me.

On a more positive note, Anton took me to view lions on foot with Elvis the other day. I quickly understood why Elvis came along. His tracking skills are superb and his calmness under pressure is amazing. Anton made me walk up front with Elvis while he walked behind with the rifle. A clear case of 'follow me, boys, I'm right behind you'. Apparently, the trainee always walks in front of the rifle in these 'pressure testing' walks.

We picked up the tracks of four young males and followed them into quite a dense mopane thicket. After about an hour of weaving through the trees, Elvis suddenly froze. My breakfast arrived back in my mouth, so hard was the adrenalin surging through my system.

There was a deep-throated growl emanating from behind a kooboo-berry bush just 20 metres in front of us. Elvis held up his hand for us to stop. This was unnecessary as I couldn't have moved if I'd wanted to. My face went cold and hot at the same time and my mouth went instantly dry as I tried to see around the vast frame of our tracker.

'Don't ... fokken ... move!' hissed Anton from behind me, the rifle on his shoulder. 'If those puppies come, they're going down.' Even in my agitated state there were a few things that worried me about this assertion.

Firstly, Elvis and I were in front of him. He would thus have had to shoot through us to hit the lions.

Secondly, a lion, I'm reliably told, can cover 100 metres in just under six seconds. That means 20 metres in 1.2 seconds. If all four decided to massacre us, Anton would have 1.2 seconds to chamber a round and shoot accurately four times while avoiding the two people in front of him. I quickly put my faith in Elvis and decided I'd do what he did and not what goon Anton instructed.

The growl became louder. Elvis turned his large hand and waved backwards slowly.

'Moving back slow!' he whispered. He took a step back and I did the same. I stood on Anton's foot.

'I said don't fokken move!' he snarled. At this Elvis turned around and glared at his boss. Anton withered visibly.

'Back, now!' Elvis reiterated as the first lion burst out of the bush in a flurry of snarls.

'Fok it!' yelled Anton, making to load his rifle but dropping it in the process. Elvis turned back to face the irate cat. It came forward two steps and then turned and ran into the undergrowth. This is fairly standard behaviour for a young lion, he told me afterwards. The birds started calling again as I fought my breakfast back down. Elvis shook his head, picked up the rifle and stalked out of the thicket. Anton did not mention the incident again.

I'll tell you about my walks next week if I survive unmolested – by human or animal – till then.

Your brother,

Angus, 'the loverboy'

P.S. I am obviously going to take revenge on String Bean. He really is an idiot. He knows I'm far nastier than him.

From: 'Hugh MacNaughton'
Sent: 13 February, 18h26
To: 'Jules'
Subject: Littley bottlees and ruskeys

Hey Jules,

Angus is not talking to me. This, of course, suits me perfectly as I have no desire to engage with him either, but I'm now feeling slightly bad about the mess I have caused. I had no idea that Melissa had such strong feelings for him. He has had quite a time brushing her off and it turns out he was helping Simone with some kids' furniture in the maintenance shed, so perhaps he said nothing about me soiling myself. He's been completing his 10 days of unarmed walking – a challenge probably less daunting than facing the slobbering beast Melissa after returning to camp in the evenings.

His roommate Jeff came to me the other day and enquired, with some concern, as to whether, if pushed too far, Angus was capable of murder. I told him that with Angus, nothing was completely out of the question and that from what I had heard, Melissa was about to set that ball in motion. Later that evening, when Angus had returned from the bush, Jeff watched him polishing the barrel of a rifle in the Rangers' Room. It terrified him. Poor old Jeff. Ironically, it would actually be Jeff and Melissa who would make quite a good couple.

I am still enjoying Tamboti Camp, but September's management participation dwindles by the day. PJ asked me the other day whether I was confident enough to run the camp on my own while September took his 2 weeks' leave. I wanted to reply by saying I had not seen anybody by that name for days, but I held my tongue and simply said that I would be delighted to have the opportunity. So, as of next week I will be the Acting Manager of Tamboti Camp and I am really looking forward to it.

Incredible (he who is everything but) has continued to amaze me this week. Fortunately, I find his manner so amusing that I am able to forgive the fact that he is about as much a Butler as The Major is an alpine slalom champion. The most amusing thing about him is his idiosyncratic pronunciation. His recent account of a baboon raid on 1 of the rooms at Tamboti Camp earlier this week brought me to hysterical convulsions.

I arrived at the camp to find Incredible looking more perplexed than usual.

"What seems to be the matter, Incredible? Why are you looking so perturbed?" I asked. He became noticeably more confused and asked who Peter was. I said that I had no idea who Peter was but wanted to know if there was a problem. He responded as follows:

"Mfo, I just want to show you some small, littley problems." I told him to go ahead and he gestured that we should make our way to Room 3. He continued, "You see, early in the morning, immediately when I get here, I just seen those naughty ones breaking into the room." He then giggled. I asked who precisely the "naughty ones" were. "No, just those littley baboons."

You should be made aware at this stage that any word ending in TLE is pronounced TLEY. Bottle becomes "bottley", for example. Little becomes "littley." For some reason Rusk also becomes "ruskey".

I asked him the extent of the damage, to which he replied, "No, they just stealing those box of littley ruskeys and also getting those teas, most specially that Early Grey."

By this stage we had arrived at the entrance to Room 3 and the sight which met my eyes was horrific. I got the same feeling as I did years ago when we returned to our burgled home after that Kenton holiday. The place was in a horrendous state. The mini bar had been opened, there were bite-marked beer cans strewn across the room, baboon faeces everywhere, and the place smelled like a bikers' bar just before closing. The situation was exacerbated by the fact that the villains had helped themselves to a good dose of the Guests' malaria prophylactics and hormone pills. Fortunately, they (the Guests as opposed to the baboons) took the potentially upsetting news rather well. I am sure there were a few baboons acting somewhat out of sorts in the bush for the rest of that day.

There is nothing further to report other than the fact that I still long for the fair Simone. I think I'm going to make a solid move soon.

Cheer ho,

Hugh

From: 'Angus MacNaughton'
Sent: 14 February, 18h48
To: 'Julia MacNaughton'
Subject: Unarmed in the Mean Green

Dear Julia,

A few things to report in this week's edition.

Firstly, with regard to the deranged and copiously spitting Melitha, I have not had a chance to dissuade her of the notion that I wrote that horrifically sappy letter. I've been in the field all day doing unarmed walks and daren't go remotely near her at night for fear that she might think I wish to commence nocturnal coitus.

Even if the opportunity were to arise, it's impossible to have a conversation with her because a conversation for her consists of blethering incoherent drivel without pause for breath. Listening to her feels like swimming up the Zambezi with your arms tied. I probably need to catch her when her mouth is full of food. Although I'm not sure she wouldn't just eject this along with whatever bilious nonsense first comes into her head. Perhaps I'll just write her 'another' letter.

Obviously, the door to the bat cave doesn't have a lock on it, so before I retire every night, I push the bed up against it and pretend I'm not there when she comes knocking as she did two nights ago. A gentle knock accompanied by, 'Anguth ... oh, Anguth!' When no response is forthcoming, 'Oh, Anguth, I know you're inthide! You're cauthing me a lot of anguith!' Eventually, she gives up and buggers off. Needless to say, my alertness in the morning while walking the reserve unarmed has been compromised by lack of sleep.

This brings me to my next topic – the unarmed walks. Each morning for the last two weeks I have left the lodge at first light, armed with a dodgy radio, a map, the first aid kit and a stick. I have fashioned the stick into a spear of sorts. It's made of leadwood and has a viciously sharp point. Obviously, the implement is entirely useless given the fact that a charging lion or buffalo will snap it like a toothpick. The map is the greatest work of fiction since the Zimbabwean elections of 2008. It looks like it was hand drawn by a small child with a blunt wax crayon. I have thus, more accurately, been lost for the last two weeks.

While I initially considered the unarmed walking a ridiculous idea, I actually quite enjoy spending the whole day in the bush. I don't have to clean the Twin Palms, run errands for Anton or spend any time with the rest of the nutters at the lodge. I walk the wilds, looking at birds and sitting on termite mounds watching giraffe and wildebeest. Every afternoon, I treat myself to a kip under a tree – one eye open for murderous creatures. As far as big game goes, I've seen elephants and buffalo but no cats yet.

Of course, the return to the lodge at sundown brings my buoyant mood right back to normal. After I have wolfed some food down, I have a debrief session with Anton and a few of the other rangers. These are sessions where Anton delivers monologues of profoundly worthless advice. Following his pointers would result in certain death. His last pearl went as follows:

'So what big and hairies you see today?' He picked his teeth with his Leatherman.

'Elephant,' was my flat reply.

'What you do when you saw 'im?' He started shaving the hairs off his left arm with the blade.

'I puked with fear, screamed and then ran away waving my arms,' I said. One of the other rangers, Duncan, stifled a laugh. The sarcasm flew right over Anton's head. He sat up and stabbed the Leatherman into the table.

'No bru, why'd you run? Next time you see an ele just pick up some rocks and throw him with them. Show it who's boss. I've never runned away from a animal, that's how I've survived out here.'

Personally, I'm under no illusions when it comes to who's boss. Neither is the elephant as he comes hurtling towards me. Thankfully, Duncan took me aside and gave me a few useful tips when the debriefing was over.

That's it for this week. With the walks occupying my time, I have yet to take my revenge on Hugh – he thinks I've forgotten.

Fool.

Bye bye,

Angus

JAMES HENDRY

From: 'Hugh MacNaughton'
Sent: 20 February, 17h00
To: 'Jules'
Subject: Guest fruit salad

Hey Jules,

It is amazing how tricky life becomes when you are solely responsible for the goings on at a camp. Very few things went awry while September was in charge. The fact that he had been spending a sum total of 12 hours a week physically at the camp is neither here nor there when PJ assesses his ability over the course of a hiccupless week. I'm not sure if "hiccupless" is even a word but on the day I was made responsible, Murphy's Law ensured that everything went wrong and after only a single day in charge, my nose is barely above water.

We had a group in camp over the weekend (not that weekends even exist out here) and, after they departed, September went on his merry way to enjoy 2 weeks of recuperation. The group departure meant that Tamboti Camp was completely emptied. This paved the way for a full camp of new arrivals the following day. This is where things began to get difficult. The diversity in character, culture, upbringing, religion and political standpoint of the Guests meant that they paired about as well as Cabernet Sauvignon and hake fillets. It was a bit like hosting Osama Bin Laden and George Bush or drinking an aperitif with Wayne Rooney and a new recruit from the Google Corporation.

There were 5 sets of Guests. First was a group of 4 extremely jolly Indian gentlemen who had won a prize from their employer in Mumbai. During their stay, Raj, Pravesh, Gupell and Sachin were hugely fun and mostly shit-faced. Our all-inclusive policy was abused so cruelly that PJ had to send a vehicle into town to collect fresh supplies of Captain Morgan Island Rum and coconut milk for them to make their own cocktails. The Indians were also partial to the odd box of Marlboros and 3 or 4 fingers of single malt in the late evening.

The next set was a New York honeymoon couple. Christian works on Wall Street, and Rachel runs a successful catering service. They were an incredibly attractive and intelligent couple in their mid-thirties who met on an MBA course at Harvard. It was their first visit to Africa and they were unspeakably excited to be in the bush.

The third set was a couple from Texas in their late seventies. Edna and Henry (quickly dubbed "Horrible Henry" by me and then referred to as such by the Tamboti Camp Butlers) are fiercely well travelled. They only stay at luxurious *Relais et Chateaux* properties and were as fussy as all hell. They had just spent 3 days at another property in the area, so I phoned to gather some information on them before their arrival. You may recall Kate, a friend of mine from school? Well, she works there and she explained that in addition to a plethora of demands, they complained loudly and often about everything.

Their demands at Sasekile included:

1. **Private Land Rover:** This means that Henry and his wife refused to be on the same vehicle as anybody else and demanded to have their own Ranger. Normally, we charge a premium for this sort of thing but they expected it for free.

2. **06:00 wakeup call:** In summer, we normally wake our Guests at 05:00 in order for them to leave at 05:30. If we declined this couple the joy of a *mahala* [free] private vehicle and forced them to drive with other Guests, their delayed wakeup call would cause some trouble.

3. **Deluxe coffees and cereal at 06:00:** Normally, we offer our Guests either tea or coffee when they are woken, but of course this was not satisfactory for Henry and Edna. They wanted macchiatos, lattes and muesli with Bulgarian yoghurt to greet them as they rose. Israel, from security, who prepares the morning coffee, is an excellent guard but he is no barista. He simply wouldn't be able to cope with the complicated order. His version of a skimmed milk latte was about as fat free as Mama Flora's Death by Chocolate Cake.

4. **Freshly squeezed orange juice at breakfast:** Amazingly, this we could do!

The fourth set of Guests came in the form of a family from the UK. Toby and Emma are relatively young parents who have made a mint from Toby's career as a professional football player. Unfortunately, he sustained a very serious injury and can no longer play at the top level.

He is bitter about it, she is bitter about it, and as for their 2 kids, they were simply born bitter. Max and Oli are 13-year-old twins and display the manners of 2 marauding yobbos. They all chose to be crowded into 1 room.

The last Guest was travelling on her own. Andrea is a young American woman in her late twenties. She was a Victoria's Secret model in her past, which in layman's terms means 3 things: (1) she has an indescribably beautiful face, (2) she has a body like a McLaren F1, and (3) she is not short of money. Andrea left the States to "get away from it all" and spent 5 days in camp.

All of the above arrived during the course of my first day in charge. Things ran relatively smoothly to begin with. I spent over an hour listening to Henry and Edna explain how important they are and figured, having seen who had already passed through the doors of Tamboti Camp, it was in my best interests to cut a deal with the private Land Rover. I offered it to them for 50% of the usual cost and, begrudgingly, they accepted.

So by tea time that afternoon, the game drive groupings were as follows:

· Darren driving Henry and Edna on a private Land Rover.
· Duncan driving the bitter football family with the honeymooners.
· Jamie driving the Bombay prize winners with the supermodel.

The scene at tea set the tone for the next few days. Keen to get out before the rest, Henry and Edna arrived first. Being sensitive to the sun, Edna had caked herself with so much sun cream that I barely recognised her. She looked like a yeti. Henry's attire and equipment indicated that he plans to be the globe's next great wildlife photographer. They ambled through and I introduced them to Darren. As they began to repeat the same insufferable speech that I had been subjected to earlier that afternoon, they were interrupted by the yobbo twins.

Max and Oli came careening round the corner and onto the deck at full sprint. They ran straight between Darren and his Guests, putting a stop to any further self-celebratory drawl from the yeti or the photography genius.

"Ay, skinny, you go' any cake for us?" Max yelled at me in high-pitched cockney. There was a stunned silence and although I was happy that

Darren had been spared, I was completely shocked at what I thought I had just heard.

"Sorry, what was that?" I responded.

"I said, 'av you go' any cake for us, you skinny wai'er?"

"Ja," I said shakily, "over there next to the tea." They proceeded to attack the chocolate cake with forks. I decided not to step in as the large mouthfuls of cake were muffling their vulgar conversation about a "cracking young slapper" who they had spotted in the camp and upon whom they wanted to perform foul unmentionables. Let me remind you that these terrors were only 13 years old!

The honeymooners arrived next with the parents of the rudest children on Earth. They made awkward conversation as they walked onto the deck and I greeted them with teeth clenched.

"Some tea and cake?" I asked. "If there's any left," under my breath. Fortunately, Redman and Mattress came to my rescue with a plate of biscuits.

Next to arrive was Andrea, pursued hotly by the Mumbai 4 who, after 6 cocktails each, had lost all inhibitions. Andrea swooped onto the deck at a semi-canter in order to evade them.

I had to forgive the men from Mumbai, as the attire, or lack thereof, worn by this woman was almost too much for us to bear. She was sporting a pair of the sexiest little hot pants I have ever had the privilege of seeing. They covered maybe an 8th of her long legs. Her top was more a modified bra than anything else. She may as well have been back on the runways of Milan. The whole deck fell silent and open-mouthed as this goddess floated in.

The shock made me drop my glass of iced tea but I found the presence of mind to gesture towards the vehicles and splutter,

"The Rangers are waiting for you up in the car park." The half-naked, 6-foot bombshell had overwhelmed everybody and they all just nodded and made for the vehicles. I chuckled, wondering how Jamie was going to concentrate in close proximity to Andrea for the next 3 hours. At least they are out of my hair for a while, but I have no doubt that there will be more to report on this lot in my next mail.

More importantly, I feel I should mention that the fair Simone has been acting a little out of sorts. Whereas in the past she hasn't really given me the time of day, now she keeps looking at me slightly strangely. I don't know what the hell is going on, but it is as though she knows something that I don't.

Although I can't work out what she's thinking, or what has inspired this funny look, I feel that I need to make a solid move. If she likes me, then great; if not, then I'm in for an incredibly awkward year, but either way it is killing me just sitting around wondering. When the next opportunity presents itself, I will take action. I have to, for my own sanity.

I look forward to reporting on all that is going on next week – hopefully with positive news.

Our brother and I have yet to communicate.

Much love,

Hugh

From: 'Angus MacNaughton'
Sent: 20 February, 18h15
To: 'Julia MacNaughton'
Subject: Cruel universe

Dear Julia,

Unbelievably, life took on new lows this week. I took revenge on String Bean, although 'revenge' was hardly the result. I am thoroughly convinced that fate, the universe, some vengeful pantheon or a combination of these hate me with an unquenchable rage.

First, things with SB. My 'revenge' was to give Simone a pill so vile to digest that she'd not be able to look at my brother without the revulsion he so richly deserves. The opportunity presented itself one night at dinner. SB was working at Tamboti Camp and I was eating in the Avusheni Eatery. Simone arrived and sat next to me (this is unusual – no one sits next to me at meal times). She presented me with the following bleached canvas on which to paint my reprisal.

'So, tell me a bit about you two brothers. How did you end up here in the bush?' Obviously, fishing for info on SB.

'Well,' says I, thinking double-time, 'poor Hugh. You know many people seem to come to the bush to forget a painful memory? He's no different.' I took a mouthful of oily chicken. Her interest was piqued, barely containable.

'Oh, what happened?' she asked with sweet 21-year-old innocence.

'Oh, I can't possibly tell you.' I looked away, putting on an Oscar-winning face of anguish. She took a bite of her food but I knew she wasn't going to be able to leave it there.

'Oh, please tell me, it can't be that bad,' she implored.

'Well, OK,' I said, 'but just between you and me.' I looked around, checking for prying ears, hunched my shoulders, turned back to her and whispered with furrowed brow, 'Hugh, you see, contracted a rare disease a while back.' I chewed thoughtfully as the smile disappeared from her face. I continued, 'He picked it up in Thailand from a night of filth with one of those, um ... ping pong girls.

Horrible thing, keeps manifesting itself in a rash on his ... um ... you know.'

By the time I reached the climax of my story, her face was paler than the snowy slopes of Kilimanjaro. I pressed on. 'Oh, yes, and he's prone to wild mood swings that manifest as long bouts of mournful wailing – they go on for hours sometimes. Dreadful misfortune. Incurable, they say.'

I took another mouthful in order to hide the smile that was fighting to envelop my face.

'Oh, poor Hugh! My cousin Richard was seduced by one of those disgusting women. Poor, poor Hugh,' she said.

Before I could dissuade her of SB's innocence, she stood up, grabbed her plate and left with the words,

'I won't say a thing to anyone ... I promise. Poor, poor Hugh.'

That my incredibly quick-thinking wit should be so punished is further proof of the universe's disdain for me.

I have had no further visits from Melitha. Quite to the contrary, she's told everyone in camp that I am born of the devil. The other night, Jenny and Melitha were having a drink at the Main Camp bar before the guests arrived for dinner. I walked in with a cheese platter for the buffet. Melitha had her back to the buffet and so couldn't see me. Jenny, however, had a perfect view of my horrified face over Melitha's shoulder.

'Oh, Jenny, I think that I find him tho attractive becauth he ith tho evil. I've made up my mind to not make an effort. He'll be thorry, you know,' said Melitha.

Jenny wiped the spittle from her face. She saw the look of disgust I wore, smiled and replied,

'Melissa, I reckon he's just playing hard to get. I think you need to persevere. He'll break eventually, you just keep at it.' Jenny obviously wants to remain my enemy for life.

On a positive note, I had a fantastic experience on the last day of my unarmed walks. I was sipping a cup of coffee, mercifully alone, outside the rangers' room in pre-dawn darkness. The lodge was just beginning to stir and off to the far north-east of the reserve, some lions called.

As usual, I left the lodge at 05:00 armed with stick and radio. The darkness broke into a beautiful morning. About an hour along my route, I stepped into a drainage line bathed in a ginger dawn mist that was rising off the dew-covered sand. Then, only about 50 metres ahead, a lion roared. I froze, determined the direction of the great cat and quickly changed course towards a koppie east of me. I scrambled to the top and found a comfortable rock to sit on. I took out my breakfast (apple) and waited. The lion called twice more before he emerged from the mist just west of and below the koppie. He didn't see me initially because I was a good 100 metres above and to the east of him. He paused to spray a bush and then looked up. He froze as my scent touched him and he picked out my silhouette against the rocks high above. We looked at each other for a few moments before he turned slowly and carried on his way. I stayed there for another hour as his calls receded into the distance. I think this was the first sense of happiness I've experienced in this place.

My mood soured again that night, however. In reception works a woman I have not yet described to you. Candice. She is a 25-year-old bottle blonde with an accent straight from the bowels of Boksburg. There are termites who could answer a phone more efficiently than Candice and she is looser than a Mugabe promise. Her latest victim is Jeff. I am thus also, indirectly, her latest victim. The noises emanating from Jeff or Candice (I can't tell which) deep into the night are like those one might expect to hear in a Siberian torture chamber. If she spends another night in Jeff's room, I swear his bed is going to come crashing through the wall into the bat cave.

So that's this week's episode from the bushveld soapie.

Angus

P.S. I should state at this juncture that I handed that work of fantasy (the 'map') to a particularly moronic South African guest who claimed to be Paul Kruger's great grandson. I told him it leads to the lost Kruger millions. He'll be lost in the greater Kruger National Park for years.

From: 'Julia MacNaughton'
Sent: 21 February, 16h43
To: 'Brother A'
Subject: Maternal relief!

Hey Angus,

Just a quick note to say that all present members of the MacNaughton household have breathed a collective sigh of relief that you have successfully completed your walking trial! Even tubby Trubby seemed especially at ease as he took his afternoon nap on the sofa. (This despite Dad's pathetic efforts to discipline the dog: 'Trubshaw, get off the bloody sofa! ... Ah well, if you're already up there, just make sure you keep your paws off Mum's new cushions.')

Somewhat predictably, Mum burst into tears when I told her your latest news. My goodness, she does worry about her 'precious baby boy'! The Major was round for his weekly dinner the other night and he could not fathom what all the fuss was about. He did, however, proffer several Second World War anecdotes about his time stationed in North Africa and reminded us that his mother kept 'a bloody good stiff upper lip'.

Anyhow, I'm quite glad that you made it through in one piece.

Love,

Jules

From: 'Hugh MacNaughton'
Sent: 27 February, 17h59
To: 'Jules'
Subject: Legal eagle

Hey Jules,

Angus and I are on speaking terms once more.

This comparatively major breakthrough in our relationship has not, as I'm sure you can imagine, come effortlessly. Rather, it is a result of the most drama-packed week yet of our short time at Sasekile. Ridge Forrester and Barker Haines in their respective soap operas have got nothing on your eldest unmarried brother this week.

First, let me give you a brief update on the Guests I told you about last week. The Indians turned out to be a huge amount of fun and I woke each morning of their 3-day stay with a terrible hangover. After dinner every night, they insisted I join them as they sampled large volumes of malt whisky and told hilarious stories about growing up in Mumbai. The evenings were made more pleasant by the stunning Andrea who sat up with us, sharing her experiences from the ramps of Milan. By the end of their stay, Raj had convinced Andrea to visit him in India and Efficient (the Security Guard) says he saw Raj emerge from her room before game drive on the last day.

The footballer and his family were less entertaining but I managed to keep them satisfied. I don't think they'll do another Safari – somewhere with casinos is more their style. They have headed off to Sun City on my recommendation.

Horrible Henry and his beastly wife just got worse and worse. Their demands never ended and their attitude soured the atmosphere around the camp. Everything was compared with bigger and better versions of things in the US. After viewing a huge male lion roaring 1 evening Henry remarked that he wasn't that impressed because bears are much bigger than lions. They did provide some entertainment for us, however. Each day after breakfast they took to the pool to swim lengths ... the pool is about 15 metres long and I think it took the yeti-shaped and coloured

Edna at least 5 minutes to flop from 1 side to the other. Incredible was beside himself as he watched.

Back to the trials (I mean in the literal sense) of Angus. While I have been holding up the family name by running Tamboti Camp all on my own, Angus has managed to insult Jenny so horribly that she had to take a day's leave. Although I am often amused by his arsenal of remarks directed at the mentally challenged Melissa, there is no denying that he crossed the boundary during his latest attack on Jenny.

Now, like any bit of gossip in this isolated small community, word of what had happened did the rounds within an hour of the event. From what I gathered, Angus made a comment about Jenny's weight, which could have been classed as just very distasteful had it not been for the fact that she is a recovering bulimic. Because of this minor detail, the unrelenting stream of Jenny's tears and the fact that the happiness of the Lodge community is so crucial to our operations, PJ took the matter very seriously indeed. So seriously, in fact, that before the day was out he had provided Angus with written notice to attend a disciplinary hearing the following afternoon.

This, of course, is where I came in, as Angus is about as much a lawyer as I am a Casanova – although this week I'm not doing too badly on that front! He came to me in desperation, begging me to apply the knowledge I gained in the labour relations component of my Hotel School degree to his dismal state of affairs.

My initial thought was to let him suffer and deal with the fallout of his offensive and inappropriate behaviour alone. But I could see that he had genuinely not intended to create such a mess, and after negotiating a small favour in return, I agreed to help.

Angus was accused of gross misconduct, and although sanctions such as immediate dismissal were out of the question, a final written warning would not look good on his record. In order to help his cause, I advised Angus that he should take an apologetic stance. I suggested we mention his high stress levels due to the unarmed walks and the additional problem of his attention deficit disorder. And that is exactly what we did.

Angus drafted and sent 2 apology letters, 1 to Jenny and 1 to PJ and the general staff before we even arrived at the hearing. We spent the first part of the hearing apologising and agreeing that his behaviour was unacceptable. As they had expected Angus to come out all guns blazing, our opening gambit subdued everybody significantly. Once there was nothing left to argue, I made a few comments about his unarmed-walking stress and nonchalantly slipped his last Ritalin prescription across the table. Even Jenny was feeling bad about the whole thing after that, and Angus escaped with a verbal warning and an instruction to watch his mouth in future. We both knew that the latter was an impossible request to honour, but accepted graciously nevertheless.

Ironically, Angus's little ordeal turned out rather well for me. In return for my help and the gentle outcome of the hearing, Angus provided me with the combination to the safe housing the Lodge's Land Rover keys. Part of the Ranger's code is to keep this combination secret and, as a trainee, Angus would have been brutally punished and probably tortured by Anton if anyone found out that he had divulged the numbers. But Angus owed me, so he sheepishly wrote down the combination and advised me which vehicle to take in order to minimise the chance of being caught. Armed with this information, I decided that the time for my move on Simone was ripe ...

While hosting dinner at Tamboti Camp I learned from the Rangers that 5 of the biggest male lions on the property were sitting on the airstrip. The lions are known as the Granite Coalition, as they were born on a secluded granite rock somewhere on the Tsessebe River. Guests and Rangers raved about them all through dinner and I was damned if I wasn't going to use them to woo the fair Simone.

After dinner I walked back towards my room via a path past Simone's residence. To my delight her light was still on and after 15 to 20 minutes of telling myself "I can do this", I knocked. There was no reply, so in order to check that she was there, I tried the door. It gave way easily and I saw her tucked up in bed, book to 1 side, fast asleep with her light still on. I gazed at her for close on a minute. I was about to give up on our illegal foray into the bush to look at great flesh-guzzling beasts, when the peaceful moment was rudely interrupted by loud banging.

A goddamn genet had leapt onto the tin roof from a nearby tree. The noise woke her and she started screaming when she saw me lurking between the wall and door like a beastly voyeur.

"Huh ... No ... this is not what it looks like," I spluttered, trying to rescue the situation. Horrified, she snatched her duvet around her and stared at me. "Do you like lions?" I squawked, figuring honesty had to be the best policy, despite the bizarre circumstances.

"What?"

"Do you like lions?" My pitch ascended in anticipation of imminent rejection.

"Yes, I do," she whispered, obviously feeling a little self-conscious about the noise that had emanated from her quarters.

"I know this is a big ask, but do you want to come with me to see some?" I said with a bit of unexpected confidence. "Obviously, you don't have to if you're not up for it," I followed in a more doubtful tone. There was a lengthy pause, which of course felt considerably longer than it was, and then, "Yes, OK," finally followed.

Of course, at this point I deserved a medal for the self-control it took not to dance around like a raver after too much speed. Instead I told her to meet me at the Land Rovers in 5 minutes. Amazing. I couldn't, and still can't, believe that after rudely waking her from her slumber, she accepted my invitation.

I grabbed a jersey and my torch and made my way to the Rangers' Room. The code worked like a dream and, following Angus's advice, I took Bradley's vehicle because he wasn't driving the following morning. I made my way to the vehicles where, much to my relief, Simone was waiting – albeit with a mild look of anxiety. I dishonestly persuaded her that I knew what I was doing. A little while later we spluttered out of the Lodge towards the airstrip.

The Rangers had explained that the lions were on the northern side of the tarmac, so imagine my joy when the only forms of life to be seen were a sleeping wildebeest and a scrub hare desperately trying to evade my lights. I was just beginning an apology for wasting her time when the first of the lions began to roar. Filled with enthusiasm once more, I drove down the airstrip to find all 5 on the southern end. They were utterly magnificent, but it was Simone's quiet whimper of nervous joy that made the moment so special.

We stayed with them for about 40 minutes or so before they loped off into the bush and, instead of circling around and ending up lost, I decided to quit while I was ahead and headed back to the Lodge.

I parked the vehicle, returned Brad's keys to the safe and walked Simone back to her room.

"Goodnight," I said.

"Goodnight," she said and then kissed me on the cheek. "Thank you, Hugh."

Sweet lord, was that a breakthrough or what?

What a week!

Lots of love,

Your notorious, woman-slaying, lion-finding, Land Rover-thieving brother,

Hugh

From: 'Angus MacNaughton'
Sent: 27 February, 18h34
To: 'Julia MacNaughton'
Subject: Disciplinary

Dear Julia,

As any dodo, kwagga or woolly mammoth will tell you, humans are by far the most dangerous organisms in creation. You'd expect that life couldn't get much more dangerous than walking the wilds of the Lowveld unarmed. Not so. My employment (bondage?) here was nearly ended this week. Jenny and I had another contretemps. The upshot of the incident was that I was extended the privilege of a disciplinary hearing. The worst part of it was having to enlist Hugh's services and – can't believe I'm going to say this – he was actually almost good.

I had just cleaned up in the repulsive den of Lucifer (Twin Palms) where there had been a birthday party the night before. Consequently unimpressed, I was walking towards the dustbin area with a bag of cans, bottles and someone's underpants when Jenny emerged from the kitchen bearing a bowl of large muffins. She winked at me, pouted and said,

'Hey there, loverboy. Have you finally stopped playing hard to get with Melissa?' I spun round and glared at her.

'What did you just say?' I hissed.

'Or have you decided to come out with your feelings for Hilda? I've seen the way you look at her.' Her smile spread as she saw the blood rise in my face. 'Ooh,' said she, as though talking to a toddler, 'does that make you cross?'

'Look here,' I replied slowly, 'why don't you go and feed yourself those muffins one by one. Then, take a toothbrush, shove it down your throat and vomit them all up. That way you'll be able to maintain your figure which, I notice, approximates that of a particularly starved broomstick. Huh? Good idea?' I gave her a special sarcastic grin.

The effect of this outburst was profound. Her bottom lip started to quiver, tears welled in her eyes, the bowl of muffins crashed to the floor and she ran off.

I shrugged and continued on my way.

A while later I was reading in the bat cave when the figure of Anton filled the door. He was in a rage.

'I don't know what you fokken did this time, Shark Crap, but you've really pissed off PJ.' He barged his way in, shoved a piece of paper in my face and stormed out, slamming the door. I brushed the guano that had fallen with the slam off the paper and perused it. (The offending missive, which I scanned for you, is inserted below.)

DISCIPLINARY PROCEDURE

NOTICE TO ATTEND A DISCIPLINARY ENQUIRY

TO: ___Angus MacNaughton_____

FROM: PJ Woodstock (General Manager)

DATE & TIME & PLACE __03/03 Meeting room__14h00

ALLEGED MISCONDUCT LEVEL: _Level_A Gross Misconduct (possible final warning offence)

You are accused of intentionally treating a fellow staff member with a level of disrespect that was hurtful and insensitive. The staff member in question is Jenny Sutherland.

NOTE:

AT THE ENQUIRY, YOU WILL BE ENTITLED TO:

1. Be represented by a fellow employee of your choice (STRONGLY SUGGESTED)

2. Call witnesses to give evidence on your behalf

3. An interpreter (YES/NO)

Obviously, given my level of popularity around here, finding the 'strongly suggested' staff representative was going to be impossible. I had no choice but to ask bloody String Bean to help me out.

I went to Tamboti Camp to explain. When I arrived, he was polishing a silver candelabrum on the deck and whistling contentedly to himself (smug git). He looked surprised to see me. I handed him the paper and said, 'Much as it burns me deep within my core to say this ...' I paused as my throat closed. I clenched my teeth. 'I need your help.'

SB looked confused as he read the paper. Five minutes later, when he had finally stopped guffawing like an inebriated hyena, he said, 'You'd better tell me about it.'

I explained the morning's events and expressed my dismay that Jenny could be so pathetically over-sensitive. SB said, 'Oh, God, you don't know what you've done ... do you?'

'Of course not,' I snapped. 'Bloody woman must be mad!'

'No, Angus,' said Hugh seriously, 'she's a recovering bulimic.'

'Ah,' I said, the penny clanging loudly. A scrub-robin called from the heat of the February midday.

Suffice it to say, I'm still here. SB actually did a rather good job of getting my possible sentence reduced to an unlikely mild verbal warning. He did an even better job of keeping me quiet in the hearing. Every time I almost lost my temper he stuck his pen in my leg. So, at the end of it I'm sporting a large hole in my right quad but I still have a job.

My training has moved to the next phase now. I have some written exams to complete next week. Anton says these are going be 'blerrie-fokken tough'. As he is doing the marking, I'm not expecting anything particularly cerebrally challenging.

That's it for this torrid episode.

Your thankfully off-the-hook brother,

Angus

A YEAR IN THE WILD

From: 'Jules'
Sent: 01 March, 14h07
To: 'Brother H'
Subject: Well done x 2

Hey Hugh-go,

Wow – looks like you had quite the week out there in the wilderness!

First off, you've shown some excellent game in your pursuance of the fair Simone – apart from the creepy hanging in her doorway thing. She must think you're really gutsy. I think you would have ticked most boxes. Doubly well done for not pushing it too far after you walked her home. Let her hang for a while!

Secondly, defending your 'big' brother – that guy is so inappropriate sometimes. I related the story to Dad, who I found completing his gardening chores. He peered up from under that ridiculous straw sunhat and shook his head, almost toppling the rose he was relocating for Mum.

'I sometimes wonder if that boy will ever learn,' he muttered, returning to his horticultural task, only to be accosted by Trubshaw, come to investigate. As I wandered back to the kitchen that familiar phrase 'Bugger off, Trubshaw!' was heard from the depths of Mum's new flowerbed.

I haven't told Mum – never a good idea to let on such combustible information just before the country club bridge tournament.

Lots of love,

Jules

From: 'Hugh MacNaughton'
Sent: 06 March, 17h58
To: 'Jules'
Subject: Quintessential House

Hey Jules,

I'm not writing to you this week from the middle of the bush, but rather from the comforts of a 5-star luxury guest house about an hour and a half from the reserve.

Because PJ has become increasingly agitated by the lack of attention to detail in the camps at Sasekile, he struck a deal with a nearby guest house. He plans to send every Camp Manager through the doors of Quintessential House over the next little while in order to expose us to the standards at which we should be operating.

Fantastic is what I'm sure you are thinking. What could be better than spending 2 nights away from the Lodge in 1 of South Africa's most sought-after retreats? Well, it would have been fantastic, but due to the 24/7 nature of the lodge business, we were not all able to go away together. We were put into pairs. And who was I destined to travel with?

Oh, yes, you guessed it – Melissa!

Imagine the contrast between my excitement at being told about this amazing getaway, complete with learning and luxury, and the deep shock of hearing it would be shared with Melissa. Even as I sit writing to you, I can see her outside the room mimicking the panting of the resident spaniel which she accosted on the veranda outside our suite.

When the amazing combination of Guests – model, brilliant Indians, footballer family, Yeti and husband – finally departed, Tamboti Camp cleared for 3 days. I was left with an empty camp and put on the list for a trip to Quintessential House. Exceptionally poor fortune dictated that Melissa, who was due to go on leave the same day, was offered the same opportunity.

"Of course, I'll go with little Hughey," was her lisped response. And so it was that we drove up here 2 days ago – together.

The car trip was horrific. The hour and a half journey felt like the better part of a month as Melissa voiced her excitement from beginning to end.

"Yay, yay, hip hip hooray! Little Hughey and I are going away!" was the embarrassing ditty I was exposed to as we left Sasekile. I felt nauseous.

Next, in a pathetic attempt at charades, she pretended that she was a wealthy billionaire from London and that I was her chauffeur.

"Quicker, quicker," she squawked. "I must get there with enough time to pamper myself and powder my nose before dinner." Unfortunately, her little act was not confined to the car. It has continued throughout our stay!

We drove through the gates and up the long and exquisite cobblestone driveway. It was flanked by tall pine trees and backed by the breathtaking, jagged northern Drakensberg. (Astounding to think that this great mountain range extends all the way into Mpumalanga and Limpopo.) A fine evening mist, which was beginning to settle around us, completed the stunning effect. The air was fresh and the gardens impeccably well kept.

Staff in neat uniforms greeted us with pleasant waves and warm smiles from wherever they were working and the signs indicating the way to the reception were polished to the extent that I could see in them the blue reflection of our humble Toyota Tazz. The place simply oozed professionalism and class even before we'd climbed out of the car. For a brief moment I was in peaceful awe of my surroundings and understood precisely PJ's motivation for sending us. Of course, this peace was short-lived. When I turned off the engine my dream-like state was rudely disturbed by my dim-witted companion.

She exited the vehicle with not so much as a thank you and swanned up towards the reception area. As you can imagine, check-in was an immensely awkward affair with Melissa insisting on her charade.

"Good afternoon. I am Lady Melissa, and here," she gestured towards me, "is my private Butler, Hughey."

I cannot even begin to describe my embarrassment at this point. I was feeling so uncomfortable that I couldn't even look our hosts in the eye.

I just stared glumly at the polished marble floor beneath me while she asked endless stupid questions.

We eventually received our keys. I don't think I could have handled 1 more idiotic question followed by that wheezy witch-like cackle. It made her sound more like Muttley from the Cartoon Network than the English aristocrat she was so poorly pretending to be.

"Carry my bags to the room for me, you slave," was the last order those poor people heard as we made our way to the cottages. Fortunately, her command was directed at me and not the staff. Of course, there was more chance of Angus copulating with this lunatic than there was of me carrying her bags. Not wanting to cause a scene, despite the fact that we most certainly already had, I refrained from comment and just walked out with my own bag.

I was overjoyed to find that we had a 2-room suite. Our separate bedrooms lightened my mood dramatically. And so it was in my own room that I remained until dinner, making notes and thinking about certain details in the room which, until now, I had not considered. I am looking forward to introducing a few of these little features to Tamboti Camp and showing the staff the photographs I've taken to help them understand what the next level is all about.

Although I am sure you are wondering what transpired during dinner last night, I truly don't have the energy to regale you with the tale. Let's just say that I am dreading the return trip to the Lodge.

Unfortunately, no news from Simone. Maybe I should get hold of her number and SMS her?

Lots of love,

Hugh – although I feel like Angus

From: 'Angus MacNaughton'
Sent: 06 March, 18h27
To: 'Julia MacNaughton'
Subject: Written exams
Attachments: Big5exam.docx

Dear Julia,

I've managed to keep myself out of trouble this week insomuch as no one's complained about me. This is probably because Melitha is on leave.

SB is away for two nights. In his absence, I've had to listen to Simone babble incessantly to Jenny and Anna at the Avusheni Eatery about how wonderful he is. Silly trollop. If I have to hear about how 'romantic and sweet' he is once more, I'll be ill.

Anyway, the week has been filled with the written knowledge exams. These have covered all aspects of field knowledge (vegetation, mammals, birds, stars, history, etc.) that I've been studying since my arrival in Hades. The tests were clearly not set by Anton as they were in a comprehensible form of English and the questions were actually quite challenging. All but one, that is. As he handed me the 'big five' test, he said, 'Shark Crap, this test I wrote myself.'

This was patently obvious. It was hand-written on a piece of foolscap paper decorated with three coffee stains and the phone number of Teaser's in Johannesburg scrawled on the bottom right-hand corner. He continued, 'I like to make up this test on my own. It's the most important 'cos those puppies are the one that'll kill you and your pax in the bush. Pass mark is 85%, so don't blerrie fok it up.'

The test contained not one biological inquiry. I have scanned and attached this profound examination.

The next highlight of the week was my first game drive on the reserve. Hilda (she of mountainous proportions from the finance office) had her parents and sister to stay. As they were not considered real guests, I was given the pleasure of driving them. These incredible specimens made Hilda look like a starved twig. They hail from some backwater in the Karoo that civilisation has yet to touch.

BIG FIVE TEST

by ANTON MULLER

① Where can you ~~like to~~ like to
shoot a elephant — draw a
picture

② You are making a walk on foot with
some 8 pax. A lion charges to
kill you. Describe how you can
put ~~him~~ down that lion?

③ What is the most dangeruss
and agresiv is the buffalo.
When can you kill him with your
pax?

④ What is the calibers of the
rifles we are carrying to protect
our pax?

⑤ What is the muzzil velositeo
of the .658 Express?

⑥ Name 10 diffirent kinds of
rifles for hunting big game?

⑦ Where is the right places to
shoot on a rhino (black one
& white one)?

I arrived on the Main Camp deck early as it was my first game drive and I didn't really know the procedure. The result of this was that I had to spend an awkward half hour alone with Jenny. Things are a little strained between us since the bulimia incident. We exchanged civil greetings and I then pretended to become engrossed in the activities of an ant carrying away a cake crumb. Meanwhile, she made an attempt to write important notes on her daysheet. I was relieved when the guests arrived.

The relief was short-lived.

The deck creaked and groaned as Hilda's family, with a combined mass of over three tonnes, waddled towards the tea table, their eyes aglow at the sight of the chocolate cake. I stared dumbfounded.

'Angus,' hissed Jenny, 'stop staring!' I came out of my trance.

'Hullo,' said the bear-like form of Jakobus Botha, '*Praat jy Afrikaans?*' [Do you speak Afrikaans?] He proffered a large ham with this.

I shook his hand and replied, 'No, only the King's English here.'

'Oh, really?' asked his wife, helping herself to half the cake. 'Not fery good Souf African!' A piece of icing fell from the corner of her cavernous mouth onto the white tent struggling to contain her belly.

The game drive was torturous. The Botha clan thought they'd aid my training by recounting every ridiculous safari cliché, including,

'You know vat ve elephants is gets drunk on vose maroelas?' (Translation: Are you aware that elephants can become intoxicated by eating marula fruit?)

Naturally, they left a tip inversely proportionate to their size. On departure, Jakobus removed a five rand coin from a small leather pouch. He winked and said,

'Here's for you, little English, get a beer.' He and his ilk then climbed into their ox-wagon (cunningly disguised as a Toyota Hilux) and departed.

Not a good start to my ranging career.

Your almost-ranger brother,

Angus

57

From: 'Hugh MacNaughton'
Sent: 13 March, 17h30
To: 'Jules'
Subject: Camp MANAGER!!!!

Hey Jules,

Possible celebration...

After my ordeal with Melissa and the inordinately awkward experience at Quintessential House, this week has been a far more pleasant 1 down in the Lowveld. I eventually reached the end of my tether with the demented woman after dinner on our last evening. She spent a good half hour telling the Manager on duty (clearly a man of Indian roots) that she couldn't understand why "people of the East have to have so many babies". Can you believe I managed to put up with her for 2 days? Such a cringe.

After this I took the decision to simply stop talking back to her and became a mute for the rest of our "educational holiday". I could no longer stoop to having any further part in her brainless conversation. Fortunately, I had the return journey in comparative peace and quiet after she caught a shuttle to Kruger Airport. She flew back to her home in Port Elizabeth for a wedding so, thankfully, I was on my own in the car for the return trip to Sasekile.

As far as news from the Lodge goes, I can report only good things – at least for me, anyway. There has been a fair amount of drama over the course of the week but the immediate dismissal of 1 of our staff on Tuesday probably took centre stage. Don't worry, it wasn't Angus.

Andrew Jackson, Manager of Main Camp, worked at the Lodge for the better part of 5 years. I hadn't really gotten to know him that well but he seemed like a fun young guy and pretty good at his job. He did, however, have a distinct shadiness about him. I suppose he struck me as the sort who would generously offer to pay for your dinner with the money he had just thieved from your wallet while you were in the bathroom; or someone who might offer to look after your house, but then rent it out to refugees. In short, he certainly wasn't going to overtake Mother Teresa on the highway to heaven.

Anyway, my instincts were not completely off the mark in that Andrew was dismissed for possibly misinterpreting his brief on "Guest Delight". In fact, so desperate was Andrew to ensure the delight of the recently wedded Kerry Saunders, that, after way too much Glenfiddich in the Main Camp boma, he offered to extend his hospitality deep into the night.

Darren, the Saunders's Ranger, offered to take them out after dinner to find the lions that had been roaring all evening. Mark – new husband and financier of the lavish honeymoon – decided this was a great idea. Kerry declined on account of "fatigue".

Darren didn't take the Main Camp Manager's instruction to "please radio before arriving back at Camp" as seriously as he might have. After successfully finding the Granite Pride and watching it demolish a wildebeest on Jabulani's clearing, Darren felt only too happy to accept Mark's offer of a celebratory night cap.

Back in camp, the main bar was locked up, however, so not wanting to disturb Mark's sleeping wife, Darren suggested that they pop into Room 1, which was vacant, and enjoy something out of the mini bar to celebrate the wildebeest's demise. Cheerfully, Mark agreed that this was a marvellous plan, but you can imagine how promptly his demeanour transformed when the sight that greeted them in Room 1 resembled the mating leopards found on game drive the day before. They stumbled onto Andrew and Kerry engaged in anything but the missionary position. Andrew was screwed – both literally and figuratively.

Apparently, had it not been for home advantage and the fact that he knew of an alternative exit to the 1 Kerry's enraged husband was blocking, Andrew would most definitely have been murdered. The risk of hurling himself off the deck into the wild African bush at 11:00 at night was one that Andrew Jackson was more than happy to take when presented with the alternative.

Deservedly, I suppose, he did not escape entirely unharmed as his home advantage failed to remind him of an ill-positioned Ziziphus thicket below the deck. This is not the kind of tree you want to even brush past on account of its fang-like thorns. Andrew Jackson landed right in the middle of this vicious lot, so it was not surprising that he resembled the Lodge dustbin after a hyena raid when he awoke the following morning.

PJ was hauled in the next day and verbally assaulted by Mark Saunders for a number of hours. Fortunately, the couple was due to leave that day anyway, but PJ felt the wrath of Saunders right up until the bitter end. Not even PJ could salvage anything from the decidedly awkward incident. In his defence, it would have been tricky for anyone to justify Main Camp's trusty host mounting Mrs Saunders on their final night of honeymoon.

Andrew was promptly fired and instructed to leave the property before the end of the day. It made for a funny feeling around the Lodge and I felt like I was back at boarding school on the day that Johan Naude was expelled for trying to ignite the headmaster's cat. The whole Lodge was a babble of chatter and skinder with any number of embellished versions of the goings on. What remained undeniable was that Andrew had left the reserve and after some management reshuffles, September was moved to Main Camp and...

Yours truly was appointed the new Manager of Tamboti Camp!

Can you believe it? I couldn't at first, but to be fair, while obviously not wanting to take anything away from my major achievement, they didn't really have too many other options. Andrew was gone and PJ needed a new Camp Manager. To be honest, he said as much when he called me in, but he also made it clear that he had faith in me and was not simply filling a gap until he found somebody more qualified. He said that my presentation on Quintessential House was impressive and that he had been watching my progress at Tamboti Camp with keen interest. He added that he had heard only positive feedback from Guests and staff alike and that he felt, despite my inexperience, I deserved the opportunity.

Of course, I am elated with the news, mainly because I am now far superior to Angus and will continue to be, even if he qualifies as a Ranger.

Speaking of my brother, I understand that he is due to take his evaluation drive this evening. This is a game drive where a Trainee Ranger takes Anton and a host of other senior Rangers out in order for them to assess his knowledge and guiding skill. It's normally pretty difficult. Most guys almost always fail the first 1, but Angus seems surprisingly confident. If he can overcome the impossible task of putting his sarcasm on hold for the duration of the drive he might have a chance. He is obviously desperately unhappy about my promotion so there is the added pressure of keeping up with his taller brother, a thought which I know is flying around his cynical head. I suppose I'll wish him luck.

Oh, incidentally, I went ahead and sent Simone that text message from Quintessential House. Of course there was no reply which got me into such a state that I was forced to hide my phone away from myself for long periods before periodically checking in the hope that there had been a hit. On the occasion that I did, after 5 hours, return to an awaiting message, it was 1 of those god-forsaken group messages from some beastly night club in Cape Town informing me of their student night discount. It didn't help that Melissa was raking in messages all the way to the airport while I was feeling ill at the prospect of Simone shacked up with Arno van der Vyfer, the chain-smoking Maintenance Manager. She has also not said a word to me since I've been back at the Lodge – despite my promotion! Maybe it's all over. I'll keep you posted.

Lots of love,

Your taller, younger and more senior brother,

Hugh

From: 'Angus MacNaughton'
Sent: 13 March, 20h05
To: 'Julia MacNaughton'
Subject: In the shadows

Dear Julia,

It's 20:00. I'm sitting with my laptop in the shadows of an old mahogany tree just outside camp. Wireless signal is weak. The full moon casts a blue light on the land so I can see all around but I'm hidden by the shadows. There is a giraffe, silhouetted in the clearing opposite, browsing on a knobthorn in the moonlight. This may be my last communication. As I write, Anton is prowling the camp looking for me.

You'll be pleased to know I did well in my tests, all except Anton's Big Five test, which he said was 'blerrie kak' and then muttered something about my imminent 'ironing by a big hairy'. My success with the tests meant that it was time for me to take the dreaded evaluation drive, where a trainee takes a number of senior rangers, other staff and the general manager on a game drive. It is the culmination of training and a rather big deal is made of it. The staff all role-play as guests of various descriptions while the trainee tries to deal with any curve balls they throw at him. Such curve balls might include trying to climb out of the Land Rover at a lion sighting or asking ridiculous questions.

Jeff has, unsurprisingly, failed six evaluation drives to date. On his last he climbed from the car to show his guests a dung beetle. Squatting on his haunches, he quickly became engrossed in a deep explanation of the beetle's behaviour. Unfortunately, he had parked on a slope and neglected to engage the handbrake. He was so absorbed with his monologue that he failed to note his Land Rover and six screaming guests (including PJ) disappearing down the hill into a dam. His latest near-homicidal mistake did not, however, deter him from lavishing advice on me for my first attempt. Jeff has been placed on staff loo cleaning for the next month.

I was further inspired to pass the evaluation because of SB's elevation to the rank of camp manager. They're really scraping the barrel there. String Bean could scarcely manage a group of ultra-compliant sloths. His promotion has been accompanied by a move to even better digs than before while I continue to live in the guano-befouled bat cave. He's more full of himself than ever now.

This afternoon I arrived, freshly spruced, though smelling faintly of guano, on the Main Camp deck. The real guests were enjoying tea and cake as they gazed out over the spectacular view afforded from the Main Camp deck. Jenny and September were chatting and serving iced coffee to an old couple. It was all rather peaceful and I felt prepared and ready. This feeling of general well-being was, as usual, short-lived, however.

Anton and Melitha were the first of my 'guests' to arrive. For intelligent people, guest role-playing extends no further than dressing normally and asking difficult questions that a real guest might. Anton and Melitha, being without intelligence, treated the evaluation as an opportunity for fancy dress and bad acting. He was dressed in leather pants and a tiny Iron Maiden T-shirt, his sagging, hairy, midriff protruding slightly from the bottom. Melitha was decked in an amorphous mass of white fabric and topped with a pith helmet.

'Ah, Melissa,' I said, 'are you here to audition for a part in the parody of Arabian Nights?'

'Shark Crap,' warned Anton, 'careful how you talk to your pax!'

Presently Duncan, PJ, Jamie, Hilda and Jenny joined us and I was spared further interaction with the two idiots. I helped them all to some tea and, in Hilda's case, a brick-sized slice of cake.

It was at this point that the assessment proper began. I gathered them all around the orientation board, pointed out various features on the map and spoke a bit about what to expect on the game drive. PJ and Duncan asked a few questions about the reserve. I was midway through a quick explanation of the geology when the following pearl emerged from beneath the pith helmet of Melitha, who felt the need to test me.

'Ranger, are the rockth thoft, medium or hard?'

'What?' I stared at her. There was an awkward moment as the immensity of her stupidity permeated the Lowveld afternoon.

'The rockth. Are they thoft, medium or hard?' She looked at me smugly, mistaking the silence for my being stumped by the intellectual, rather than inane, nature of her question.

'Well, they're obviously nothing like as hard as the ones in your head,' I replied without thinking. The effect was amazing. Jenny spat a mouthful of tea over the map and ran out pretending to cough. Jamie and Duncan stifled guffaws, Hilda took another mouthful of cake, PJ observed quietly and, predictably, Anton nearly lost it.

'Shark Crap! This is not a joke, this is your pax! You will treat them like real pax or we stop this evaluation right now!' Seeing another six months in the bat cave flash before my eyes, I retreated.

'I'm sorry, no offence intended.' I held up my hands. Melitha glared at me through narrowed eyes.

From the deck we moved to the car park where the Land Rover was waiting with Elvis who was tracking for me. The road out of Main Camp heads around a picturesque waterhole surrounded by lush vegetation. There are hippos, crocs and a multitude of birds to see. Weavers building their nests, kingfishers hunting and fish eagles looking for food, motionless herons and many others. It's a perfect place for a new ranger to showcase his knowledge.

I stopped in the shade and began pointing out birds and explaining bits about their behaviour. A hippo surfaced with a splash and I explained that they normally stay under for about a minute at a time. All was going swimmingly until a kingfisher flew over and disappeared behind a sweet thorn tree.

'Ah, pied kingfisher,' said I. Duncan gave an affirming nod and made a note in his notebook.

'Giant, not pied,' sniped Anton. There was a pause.

'Pretty sure it was a pied,' I said, turning round to see Anton examining his bicep.

'Giant, bru,' he said dismissively. 'Don't contradict your pax, specially if it's me.'

'With due respect, that bird was less than half the size of a giant kingfisher.' There was a hush on the vehicle as the 'guests' felt the tension building. Duncan looked awkward – unsure of whether to side with right or might. He chose neither.

'Shark Crap, I been in the bush 12 years here. What you thinking? If I say it's giant, it's giant. End of story!' He took his eyes off his bicep and glared at me. My patience (and any chance of passing the assessment) evaporated at this point.

'Anton, one might confuse other sorts of kingfishers with each other. For example, a malachite and a pygmy, but that bird was less a giant of the kingfisher world than you are a giant to the world of astrophysics.'

Jenny, Jamie and Duncan couldn't contain themselves. They began laughing hysterically. PJ, as ever, just observed. Melitha looked confused and Hilda, wide-eyed, pushed four Jelly Babies into her mouth. I'd pushed Anton too far and he went ballistic.

'Shark Crap, you've gone too fokken far this time!' he screamed, going puce. He leapt out of the back seat and scrambled over the two rows of seats between us. Hilda's Jelly Baby packet went flying. I jumped up out of the driver's seat, over the dash and onto the bonnet. 'Come fokken down from there, right now!' he yelled.

'Calm down, man! It's just a bird!' I said and then jumped off the front of the car as he made it onto the driver's seat and then the bonnet.

'I'm gonna blerrie moer you, you private school sissie!' he screamed, making to leap off the bonnet after me. Unfortunately for him, Elvis stuck out a foot from his perch on the tracker's seat. Anton tripped, hit the ground with a thud and rolled into the dam. This galvanised Jamie and Duncan. They launched from their seats to pull him out of the water.

'Angus, I think you'd better walk back to the lodge before they get him out,' PJ suggested quietly. I acquiesced.

That was about three hours ago. I've been under this tree ever since. I'll probably sleep in the branches tonight.

Wish me luck,

Angus

P.S. If I do make it through the night, I'll still be in the bat cave for the next while.

From: 'Dad'
Sent: 14 March, 12h17
To: 'Hugh'
Subject: Very proud

Dear Hugh,

Congratulations on your promotion to Camp Manager. Your mother and I are extremely proud of you. We think it is extremely impressive that you have been elevated to the position in such a short time and are so pleased that you have found such a happy niche.

I believe your brother has not impressed management in quite the same way.

Anyway, well done, and good luck with the new responsibility.

Love,

Your very proud parents

From: 'Hugh MacNaughton'
Sent: 20 March, 18h03
To: 'Jules'
Subject: Leave!

Hey Jules,

This is just a short note informing you that I have been granted my first leave. PJ is adamant that I need a rest before taking full charge of Tamboti Camp, so Holly Jones, the Relief Manager, is going to cover for me while I go away for 2 weeks. From now on I'll be working 6 weeks on and 2 weeks off. This is the arrangement for all of the staff who live far away from the property, but an initially long probationary cycle is normal. So it is with great excitement that after 10 weeks, I will be seeing you tomorrow!

As you can imagine, Angus is decidedly bitter about this arrangement. The whole idea of my taking a holiday has enraged him deeply. I feel that this is simply another avenue for him to vent frustration after his disastrous evaluation drive. He is so petrified of being brutally savaged by an enraged Anton (who, from what I have gathered, he personally insulted on the drive) that he went into hiding.

Simone congratulated me on my promotion this morning which made for a particularly good start to the day. The only drawback of going away for 2 weeks will be missing her. I am convinced that I am in love with her but, alas, I am still unsure of where her heart lies. I pine for her so, and pray to the gods on a nightly basis that she too will 1 day pine for me.

I am really looking forward to seeing you tomorrow and catching up face-to-face. I will be leaving at first light so I should be home at lunchtime. Let's have a drink when you finish work in the evening.

Lots of love,

Your home-bound brother,

Hugh

From: 'Angus MacNaughton'
Sent: 20 March, 18h40
To: 'Julia MacNaughton'
Subject: Meeting the apothecary

Dear Julia,

I'm not dead.

It was a close shave, though. At midnight on the eve of my ill-fated assessment drive, I emerged from my hiding place in the mahogany tree. I had only my right shoe by this stage – I removed my boots at the base of the tree when I climbed into the shadows and a hyena made off with the left one. Naturally, this was my only pair. So it was that I hopped back into camp through the shadows cast by the setting moon. I then did a very strange thing, very strange indeed. I made for Melitha's room – she is on her allotted two weeks of leave and I knew Anton would never think to look for me there.

Her room is in a block of three, shared by Anna and Jenny, close to Anton's filthy palace. I gained careful, silent entry with my superb burglary skills and rested there until first light – but not before I'd removed the hundreds of ridiculous stuffed toys Melitha has arranged on her bed. (The most bizarre of these is a four-foot pink penguin.) Anyhow, my clothes smelled of her when I woke ... Sick.

As the dawn broke, I decided to seek counsel. PJ was by far the most rational choice given that the worst he'd do was fire me. I was about to hop out into the pale dawn light when an engine began roaring mightily from nearby. I opened the door a fraction and poked my head out. Anton's bright yellow 4x4 (what other colour would that git have?) was belching oily smoke into the air. He was pumping the accelerator viciously. The car spluttered, coughed and gave up.

'Blerrie fokken kak!' he screamed, smashing his fists against the fake wooden steering wheel. He turned the key again. The engine brayed and died again and he threw another tantrum. It was all rather amusing until I heard a voice from the room next door.

'What, my boy, could you possibly be doing here?' it said huskily. I wheeled around and, in my haste, tripped on my untied right shoelace. I tried to balance on my socked left foot but it found no purchase on the polished concrete veranda. My feet slipped out in front of me and I back-flipped out of the door, cracking my head as I crashed to the floor. I opened my eyes groggily in time to see Anton's car door opening – he was still cursing violently. I was now in imminent danger of being spotted by this murderous bonehead. I lay prostrate between the car and his room. Thankfully, he turned to mete out a savage kick to the vehicle. The idiot then fell on the ground, holding his damaged foot, in an even deeper rage. His limited intellect failed to find vocabulary vile enough for this new level of fury, so he just bellowed like a wounded buffalo.

Meanwhile, I was prone, blood seeping from a wound on the back of my head and groggy from the combined effects of a bang to the head, little sleep and no food since lunch the day before.

The feline owner of the voice, Anna (aged roughly 32 with deep cocoa hair and black eyes), realised that if Anton saw me, he would take the opportunity to vent his anger by delivering a level of physical trauma enough to frighten the Spanish Inquisition. She grabbed my hand, helped me to sit up and whispered with husky urgency, 'Quickly ... stand up ... come.'

She helped me to my feet, put my arm around her neck and half dragged me as I staggered into her room. She shut the door just as Anton raised himself and stomped past, yelling, 'Fok blerrie [unrepeatable words describing female anatomy], bakkie [unrepeatable words describing male anatomy].' A few moments later there was some loud banging at his car, the engine turned and mercifully he and his custard-coloured idiot-mobile buggered off.

So there I was, bleeding and concussed in the room of this mysterious woman. I passed out soon after I heard Anton depart and opened my eyes somewhere around noon. I only woke up because Anna walked into the room. She placed a glass of Coke and ice on the side of her bed and sat down next to me. She regarded me for an awkward minute and smiled.

'Silly boy,' she said in her upper-class English accent, 'how are you feeling?' She is, without question, the most self-assured person I've ever come across.

'What's the time?' I asked groggily, sitting up and pulling the covers off. I twice as quickly pulled them back up when I realised I was clothed in nothing but a holey pair of Woolworths cotton briefs. 'My clothes?' I stammered.

'Over there, on the chair,' she pointed over to a pile on an armchair at the far side of the room. 'I wasn't about to put you in my bed in those filthy rags. Just relax and drink this.' She tipped a few drops of something from a dark brown bottle into the glass. I regarded it doubtfully.

'You an apothecary too?' I raised my eyebrows, my cut stinging as I leaned my head on the wall behind me. I winced as my hand went up to the neatly cleaned wound.

'Just do as I say, and you'll feel much better.' I took the glass and sipped. Waves of relief surged through my body and I drank thirstily while she spoke.

'I've spoken to PJ. He seemed quite amused about yesterday. Apparently, Anton has been sent off on leave early ... to recover from the mood you induced. You're safe for the meanwhile.' She smiled again and stood up. 'Your colour's a bit better now but your head has a nasty egg on it.' She slinked over to her cupboard and in one smooth movement removed the top she was wearing, exposing her shapely back. She carried on talking normally, as she took out a T-shirt and pulled it on. 'Stay here as long as you like, I must go back to camp.' With that she walked out.

'Thanks,' I said, wide-eyed as the door closed.

I left shortly afterwards and returned to the bat cave. My head throbbed and I had a strange floating sensation — presumably a result of Anna's apothecary drops. It felt like I'd been gone for weeks. Just as I sat on my bed, head in my hands, my gormless neighbour walked in without knocking.

'Hey, hey, Angy! What's up with you in the house?'

'What?' I glowered at him. He was holding a *National Geographic* magazine with a gorilla on the cover.

'Cousin of yours?' I asked.

'Huh?'

'Never mind,' said I, clearing a small pile of guano from my bed and assuming the foetal position. 'What do you want?'

'Oh, can't believe we're so lucky! This guy Russell Aspen-Mills is coming to drive 'cos the rangers' team is a bit short at the moment 'cos Anton's taken some leave. He's my hero, Russell, I mean. I've got all his videos. *Hunting Lion with Knives, Alone in the Wilderness – Me and My Swiss Army Knife,* and *Saving the Rhino Single-Handed*.'

'He sounds marvellous. Now, bugger off,' I replied.

Then the name registered. Couldn't be the same Russell Aspen-Mills ... could it?

Until next time ... if there is a next time.

Angus

From: 'Angus MacNaughton'
Sent: 27 March, 18h55
To: 'Julia MacNaughton'
Subject: The Love Muscle

Dear Julia,

Still extant – Anton has not returned and SB is mercifully still on leave.

Hooray.

The egg on my head has gone down since last week and I have a scar which Anna says will go eventually. Her deep black eyes leave me speechless. I think she may be a witch.

I related briefly last week how I learned from Jeff that Russell Aspen-Mills was about to arrive. He apparently cut his bush teeth here many years ago and so was an obvious temporary replacement for Anton. I hoped that this was a different Russell Aspen-Mills although I knew the chances were negligible – he's the very same.

He arrived by plane with some guests shortly after my last missive and I was assigned to go and fetch him. I drove up to the strip early in order to have some solitude in the bush. There, I lay peacefully on the Land Rover bonnet in the shade, chewing on a piece of grass and listening to a white-browed scrub-robin calling in the lazy, mid-morning heat. A swarm of stingless-bees flew in and out of their hive in a knot halfway up the huge mopane tree I was under.

The whine of an approaching airplane disturbed my day-dreaming about the strange and not entirely unpleasant experience in Anna's room last week.

I stood up and straightened my uniform as the plane came to a halt on the apron. The door opened, making a loud 'pshhh' as the cabin decompressed. A wisp of vapour escaped from the dark interior and floated into the Lowveld. There was silence.

A well-built, tall man stepped out into the sunshine at the top of the steps of the plane. My jaw clenched immediately. He was clothed in neatly pressed khakis. On his head sat a wide-brimmed leather hat which he removed to reveal greased-back blond hair. His face sported precise designer stubble. His boots were shiny brown (obviously slip-on). Completing his attire was a ridiculous hunting knife that would have made Excalibur jealous.

The great white hunter paused and surveyed the surrounds with an arrogant air. I stared in disbelief. It was, indeed, that utter wanker, Russell 'The Love Muscle' Aspen-Mills. Remember him? He was at school with us – two years my senior. I'm sure you remember the various injuries (physical and mental) he inflicted on me at Eagle's Cross College. SB was spared him but I'm led to believe the girls in your class weren't.

'Ah, Aspen-Mills,' said I, forcing a smile and offering a hand. 'It's been a while.'

'Have we met?' he asked as though addressing a tick attached to his nethers.

Without waiting for a response, he passed me his hand luggage and climbed onto the Land Rover with the new guests.

I unpacked all of the luggage from the plane while Russell regaled the guests with a yarn about the time he saved a woman from a mamba with his bare hands. It is my belief that spending a minute with Russell is worse than suffering a dirty weekend away with Melitha.

'Come on!' he said to me as I struggled under the mass of his five matching pieces of safari-style luggage.

'I'm so sorry to keep you. You must be exhausted after your hour-long flight,' I snarled sarcastically. He regarded me suspiciously. 'No, really, not to worry, don't move a muscle!' I said.

Russell does not have staff accommodation, which means he is living in a guest room. Me in the bat cave, Russell in Main Camp Room 10. Clearly, the wheel is still turning comfortably in his direction.

Other than that, it has been a pleasant week (relatively speaking). I have been out on training drives with Duncan, one of the senior rangers, and have learned a lot about taking game drives and walks. My highlight of the week was a walk I went on with Elvis. We tracked a rhino for about two hours early one morning. He showed me how the rhino's feet broke the dew and how its grazing caused the fresh grass to 'bleed'. I felt rather privileged to be watching the great animal with Elvis. I hope he is my tracker if I ever qualify.

Till next,

Angus

From: 'Hugh MacNaughton'
Sent: 27 March, 19h30
To: 'Angus'
Subject: Worried

Dear Angus,

I have just read your latest email to Julia and am mildly perturbed to read that Russell Aspen-Mills has temporarily joined the Rangers' team. How long is he there for?

I remember this guy from school. I remember many of the girls in my class – all several years his junior – boasting about losing their virginity to him. Apparently, he is hung like a zebra. Rumour had it that before matriculating, he had notched over 100 conquests in his belt.

I didn't know that he had made a career in game ranging, did you? And I was certainly unaware that he had ever worked a day at Sasekile.

Angus, I would appreciate it if you would keep me updated about this gigolo in disguise. If his filthy seductive techniques managed to infiltrate Simone's pure spirit I don't think that I would have the strength to carry on.

Thanks, Angus,

Hugh

From: 'Angus MacNaughton'
Sent: 03 April, 14h00
To: 'Julia MacNaughton'; 'Hugh MacNaughton'
Subject: Love Muscle and his mark . . .

Dear Julia and Jealous SB,

This week in the lodge has been dominated by the antics of Russell Aspen-Mills and the return of Anton. I would like to report on the former first.

For your edification, SB, the following should be noted:

+ Russell sits next to Simone at all meals;
+ Russell tells really dumb jokes which Simone laughs at;
+ Russell has offered to help Simone with the children's programme; and
+ Everyone in the lodge is talking about the size of his whatnot – the question is: who is giving them this intimate information? Surely not sweet, innocent, virginal(?) Simone?

I've had to suffer the cad more than most. Because he arrived here with such a reputation, PJ decided that I should spend some time shadowing him – for the sake of training. He treats me like his personal dogsbody as Anton has informed him that this is precisely what I am. I've accompanied him on a number of insufferable game drives. The amount of schmoozing and sliming he does is nauseating. What is even more sickening is the fact that women lap it up so readily.

Two days ago, I went on drive with him and six guests, two of whom were a honeymoon couple. She was a plastic American with a set of vast, stand-to-attention boobs that nature did not give her. Russell made sure that she sat next to him in the Land Rover with the following words,

'Hey, beautiful, saved this place next to me so I can look after you ... personally.' He then winked and clicked his tongue.

I sat next to her husband in the front row. Our ranger spent most of the drive hitting bumps too hard and then squinting left towards the giggling, bouncing cleavage. Her timid husband sat looking glum. I thought it all rather amusing until he ran over a francolin.

'Watch out!' shouted One-eyed Joe, the tracker, and I together.

'Huh?' said Russell.

'Francolin, you arse!' I pointed, but it was too late.

There was a loud pop and a puff of feathers as a large Natal francolin disappeared under the front left tyre. Russell hit the brakes so hard that Joe went Superman into a buffalo-thorn tree.

'Oh, my Gaaad, you killed that partridge,' yelled Boobs Malone.

'Blud fool!' bellowed Joe, suspended in the thorns.

'Not a partridge,' I corrected. 'Our fearless ranger exploded a ... *francolin* not a partridge ... subtle difference.'

Silence.

Russell wheeled round.

'Why didn't you tell me it was there? I can't do everything! I'm busy risking my life to show these guests the most dangerous animals on planet Earth! You can't even spot a bird on the road? Can you imagine if I kept my eyes on the road what would happen? Huh? We'd be flattened, killed stone dead by elephants. I can't afford to keep my eyes on the road!'

'I'm sorry?' I said, confused.

'Look here, trainee boy,' said he, getting riled, 'you think it's easy having the lives of nine people on your shoulders? A little help from someone who is supposed to be a ranger would be nice!'

I stared at him. 'Well, you nearly lost one of those nine,' said I, pointing at Joe.

Joe by this stage had extricated himself from the buffalo thorn. He was mad as a snake, his uniform in tatters. He only just managed to return to his perch before Russell drove off in a rage. There was stony silence all the way back to the lodge.

On a more bizarre note – Anton's return. He came back a week early, claiming to have embraced Buddhism with the aid of a collection of books called *Enlightenment in Three Volumes and Just Three Months*. He carries these with him everywhere. My bet is that he found them in the self-help section at a bargain book sale. Apart from their dubious origin, they must be of limited use because I'll bet that idiot has never finished reading a publication in his life – other than his *Guns and Rifles* magazine (which is mostly pictures). He says he has found 'Zen' and will thus not kill me – we'll see how long this lasts.

So, I survive another week ...

Angus

P.S. String Bean, I suggest you buy copies of Anton's books in order to achieve peace with Russell and Simone's blossoming romance/sexual infatuation.

From: 'Hugh MacNaughton'
Sent: 03 April, 20h00
To: 'Angus'
Subject: Fuck you!

Angus,

Although you are just as depressed as I am about the fact that we are both destined to an eternity of sibling-ship, I would think (but I suppose you wouldn't) that you might have a modicum of understanding for my romantic predicament. I have made it more than obvious to you how important the prospect of a relationship with Simone is, yet you toy with my emotions without regard.

You are – just like *everyone* says – a prick!

Hugh

From: 'Hugh MacNaughton'
Sent: 04 April, 01h00
To: 'Angus'
Subject: Sorry

Dear Angus,

I'm sorry.

I apologise for those harsh words, but I'm going into a mild decline here. The thought of returning to the news that Simone's depths have been plundered by Russell and his god-forsaken love muscle is driving me mad.

How much of what you said is true? Are the 2 of them really sitting next to each other at every occasion, and does she honestly find that creature amusing? I simply want an honest account of the happenings between Simone and Russell. Is that really too much to ask?

I am convinced that your words are untrue, but I need to know for sure. If the worst is in fact a reality, then I need to start making some pretty serious decisions. I really don't think that I will come back.

Do you have PJ's cell number? Maybe I should suggest he start looking for an alternative to run Tamboti?

Perhaps a message to Simone herself? Would that change her mind or is she beyond rescue from Russell's promiscuous hypnosis?

Angus, I am going berserk!

Help me – please.

Your loving brother,

Hugh

From: 'Angus MacNaughton'
Sent: 04 April 10h00
To: 'Hugh MacNaughton'
Subject: Simone's flower

SB,

Thanks for your apology, which was sweet ...

Unfortunately for you, I do not give a shit whether you hate me or not. Swearing at me or apologising is going to have absolutely no effect on me as I do not consider your opinion worth the air it took to form.

It is also going to have no effect on Russell or his seemingly imminent plucking of Simone's flower.

Cheers,

Angus

From: 'Hugh MacNaughton'
Sent: 10 April, 18h01
To: 'Jules'
Subject: It was all a lie!

Hey Jules,

Russell and Simone are not together – thank god!

It was great seeing you again and catching up properly.

You will be happy to hear that I have arrived back safely. After my short time away I am left agog at the sheer absurdity of the events which transpire here on such a frequent basis.

I met with PJ on my first morning back. After a short chat packed with motivation and inspiration, he made my position as Tamboti Manager official. There were a few raised eyebrows at my promotion amongst some of the senior staff, but I am determined to prove myself and silence their doubts by making a serious contribution to the far-eastern section of the Lodge.

Of course, it would have to be Russell driving the Tamboti Guests who arrived 3 mornings after my return. He is more slippery than your average catfish and it is pretty sickening having to converse with him. He constantly feels the desire to "mentor" me on the various techniques involved in getting laid on a 1-night-stand and is also intent on gleaning the physical status of my relationship with Simone. Fortunately, despite Angus's efforts to make me believe otherwise, nothing has happened between the 2 of them. In fact, quite to the contrary, Simone thinks almost less of the Love Muscle than I do.

"Guys who simply see chicks as numbers are so lame," she remarked with a scowl when I asked her about him. Having slept with a grand total of zero women myself, I was delighted to hear those words.

Tamboti Camp is hosting an English family for a few days. They are a multi-generational family with everything going on: engaged adult daughter and fiancé who have been forced into separate living quarters by conservative mother of the future bride; promiscuous younger daughter who is still in school and who seems – quite amazingly – to have taken a shine to Angus; reasonably level-headed older parents with aristocratic heritage; and an eccentric old grandfather who reminds me of The Major. Finally, there is the beastly younger son, William, who is the kind of boy that would have had the stuffing knocked out of him at my school – such an attitude.

They arrived by private jet and Angus had to help with the luggage. You can imagine the satisfaction I got from watching him unload large leather suitcases in front of me in the Tamboti car park. Russell retired to look at himself in the side mirror of the Land Rover while I helped the Guests off the vehicle.

I got on well with all of them from the start, but I have grown particularly fond of the old bullet named Walter, who – coincidently – insists on being called "Major". He refers to me as "Private" and enjoys exchanging salutes when we pass each other. He is also particularly grateful for the generous measures of scotch I give him – apparently they are somewhat larger than the ones his daughter pours back home in England.

Their stay has gone well thus far, but they are still in camp for a further 5 days. The only mildly worrying element is Russell's constant "hitting" on Jackie, who is the daughter travelling with her fiancé Mathew. He has been anything but discreet about it. Admittedly, Mathew is a bit of a wet blanket but how he hasn't reacted to some of the crap coming out of Russell's mouth is a mystery to me. Last night at dinner he dropped the following clanger.

"Hey, Jackie, feel the sleeve of my Ranger's shirt," he said, with a sultry sickliness. Playing to his little game in an effort, perhaps, to piss off her loving fiancé (as only women get a kick out of doing), she rubbed the sleeve of his shirt between her fingers. "You know what material that is, hey?" he asked.

"Tell me, Russell, I have no idea," she cooed rather pathetically.

"It's marriage material," he chortled.

Can you believe that those words actually passed through the lips of a human being? Jackie and her sister chuckled, but Mathew remained as cool as a cucumber. Amazing. Maybe he didn't hear, though, as, at the same time, Walter was loudly coughing up a slightly undercooked carrot.

News on other fronts includes a welcome-back note to me from Simone which I found on my bed. Part of the loving note included a comment that she had missed me. Pretty good stuff, don't you think? We are getting on better than ever since my return, which is terrific.

Finally, PJ has called for a meeting with me to discuss a big group – the Travel Luxury Company. It is to be the most important group of the year so we will need to plan their stay, game drives and entertainment quite carefully. I think that PJ wants me to get on top of all of it early so that nothing goes wrong closer to the time.

That's it from me for this week.

Lots of love,

Hugh

Tamboti Camp Manager!

From: 'Angus MacNaughton'
Sent: 11 April, 18h29
To: 'Julia MacNaughton'
Subject: The Cad, The Slut and The Army Man

Dear Julia,

Zen Master Anton sent me up to the airstrip with Greasy Russell to fetch some guests the other day. My function was purely that of porter. Thankfully, the plane landed soon after we arrived so I didn't have to suffer conversation with Russell. He was leaning on the Land Rover sharpening his knife as the plane door opened.

Lord Fulton, in his early sixties, stepped out into the sunlight. He was half way down the stairs when Russell held up his left clenched fist in the 'freeze' position.

'Wait!' he shouted. 'I need to survey the surrounds.' He squinted from his ridiculous leaning position, peering left to right into the fringing bush, his hat tipped over his eyes. He checked the sharpness of Excalibur with his thumb. Lord Fulton froze, presumably expecting to see a savage beast come hurtling out of the vegetation.

A chinspot batis called from a bushwillow tree nearby.

I coughed.

'It's OK,' said Russell presently, 'safe to come out.' He replaced the sword in his belt, smiled and smarmed over to the guests as they filed from the plane. They consisted of:

+ Lord and Lady Fulton – similar ages. His chinless bottom jaw indicated that his title was born of genetics rather than a purchase.
+ Chloe, their slutty-looking 16-year-old daughter.
+ Jackie, their other daughter (28-odd), travelling with her fiancé Mathew (30-odd – also undershot bottom mandible). The sight of Jackie increased the level of grease in Russell by an order of magnitude.

- Brainless William (17). He was attached to an enormous pair of earphones. Calvin Klein boxer shorts stuck out of his trousers which were made for someone with the backside of a hippo. His first utterance went something like, 'Yeah, my mother's a damn ass who ...' as he sang along to the mindless crap coming out of his earphones.
- Last out of the plane came a man approaching 250 years. His eyebrows were so impressive that I thought he'd attached two hedgehogs to his forehead.

Lady Fulton whispered, 'This is my senile old father, Major Walter Thesiger. He's not quite right, I'm afraid.'

The old man tottered up to the group wide-eyed. 'Morning all!' he said, rather too loudly. He ignored Russell and stared at me standing in the background. 'I rather like the cut of your jib! What's your name?' he bellowed.

'Right, back to the lodge,' said Russell before I could reply. He waved the guests towards the waiting Land Rover. For the second time in less than a week, I was loading mountains of luggage unassisted. (Again, please ask Mum and Dad if this is what they intended when they paid for my degree.) Chloe eyed me and licked her lips from the back seat as I loaded the trailer. I made as if to vomit and she turned around.

Russell drove back to camp while I lay on top of the luggage, trying to prevent it bouncing out of the trailer. On arrival at Tamboti Camp, SB was waiting, all spruced up and cheerful. He's such a geek. I helped Incredible (a butler not blessed with a frontal lobe) carry the bags to the rooms. As I dropped off Chloe's suitcase she appeared at the door to her room, blocking my exit. She stared at me suggestively.

'May I be of further assistance?' I asked tiredly.

'Ooh, what's on your mind?' she said, slinking into the room.

'Right now?' I replied with a sigh. 'Right now, I'm wondering how many times you've ignored the legal age of consent. Now step aside.' I pushed past her and made my escape.

The rest of my week has been similarly painful. I've had to go with Russell on every game drive and there are fresh oysters less slimy than him. His knowledge of the bush is poor at best. He covers this deficiency by deferring many questions to me in order to 'test my knowledge'. His other tactic is to ignore the question asked and launch into a ridiculously far-fetched story from his days as a 'daring' wildlife filmmaker. I make sure I sit in the back of the Land Rover so I can roll my eyes heavenward without being observed.

One piece of positive news is that the coital noises emanating from my neighbour and Candice have stopped. Jeff is looking morose and has not spoken in days (one must be grateful for small mercies). Candice, on the other hand, is irritatingly bubbly. This can only mean that she is bonking someone else because she is unable to be without sex. I found Jeff's entire DVD collection of *Russell Braves Africa* in the bin yesterday, so my guess is that our receptionist is being serviced by the great Love Muscle himself.

What a wonderful life ...

Angus

From: 'Hugh MacNaughton'
Sent: 17 April, 14h55
To: 'Jules'
Subject: Pure joy

Hey Jules,

It is with great glee, abundant joy and furious enthusiasm that I report this week on a major development in my relationship with Simone. At last we have kissed and for the first time it has been for an extended period. "French kissing", "coming right", "sucking face" – call it what you will but the fact remains that I and Simone have engaged in a passionate embrace and I am chuffed beyond speech.

True to form, however, the circumstances were outrageous – or better put, they became outrageous. I had finished with dinner at Tamboti Camp where things had gone reasonably well. I say "reasonably" given that the stationed Security Guard, unsuitably named Efficient, was fast asleep in the boma when I arrived. After I shook him back to life, it quickly became evident that he had spent the afternoon indulging in a generous tasting of the Lodge's finest vodkas. Despite the pungent alcoholic fumes and red eyes, he assured me that he had not touched a drop of anything other than water and a Coke. The sheer sincerity of this foul and contemptible mistruth was staggering. I made him a massively strong plunger of coffee and forced him to drink it all before the Guests returned from drive.

I suppose that the remainder of the dinner fitted into the "well" category. Walter was his usual eccentric self and regaled those who cared to listen (or didn't, for that matter) with stories of his many successful advances on enemy lines. Chloe occupied herself for most of the meal with hoisting cocktail olives into the air and attempting to catch them between her rapidly developing boobs. Russell found contentment in smothering Jackie with as many compliments as possible while the parents chatted with me. Mathew and William added very little – William, of course, was distracted by the sound of "smack my bitch up" playing through his oversized earphones.

After dinner I plucked up the courage to make my move. I had been waiting to invite Simone round to my new residence for some time, but wanted to be sure to pick the right moment. I neglected to mention in last week's email that with my recent promotion has come even grander living quarters than before – an expansive suite just behind Tamboti Camp is my new abode. Need I mention that Angus is still in what he refers to as the bat cave?

Anyway, Simone had been looking after a horde of young terrors over at Main Camp for the evening and was still at it when I arrived to see how she was doing. Mercifully, it was not long after I got there that they moved on to bed and I had my opportunity. She was in good spirits when I started talking to her and, having had a few drinks already, she was more than up for my invitation to have a glass of wine and a look around my house.

Unexpectedly, things between us were rather easy to begin with. She laughed at my jokes, complimented the wine I had chosen and remarked frequently on how nice my new house was. We chatted for ages and I really couldn't put a foot wrong, to be honest. I topped her glass up liberally and frequently to up my chances. When we found ourselves cornered between my makeshift wine rack and a protruding window I categorically knew that I had to act. I briefly reflected on the strategy of "Go 90 and wait for her to come 10" but unfortunately could no longer contain myself. I put my head on her forehead, paused for a moment, and then kissed her.

It was wonderful and a deep sense of contentment enveloped me from head to toe. It was bliss.

Of course, as the madness in this place always dictates, our passionate embrace could not last. Just as I felt that I had entered a realm of ecstasy that could not be matched, Simone and I were forced apart by the deafening sound of 3 rapid gunshots. From the volume I knew that they were close by. Leaving Simone in a mild panic, I dashed from my residence with torch in hand to find out what all the commotion was about. I arrived on the scene – outside Room 1 – to something that nobody will ever believe: old boy Walter on his patio, without clothes and carrying 2 hand guns! His family arrived shortly after me.

My immediate thought was that he was sleepwalking in a past memory and thought he was under attack by the advancing enemy. He kept squawking on about some "god-forsaken Bolshevik agitator". I enquired as to the whereabouts of the alleged offender. He gestured viciously into the darkness with the barrels of his archaic revolvers, so I thought it best to at least offer to search the camp. In so doing, I ensured that none of the Guests received a full metal jacket to the shoulder.

The hung-over Efficient had emerged by this stage so we set off together. Efficient looped slowly around the room but found nothing. Fortunately, Lady Fulton had become a little more assertive by this stage. She took control of her father and the rest of the family. She apologised embarrassedly about her demented parent and sent him back to his room to check on Chloe, who was sharing the double room with him after William refused to. I apologised in general for the unfortunate circumstances and we all headed back to bed.

When I returned to my house Simone was still there. I recounted the bizarre events and she smiled.

"Very brave for someone so young!" she said with a slight cheekiness. I smiled back and cast my eyes towards the heavens. "May I stay with you tonight?" she asked. "I don't want to move too fast with all of this, but I am not too keen on being shot either," she said.

"Of course," I answered, "but only in the interests of not being shot."

We shared a final cup of tea together on my couch before she fell asleep with her head on my shoulder. I lowered her onto the couch and put a blanket over her. She made a few grumbling noises, which took me by surprise, but did not wake up. She is truly beautiful.

I am desperately in love,

Hugh

From: 'Jules'
Sent: 17 April, 16h05
To: 'Brother H'
Subject: Well done, Casanova

Young man!

Congrats! Who was it who said that patience would yield the ultimate reward? I trust Simone appreciates the special man who has been wooing her all these months. You must be out of your boots with excitement!

Now remember, the game is still *muchos importantes* from here on out. My advice is that you should play the aloof card every now and then, just to keep her keen. This is no doubt irrational to you (and the rest of men) but what can I say, it works!

Very proud to be your sister!

Love,

Jules

P.S. Also heaps relieved that you did not get yourself shot!

From: 'Angus MacNaughton'
Sent: 17 April, 18h32
To: 'Julia MacNaughton'
Subject: Sweet revenge

Dear Julia,

Finally, some bloody satisfaction. Revenge may be childish but it can be just as sweet as the clichés suggest. SB, for once in his miserable life, will be rather pleased with his big brother's efforts. Russell the knobhead finally received the comeuppance he so richly deserved since he flushed my head in the house loos all those years back.

But I must go back 2 days to explain ...

At about 00:30 two nights ago, the camp was quiet, bathed in the shadows cast by a big moon. I was asleep in the bat cave, dreaming of playing at the Royal Albert Hall with Eric Clapton. Suddenly Eric's guitar morphed into a cobra. I stood frozen as the snake attempted to climb into my ear.

The fright woke me. Instead of a snake, I found a mouth nibbling my left earlobe. I flung myself out of bed and flicked on the bedside lamp.

There, stretched out on my bed, in a minute T-shirt and a pair of equally minute pink shorts, was the harlot Chloe Fulton. A powerful blast of perfume slapped my face.

'Just little me,' she said cattishly, 'come back to bed.' She pouted her full, glossed lips and pushed out her pert chest.

'I'd sooner go to bed with a rabid mamba,' I snarled. 'How d'you get here?'

'Don't you think I'm attractive?' she said, rolling over towards me, squeezing her cleavage together.

'You smell like the depths of a Turkish brothel, you are 16, and quite honestly I don't know where you've been. I ask again, how did you get here?'

'I walked here on my own.' She started lifting her shirt to reveal a well-toned, bronzed stomach. 'I'm not a virgin, you know.'

'Really? What an immense surprise,' I said flatly. 'Now get up quietly. I'm taking you back to your room.' The thought of being caught with her in my cave and having to explain the situation was too awful. I decided to take her back myself rather than have her mauled by a buffalo on the return journey.

A few minutes later, my admiring teenager and I were sneaking back through the camp trying to avoid being spotted by Efficient Nkuna. She was sharing a room with her grandfather. As we approached the room, I spotted Efficient's torchlight. I grabbed Chloe's arm and yanked her down behind a plumbago bush to the side of the room and under the bathroom window.

'Now, sit still,' I said, holding her against the wall. Efficient's torch beam, shining inefficiently from side to side, passed over the top of the bush as he headed down the path.

I stood up.

'Let's go ... quickly,' I said, pulling Chloe by the wrist and carefully watching Efficient's beam recede. As we emerged from behind the room, we collided with someone.

The moonlight revealed the tart – Candice. She let out a squeak which stopped Efficient in his tracks. I grabbed both women and dived back behind the plumbago as the security guard turned around. I covered Candice's mouth with my hand as the torch beam passed once more over the top of the bush. Efficient (being anything but) decided against investigating the noise and went on his way.

'What the bloody hell are you doing here?' I hissed, releasing my grip.

'I thought Russell might like to see my new Wonderbra,' she replied defensively. So my guess that Candice had been servicing Russell was correct. She was dressed in a leopard-print coat and ridiculous, clear plastic high heels. There was a sprinkling of glitter on her spectacularly augmented cleavage.

'Anyway, I might ask you the same thing!' She looked at Chloe, who had tucked her arm into mine.

'Oh, shut up,' I snapped, poking my head out to look out for Efficient. I was about to stand up and move again when, if you can believe it, Jackie appeared, apparently sneaking to her fiancé's room.

As she was about to pass our hiding place, there was a whistling. The sound made me shudder. I remembered it so clearly from my days at school. It was the same tune that Russell used to whistle on his way into the house common room – *La Marseillaise*. It used to send the juniors scattering for fear of the Russell bogwash.

Jackie froze right in front of the plumbago bush, straining to find the direction of the whistle. From the shadows, the figure of Russell appeared on the path. His seductive nocturnal clothing took the cake – crotch-hugging Polo Sport hot pants, unlaced boots, leather hat and knife strapped around his waist. He carried a bottle of champagne and two glasses. Jackie ducked to the side of the room and crouched down, next to the plumbago, watching Russell. It took her about three seconds to realise she was not alone.

'What the …?'

'Shut it,' I hissed, and held a finger to my lips.

Russell wandered past the bush and onto the room's veranda. He pulled the door open with a flourish.

'Hello, Jackie baby!' he bawled and swaggered in. The greasy fool had mistaken Thesiger and Chloe's room for Jackie's.

'Oh!' said Jackie and Candice in unison.

'What a bloody idiot,' said I, holding my head in my hands. 'This, incredibly, can only get worse.'

'What the devil?' I heard Thesiger wake suddenly. 'Who's there?' He flicked on the light and I could imagine the wide-eyed and absurdly dressed figure of Russell standing, rooted in confusion. There was a scrabbling noise.

'Damn!' cursed Thesiger as his glasses tinkled to the floor. Chloe started giggling.

'I, umm ...' began Russell, but that was all he managed. There was a mighty crash of breaking glass.

'Take that, commie swine!' bellowed Thesiger as two halves of a crystal sherry decanter came flying out of the door, followed closely by a dazed Russell holding his bleeding forehead. There was more scuffling in the room and then Thesiger yelled, 'I'll blow your bally noggin off, anarchist bastard!'

Three shots rang out.

I realised that there was going to be a death in the camp if I didn't act fast. I leapt from the plumbago, grabbed Russell as he lurched off the porch and pulled him into the hiding place.

'But what ... you ... them ...' He looked groggily from me to the three women in various states of undress. I pointed a finger at him menacingly.

'You just shut your gob and lie still.'

Thesiger emerged from his room, stark naked, brandishing two revolvers as Efficient came running in a mystified froth.

'What is shooting and where is clothes?' he demanded.

'Bloody Bolshevik agitator!' shouted Thesiger. 'Don't worry, think I offed him! Was in my room, don't you know!' Efficient, predictably, had absolutely no idea what the naked geriatric was on about.

The shots woke everybody else in Tamboti Camp including SB, whose mansion is nearby. The Fultons, Mathew and SB arrived simultaneously in animated bewilderment. Thesiger walked down from the porch and glared into the darkness. Everyone was stunned silent by the unclothed figure and his two smoking guns.

'Oh, Daddy!' cried Lady Fulton at the sight of her revolver-brandishing, naked father.

'What have you been shooting at?' asked SB, making an attempt to take control of the situation.

'Intruder!' replied Thesiger, apparently unaware that he had nothing on. 'Probably some sort of communist dissenter. Damn his eyes! DAMN HIS EYES!'

'Um ... Well, we better have a look around,' said SB trying to ease the awkward atmosphere. Efficient flicked his torch from side to side.

'I walk around!' he said, feigning enthusiasm. His footsteps headed off towards the opposite side of the room from my plumbago.

'Oh, crap,' I hissed. Explaining my presence behind the room with three semi-clad women and a bleeding Russell was not an option. I noticed the open bathroom window above us. 'Get in the bloody window!' I whispered as loudly as I dared.

It was at this point that Lady Fulton remembered her youngest daughter.

'Daddy, where's Chloe?' she asked, suddenly panicked.

'In the room, of course!' he answered.

'Hurry up!' I whispered and pushed Chloe through the window. Lady Fulton rushed onto the porch and into the room as Chloe emerged from the bathroom, closing the door behind her.

'What's going on?' I heard her ask her panicked mother, feigning a yawn.

Meanwhile, Jackie and Candice scrabbled up into the bathroom. Russell was almost comatose from the blow to his head. I pushed him up from behind while the two girls pulled from the inside. We stuffed him through the window and I followed, just as Efficient came round the corner from the back of the room. He returned to the waiting group.

'I find nothing,' he reported sourly.

'Chloe seems to have slept through the whole thing!' exclaimed Lady Fulton, going back out onto the veranda. 'Father, really! You must've imagined the whole episode. How awfully embarrassing. Where on Earth did you get those hideous weapons?'

'Good army man always carries protection!' he snapped.

'Please go back inside. And at least put something on. My daughter is sleeping in there!' said she, blissfully unaware that her daughter was less chaste than a horny scrub hare.

'Exactly, that's why I carry these trusty things. Hadn't been for me, that swine would've plucked her purity!'

'Please forgive him, he's going rather senile,' said Lady Fulton apologetically. The onlookers muttered goodnights to each other and dispersed.

Back in the bathroom, Russell had collapsed in a heap, his head on the loo. Chloe walked back in.

'They've all gone,' she whispered. There was a knock on the door. 'Be out in a sec, granddad,' she shrilled.

'You two get out of the window.' I pointed at Jackie and Candice. They scurried out.

'Is there someone in there with you?' Thesiger asked suspiciously. 'Who's that I can hear?'

'No, of course not, granddad!' Chloe said. I clipped Russell over the back of his head but he didn't move. 'He can't stay here!' whispered Chloe, getting hysterical.

'Yes, thank you, I'm well aware of that!' I replied through clenched teeth, looking at Russell. I smiled, and kicked his groggy head over the lip of the loo bowl and flushed. 'There you are, knobhead, how does that feel?' Russell spluttered and regained enough consciousness for Chloe and me to heave him out of the window. There was more banging on the door.

'What the devil's going on in there?' bellowed Thesiger. As I was about to follow out the window Chloe grabbed my face and planted her full lips on mine.

'I'm coming in!' yelled the old boy as I managed to free myself from her clutches and leap out.

'Really granddad, can't a girl have any privacy?' I heard her ask.

As I walked home (alone) in the dim moonlight, I chuckled merrily at the thought of Russell's bleeding head flushing in the porcelain bowl.

In other news, Anton announced that I would be going on my second assessment drive next week. He's still on his Buddhist kick but the cracks are beginning to appear. He threatened Clifford the butler with violence three days ago.

The edge of the summer heat has come off, which makes for long, pleasant days. I went tracking with Elvis again the other day and we managed to find a leopard basking in the shade of a jackalberry tree on the banks of a dry watercourse. We watched her sleep from a distance and she was completely unaware of us. It's at times like those that I'm grateful for being here. At other times, like the other night, I'm obviously not.

So ends yet another ridiculous week in this place. I shall report on my assessment drive with the Dalai Lama in the next email.

Angus

From: 'Hugh MacNaughton'
Sent: 24 April, 17h45
To: 'Jules'
Subject: Arno

Hey Jules,

I am still utterly disbelieving of the events (unbeknownst to me at the time) which transpired on Monday last week. I doubt that the best script writers in Hollywood could have constructed the twists and turns of the Fulton debacle – I, for 1, was certainly caught unawares. I must say though that the sight of Russell leaving us for good – bandaged head and all, and delivered to the airstrip by none other than Angus – gave me gratification second only to the kissing of Simone.

As you can imagine, I am still all aflutter about the development of our relationship. We have been "together" for a little over a week now, so this liaison records as my longest to date – not a difficult feat given that my previous "relationship" summed all of 1 evening on Clarke's field playing spin-the-bottle with Clarisse Potgieter back in Standard 9. I am really so fond of her (Simone, not Clarisse) mostly because we get on with such ease. We truly enjoy one another's company.

Of course, the whole Lodge has been skindering away as usual, which has been awkward at times, but Simone and I are able to joke about it when we get our opportunities alone. We've put on brave faces while the comments have flown at us in open forum.

There must, however, always be 1 who pushes the envelope just that fraction too far. This week it was Arno van der Vyfer, the desperately miserable Maintenance Manager. To set the scene before explaining what transpired, it would be remiss of me not to humour you with a brief description of this man.

Tall and severe, Arno wears a weathered face for a man in his mid-thirties. Veins protrude from his neck when he gets angry, and he is angry most of the time. Dark black hair with abundant flecks of grey is pulled back off his wiry face into a greasy ponytail. A thin beard of similar colour and texture grows in a vertical stripe between the middle of his bottom lip and chin – I have heard facial growth in this style humorously referred to as a "womb broom". Arno does not talk much but shouts often. His speech is always punctuated with a healthy use of the F-word.

He wears only black attire which is often dirtied by oil stains and complemented, on exceptionally cold days, by a dark brown woollen jersey which looks as if it was knitted by the quivering and arthritic hands of a woman in her 100s.

But Arno's most noteworthy trait must be his addiction to nicotine. I have watched him comfortably put away 10 cigarettes over a 30-minute lunch break and in the time that I have been here, I haven't once seen him not lighting, holding or inhaling a cigarette. This has led to a consistently foul odour about him and an immovable yellow stain around his pursed lips and womb broom.

He is not a nice man.

I'm sure that you will appreciate how little I cared for his tasteless humour the other day while retrieving a packet of nails and a hammer from the workshop. Doing everything by the book – as pedantic as it was – I radioed Arno and asked if I could meet with him in order to sign out the tools I wished to use. (I wanted to create a place to hang the many lanterns that we use of an evening in the camp.)

"Be wiff you in 5," was the answer that came back through the airwaves.

Arno arrived on time looking his usual dishevelled self.

"OK, waddoo you need, bru?" formed his opening exchange.

"Yes, good morning to you too, Arno," I responded. He glared back at me but said nothing. I continued, "I wish to borrow some nails and a hammer." There was long pause. Becoming mildly frustrated now, I ventured, "Arno, if it's all the same to you, I would appreciate the opportunity to get to work at some stage before sunset."

Arno was clearly not amused by my light humour. Still mute, he turned away from me and began to rummage around in his storeroom. He emerged with the tools and a form for me to sign. I began to thank him, but he interrupted me.

"Be careful, bru," he said.

I assured him that I had, in fact, used a hammer many times before, but the sarcasm seemed lost on him.

"No, idiot!" he shouted. "You must be careful. That Simone is a nice piece of ass." I stiffened suddenly and looked back at him. "Don't think I won't show her what a real man is capable of when I next catch her off guard."

A feeling of rage began to boil deep within me. It rose from my core, ran up my back and coursed through my veins. It enveloped me as I watched the threatening words leave his yellow, puckered lips. I exploded internally – but not on the outside. I took a deep breath, thanked Arno for the tools, turned away and took a single step.

I paused.

I could have walked away but my body wouldn't allow it. I spun round in a flash while lowering my centre of gravity and struck Arno so hard below his knee with the hammer that it might have broken his leg. He let out a blood-curdling yell – a mixture of the F-word and ahh.

"Fuaaaaahk!" he bellowed.

I said nothing and walked away.

I am not sure what will come of this or of the state of Arno's left leg.

I don't care, though.

Hugh

From: 'Angus MacNaughton'
Sent: 24 April, 18h36
To: 'Julia MacNaughton'
Subject: Second evaluation drive – the apothecary strikes again

---

Dear Julia,

I write this in the aftermath of my second assessment drive this afternoon. The line-up of 'guests' on the drive consisted of the following people:

+ PJ – normal dress and behaviour;
+ Duncan (who has been helping out with my training since the departure of Russell) – normal dress and behaviour;
+ Anna – normal dress and typically dark feline behaviour;
+ Arno (maintenance man) – limping, normal dress and behaviour (for a bone-head, of course);
+ Anton – shaved head in the fashion of a Buddhist monk, loose-fitting khaki clothes and hideous sandals;
+ Candice – miserable and silent since the departure of her Love Muscle.

I arrived on the Main Camp deck 15 minutes early, spruced and ready, a task not made easy by the fact that half the ceiling in the bat cave collapsed last night – onto my head. I woke with a mouthful of guano and a thousand bats swarming around the room in panicked delirium. I turned on the lamp and my face was immediately covered by at least ten of the diseased things. Wings flapped all over my head and their mouths investigated my ears and nose. I ran for the door and gasped out into the night. *All* of my stuff smells like bat crap now ... But I digress.

September was serving the Main Camp guests their tea as they watched the river's lazy path in front of the lodge. Jenny was chatting to a happy old couple in the corner. It was all very peaceful.

Anna arrived first. She carried with her a small black envelope which she handed to me on her way to the tea table.

'Angus' was written on the front of the envelope in fine handwriting. I moved to a secluded part of the deck and opened it. On expensive black paper, written in white ink, was the following.

Dear Angus,

A short missive to wish you the best for your drive. There is no doubt you have the talent to do an excellent job. While some find your dry sarcasm amusing at times – they are few and far between. For your own sake, leave it behind today and try to be more like your brother on this occasion.

Good luck,

Anna

P.S. I have added a ready-mixed cocktail to your cooler box for the drinks stop. It is always fun to give your guests something special to drink.

She is, without question, the only living organism that could get away with telling me to be more like the snivelling SB. I'm convinced she has extensive contact with the underworld. I took her advice to heart and resolved to bite my tongue.

The others arrived presently and tea proceeded without incident (Hilda wasn't around to devour the entire cake, and Melitha was also mercifully absent). The orientation talk and safety briefing were seamless and we continued to the car park. So far, so good.

Unfortunately, there was no tracker available to me for that afternoon. Instead of Elvis, I was forced to make do with the cretinous Jeff on the front left of the car. I introduced him to the 'guests' as my tracker, which made him grin stupidly. Despite the warmth of the afternoon, he had a thick beanie on his head and sweat beads dripped down his forehead from beneath it.

I realised I was on my own.

I announced myself on the radio and Jamie replied that there was a pride of six lions lying in an area to the east of the reserve. In an effort to include Jeff, I informed him of the location and asked what he thought was the best route to the area. He replied with a convoluted route that would have fetched us up at the far *west* of the reserve. For interest's sake I asked him from which direction he thought the sun rose. He closed one eye, looked for the sun and then placed his thumb on his nose, pinkie finger outstretched. He faced his open eye into the sun and then pointed due north. Utter moron. I didn't bother to talk to him for the rest of the afternoon.

We headed off and I pointed out various birds and trees as we went. Arno thought this was very boring and kept asking,

'Is we going to see a kill?'

Anton had no quibbles with my identification of the birds. This time around he just looked wistfully at the vegetation and said things like,

'Blessings on that tree.'

It took roughly an hour to get to Jack's Road where the lions were supposed to be resting in obvious view. There was nothing there, just empty shade. In keeping with my general good luck in this place, and contrary to all hitherto recorded lion behaviour, *this* pride decided to bugger off with the sun still well in the sky. I told the 'guests' that the animals must be nearby because they tend not to move in the heat of the day. We headed off-road.

An hour later we were lodged in the middle of a flaky thorn thicket denser than the Bwindi Impenetrable Forest. It was an utter disaster. The car was so covered in loose vegetation that it resembled a garden compost heap. In addition, Candice had failed to heed one of my many warnings to watch out and had ripped her shirt on a buffalo thorn. This revealed a luminous pink Wonderbra.

'Eeeeek! Angus, what are you doing?' she squealed. 'You've torn my shirt!'

I turned around to look at the damage and probably stared too long because I failed to notice an overhanging sweet thorn branch. Jeff saw it and leapt off his perch on the tracker's seat. His yelp made me look up but not before the offending limb had cleared me and caught Anton square upside the head.

Buddhist goodwill evaporated instantly.

'Aaargh, blerrie fokken kak!' he bellowed. I stopped immediately and turned to see three long white thorns protruding from his bald head.

'Hey, Shark Crap ...' he began menacingly but tailed off as the pain became too great. Candice tried to console him. I offered to remove the thorns with my Leatherman but he just glared at me, shaking his finger. 'Don't ... fokken ... come ... near ... me!' he hissed.

PJ suggested that we had been 'wasting our time' for long enough and that we could all use a drink. This was gleefully accepted by all 'guests'. I heard Duncan whisper,

'Thank god!'

Things were not looking rosy.

I extricated the vehicle from the thicket and drove to the top of a ridge that afforded a superb view of the northern Drakensberg glowing in the last embers of the day. Everyone climbed off in stony silence. I tried to make a show of the cocktails Anna supplied but everyone was too enthralled by Anton's injuries. I poured six glasses and handed them out as fast as possible.

What she had put in the mixture is not clear but its effect was noticeable in just ten minutes. The hostility to my thus-far horrendous drive disappeared. People started joking and slapping each other on the back. Anton told PJ that he wanted to be his best friend. Candice forgot Russell and used the tear in her shirt to good effect as she sidled up to Arno. I looked over to Anna who shrugged her shoulders.

We bumped into the lions shortly afterwards. They were walking through a clearing, enjoying the last of the day's warmth. The three-month-old cubs rubbed themselves up against the lionesses and pounced on each other in the twilight. It was pure magic. The guests, pissed or high as they were, believed it was all my doing. They heaped so much praise on me that I began to feel squeamish.

I will be receiving my feedback and results tomorrow morning. I suspect I may need to thank Anna.

Your expectant brother,

Angus

P.S. Russell left in shame the morning after his incident. The vile lizard was still groggy and had a bandage around his head when I took him up to the airstrip. As we climbed out of the car, I said, 'It would seem, Russell, that the wheel does indeed turn.' Russell looked confused. I tossed his bag on the tarmac. 'Now piss off back to whatever rock you crawled out from under.'

From: 'Angus MacNaughton'
Sent: 25 April, 18h15
To: 'Julia MacNaughton'; 'Dad MacNaughton'; 'Mother MacNaughton'
Subject: Release from Hades

Dear Mum, Dad and Julia,

Joy and rapture unforeseen.

I have passed my assessment drive and have thus been granted a two-week reprieve from the hell that is my job. I will be home tomorrow. I'll be there around lunchtime so tell Trubshaw to be on good form. I would love to be doing something exotic on leave but my salary is so paltry that I can barely afford the trip home. This is unlike SB who is planning adventurous tours with some of the cretins he calls his 'legendary lodge friends'. He clearly earns my salary to the power of five. Thankfully, on my return to Hades I will earn gratuities in addition to the joke they call my salary.

My assessment feedback wasn't entirely complimentary. PJ and Anton commented more on my character than on the drive, which it seems they hardly remembered at all (thanks to Anna). Anton had a very fuzzy recollection of how he received the scratches on his head.

PJ said that despite my good bush knowledge, I was arrogant, sarcastic, obtuse and unpleasant to people I felt were not as intelligent as I am (this means everyone here). He said I had shown flashes of potential but that I would need to make sure that there were more of these.

It would seem that there are two main reasons that I passed this drive. The first is that they are now a bit desperate for rangers. The village idiot, Jeff, has been training for eight months now and shows no sign of being able to conduct anything remotely resembling a game drive. Personally, I think his DNA is so poorly configured that he is better suited for the job of gnome in the Main Camp garden.

The second reason is that Elvis has requested me to be his ranger. This fills me with a deep sense of relief (and some pride) as I think we may be able to tolerate each other.

So there it is. Home to freedom, tomorrow. See you then.

Your happy (for once) son and brother,

Angus

P.S. Mum, please don't have your bridge ladies round tomorrow. Dealing with those women after 17 weeks in purgatory is more than I could bear.

From: 'Hugh MacNaughton'
Sent: 01 May, 17h00
To: 'Jules'
Subject: Big responsibility

Hey Jules,

It seems that my brutal blow to Arno's upper shin was not as powerful as I'd hoped. I suppose that the somewhat gentler consequence is better for me and the lodge's maintenance. Notwithstanding the glee I'd have got out of putting him in Tintswalo Hospital after his despicable threats to Simone, his hobbling around with a simple crepe bandage has kept me out of trouble and prevented some hefty medical bills. Unfortunately – or perhaps fortunately – not a single other staff member saw the great blow and so nobody has any idea what happened.

Arno's ego is simply not capable of accepting that a boy in his early twenties outdid him. He hasn't said anything to me about the incident. In fact, we haven't exchanged a word. Zero communication with Arno van der Vyfer is not something to complain about so I suppose that things worked out well in my favour.

On an unhappier note, I had the gross misfortune of having to listen to Melissa drone on again this week. My move to Tamboti Camp means limited interaction with her but PJ insisted that I meet with her in order to glean whatever I could from her greater experience with large groups in camp.

I invited her round to my house during the less frenetic middle of the day. She arrived with abundant energy and 4 jam-packed Lever Arch files of unbelievable weight.

"Wow, Hugh, this house is, like, huge!" she said. "You and Simone gonna live here together now!" she followed, with a chuckle.

"No, Melissa, I have not made plans to move in with Simone – it has only been a fortnight," I said.

"But you are so in love, I know you are!" she answered between giggles.

"If we could just talk about the upcoming group, please, Melissa," I said finally – the memories of my time at Quintessential House flooding back painfully.

Mercifully, she agreed. As painful as it was listening to her blabber on about how well she had handled groups in the past, I must confess that she brought up a few good points and so I took more from the exercise than a saliva-showered face.

She echoed the point that PJ had brought up with me weeks ago when he first introduced me to the importance of this group. Night-time entertainment was going to be a key component and although their arrival date was still a long way off, I knew that I needed to start thinking of wonderful and different forms of theatre and entertainment in order to blow this lot away.

Sadly, Simone is on leave. As irony would have it, she shares the same leave cycle as Angus. We have been in SMS contact often, though, and she seems to be having a good holiday. Her parents live in Johannesburg, but not particularly close to our home. Her family also owns a small game farm near Bela Bela which she loves. She is heading there with family and friends this weekend. God, I would love to be going there, but haven't said as much to Simone. Got to play it cool – like you've told me.

I trust that you are having an enjoyable time with Angus being home. Not likely. Tell him I say hello, though, please.

Lots of love,

Hugh

From: 'Hugh MacNaughton'
Sent: 03 May, 17h20
To: 'Angus'
Subject: Protection

Dear Angus,

I hope that you are having a nice time at home.

I write to ask a favour of you.

I also write with the trust that the contents of this favour will be taken sincerely and not in the dismissive fashion you have shown in the past.

Simone and I are getting quite serious and I feel that it would be a travesty of justice for me not to have the necessary protection should things in the bedroom develop further.

I would be most grateful if you would be so kind as to purchase me a few condoms before returning to the lodge in order to arm me with what is required to perform properly.

Please don't mention this to anybody.

Thanks, Angus,

Hugh

From: 'Angus MacNaughton'
Sent: 05 May, 12h00
To: 'Hugh MacNaughton'
Subject: Are you joking?

String Bean,

I read your email for the first time at 10:00 two days ago. I then read it again immediately to make sure that my eyes had not deceived me. Apparently, they had not. An hour later, Francina came into my room to find out why I had not appeared for my morning tea. There she found me, doubled over on the floor, laughing hysterically.

'Angus, what is the matter?' she asked, distressed. Alas, I was unable to answer and she eventually rushed off to fetch Mum because she thought I was having a seizure.

I find the fact that you think your virginity is about to end in the arms of Simone mirthful to say the least. The image of your awkwardness while trying to figure out how to apply a newly acquired 'gumboot' in the *moment critique* is causing my fit to return.

I was at the Jolly Roger having a drink the other night when who should walk through the door but the lovely Simone with a large bunch of pre-humans. My group was seated in a dingy corner so I was able to watch proceedings undetected. Your Simone spent most of the evening talking to a hominid resembling a Colombian drug lord – named Carlos, perhaps. Naturally, he was dressed in a black leather jacket and his hair had more grease in it than the lodge workshop. I assume there was a thick gold chain nestled in his ample chest hair and no doubt a Glock tucked into the back of his beautiful torn black jeans.

Quite what Simone was doing with *Homo erectus*, I'm not sure, but I thought it best to create worry and doubt in your mind before complying with your request. This will make the *moment critique* even more hilarious. Do you think that Simone's flower remains unplucked? Surely not for long if Carlos has his way.

Well on that note, have a nice day.

Angus

P.S. There was a dispenser of free government-issue 'gumboots' in the gents at the Jolly Roger so I got you some of those. I'm told that donning one of them allows about as much sensation as a cricket pad.

From: 'Hugh MacNaughton'
Sent: 07 May, 15h00
To: 'Angus'
Subject: Fuck you – again!

Angus,

You are not a human being and I will never call you my brother – not today, not ever!

I don't believe a word of what you described in your email (Jolly Roger, Carlos, etc.). I find the fact that you use my love for Simone as a source of humour for your childish heartlessness, insensitive and unbecoming of a brother.

Why are you so nasty?

Did something go awry in your early childhood before I was around? Perhaps you were molested by an old man "selling sweets"?

Only something that horrific could explain the way you choose to conduct yourself.

I am not even angry.

I feel sad for you.

You are truly awful.

Hugh

From: 'Angus MacNaughton'
Sent: 07 May, 16h27
To: 'Hugh MacNaughton'
Subject: Gumboots

Hugh,

It's your lucky day.

Julia says I'm being mean and insensitive – I had to share your email with her. It was too funny to keep to myself.

I will bring you your gumboots (unused though they will remain) on one condition. Get one of your Tamboti Camp housekeepers to clean the bat cave. Also, have your new BFF, Arno, fix the place where the roof broke before my assessment drive. Make sure he gets rid of the bloody flying mice. For this favour, Hugh, Simone and your whatnot will remain protected.

Thanks awfully,

Angus (your 'overexcited-about-returning' brother)

P.S. What sort do you want – ribbed, studded, featherlite, stamina increase or something I saw the other day ... tingle? Let me know or I will choose myself.

From: 'Hugh MacNaughton'
Sent: 08 May, 18h12
To: 'Jules'
Subject: Holiday plans!

Hey Jules,

It has been a good week at Sasekile, but I have missed Simone. We have continued our contact over SMS, but it's not the same as having her around all the time. She seems to have had a wonderful holiday, though, with a long weekend at their family farm being the highlight. She talks of it being so peaceful there and has expressed an interest in my going with her on the next occasion. This is, of course, brilliant news, but the sheer thought of spending a romantic weekend with her alone at their farm sparks a yearning in my heart to see her.

Unfortunately, the situation is made worse by the fact that it will still be some time before I do see her. I am due to go on leave next week and we are leaving early on the morning of her return.

By "we" I refer to what has been coined "The Mozam Dream Team". A group of 8 of us have decided that spending 2 weeks on the pristine beaches around Guinjata Bay in Mozambique may not be the worst idea. Research has shown beach, bar, pool and ocean all within a 100-metre radius of one another and all at a reasonably affordable rate. The accommodation seems basic but comfortable and there is a dive centre close by. Seven people from the Lodge (a few Rangers, 2 Student Chefs and 1 of the Accountants) have been planning this trip for months which has made for great excitement (as well as a fair bit of jealousy) around the camp.

Jamie (1 of the Rangers) was telling me about the trip at lunch the other day and upon realising that I would be on leave at the same time, he extended the invitation to me.

"We actually need an 8th member for the crew," he said excitedly. "The Baraka [meaning palm thatched house, I think] sleeps 8, so if you come along as well, it will bring the price down even further. Come on, Hugh, it's going to be the most sick, killer party ever – you'll dig it, bru."

"I suppose I don't have any other plans," I replied.

"Pha-Nom-A-Nal!" yelled Jamie. "I'll tell the rest of the Dream Team that you're in."

I told PJ the news and he seemed happy for me, but questioned my progress surrounding the planning for the big group arriving not too long after my return. I offered to sit down with him and present what I had planned so that he'd know I am completely on top of things.

I gave him a comprehensive briefing on each Travel Luxury member and their respective partners. I laid out the day-to-day plan for the stay and also outlined the all-important evening entertainment. This will include a local entertainment crew – the Magical Marimba Band – from the nearby communities to perform on the last night. I have also arranged for us to eat in the bush on the first night and in the boma on the second. I have asked the massage therapists to be on standby for treatments throughout their stay and persuaded Jonesy to do his Wild Dog presentation on 1 of the evenings.

PJ was wonderfully impressed and congratulated me on an excellent job thus far. He said that I had clearly made a big effort and deserved a good holiday.

On the strength of that I have confirmed my intention to join the team on their adventure to Mozambique. Fortunately, I have done reasonably well in the tips department this last cycle (mostly on account of old boy Thesiger very kindly leaving me £250) so I will have plenty of money for diving, dining and drinking.

Please would you ask Angus to bring my passport down with him when he returns?

Lots of love,

Your beach-bound brother,

Hugh

From: 'Hugh MacNaughton'
Sent: 13 May, 18h20
To: 'Angus'
Subject: Passport meeting

Dear Angus,

Although it was unexpected, I'm grateful for your reply. Maybe you are indeed capable of behaving like a human being on the odd occasion after all.

I will have my housekeepers clean out your room, but I'm sure that even you can appreciate my hesitation in speaking to Arno. I will have a word with PJ, though, and ask him to speak to Arno about driving out the bats.

As far as the design/make/cultivar, etc. of the condoms go, I really don't give a shit. All I want is a god-forsaken raincoat should the unlikely event of sex occur between Simone and me. However, if you must push me to make a decision, I suppose "Durex Fetherlite" would be my choice.

I also need my passport. I know it will sicken you to hear this but I am now part of "The Mozam Dream Team" and we will be leaving for Mozambique in just under a week. As we will be leaving early on the day you return, I would be grateful if we could meet you on the road.

There is a little farm stall at the fork in the R40/Hoedspruit road. It's called Ouma se Lekker Vars Veggies en Vetkoek. We'll be heading towards the Orpen Gate in Kruger from there. You will, of course, be driving right past this point so I don't think it's too much to ask for us to synchronise our respective journeys. If we could meet there at 09:00 I would be grateful.

It is embarrassing that I even need to write this final paragraph, but if you feel that you are unable to accommodate this humble request, please have the courtesy to give me fair warning so that I may ask the folks to courier my green mamba to me in the next day or 2. This option will, of course, be decidedly pricier.

Thanks,

Hugh

From: 'Hugh MacNaughton'
Sent: 15 May, 11h02
To: 'Jules'
Subject: Mozam Dream Team departs!

Hey Jules,

I am in the car and en route to Mozambique. Jamie has a BlackBerry which he has lent me to write you a quick message.

Just seen Angus at Ouma se Lekker Vars Veggies en Vetkoek but you won't believe who was with him.

Simone!

I can't believe that nobody told me that she was bumped off her flight. I also can't believe that her only option for a lift was with Angus.

She had mentioned nothing by SMS and it was the most wonderful surprise – amazing to see her again. I feel on top of the world.

We shared a chocolate milkshake together at the farm stall and briefly caught up on her holiday. She gave me a big kiss and said that she had missed me lots and lots.

It was heavenly.

Angus was in a rage, though.

While I was talking to Simone, a member of "The Mozam Dream Team", already drunk, spilt beer all over him. When Jonesy (the drunken guy) attempted an apology by slobbering directly into Angus's left ear drum, I thought there was going to be murder.

I will try and send you another message from Mozambique but not sure if I will get signal.

Send love to Mum and Dad and tell them I miss them.

Hugh

From: 'Angus MacNaughton'
Sent: 15 May, 21h00
To: 'Julia MacNaughton'
Subject: Return to Hades

Dear Julia,

I returned to find the roof of the bat cave fixed and the room spotless, thanks to the gumboot negotiation with SB. There are, however, tell-tale ultrasonic squeaks at night which means that Arno has failed to remove the heathen bats.

The trip back with Simone was OK. I enjoyed the drive as the countryside is beautiful in the late autumn. She slept most of the way so I wasn't forced to make small talk about SB's childhood and his merits (which she has failed to realise are unquestionably lacking).

As I'm sure Hugh has waffled to you, we met 'the Mozam Dream Team' next to a farm stall on their way to the border for the passport handover. They were sickeningly full of backslapping 'we-gonna-drink-so-much-rum-buddy' team spirit. I can think of nothing worse than a 'Team Holiday' with that bunch. I've no doubt Hugh will detail the gang to you, describing them in hyperbolic terms such as, 'Geez, that guy is such a legend'.

Puke.

I've been driving guests since my arrival, which is good because it means I'm no longer cleaning the Twin Palms. I also no longer have to meet Anton every morning at 07:00 for an update on subjects including British atrocities during the Boer War, hunting rifle ballistics, and the merits of technical colleges versus private schooling. Instead I've been out with my guests from 05:30 every morning (when it is chilly this time of the year).

My current guests are generally tolerable. They are a family of six Americans – the Jeffersons from Philadelphia. Todd and Jody, their two sons, Jack (12) and Bill (9), and Todd's parents, Betty and Jerry (aged 465 and 468). They are interested in many things so it's not hard to keep them entertained although some of the kids' questions are fairly special (e.g., 'Hey, Angus, it's May back home, what month is it here?'). Apparently American schooling has taken a leaf from the book of whatever technical college Anton attended during his abominable youth.

Elvis has been incredible and finds an astounding number of animals. I've had huge fun tracking with him but he's not a particularly talkative person (in fact, I've seen more verbose road kill). I have to learn by watching.

This morning we had a marvellous, life-threatening situation. The sun had just come over the horizon but it was still cold. From his perch on the bonnet, Elvis raised his large right hand slightly. This means: *'Stop immediately!'*

We climbed off the car to examine some leopard tracks crossing the dusty track.

'Very fresh,' he mumbled and walked off on the tracks. This means: *'Fetch the rifle and the radio, tell the guests to sit tight, and hurry up.'*

About 15 minutes later, we found ourselves in a dry riverbed, flanked by thick evergreen trees. Elvis told me to walk very carefully. He did this by turning round and glaring at me and then my shoes. It is surprising that so vast a human being can walk so quietly. The tracks were very fresh – even I could tell that because the dew on the surface of the riverbed had been broken.

I walked very carefully behind and to the right of the 120 kg tracker.

(I should point out that this positioning is contrary to Anton's strict instructions.)

'Shark Crap,' he told me, 'the gun is in front always. When the shooting starts, you can't be getting your tracker out the way.' This, of course, makes no sense because the tracker can see nothing if an inexperienced ranger like me is walking all over the tracks. Besides which, Elvis has told me where I am to walk and I'm not about to argue with him.

Anyway, a few minutes later, I noticed the birds were quieter and all I could hear was my own breathing and the steadily increasing thump in my chest. There was a palpable tension in the air. I looked on the ground, to the sides of the drainage line and in front of Elvis.

Suddenly he froze. I followed suit, at the same time peering frantically into the undergrowth flanking the river.

Nothing.

As I was about to relax, there was a flash and a growl as she exploded from the bush to the front and right of me. My training kicked in and, in what felt like an instant, the rifle was on my shoulder and a round in the chamber. I took aim.

But there was nothing to aim at. Just the returning sounds of the birds and the settling autumn dust. I stared in disbelief, scarcely able to move as my eyes scanned the area.

'Hmm,' said Elvis as he turned to stroll back to the car.

I fought my heart back down my throat, took the weapon off my shoulder, removed the round and made the rifle safe. I then hurried after Elvis, who was whistling a tune to himself as he wandered back along the drainage line. I realised the leopard could have savaged us both before I'd even thought of the rifle.

'That was close,' I said to him, trying to sound casual.

'Ja,' he said in the same way he might when asked whether he'd like milk in his tea. We returned to the vehicle where the guests were waiting. I was still shaking as I climbed into the driver's seat.

'Well, we found her,' I said. 'She, um, moved off when she saw us, though.' I paused to breathe heavily, trying to disguise my gasping need for oxygen with a sigh. 'We'll try and have a look in the vehicle.' It took me a while to start the engine as my left leg was shaking so much I could hardly depress the clutch.

After some bashing through the bush in the Land Rover, we did eventually find the leopardess, lying on a rock. The reason for her earlier aggression became apparent as two small cubs emerged from a gap in the rocks behind her and began to suckle. The guests were utterly amazed. We sat with her for about an hour until the sun-bathed rock surface became too warm for them. The cubs disappeared back into the safety of their little cave and their mother headed off to lie in the shade. On mornings like this, I really enjoy it here.

My happiness is difficult to maintain in camp. Unfortunately, I've been assigned to drive guests out of Kingfisher Camp where the delightful Melitha is manager. She has been full of instructions and advice for me being the 'newbie' as she has taken to calling me. She introduced me to the Jeffersons and then told them I'd been a ranger for 'thix thecondth' – just the thing to inspire confidence in the person about to take you out into the wilds of Africa.

Dinner was an appalling experience. I've not seen Melitha's evening attire before but on this occasion it consisted of an obscenely short red dress and some wicker platform heels perhaps made from the remnants of an ancient picnic basket. She had on enormous amounts of red lipstick and hairspray, which made her resemble something from a Bon Jovi concert in the mid-eighties.

Appearance aside, her conversation at the dinner table was profoundly idiotic. The low point was her attempt to engage on the subject of American politics, about which I was learning quite a lot from old Jefferson. She asked the following clanger: 'Why did the Americanth vote for a muthlim for prethident when they know that the muthlimth don't like them?' Presumably referring to Barack Obama.

Enough said.

Until next week ...

Your ranger brother,

Angus

A YEAR IN THE WILD

From: 'Hugh MacNaughton'
Sent: 22 May, 18h01
To: 'Jules'
Subject: Mozam will never be the same!

Hey Jules,

I have finally managed to find a spot where this bloody BB gets signal.

Mozambique doesn't know what has hit it!

It hasn't been since "Matric Rave" that I've been around a group of people so intent on defining inebriation. We're just over a week into this holiday and the circumstances of the Mozam Dream Team are as follows:

Jamie (Ranger and leader of the trip) has had sex with Natasha (Student Chef #1).

Jonesy (Ranger and the guy who spilt beer over Angus at the farm stall) and Jabu (Ranger) had their wallets stolen on the first night after passing out on a sand dune.

Albert (Accountant), who is completely whipped for Ashleigh (Student Chef #2), has been rejected by her for the 5th time now.

Ashleigh had sex with a dive instructor last night, although apart from Ashleigh and the dive instructor, I am the only one who knows about this.

Brandon is missing. He was last seen walking aimlessly down the beach with a local fisherman.

And I am the new Guinjata "down-down" champion after I slugged back a Manica quart in just less than 10 seconds 2 nights ago.

I am going to send a message to Simone now.

Lots of love,

Hugh

From: 'Angus MacNaughton'
Sent: 22 May, 18h27
To: 'Julia MacNaughton'
Subject: Invasion of the Goths

Dear Julia,

I am pleased to report that I've not been driving out of Kingfisher Camp this week. Instead, I've been driving out of Main Camp where September and Jenny run the show and there is an assortment of excellent to utterly useless butlers. More about one of them later.

What Jenny lacks in hospitality training, she makes up for by being well-spoken and not entirely unpleasant on the eye – she is blonde and brown-eyed.

Unfortunately, the standard of my guests has plummeted. The whole camp (10 rooms) was taken over by an incentive group the other day. This means that they were sent here by their employer for their contributions to the corporate bottom line. It therefore also means that they have not chosen to be here – a whole lot of goal-oriented, Type A Chermans with no real desire to be in the wilderness. Staring at me from the pages of the daysheet were those tell-tale names with far too many consonants – Kupferschmidt, Schnyder, Kappelhoff, Schwarzkopf, etc.

There were four of us driving them: Sipho, Carrie, the delightful Anton and me. I have not described Carrie to you before. She is the only female ranger here. Unfortunately, she is not built like Jenny. She is the sort of person you might describe as having nice elbows or good handwriting. She is pleasant enough to talk to, however.

While the guests were having their tea on the first day, Anton nominated me to give the orientation talk because I am the newest ranger. Thus instructed, I placed the orientation board in front of ze Chermans, who were all seated on the deck. They looked disappointed by the lack of knockwurst and sauerkraut on the tea table. A sea of unsmiling faces regarded me so I thought I'd try and lighten the mood.

'The only German I know,' I paused for effect, 'is ... *Achtung, Schpitfire*.'

They didn't seem to think this was amusing in the slightest. They just stared at me. The rangers, who were standing behind the group, were dumbfounded for some reason. Their jaws dropped. I thought I'd better try again.

'Oh, and also ... *Ich bin ein Deutscher soldat.*' This means I am a German Soldier. Similar response from all concerned. I gave up and simply continued with the orientation. Ze Chermans are truly a nation without humour.

I finished the talk and walked over to the tea table. Jenny was standing there looking disturbed. I smiled and cut myself a piece of orange cake.

'Do you have any idea what you just said?' She seemed nonplussed.

'What?' I said, becoming confused.

'You can't say stuff like that! People are sensitive!' she hissed.

'Stuff like what?' I asked biting, into what is, unquestionably, the best cake in the world.

'Stuff like *Achtung, Schpitfire!* This is not *Fawlty Towers*, this is real life, Angus! You are going to cause huge offence talking like that.'

'Come on,' I replied, 'surely they must be over it by now.'

'They're on holiday, Angus! Paying to be here! War jokes are not funny for Germans on holiday!'

'Well, they should have thought of that before they shelled Gdansk.' I walked off with my cake to the peace of the area behind the kitchen. Silly girl really seemed quite miffed. Perhaps she has some German ancestry.

Ten minutes later the guests began arriving in the car park. They climbed onto all the Land Rovers but mine. One by one the other rangers departed on game drive while Elvis and I were left waiting in the dust.

Six stragglers eventually emerged from the lodge and reluctantly climbed onto our Landy. The last one sat down directly behind me and said, 'You've vatched a lot of var movies, haven't you?'

'A few,' I replied.

About half an hour later we were driving through the beautiful autumnal afternoon. I wasn't saying much – just enjoying the general scenery. Elvis suddenly raised his right hand. I stopped immediately and climbed out to investigate the apparently bare piece of earth he was indicating. Closer inspection revealed that the area was actually a flurry of activity – there was a violent battle in progress. Two swarms of ants (one slightly red, the other black) were locked in desperate combat. The black army was taking an awful pasting. All around the area each black soldier was being savaged by two or three red combatants. In the background, other red ants were emerging from the black ant nest carrying eggs – the spoils of war for the victorious red army. It was a sad and sorry state of affairs for the black colony.

The scene was electrifying. I suggested the guests jump out of the car to look as I explained how the war was unfolding. A few sentences into my enthusiastic treatise, I noticed silence. I looked up to see ze Chermans glaring at me. Hans Kupferschmidt pointed a finger at me.

'Ve are here for ze catz ... not ze bugz!' He flicked his spindly finger towards the road, 'Drive on!' I drove reluctantly to a comatose pride of fat lions that Sipho had found in the morning. They were so boring compared with the ant war, just lying about in the long grass, more asleep than Rip van Winkle. Ze Chermans seemed satisfied, although Hans did ask,

'Vhy zey are not killing somesing?'

'The lions are vegetarian out here,' I muttered under my breath.

'Vhat?' he snapped.

'They've just eaten a scrub hare,' I replied loudly.

Dinner that night was in the boma. I arrived just before ze Chermans and retrieved a scotch from the bar where Jenny and Jackson (the barman) were tipping champagne into crystal flutes. She asked if I'd made any more faux pas (not that I acknowledge making one in the first place) and how my game drive was. I told her about the ants which, unlike the Goths, she found fascinating. Halfway through my story, I was distracted by an amazing scene unfolding in the middle of the boma.

One of the butlers, a ridiculous individual going by the name of Clifford, was attempting to light the fire. He emptied a five-litre plastic bottle of diesel onto the towering wood pile. He then took a box of matches from his pocket, absently struck one and flicked it into the fire wok.

The result was impressive.

For a second, I lost sight of the idiot as the flames exploded out of the fire wok. The whooshing sound of the ignition made Jenny swing around and knock over three flutes.

'Clifford!' she screamed as he emerged from the inferno in a horizontal dive. 'Are you OK?'

'Oh, yeees! A great FIRE!' he replied, dusting himself off and continuing with his other duties.

'He just doesn't seem to understand,' she said to me, mopping up the spilled Graham Beck Brut. 'He keeps doing silly things like that. He's going to hurt himself.'

'Or better still, wipe himself out,' I replied.

The other noteworthy piece of news is that I've been informed that I will be going to shoot my impala within the next week. This is the final test before a trainee is elevated to the status of 'just better than Shark Crap', as Anton puts it. I have to go out on foot and shoot an impala at least two kilometres from the camp and then carry or drag it back to the lodge. This will be my final ordeal and then I will hopefully be able to move out of the bat cave.

Your hunter brother,

Angus

From: 'Jules'
Sent: 27 May, 15h02
To: 'Brother H'
Subject: Trubshaw's beach holiday

Hello Hugh,

Sounds like you guys are having a marvellous time out there in Mozambique! Much better than the corporate legal halls I am forced to inhabit on a daily basis. A little trip to the coast sounds marvellous.

Speaking of which, the folks just returned from a week in Kenton. Apparently, Mum convinced Dad, against his better judgement, to take Trubshaw to the beach. The hound took one look at the sea and hurled himself at the waves with reckless abandon. As you know, Trubby is not a skinny beast and swimming is not his strong suit. Dad had to rush into the freezing winter water to retrieve his 'best friend'.

Trubby escaped a further three times and repeated his marine attack each time. They only thing keeping Dad warm on the walk home was the rage he felt for his ill-mannered dog.

He is still coughing up sea water.

Lots of love,

Jules

From: 'Hugh MacNaughton'
Sent: 29 May, 18h00
To: 'Jules'
Subject: Return of the Dream Team

Hey Jules,

You will be happy to hear that all members of The Mozam Dream Team have returned to the Lodge in 1 piece. It was a fantastic holiday, and I was named "man of the tour" for my down-down victory and for negotiating a considerable discount on our bar tab. I am, however, relieved to be back as the heavy drinking and late-night partying were beginning to take their toll.

We eventually found Brandon about 10 km down the beach staying with a rural fishing family. When asked why he hadn't bothered to tell any of us, he said that he had lost track of time. It's no wonder he gets back so late from his game drives. Jamie was furious with him, but given the amount of time he and Natasha have spent in his bedroom, it's a wonder he even noticed our dozy friend was gone. Brandon did apologise, though, and made amends by cooking us the most delicious tuna which he had caught with his new friends.

The journey back was arduous, given that 8 of us were crammed into 1 double-cab and that the excitement of the holiday was no longer a factor. Albert farted the entire way back which did him no favours in his endless pursuit of Ashleigh, who, after her last night with the dive instructor, looks like she spent her leave on horseback. After 10 long hours we eventually arrived back late into the evening.

Seeing Simone again was obviously a highlight. She had managed to get the night off for my return so we spent the evening at my house catching up on each other's respective holidays. I told her all the skinder from Mozambique which she found profoundly amusing, but it was Brandon's going AWOL that she giggled at the most.

"How that guy is still alive is a mystery to me," she said with a chuckle.

On the work side, things are beginning to hot up for the Travel Luxury group. I got an email from Dorothy McDonald (Managing Director) yesterday informing me that 1 of her Guests had broken his ankle, but would still be coming. I offered to swap a few rooms around in order to keep him closest to the deck, which she accepted gratefully. She also informed me that Tamboti Camp is going to be the last stop on their itinerary so she wants their last night to be a particularly special 1. Should be a cracker evening in the boma with the Magical Marimba Band and their dancers, so I am not too fazed by the pressure.

Angus is trying to shoot an impala at the moment. This is the final Trainee Ranger task. Simone says he is having a torrid time. He is going out again in the morning to hazard another attempt. I think that he's almost out of bullets.

Lots of love,

Your seriously organised and on-top-of-things brother,

Hugh

From: 'Angus MacNaughton'
Sent: 29 May, 18h38
To: 'Julia MacNaughton'
Subject: Impala hunt

Dear Julia,

Yesterday I finished driving some 'no eenglesh' Italians who kindly tipped Elvis and me a very generous R50 ... to share.

'You!' Paolo pointed at Elvis and me in turn as he was leaving. 'Dreenk sum beear!' He gave us a greasy thumbs-up and handed the single note to me. It's no wonder they got on so well with the Germans. Elvis just glared at him.

In the afternoon, I appeared before a panel of senior rangers who briefed me on the impala hunt – my final test. Anton is on leave again so I actually received a logical briefing. There are a number of reasons for the hunt. The most important is that we need to know that we'll be able to shoot an animal in an emergency situation because few of us have shot anything other than a box. (This doesn't apply to Anton, of course. He's been murdering hapless creatures since his mother gave him a catapult for his first birthday.)

The hunt is a traditional rite of passage at the lodge and I think it will be a valuable lesson for me. I'm allowed only three rounds (bullets to the layman) to complete the task. If I miss with these – employment is terminated ...

The night before the hunt, I packed my small satchel with some condensed milk, apples, a first aid kit and a bottle of water. I was placing my radio on its charger when there was a knock at the door.

'Yes!' I snapped, thinking it was Jeff with more advice based on his many profoundly unsuccessful misadventures.

'That's very friendly,' the voice replied. The door opened and Anna walked straight in. I was dressed in only a towel but she took no notice. She had been hosting dinner in her camp and was dressed in a black dress, her hair carelessly tied up with a pencil.

'I've come to wish you luck for your hunt tomorrow,' she said, 'and to give you this.' She held out her left hand which contained an old and dented wooden box. I looked at it, unmoving. 'Go on, have a look!' she said. I snapped out of my funk, took the box and prised it open. There, nestled in a bed of ancient cotton wool, was an old folded hunting knife.

'My grandfather gave this to me just before he died. I've never used it and you might find it useful tomorrow.' I looked at her and then the knife. There was something completely matter-of-fact and supremely confident about the way she gave it to me.

'To borrow ...' I said rhetorically.

'No, I'd like you to have it,' she said. 'You remind me of him. I'm told that, as a young man, he was a cuttingly sarcastic and cynical bastard.' She paused.

'Gee, thanks,' I said.

'Thankfully, he softened to a hilarious old man. I'd like you to have this as a token of the regard I have for your potential.' Normally a conversation like this would make me squirm but Anna is so comfortable with everything she does that I felt no more awkward than if we'd been discussing the weather.

'Thank you,' I replied, closing the box.

'Good luck, Angus,' she said, stepping forward, kissing me gently on the cheek and squeezing my empty hand.

Then she was gone. I removed the knife from the box and packed it into the side pocket of my satchel and sat down on the bed. I touched my cheek where she'd kissed it and realised that I was sad she had left. Something in me wanted to charge out of the bat cave after her.

This morning I walked out of camp just as the chilly dawn arrived in the Lowveld. I stuck to the roads to begin with, moving at a leisurely pace. I headed for a big clearing where there are often herds of impala. At this time of the year, the males are rutting. They tend to forget about eating and predators – all they think about is sex. This, apparently, makes them easier to hunt.

I came alongside the clearing about an hour later, and there was an enormous herd of females guarded by one male at the western end of the clearing and a whole bachelor herd on the other side, roughly 40 metres from me. The males were chasing each other round, making their ridiculous snorting roars. They hardly looked at me despite the fact that I was standing in the open. Easy as pie, I thought.

I shouldered my rifle, cycled the bolt and pushed a round into the chamber. The rifle clicked and the bolt closed.

The impala reacted to this sound as if they had been conditioned to its meaning since time began. They exploded in a hundred directions and before I could aim there was nothing but dust hanging in the cool morning air.

Not so easy, then.

I tried a more stealthy approach by going around the back end of the flanking bush into which area the herd had run. All I saw were tracks indicating that the wily antelope had been running fast when they came through the thicket. After an incredibly frustrating two hours of tracking them and seeing fleeting glimpses as they fled on sight, sound or smell of me, I gave up on this particular herd and went in search of a spot to have my breakfast.

I found a termite mound shaded by an enormous brown ivory tree. There I sat against its ancient trunk while I ate an apple and sipped on my condensed milk. I sat for half an hour, scouring the land for signs of impala while the sun warmed my feet. I really do enjoy just being out here on my own. It's so peaceful. I have to admit that my mind wandered to Anna as I cut my apple with the knife she gave me.

After my breakfast, I became increasingly frustrated. The sun warmed the land and the animals disappeared into the deep shade. From the time I left the mound to 16:00 I stalked any number of what I have decided are the slyest and most devious creatures on god's Earth. Time after time I followed tracks as quietly as possible into thickets. I leopard-crawled, shredding my legs and stomach on the thorns. Each time I caught a glimpse of an animal, the bloody thing was staring straight at me as if I'd approached thrashing a metal drum.

In short, I didn't even get close. At 16:00 I gave up and headed home. I'd not aimed, let alone taken a shot. It is beyond me how the hell these things are devoured with gay abandon by every predator on the reserve. I seem to be the only thing in the world capable of deterring an impala ram from his pursuit of sex.

On my return this evening my mood was further sullied by the company I was forced to endure while eating at the Avusheni Eatery. Melitha and Hilda were there (the latter eating an enormous mound of stew with a fork in one hand and a bottle of chutney in the other). She saw fit to spew free advice on me while Melitha giggled.

'On my faahm, we just sit on rocks wiff some byas [beers] and a worker is chasing bucks to us and we shoot on them from there. My brovver [brother] Baksteen is the best shooter in the valley where our faahm is.'

Hopefully by next week my luck will improve.

Your frustrated and irritated brother,

Angus

From: 'Angus MacNaughton'
Sent: 05 June, 18h27
To: 'Julia MacNaughton'
Subject: Hunter

Dear Julia,

My second day of hunting was as pathetic as the first. Every impala I spotted was staring at me suspiciously. My frustration on return to camp was elevated by Anton's return from leave. The great leader's words of encouragement were,

'Shark Crap, gotta take the shot, can't be a baby 'bout this things. Shot my bok on day one ... 'bout 150 metres.'

Day three, four, five and six progressed in similarly disastrous fashion but for one difference. I fired one of my precious rounds on day five – and missed.

I started the day trying to leopard-crawl through various thorn-, stone- and, in one case, cobra-infested thickets. By 12:00 my belly was raw. My face was scratched to hell and crusted with dust and sweat. I sat down on a termite mound to have my lunch. As I was removing the wax paper, the peanut butter sandwich slipped from my grasp, gracefully opened, and fell in the dust – nut butter-side down.

This pissed me off thoroughly. Seething and very hungry, I continued the hunt. This is a poor frame of mind in which to be hunting with limited ammunition. A hot hour or so later I was stomping down a slope towards a shallow drainage line, muttering to myself. The other side of the depression was a clearing in which I spotted a small herd of impala grazing roughly 120 metres away.

My vision went red and my teeth clenched.

I shouldered the rifle, drove home the bolt, took aim and fired. The report of the rifle echoed off the banks of the drainage line and the impala exploded into the flanking thickets. I ran across the riverbed, knowing all the time that I'd missed but irrationally hoping to find a limp carcass lying in the evacuated clearing. Naturally, there was no such luck. The rifles we use are only ever tested at less than 30 metres so it was a ridiculous attempt. I was two rounds from ending my employment. I didn't consider this a necessarily bad thing but for the fact that it would give Anton such immense pleasure to see me fail.

Later that afternoon, I decided on a different strategy. I was sitting in a low tamboti tree grove, sucking on the last of my condensed milk. A herd of impala came wandering along a game path about 100 metres off, probably on the way to water. They were oblivious. I resolved to find a suitable thicket or mound close to the path in the morning and posit myself there for the day – like a leopard might.

That night I went to dinner later than usual, hoping to avoid Anton. He wasn't there, but Melitha, Jenny and Anna were. They were sitting drinking tea on the Avusheni Eatery veranda, hands cupped around their mugs against the evening chill. I sat at the other end of the table hoping to avoid conversation but it took Melitha less than a minute to begin her drivel,

'Anton thays you not brave enough to kill.' She sniggered.

'Melitha, you and Anton are not sufficiently cerebrally equipped to have an opinion on what the time is, let alone on my bush capabilities.' Jenny coughed, which egged me on. 'I would sooner heed the opinion of this oily mince than give credence to anything you or Anton could conjure up with your combined IQs barely approaching double figures.'

Jenny choked. She left the table and sped into the Avusheni Eatery, spluttering. Anna held herself together, although the corners of her mouth strained upwards in her attempt to remain composed.

'Anguth, you horrible thhit!' Melitha screeched as she slammed her mug on the table and stomped off. Anna allowed herself a chuckle.

'Angus, while she may have asked for that, you didn't necessarily have to give it to her,' she said.

This morning, I headed out feeling excited about my new strategy. I made for the same game path I'd discovered the day before. I hid myself on a termite mound surrounded by guarri bushes and waited. And waited.

And waited.

And bugger-all happened.

By 13:00 I was dropping off in the midday warmth when a warthog came ambling absently towards the mound, looking for shade or a nutritious shoot to chew. He came to within three metres of where I was sitting and paused, sensing something amiss. As his eyes fell on me, he belched loudly, exploded off the ground, achieved an instant 180-degree pirouette, and sped off like a cannon ball. I chuckled quietly.

The afternoon became quiet again. I really wanted to walk around a bit but didn't want to give up my position. I started to drift in and out of consciousness, lulled by the soporific sounds of the bush afternoon.

An hour later I reached lazily for my water bottle. As I brought it to my lips, a movement caught the corner of my eye — a bachelor herd of impala on the path.

The animals were completely unaware of me as I checked the wind carefully using an old sock filled with ash. A gentle zephyr blew from the herd to me — perfect. I fought the urge to grab my rifle quickly, despite the gripping fear that the herd would disappear before I could aim. As the bolt closed with a gentle click, I gritted my teeth, expecting the impala to turn around.

They didn't flinch.

I engaged the safety catch. There was a good-sized adult just near the back. I selected him as my mark.

I could see my shoot-point through a small gap afforded by the guarri leaves, just beneath which there was a stout branch to rest the barrel on. I slowly manoeuvred myself into position, rested my cheek on the butt, and adjusted the angle of the weapon until the bead of the front sight was nestled in the V of the rear one. One by one, the herd slowly moved past the shoot-point. First a few yearlings, then a stray ewe. I could feel the muscles all over my body tensing in anticipation and also because I was on my haunches, which was burningly uncomfortable. The herd stopped moving.

I opened my left eye, to see what had arrested them. My legs started to shake. There seemed to be no reason why the bloody things had stopped but my ram wasn't in view. A bead of sweat made its way down my forehead and onto my nose where it started to tickle. My teeth were clamped shut against the searing ache that had developed in my quads and the excruciating need to scratch the end of my nose.

The impala started to move again. My mark made his way into view. I took aim at a spot just behind his right shoulder and flicked off the safety catch. He stopped momentarily, I took a deep breath, held it, my legs froze for a second and I squeezed the trigger.

The rapport of the .375 calibre H&H Magnum shattered the peaceful afternoon into a million pieces.

The recoil sent me sprawling from my unsteady position, but I recovered quickly and charged out from the cover. I could see nothing. I must have covered that 30 metres in less than three seconds but there was nothing there. I stared at the ground in frantic disbelief.

Then, to the side of the path, I noticed a red tinge. I hadn't missed – well, not completely anyway. I stepped towards it. There was a bigger splotch just further on, and roughly ten metres beyond that, hidden by a long patch of golden winter grass, was my mark.

The ram is dead!

Then my joy faded. He lay there, his eyes open and his tongue lolling out to the side. I've never taken a life before (except for the odd bug and that rat that Trubshaw caught once). I just stood staring at him. The shot took him just behind his shoulder and shredded his heart and lungs. I felt awful.

A numbness developed as I cut the throat of the old ram in the manner I'd been instructed. The grass turned crimson. I then had to gut him. This was a grimy, vile job, but Anna's sharp knife made it relatively simple. I stank when I'd finished.

The next task was to pick the old boy up. An impala ram weighs between 60 and 70 kg ... I weigh in at a massive 68. I managed to heave him onto my back.

I stood briefly, wobbled and fell over backwards onto the lifeless weight.

There, gasping for air, I lay in the bowels of the impala. Smelly situation. Eventually, I managed to repeat the process, stood more steadily and began the slow three-kilometre trudge back to camp. It was just after 15:30. There was about an hour and a half of light left.

It was utterly exhausting but I developed a good, slow rhythm after a while. I had no water left and the sweat began to pour from my body even though the day was cooling as it does quickly at this time of the year.

At 17:00 I walked through the Sasekile delivery entrance, starting to feel particularly pleased with myself and looking forward to dumping the carcass at Anton's stinking feet. I rounded the last bend towards the offices, and there was a sight I thought I'd never see. Just about the entire staff was there, shouting and clapping. For a minute I thought there must be some sort of emergency but it turns out they were there to cheer me on the home straight. Very embarrassing.

I walked the final 20 metres through a throng of clapping people at the end of which was Anton. I dropped the carcass on his boots, leaving a gory smear on his leg. SB emerged from crowd and patted me on the back.

'Hey, Angus! Congrats,' he smiled.

PJ handed him a champagne bottle. He popped it open and began spraying me with the stuff. I almost liked him for a minute ... almost. There was a great cheer and all the rangers and trackers came to shake my hand and congratulate me for completing the final rite of passage.

Anton then made a truly gormless speech that went something along the lines of:

'There come a time in the life of a Shark Crap that he isn't a Shark Crap no more. That is time now for Angus. He is not a Shark Crap no more but a ranger – but a junior ranger of course.' He handed me a quart of beer. 'Now you must have a real ranger drink.' He started some dumb drinking chant and all the rangers joined in. This brilliant poetry went,

'Shoot a tiger

Shoot a cat

Chunder chunder on your back

Chunder chunder cotch and spew

Cotch on me

I cotch on you.'

Apparently I was supposed to down the beer in the time it took them to sing this. Needless to say, I achieved about two sips before my gag reflex kicked in. I made a valiant effort but by the time I'd finished, people were drifting off and making conversation.

As I swallowed the last drop, Anna appeared.

'Well done, Angus,' she said, kissing my cheek, ignoring the grime on it. Then she was gone.

Ah, how the universe hath smiled on me with great and abundant blessings – for once.

That's it from your impala slaying, not-Shark-Crap-any-more brother,

Angus

From: 'Hugh MacNaughton'
Sent: 05 June, 18h46
To: 'Jules'
Subject: Our brother qualifies

Hey Jules,

Angus has qualified!!

He finally managed to shoot that impala he has been hunting for the last week. I must say I am really chuffed. Even the rest of the Lodge was quite upbeat about the news. Of course, his recent feat is destined to result in a big party where Angus will be forced to drink and retell the tale of his great hunt. If they make the punch too strong he probably won't last till the end of the evening. We will have to wait and see, though.

My preparation for the group is still going along swimmingly. It is only 3 weeks before their arrival and everything is in place. I have brought in extra wine and spirits for a more diverse drinks selection in the evenings. I've been through the dietaries with the Head Chef for the third time now; and I've booked probably the most reliable entertainment group in the Lowveld. I love being organised like this and I am actually looking forward to the day of the grand arrival. I can't wait to prove myself once and for all to the critics who think I'm too young for the pressure of Tamboti Camp.

On a slightly duller note, Simone is being ridiculous. Word has got out about my behaviour during one of the evenings in Mozambique, and she is not pleased. Personally, I really don't see what all the fuss is. I have at least 3 mates from varsity who regularly remove all their clothes in front of large crowds, so why should my performance at Rosa's Restaurant in Mozambique be considered any different? She wasn't even there! The Mozam Dream Team thought it was the highlight of the holiday and even the owner of the restaurant saw the amusing side of it. It was all just good clean fun, but unfortunately she doesn't see it that way. She thinks it's selfish and immature. Whatever!

Furthermore, she had the audacity to attack me the other day about how hard I've been working. Since when does hard work land you in the dog box? I would have thought she'd have been impressed with my work ethic and organisation at the camp, but she says that I only have time for things involving the Lodge and that we never talk about "other stuff". What "other stuff" could possibly be more important than my upcoming Travel Luxury group?

Also, she thinks that I drink too much! Can you believe it? My recent feedback from Guests has included rave reviews about my wine knowledge and food pairing recommendations. How am I supposed to achieve that by drinking passion fruit and water the whole evening? Sometimes I think she forgets that you should actually enjoy the work you do. Last night I stopped by her house with a little ramekin of chocolate mousse that was left over from dinner. I know how much she likes chocolate so I thought it would be a nice gesture. I even brought her a little teaspoon with which to eat it. She had just got into bed when I arrived, so I sat down next to her. The bed is quite springy so my first attempt sent me crashing into her bedside table and, ultimately, onto the floor. I managed to stabilise myself and present the dessert.

"You smell like a brewery," was the extent of her appreciation for my efforts!

"Fine," I said, and scoffed the whole thing myself on the way back to my room. Admittedly, I spent the rest of the night alone.

I suppose that these are the highs and lows, the peaks and troughs, the magic and misery of relationships. You've warned me about all of this so it seems silly getting too worked up. Next week she will, no doubt, see me once again as her knight in shining armour. Her birthday is coming up towards the end of the month so perhaps I'll help things back on track with a thoughtful gift. Something out of the ordinary and specific to her should do the trick. She likes children, but I don't think I'm quite ready to give her 1 of those yet and chocolate mousse is definitely out of the question. Perhaps something for her garden, but I'll have to give it some thought.

Should you have any further pearls of wisdom regarding the unexplainable dynamics that exist between 2 people who like each other, I would be most grateful for a few. I have no clue how to deal with Simone's sudden change of heart, despite my belief that it is nothing but a passing mood swing mixed with some jealousy about my trip to Mozambique.

Lots of love,

Your currently-unloved-and-neglected-but-still-seriously-organised brother,

Hugh

JAMES HENDRY

Dear Angus,

A short message from your mother and me to congratulate you on qualifying as a ranger. I am sure that you will make a success of it if you manage to hold your tongue.

You are not a run-of-the-mill sort of fellow so being in such a small, closed community cannot be easy for you. But it would seem that despite the odd setback, you are managing very well and we are very pleased that you are forging ahead in the bush – a niche we feel is ideal for you.

All love,

Mum and Dad

From: 'Hugh MacNaughton'
Sent: 12 June, 17h47
To: 'Jules'
Subject: Patching things up with Simone

Hey Jules,

Angus was subjected to his Rite of Passage Impala Party at the Staff Shop this week. Everybody arrived in high spirits after their Guests had finished dinner and gone to bed. With the party themed "Completely Inappropriate", you can just imagine what some of the characters in this place came dressed as. One girl had on only her underwear, while many of the guys chose to augment their "Mackenzies" with socks. There were endless buckets of punch which Jamie (leader of the Mozam Dream Team, if you recall) had spiked with bottles of Tequila. The ultraviolet lights made everything look even more risqué. I think the highlight for me, though, was watching Albert drooling over Ashleigh, who had come dressed as a Playboy bunny. When she and her partner Natasha (also clad in bunny ears and not much else) performed an entwined version of the Macarena in the middle of the dance floor, Albert collapsed. Jonesy had to pour ice water over him to bring him back to life. Gladys, the village cleaner, shook her head in disgust.

I had a picture of a naked woman pinned to the front of my shirt. The guys thought it was hilarious but all the girls stared at me and shook their heads. Exceptionally inappropriate!

I arrived at the party slightly later than most of the staff. I'd had 4 Irish international rugby players in camp for 3 nights and didn't want to miss their last evening. As it was the same night as the party, Melissa offered to cover for me as Kingfisher Camp was closed, but I courteously declined her offer. I simply felt too bad at the thought of subjecting the 4 lads to remarks like, "Oh my gosh, you guys are so strong and muscular," etc.

The guys stayed up late, so when I eventually did pitch up at the Staff Shop, the party was well under way. I was informed that Angus had already told his tale of glory and that it had been surprisingly captivating. He must have had a lot of punch! He was comatose by this stage and in the foetal position which he usually adopts after anything more than 2 beers.

Simone was nowhere to be seen at first, but when my eyes adjusted to the light, I spotted her at the end of the open shop veranda. After last week's events we had a huge fight about all the things I mentioned in my last email and we hadn't spoken for 2 days. With neither of us wanting to be the first to try to fix things up, we simply avoided each other around camp. As a result, I was hesitant to go over, but I figured that it had to be as good a time as any to make peace. I made my way across the dance floor, thinking about what the hell I was going to say, but as I arrived and she looked up at me from where she was sitting, the 2 Playboy bunnies leapt on me from both sides.

"Are we gonna see you with no clothes on again tonight, Hughey?" they cooed. "Just like in Mozams. C'mon Hugh, we know you'll do it again!"

This was not a good start!

"Not tonight, girls," I said. "Maybe another time."

Simone glared at me. Mercifully, the bunnies moved on. We still said nothing. I looked into her sad brown eyes and felt a sweeping sense of guilt about what I had done in Mozambique. I didn't intend it at the time, but I had been inconsiderate and I realised that then. (Thank you for your pushing me gently to this realisation with your last mail.)

As if by some telepathic magic, she seemed to understand what I had just realised and she was the first to speak.

"I hate fighting with you," she said, above the noise.

Another long pause followed.

"Me too," I replied. "I'm sorry."

"What are you supposed to be?" I enquired. She was dressed in tatty jeans and an old white shirt. In her hand she clutched a brown paper bag.

The faintest of wry smiles became evident as she opened the bag and jiggled the contents. It was filled with sweets.

"Child molester," she replied. "Inappropriate enough for you?"

I roared with laughter. I was not expecting that answer, but I thought that it was brilliantly funny. After a while, she started laughing as well and before long tears were streaming from both of our eyes.

After that we talked for ages about how much we had missed each other and we vowed never to let things go that way again. We eventually stumbled home, in a drunken state, but happy.

Lots of love,

Your now-loved-again brother,

Hugh

From: 'Angus MacNaughton'
Sent: 13 June 18h40
To: 'Julia MacNaughton'
Subject: Evacuation of the bat cave

Dear Julia,

Unusually, the universe has cast a favourable gaze on me for two weeks in a row.

The bat cave and environs are now occupied solely by the Village Twit, Jeff. I have my own bathroom and no longer live in constant fear of foot rot, herpes or infection from bat-hosted diseases. As of yesterday, I reside in the part of the staff village where most of the general staff live. By general staff, I mean butlers, laundry ladies, maintenance people, etc. They are mostly Shangane. I am the only pale-faced person living in this area. This has upped my standing amongst the Shangane staff, as has the conversion of my school Zulu into rudimentary Shangane.

My room is a decent size – about four-by-four metres (I can no longer touch the walls when I'm in bed). There is a cupboard, a desk, a bookshelf and the floor is polished concrete. The only disadvantage of the bathroom is that the loo seat is plastic, which makes for uncomfortable post-lunch sessions with my *National Geographic*.

I wish now to describe the ordeal that constituted my Rite of Passage Party three nights ago. The Rite of Passage Party is a traditional celebration supposedly in honour of a newly qualified ranger. In actual fact it's an excuse for the monkeys here to express the lower primate DNA embedded in their makeup. (It is simply incongruous, given my level of popularity, that a party should be thrown in my honour.)

The deep sense of foreboding I felt before the event was made worse by the party's designation as a themed evening. As you are well aware, I'd sooner bath in a septic tank than engage in fancy dress. The theme was *'Inappropriate'* which gave extra licence (as if they needed any) for most of the staff to behave like gormless *Australopithecines*.

The only items in my cupboard are khaki clothes, some socks, unfashionable underpants, two pairs of sleeping shorts and my running kit. My running kit includes an old red T-shirt. On the front it says, 'I find you offensive ...' On the back, there is a picture of a raised middle finger with the caption, '... so piss off'. This, I felt, was ideal.

The festivities began at about 19:00 when my impala (and a supplementary one) had been sufficiently cooked over a spit at the Staff Shop. All the staff not at work in the camps were served a chunk of roasted antelope, some pap and coleslaw. Everything was quite pleasant. Elvis and I sat by the fire and ate. Unfortunately, the tame and pleasant atmosphere did not last.

At around 21:00, the staff who had been hosting dinner in the camps began to arrive at the Staff Shop and the nonsense commenced. Each person collected a 500 ml plastic mug on arrival. These they used to help themselves to punch from an old enamel bath at the far end of the veranda. The bath was brimming with a concoction of vodka, tequila, lemonade, fresh lemons, orange squash and ice. I helped myself to a glass and observed proceedings from a dark corner. Booze flowed into the staff at roughly the same rate as water gushing from the sluices on the Three Gorges Dam.

Anton (wearing a pair of candy-striped hot pants and his boots) downed four mugs in quick succession. This made him amorous. He made a beeline for Jenny who looked like she might be ill and melted into the burgeoning crowd. She was dressed in blue worker's overalls, cut off at the upper thigh and shoulders. Her cleavage was augmented by two inflated condoms. On her face, she had bright red lipstick, black eye makeup, and teased hair.

Jeff shaved the fur off his chest for the occasion. The consequence – a horrific case of ingrown hairs. It looked like a violent pox had attacked him. Undaunted, his only attire was a pair of cotton briefs with a pair of socks tucked into the front. Across his stomach were painted the words 'COME GET SOME' with an arrow pointing down. Because Jeff is a complete imbecile, he painted himself while looking in the mirror, so no one could read the backward scribbles on his belly.

Shortly after everyone arrived, Anton turned the music off. The lights came on and I was called to the middle of the room to stand on a low platform.

'The old Shark Crap will now tell the story of how he shot that impala.' He handed me a mug of punch. 'Each time he make a mistake, what he has to do?'

JAMES HENDRY

'Drink!' screamed the entire room in unison.

'I can't hear you!' he shouted.

Drink! they yelled. All around me the crowd (about 40 people) seethed and screamed in the cramped and windowless room. I caught a glimpse of Anna in the background. She was standing next to Elvis, dressed in some sort of tight leather cat outfit. She watched with a wry smile on her face.

Anton held his hands up and the crowd went quiet. He handed me a rifle stock with a broom handle for a barrel and then surveyed the crowd for a victim. He beckoned Jenny and gave her a pair of impala horns.

'You have to play impala!' There was further cheering.

'Begin!' shouted Anton, moving off the platform.

So began my Impala Story – the self-told and acted tale of my hunt. I had no desire to be up there but played along for the sake of tradition. Every time I described making a mistake, there were loud shouts of 'drink!' from the rangers. I then had to take a gulp of punch which Anton was holding and refilling on the side of the platform. By the time I related the warthog incident, the crowd was starting to blur slightly. I was beginning to feel far more relaxed about life and getting into the acting – reliving my days in the school production of *Grease*.

Eventually, I reached the climax of the story – Act 3, 'Death of the Ram'. Jenny took her place on the stage. With great show I took aim and held my squatting pose. I shook as I described the mixed emotions of adrenalin-fuelled fear, joy, sadness and anger in the most purple language I could muster. I paused. The crowd was captivated.

'BANG!'

A huge cheer rang out as Jenny collapsed onto the floor with a loud gurgling noise. I held my hands and the rifle up above my head in victory while Anton fed me more punch. I picked Jenny up and walked off the stage. There was more clapping and the rangers and trackers came around to pat me on the back and shake my hand. I felt quite proud.

They handed me yet another mug of punch which, by that stage, tasted like a sweet elixir. It slid easily down my throat as the music started pounding and the lights dimmed. The tightness of the mob, the darkness and the booze made it feel as if everyone was moving as one. I turned and found myself face to face with Anna and then, quite suddenly, and I have no idea how, we were dancing, invisible in the crowd and very dim light.

'Well done,' she said. 'I think you won a few friends with that performance.' Her arms were wrapped gently around my back, our cheeks pressed together. There we remained for the next two songs after which we drifted away from each other into the throng.

The next day I felt horrible. Thankfully, I wasn't driving that morning. The whole staff was wearing a collective hangover. SB had to excuse himself from lunch with his guests to be sick. Jenny had to be woken for the morning meeting, and Jeff has disappeared.

Speaking of SB, he has been running around with furrowed brow and lips in an officious purse. He spends hours on the phone and goes nowhere without an enormous black file. Apparently, he is organising a very important group booking. If I had his mental capacity, I'd be terrified by such a responsibility. It's bound to be a stuff up.

I'm driving out of Anna's camp (Rhino Camp) for the next two weeks, which will be pleasant.

So that's the news from your slightly more popular brother. Please tell Trubshaw I miss him.

Angus

P.S. My impala's horns have been mounted and now reside on the Staff Shop wall next to all the other rangers' conquests. The mount bears my name and the date of my final qualification and elevation from Shark Crap – to what, I'm not sure.

From: 'Hugh MacNaughton'
Sent: 19 June, 18h12
To: 'Jules'
Subject: Oh shit!

Hey Jules,

Life has taken a drastic turn for the worse!

The setbacks presented to me over the past 3 days have rendered my planning for the Travel Luxury group completely futile. With the Guests arriving in less than a week, it is incomprehensible that so many things have gone wrong so quickly at the last minute. I feel as though I'm standing at the base of a mountain watching a great ball of snow grow larger as it gathers momentum and in no time at all I am to be smothered. Of course, this is a relatively appealing option when compared with my current situation – at least with the snowball, my fate would be sealed and my life would be over. At the moment, though, who knows what will become of me after the biggest group of the year is a dismal failure. I have absolutely no idea what to do. I wish I could dig myself a hole and disappear. If you never see me again, the contents of this email will tell you why.

Problem number 1
The Head Chef, Oliver, resigned yesterday. His long-distance girlfriend told him he leaves the Lodge or she leaves him! He was gone in 24 hours.

We have no replacement at this stage.

Problem number 2
Jonesy and Sipho, the 2 experienced Rangers who had been assigned to the group, have fallen ill with bad flu picked up from some Guests.

Problem number 3
Owing to electricity surges, the ice machine and both fridges in the camp have blown. Arno is incapable of repairing the damage.

Fuck!

Problem number 4
Two air conditioners are not working. I asked for them to be re-gassed but it seems that their PC boards have malfunctioned (whatever that means). Yesterday morning was the coldest morning we have had in 10 years.

Problem number 5
Finally, and worst of all, the "most reliable entertainment in the Lowveld" has gone out of business. They were caught stealing at a neighbouring property a few days ago while performing for Guests. The police have discovered that they have been thieving all over the Reserve under the guise of the "Magical Marimba Band". While half the group has been performing a combination of dance and song, the rest of them have been raiding the rooms.

I hate my life and I hate marimba. The only thing I can think of is talking to Angus about either playing his guitar or writing a play. He has some skill in that department but I really don't want to have to rely on my surly brother.

I am petrified to tell PJ any of this. If it were only 1 problem I wouldn't feel so bad, but having entirely committed myself to the success of this group, I fear that his disappointment will be too great. Of course, he will find out eventually, but I simply can't bring myself to speak to him at this stage.

Maybe there will be a miracle? Unlikely, though.

Your completely screwed brother,

Hugh

From: 'Angus MacNaughton'
Sent: 19 June, 18h27
To: 'Julia MacNaughton'
Subject: Being a ranger

Dear Julia,

I have started the day-to-day duties of being a ranger and no longer have to worry about anything other than my game drives and the odd walk at 11:00. This is good because it gives me time in the middle of the day to read and play the guitar – free from disturbance by Anton or Jeff's inanity. I'm thinking about trying to put my degree to use with some research. I'll do some interviewing of the Shangane staff and see what their lives are like. This will give me the opportunity to visit their homesteads in the communities and get away from the lodge for a while.

I've been driving out of Rhino Camp, which has only three rooms. The camp is the newest in the lodge and is set out beautifully. I have not yet had the pleasure of staying in one of the rooms but they look incredible. The main deck area has a stunning view of the river. It has modern furnishings but they are very tasteful (as far as someone like me can tell).

Anna is Rhino Camp's manager. This is marvellous as I do not have to make any small talk with her. We have a sort of silent understanding. She is five years my senior and I'm not entirely sure whether she looks on me as a brotherly companion or potential lover. I would be powerless to object, of course, should she make an advance. This is because I find her enchanting in the literal sense of the word – she is like an obscenely sexy Tolkienesque witch.

In the mornings, when I return from drive, my guests (six if the camp is full) sit at their own tables. Anna and I sit at another and have breakfast. This is normally one of my favourite parts of the day.

Elvis has been his usual impeccable self. His ability to find animals remains unparalleled. The other morning he spent three hours on foot, alone, tracking a leopard. It was an immense achievement but in typical Elvis style he was nonchalant about it. He just called me on the radio, told me where to find the cat and its kill, and then told me to fetch him on the road when we were finished photographing the elusive animal.

My favourite part of this week however, was SB's distress. As I'm sure he's told you, he's organising for an important group at Tamboti Camp next week. This, he feels, makes him immensely significant to the workings of the universe. One of his tasks has been to sort out entertainment for the group. Needless to say, he has buggered this up and is now blaming others for letting him down. Because his ego is so enormous, he has been unable to confess this disaster to PJ and, amazingly, came seeking help from me. I'm sure you can appreciate the level of anxiety it took for him to do so.

He knocked on my door yesterday after lunch. This was unusual as no one knocks on my door except Jeff, who wanders up to my new digs every so often in order to tell me about his latest misfortune. Anyway, SB arrived, his teeth gritted into a false smile. Geez, I think it really hurt him to come to me.

'Angus,' he spluttered, standing at the door, 'I need you to help me. You know I wouldn't ask unless I was desperate.'

'Unfortunately for you,' says I, 'there is nothing I want from you, which makes this transaction a waste of our time.' I returned to the book I was reading but SB was not about to give up, so agitated was he.

'I certainly didn't expect you to do me a favour out of brotherly love,' he replied. 'It's not like I've forgotten who you are. If you do this for me, I will organise for you to spend two nights at Quintessential House, that exquisite country retreat up in the mountains.' He paused, seeing my interest pique slightly. 'If you want to take someone with you, not that I think that is likely, then I will sort that out too.'

Well, I'd quite like to stay there, so I put my book down and told him to tell me his troubles. Turns out, his gumboot dancers or marimba players or whatever they are have cancelled their gig. He cannot find anyone else in the area who'll be able to perform on the night and so he wants me to script a little play that he and I can perform for the group. As you know, I was no mean actor and director at school and he wasn't too bad on stage either. I think, however, that this act will be slightly different from my last school performance as Strephon in Gilbert and Sullivan's *Iolanthe*.

I have penned what I consider to be a masterpiece. I call it *Fawlty Towers – The Thirteenth Episode*. It details the clearing of pudding in the boma, Fawlty

Towers style – Manuel doesn't understand anything and is generally terrified of the bush. SB looks like John Cleese and I do a rather good Manuel.

I'll update you on how it is received next week.

Angus

From: 'Hugh MacNaughton'
Sent: 27 June, 06h45
To: 'Jules'; 'Mum'; 'Dad'
Subject: I'm in trouble

Dear Mum, Dad and Jules,

There is good news and bad news.

The good news is that, with some help from PJ, I managed to solve almost all of the problems I explained last week. The bad news is that Angus and I are likely to be fired later this week.

Almost immediately after sending my previous email, I came to my senses, swallowed my pride and told PJ everything. He was perfectly calm about the setbacks, but utterly incensed that I had taken so long to bring them to his attention.

"Let's just get 1 thing straight here, Hugh," he said. "I may have made you responsible for the planning of this group, but certainly didn't make you responsible for the reputation of this business. I told you at the beginning to come to me if you were unsure at any stage. To have ignored such a simple instruction shows immaturity, arrogance and stupidity. Do you have any idea what the repercussions of this group going badly will be for us? These agents carry huge clout in the industry. These setbacks that you are so panicked about are easily overcome when approached correctly. My job is to solve these sorts of things, but a little longer than 48 hours' notice would have been nice."

PJ accepted my apology but I could see he was pissed off and I felt bad. With his help, though, we came to the following solutions:

Solution 1
PJ called in a favour from an old friend who runs a restaurant in Cape Town – she is coming up to cook for the group.

Solution 2
We swapped out the 2 sick Rangers with Jamie and Duncan.

Solution 3
We have replaced the ice machine as well as the fridges. PJ said that it blew the budget completely, but that the business we would get from this group would pay off that expense in less than a month.

Solution 4
We have cannibalised parts for the air conditioners.

Solution 5
The final problem – evening entertainment – was left up to me. PJ told me to sort this 1 out. I knew that this was my opportunity to make amends. I phoned around to all the other lodges in the area for advice, but *they* had all been using the same Magical Marimba Band now on the run from the police. I then tried the women who work in the laundry. I often hear them singing while they work and thought that they may be available to help. Unfortunately, there was to be a much-awaited soap opera screening on the same evening so I had no luck. I thus had no alternative but to appeal to Angus's limited playwriting abilities.

In hindsight, a foolish decision.

After he eventually agreed to co-operate, Angus suggested we perform a game lodge version of *Fawlty Towers*. It was a *Fawlty Towers* scene that won us the House Plays Competition back at school, so at least the characters were familiar. I agreed that it seemed as good an option as any and that if we could pull it off, it may even be slightly amusing.

Then the group arrived. Things went well from the beginning. My group check-in was good, I remembered everybody's names, the rooms had been scrupulously inspected and looked fantastic and the opening lunch was a glamorous affair. The group members were in great spirits and, despite their lofty stations in life, they were a great bunch of people. However, I didn't lose sight of the fact that they were most certainly the kinds of people who are well pleased until something goes wrong – then they go ballistic.

The game drives also started with a bang. The group watched a breeding herd of elephant feeding alongside the river as well as the Granite Pride taking down a buffalo on their first afternoon. As I was unable to produce entertainment for both evenings, Jamie and Duncan sparkled up the night with a night sky presentation on the airstrip. The talk was accompanied by warming port, cheese and Amarula hot chocolate – it was highly appreciated.

The following day also went well. During the morning the group enjoyed yoga, massages, and spent a lot of money at the gift shop. So after another amazing evening game drive, where wild dogs hunting impala provided the highlight, everything seemed to be well on track for a successful final evening.

Unfortunately, this was not to be ...

That afternoon, while the game drive was out, I began to feel enormously nervous at the prospect of performing *Fawlty Towers* in the boma for discerning travel agents. So, in order to settle my nerves, I must admit to having a few drinks to calm down. When the time for the performance arrived I was feeling much better – a bit like John Cleese himself, actually, and quite excited about the crescendo of the Travel Luxury stay.

The Guests arrived for dinner, chattering with excitement about their afternoon. After several rounds of champagne, they sat down to dinner in the boma. The 2 Rangers joined them at the table while the stories continued. Angus arrived during main course. Our cue was the start of dessert.

This was to be the beginning of the end.

Angus and I strode out into the middle of the boma, each dressed with a napkin atop our heads. We felt that this would add to the theatre of it all. After a true thespian introduction, we scuttled off and returned moments later in character.

We began.

Initially there were a few chuckles from Beth and Graham (the English couple), but not much response from the rest of the crowd. But as Beth and Graham began to laugh louder, the rest seemed to get progressively enthused and were soon roaring with laughter. However, things went quickly downhill.

Just as Basil clips Manuel over the head from time to time in the real series, so I did to Angus. I was only following *his* script, after all. The first time, Angus just glared at me, but I figured that he was simply acting to character. Full of confidence, I clipped him slightly harder the second time. The blow sent him crashing to the ground, where he stayed for a brief moment. From the sandy floor of the Tamboti boma, he glared back at me, his eyes filled with rage and hatred. He shook his head as if to clear it.

"Fuck you, Hugh," he said under his breath.

What ensued after that is very blurry. Apparently sand, fists and blood filled the air as the most discerning members of the world travel trade sat watching with horrified faces under the winter sky. Jamie told me later that Angus's first punch to my nose began an almighty battle which unfortunately continued for at least a minute before Anna, Efficient and, worst of all, PJ, split us apart. During the debacle, an incensed Dawn Wiseman – CEO and founder of Travel Luxury – led her group out of the boma.

Our disciplinary hearing is tomorrow.

We are so screwed.

Love,

Your soon-to-be-fired brother,

Hugh

From: 'Angus MacNaughton'
Sent: 27June , 07h05
To: 'Julia MacNaughton'
Subject: String Bean the arsehole

Dear Julia,

Today I have the pleasure of my second disciplinary hearing. This is because your other brother – if he is that and not the son of an errant gypsy who had an affair with a retarded greyhound – is an arrogant imbecile.

We're almost halfway through the year and I now hate him more than I did before. Please send Mum and Dad my congratulations on their idea to send us both here in order to grow our bond. It has been firmly cemented now and, along with the cement, has sunk to depths greater than those of the Mariana Trench.

The only slight positive about my life right now is that cretinous SB also has a disciplinary hearing tomorrow. Frankly, I'm astounded he wasn't fired on the spot last night.

As you know, he was organising various things for an important group, for which I wrote a superb piece of theatre. We practised this piece twice. The second time, we did it for the camp mangers who all thought it was hilarious – all, that is, except Melitha who looked confused throughout. This is not surprising as Tom and Jerry is about the limit of her intellectual ability.

SB was apparently nervous about the performance and decided to fortify himself with liquor. By the time I arrived in the boma at 21:00, he was rat-arsed and slurring his conversations with Anna, who was there helping with the group's final gala dinner. As the pudding was served, it was our turn to perform.

I pulled SB out of the boma and handed him a glass of water.

'Drink that, you idiot,' I said. 'You'd better not forget your lines!'

'I'm ... uh ... fine,' he slurred at me through half-open eyes. He then poured the glass down his shirt front. Anna appeared.

'They're ready for you,' she said, observing SB ineffectually mopping the patch on his shirt.

We placed thespian-looking napkins on our heads and entered the boma. The introduction to our show went rather well. I began to feel hopeful as we exited.

Hugh lurched back in to begin the piece. I had to wait in the wings for a while as he performed the first part of the play on his own. Amazingly, he was very good and remembered all his lines and even improvised a few which made the audience laugh. When I entered and we commenced the first dialogue, we had to stop for lengthy pauses because the laughter was so loud and long.

The atmosphere of frivolity did not last.

It came time for me to make my first attempted exit from the stage. The script specifically directs Basil to *clip Manuel on the head*. Because SB was pissed, he slapped the back of my head viciously. I swung round but managed to contain myself, although my next lines were delivered through gritted teeth. SB's slap and my reaction changed the energy of the performance. Jamie, who was playing the guest, became increasingly awkward with his lines as the pressure notched up.

PJ came into the boma at that moment. We both saw him. I, obviously, could not have cared less if John Cleese had come in to evaluate us. SB, however, has a deep desire to please PJ in everything that he does. In his inebriated state, he began to forget his words. He kept shooting nervous looks at PJ who was clearly becoming unimpressed by the bungling performance.

During my second attempt to leave the boma, this time with a guest in tow, SB slapped me so hard on the back of the head that I fell over. The guests gasped. I could take SB's idiocy no more. I stood up slowly and clocked him one on the nose. He reeled back into the boma fence. This drove him into a drunken rage. He pulled a fire torch from the fence and charged, bawling something incomprehensible. I ducked so that the first swipe missed my head, but the returning blow collected my right knee. It buckled and I went down. The impact caused the torch to break open and balls of ignited paraffin exploded in all directions. Guests screamed as fireballs hit tablecloths and trouser legs.

Hugh, undaunted by the screaming and fleeing guests, dropped the torch and leapt on top of me, still yelling in language so foul I'd be embarrassed to repeat it to a corpse. From my prone position I managed to hit him in his left kidney. He screamed and then head-butted me. Blood spurted from a cut above my right eye but I could feel nothing except the pure raging hate pounding through my body. I grabbed his head as it made for a repeat head-butt, twisted and got on top of him. My fists slammed into his face twice more before PJ, Efficient and Anna grabbed me and pulled me off.

Hugh raised himself from the ground slowly, the fight gone out of him. The realisation of possible consequences trickled into his small, drunk brain. I slowly relaxed. Anna led Hugh away and sat him down at the nearest table with a glass of water. PJ and Efficient released me. I took a singed napkin and placed it over the profusely bleeding wound. The pain above my eye was eclipsed only by the sharp stabbing sensation emanating from my right knee.

PJ was beside himself. His normally calm (some might say dozy) demeanour vanished. Through gritted teeth he yelled,

'You two will have disciplinary hearings in the morning!' Saliva flew from his mouth as he spoke and his face went bright pink. 'Efficient, take Hugh home and make sure he does not come out until morning. Anna, you make sure Angus does the same. I'm going to see if I can damage-control this mon-u-men-tal fuck-up.'

Efficient led Hugh out of the boma. I say led but 'carried' is more what he did. Hugh was virtually comatose from the booze and the punches he'd received. He didn't utter a sound.

I tried to walk out but my knee buckled and I fell over. Anna helped me to my feet and I leaned heavily on her as we stumbled back to my room in the staff village. I was pretty groggy.

I lay on my bed and she mopped the worst of the blood from my head with an old towel.

'Have you got any disinfectant?' she asked, turning her nose up at the sand-encrusted wound. I pointed at my game drive bag.

'In there,' I replied, my head starting to throb. She retrieved a small bottle of Savlon and applied it to my wound, scraping the sand out. It was exceedingly painful but it felt much better when she finally finished. She took off my shoes and helped me under the covers. The last thing she did was to place two aspirins in my old enamel tooth mug.

'Drink these,' she ordered. I did as I was told, lay down once more and fell into a deep sleep.

I woke the next day to find a letter under my door. It was the familiar sight of a notice to attend a disciplinary hearing. I shall frame it next to my other one.

We are sure to be fired this time. While I'm fairly ambivalent about my future here, the circumstances of this latest hearing irritate me because I blame Hugh entirely.

See you soon with all my bags,

Angus

From: 'Mum'
Sent: 27 June , 06h15
To: 'Angus'; 'Hugh'
Subject: What on Earth?

Boys,

Your sister printed me a copy of your last letters to her last night. As a result, I have not slept a wink. I am distraught. How on Earth could the two of you let things between you get so dreadfully awful? Can you imagine what people must think of our family with the two of you behaving like gangsters from the south of Johannesburg?

I am utterly mortified by your behaviour. I cannot imagine what your father and I could possibly have done wrong in our parenting to have created a situation where such barbarism could occur.

Frankly, as much as I miss both of you, the thought of seeing either of you fills me with anger. Unfortunately for me, you will probably be fired and I will be forced to take you into our home again.

I think I will insist that your father takes me away for a while.

I am extremely angry and ashamed of both of you.

Mother

From: 'Brother H'
Sent: 28 June, 10h14
To: 'Jules'
Subject: Postponement

Hey Jules,

Angus and I have been informed that our disciplinary is postponed.
PJ told Angus (PJ is not prepared to look at let alone speak to me at
this point) that the case warranted waiting for the owners to arrive.
Coincidentally, they are due for their annual visit next week but because
of the seriousness of our offence, they have decided to cut short their stay
in Cape Town and fly up to the Lodge.

I am now truly terrified and cannot concentrate on my job or anything
else. I feel sick.

Hugh

From: 'Hugh MacNaughton'
Sent: 03 July, 17h56
To: 'Jules'
Subject: Thank god

Hey Jules,

The outcome of the disciplinary was successful insomuch as I have not been dismissed.

The hearing itself was an ordeal.

Dennis and Nicolette Hogan are not a poor couple. Not only do they own Sasekile Private Game Reserve, they also have 5 other properties dotted about the world. Although Dennis was born in Australia and lived there most of his life, he and his South African wife now live in the Cayman Islands. Apparently, this is for tax purposes. Dennis, who is probably in his mid-fifties, is a typical Australian guy – he loves sport, worships beer and is close friends with Shane Warne. However, he is also 1 of the greatest womanisers the world has ever seen. With plenty of money and reasonably good looks, it's no wonder his wife trusts him less than a rat in the pantry. There is even a rumour that he got stuck into a couple of single Guests, simultaneously, when he was visiting the Lodge on his own last year. Otherwise, he is a laid-back, very affable guy.

By contrast his wife, Nicolette, is 1 of those people who simply seems angry with life. The old phrase "money can't buy you happiness" has never been more appropriate. She rarely smiles at anybody unless she feels that she needs to impress them. She has travelled to all the top properties in the world and acts like the global authority on service excellence, haute cuisine and housekeeping. Dennis and she have a private house on the property but she always spends at least 1 night of her yearly visit in a Lodge room. The morning after, she tears the housekeeper, Camp Manager and General Manager apart with an onslaught of ridiculously pedantic feedback.

"I am still finding bloody dirt in the front doormats," is how she starts every 1 of these little feedback sessions. It's a front door mat, for god's sake – its purpose is to collect dirt. I know that PJ has been dying to say that to her every year since he started here a decade ago.

You can just imagine her delight when she heard about *Fawlty Towers* and the fist fight.

The hearing itself and the following 2 days of deliberation around the appropriate sanction were probably the most unpleasant 48 hours of my life. By 11:00 on the day of my hearing, I was seated in the meeting room with the owners, PJ and Candice (Secretary). The full gravity of the situation really sunk in. I realised that I have become immensely fond of this place and of the many people I have met – 1 person in particular. I have learned more here in the last 6 months than I ever did at Hotel School and I continue to learn every day. I feel that life back in the city wouldn't measure up and this could be the place where I launch my career. My passions for food, wine and people are all fulfilled here and the idea of all that coming to a sudden end was more than I could deal with. Before the first words of the hearing were uttered, my bottom lip had begun to wobble and shortly after that I started to blub. I simply couldn't help myself.

There were mixed responses to this.

PJ and Dennis just sat there for a while before agreeing to move on with proceedings regardless of the sobbing. But Nicolette had no mercy.

"Oh, for god's sake, shut up! This is not a nursery school! Be a man!" she screamed, slamming her palms down on the table. I stopped after that. I think everybody got a fright.

From there on the hearing took on its normal form. There wasn't really anything to dispute. I accepted that I was completely out of line and drunk. I apologised profusely and expressed my deepest regrets, but more than that I couldn't do – apart from hope for the best. Jamie, my staff representative, put in a good word. While I was still fighting back the tears, he gave a passionate speech about my obvious regret, my love of the Lodge, the huge effort I put into my job and my sterling record thus far.

But when, after a long consultation, we were finally told that bringing the Lodge into disrepute was very rarely punished by anything other than dismissal, I was convinced that it was the end for me. I wept that whole night.

Two hellish days later, we were called back for the verdict. We weren't fired! On account of my pristine record, and due to it being my first offence, I have been put on final warning for 6 months. Likewise, Angus finds himself on final written warning. I'm not sure how we escaped dismissal but I'm convinced that PJ must have gotten through to Dennis and defended us somehow, because I'm sure that Nicolette wanted us both out of here immediately.

However, it's not all roses and cream for Angus and me. My upcoming leave has been withdrawn. This is a problem because I had promised Simone that I would go with her to her farm on our next leave. Consequently, she has already delayed her usual leave time by 2 weeks. I'm not sure how I am going to break this one to her.

As a result, I'm in line to work 2 cycles back to back. During my leave, I will be joining Angus for 2 weeks of bush clearing with the conservation foreman Jacob. This should be an interesting experience, but not a pleasant one. I really couldn't care less, though, as I am just so happy to still be here.

I am, however, very ashamed at how upset Mum was about the whole incident.

Lots of love,

Your hugely relieved brother,

Hugh

From: 'Angus MacNaughton'
Sent: 03 July, 18h28
To: 'Julia MacNaughton'
Subject: Reprieve

Dear Julia,

Astonishingly, I have not been fired – nor has your other miserable excuse for a sibling.

I'm not particularly surprised about my reprieve but that SB's drunken, orang-utan-esque behaviour has not landed him amongst the ranks of the unemployed cannot be credited. I can only think his head is so far up PJ's rear end that it would have hurt our esteemed manager too much to pull it out.

The owners of this 'fine' establishment arrived the day before our hearings. They are a mega-rich couple who flit about the world doing lord knows what. Apparently they like it here during the cooler months. Dennis is a slightly slimy Australian but seems to have spent a lot of time in the bush. Nicolette (never Nicky) is a vicious-looking South African who was probably attractive in her day. She has been running hotels all over the world since conception. They were invited to attend the hearing because the cock-up in the boma was so huge.

SB's hearing was before mine. His chosen staff representative was Jamie – the ranger who played the guest in our act. Jamie thinks SB is a 'legend' and, as a senior ranger, he holds a bit of clout. I sat outside in the sun watching through the window as the snivelling SB and Jamie pleaded the case. I could see Jamie gesticulating and pointing at SB who was so miserable that I expected him to emerge dressed in sackcloth with ash on his head. He really loves his job.

It makes me sick.

He eventually came out, all bleary eyed, sad and blowing his nose. He just looked at me and walked off. PJ came to the office door.

'Angus, come in now,' he said sternly.

My staff representative was Anna. I didn't initially want a representative but when I told her, she said matter-of-factly,

'Angus, you're less tactful than a honey badger. Do you want to be fired?'

'Not really, but I'm not spoiled for choice of legal counsel around here.'

'Well, I'll do it, if you like,' she replied. I suddenly thought that it might be quite a good thing to have her in the hearing. Everyone is wary of her – including PJ.

Anna and I walked into the office. The owners stood up to greet Anna. Nicolette shook hands formally and Dennis nearly fell over himself in his rush to kiss her hello. When he'd regained his composure, he resumed his seat next to Candice, from where he cast furtive glances at her cleavage throughout the hearing.

PJ acted as the prosecutor in the hearing, with Nicolette and Dennis there to act as judge and jury. PJ presented a scalding case for the prosecution during which he utterly failed to realise that the incident was entirely SB's fault. He went on and on about how the group was the most important to come through the camp for years and that we had ruined the relationship with them for good. He also took time to explain that I was unpopular, already on a warning, and had made no effort to integrate myself into lodge life. In summary, he said,

'Angus is an arrogant and thoroughly unhelpful member of staff. He has shown complete and utter contempt for the principles of respect that are so crucial to the functioning of a lodge. While he is clearly intelligent, and produces excellent game drives for his guests most of the time, he uses his intelligence and sarcasm to bully other members of staff. He creates a feeling of unease for many of the hardworking and dedicated people who work here. I feel this lodge, its guests and its staff would be far better off without him.'

Silence ensued after his blistering attack.

There was, however, a hole in his argument, which Anna and I had discussed beforehand.

A few moments later, Anna rose to speak. Her white lodge shirt hugged her gently and this completely mesmerised Dennis (and me).

She started slowly by admitting to my less-than-sterling record but went on to say that I was in no way solely to blame this time round. She stopped short of blaming SB because she is not that sort of person. Instead, she insisted that the situation had quickly escalated out of control and while I could and should

171

have reacted differently, it was extremely difficult. She also reiterated that my previous warning was not for a similar offence and should thus not be taken into account.

Anna paused and took a sip of water. She then delivered my saving grace – a work of crafted logic worthy of Portia in *The Merchant of Venice*.

'Angus has most certainly offended a number of staff members at the lodge with his surly attitude, sarcasm and bad temper. It would be foolish and simply disingenuous to argue otherwise. That said, he has some redeeming qualities which I believe should allow him the benefit of another chance. Firstly, as PJ mentioned, he takes a very fine game drive and this, after all, is his main function as a ranger.

'It is, contrary to what PJ has said, on the staff morale side of things that I believe the strongest case lies for his retention.'

When PJ heard that, he leapt out of his seat. I've never seen him move so fast.

'I beg your pardon!'

Dennis was so caught up in Anna's forceful delivery that he simply held up a hand. PJ slumped back into his chair as Anna continued.

'Angus lives in the general staff part of the village. All of his neighbours are Shangane people. Angus is the only white member of staff who is able to converse in passable Shangane. This is no mean feat considering he has only been here six months. Most of his colleagues have been here in excess of two years and they can barely greet their trackers in the local language. He has made every attempt to learn about the lives of his neighbours and their families. This aspect of his life here is not obvious but one has only to walk into the village on an evening that Angus is not taking a game drive to observe it. He can often be found sitting on an upturned crate, drinking a milk stout and talking or listening to the Shangane staff members discussing their lives. There are precious few other white staff members who have shown this sort of commitment to understanding the cultural divide.'

She paused. PJ's face had relaxed from the contortion it had twisted into on hearing that I am good for staff morale. Anna concluded,

'While Angus's behaviour the other night cannot be condoned and his dismissive attitude must be modified, I believe he has shown a side of himself that could be tremendously valuable to this lodge. In summary, it is my considered opinion that he should be sanctioned for his behaviour in the boma but this sanction should stop short of dismissal. Thank you.'

There was a brief silence before Nicolette spoke.

'Thank you, Anna. We'll discuss the arguments and let you know our findings. You may go.' At this we went off to lunch.

At the Avusheni Eatery, the veranda table was full of eager chatter. Obviously, there was great interest in the possible departure of the MacNaughton brothers. SB was nowhere to be seen. As I arrived there was abrupt silence. All eyes turned to me and I regarded the audience.

'You'll all be pleased to know that I have been knighted and awarded the Order of Mapungubwe. You may all address me as *Sir* Angus henceforth. Continue with your gruel.' I headed into the canteen to fetch my lunch.

Two days later, we were summoned back to the office. When I arrived, I found Hugh there, looking more terrified than an impala lamb about to be savaged by wild dogs. I actually felt a twinge of sympathy for him – can you believe it? He loves this place so much.

Nicolette read out the findings of the hearing in a measured voice while Dennis stared at Candice's boobs. PJ sat quietly to one side, clearly satisfied with the outcome. He is a reasonable man – I'll say that for him. Nicolette came straight to the point.

'We have decided that neither of you will be dismissed,' she began. Hugh let out an audible sigh of relief at this news. 'You will, however, both be put on final written warnings. What occurred in the boma I have neither experienced nor heard of in the 40 years I have been involved in game lodges. The fact that you cleared a boma of our most important agents, some with burn holes in their clothes, is without precedent.

'Hugh, in your case we felt that your complete commitment to your job and guest satisfaction warranted our giving you a second chance. Angus, it would have been far easier to fire you, given your tainted record up to this point. Anna, however, made a good case for your retention. While we are fairly confident Hugh will learn his lesson, the jury remains out on you.

'As punishment, the two of you will spend two weeks working as labourers with Jacob and the conservation team. They are working on a new clearing in the north of the property. You will also both write letters to each and every one of the guests whose experience you ruined. In your case, Angus, these will be vetted by PJ.

'That is all – you may both go.'

'Thank you so much,' said Hugh as we rose to leave.

I walked out.

So there it is. Tomorrow we begin work with the conservation team. I'm quite excited, to be honest. No guests, and bush time for two weeks. The work will be good exercise. The downside is that I won't be earning any tips.

I will thus see you in a fortnight, tanned, buff and still employed.

Angus

P.S. Please tell Mum to calm down. No one died and the family name, while it has taken a knock, is hardly about to be excluded from the Johannesburg social list.

From: 'Julia MacNaughton'
Sent: 04 July, 13h15
To: 'Brother A'; 'Brother H'
Subject: Phew …

Brothers,

I must inform you that Mum is still rabid about your little contretemps in the boma the other night. Even Dad has spouted comments of immense irritation that his offspring have behaved with less decorum than one of those English football louts.

I think he is really worried about the two of you.

No doubt the 'fight in the boma' will go down in the annals of Sasekile, and if I were not related to the two of you, I would probably find it hilarious. Unfortunately, family is one of those things that one can't choose and the way you two toddlers behave around each other, I fear that you will one day splinter our family.

Frankly, it's a bit pathetic and sad.

Jules (a deeply disappointed Jules, at that)

From: 'Hugh MacNaughton'
Sent: 10 July, 18h00
To: 'Jules'
Subject: Hard labour and angry Simone – not sure which is worse

---

Hey Jules,

I hope things at home have calmed down a bit and that you have all forgiven me.

Simone has taken the news of my punishment particularly badly. It's not the fact that I've been sentenced to bush clearing, but that my 2-week penalty lies over our planned leave together. We were meant to be going to her farm in the Waterberg.

"Shit, Hugh, what the hell am I supposed to do now?" she said when I broke the news (lately I have become quite accustomed to my name being preceded by something blasphemic or a swear word). "I hope you don't think I'm changing my leave again because of your stupid behaviour," she snapped. "And what am I supposed to tell my parents, hey? What are they going to say when I tell them that the reason you can't come any more is because you got drunk and had a fist fight with your brother in the boma during dinner? God, I don't know why I bother with you sometimes!"

"That's a little harsh, don't you think?" I replied.

"Aargh!" she howled, pulling at her hair. With that she whipped round and walked out, slamming the door hard as she left.

Viciously harsh, I thought to myself as I stood there with my ears ringing from the slam.

I decided to write PJ a letter. He has been nothing but good to me since I arrived here and I could not have wished for a better mentor, but I think that this whole episode has really disappointed him. I put it all down on paper – my regret, my fears about the group being a failure and my appreciation for his taking me under his wing. I especially wanted to thank him for backing me as the new Tamboti Camp Manager when everyone else thought I was too young and inexperienced. I don't necessarily expect it to change anything in our now-blemished relationship, but I wanted to write it anyway. I put it on his desk a few days ago, but he has yet to mention it.

Simone went home to her folks on the Waterberg farm 3 days back and I have begun my time in the bush. She decided to tell her parents that I had volunteered to work with the conservation team in order to add to my experience in the lodge industry – but she was not in the slightest bit happy about it.

"They were really looking forward to meeting you, Hugh, and now you've gone and made me bend the truth," she said just before leaving the Lodge. "See you in 2 weeks, I suppose." I didn't even get a kiss before she left.

Working for conservation is not for kids. Jacob is probably the strongest man in the world and drives a TLB (back actor and front-end loader) like he was born for it. He speaks no English – only Shangane – so communication is tricky. The rest of his crew specialises in grading roads, pumping dams, fighting fires, clearing alien bush and culling impala for staff rations. They also have a reputation for being like the camp SWAT team. Whenever there are field-related problems that no one else is capable of handling, Jacob and his men are called. Chasing elephants out of camp on foot is a regular task, for example.

Given that Jacob and his crew speak little English, I have decided to use the opportunity to improve my local linguistics – not that I have much of an option. After 3 days I can understand basic commands, but the labour has been so hard that language can't be a priority. We have done nothing but dig trenches for a new water pipe which extends from the river to a new waterhole.

Angus has been as petulant as ever and working together has been pretty awful. He has accepted no responsibility for what happened in the boma. That said, he seems to rather enjoy the work. He passes shirty little chirps my way about how stupid and useless I am. He thinks PJ will never look at me the same way again. I have done my best to ignore him, but I am getting sick of it now.

I hate him.

Anyway, that sums up what's gone on this week.

I hope that you are well, that The Major is on good form and that Trubshaw's bowels have been milder than usual.

Lots of love,

Your trenchpipe-digging brother,

Hugh

From: 'Angus MacNaughton'
Sent: 11 July, 05h28
To: 'Julia MacNaughton'
Subject: 'Punishment' with the conservation team

Dear Julia,

Well, I'm not sure that my 'punishment' could have worked out much better than it has.

SB and I are a few days into our work with the conservation team under the capable leadership of Jacob 'Spear of the Lowveld' Mkhonto. We are digging a two-kilometre trench from the Tsessebe River up to a new waterhole which will be pumped in the dry season. The pan is on the ridge opposite Main Camp so the guests there will be able to view animals coming to drink in the winter months. While the work is hard and physically punishing, I'm enjoying it. My enjoyment is further increased by the suffering of String Bean.

First, let me describe the conservation team. There are seven people under Jacob, three women and four men. They all fulfil a variety of roles in the team depending on what is required. Two of the men, Timot and Smile (yes, those are their names), drive the two red, four-wheel-drive tractors when they are not labouring. Bertie, one of the others, is an ambitious young chap about my age. He is trying to learn English so he likes to work next to me while we dig. I help him with English and he helps me with Shangane. He has a great sense of humour and we spend much of the time laughing.

I'm not convinced the three women are human. They possess the strength of Olympic weightlifters and the stamina of Kenyan marathon champions. All day long they toil with picks and shovels, moving rocks and laying pipes. The most amazing thing about them is that they don't shed an item of clothing during the day. Despite being winter, it is still warm in the midday sun and we all work up quite a sweat. These three paragons of power remain covered, complete with woolly hats, the whole day. I enquired of Doris the reason for this and she looked at me as though I were mad. In high-pitched and rapid-fire Shangane she replied that her skin would become 'dark like a Nigerian' if she exposed it to the sun. Apparently, lighter skin is much sought after among modern Shangane women.

General Jacob, as I have taken to calling him, is not a smiley man but he likes it when I stand to attention and salute him in the mornings. I know this because the right side of his mouth twitches slightly. For Jacob this is the equivalent of you or me clutching our sides in hysterics. His main function is to whip the rest of us into shape and operate the TLB. He has the build and strength of the Incredible Hulk.

Back to SB.

I don't think the lazy goon has done a stitch of exercise since he got here and all the fine food and wine consumption has withered his once passably athletic physique. Watching him wield a pickaxe is a sight to behold. He goes puce in the face and can only manage about three ineffectual swings before he needs a rest. This results in the three women laughing at him until Jacob admonishes them. After the first day, his hands were so blistered that he had to ask Jacob for plasters. Jacob, of course, didn't know what the hell he was talking about. He looked at SB's hands, clicked his teeth and then took an old oily rag from the tractor toolkit (I think it used to be a Tamboti Camp facecloth). This he tore in half with his teeth and proceeded to wrap the two halves around the bloodied hands. I thought SB was going to be ill.

By the end of the week, he seemed to be getting used to the pick and he even managed a word or two to the ladies digging next to him. The gardening gloves he now wears to work are tremendously pathetic, however.

I'd love to say that it has been plain sailing for me but despite my regular daily exercise regime, I was not prepared for the physical onslaught of digging a two-kilometre trench through stony ground with picks and shovels. The first few mornings of the work, I felt like I'd been scrumming alone against the Springbok pack. Now, however, my body is getting used to it and I feel strong and happy when I wake up.

Back at the lodge, there has been mixed reaction to the continuation of the MacNaughton employment. I think Melitha is thoroughly disappointed that I wasn't fired. Yesterday, she saw me at dinner.

'Can't believe a few people can get away with behaving like baboonth and the retht of uth work like thlaves!' she said.

I said, fresh after a week of labour in the field, 'Melitha, slavery is characterised by unpaid work, whipping, branding and negro spirituals. You are paid far too much and are not whipped or branded nearly enough. Logic tells me, therefore, that you cannot be a slave.'

Anton, obviously, can't believe I still have a job. He tells a 'when-we' story every time I'm in earshot. Something along the lines of,

'When we were new, if we'd done something like that, we'd have been fired, arrested by the police and put in jail for being a *doos*.' This is normally followed by something similar from Arno.

Anna tells me that the rest of the staff are fairly ambivalent about my stay of execution but they are relieved that popular Hugh has been given another chance.

OK, that's it. Hope all is well back home. I'll be coming home in just over a week for my leave, which will be good. Please tell Mum to make the house warm. Johannesburg is beastly this time of the year.

Your labouring brother,

Angus

From: 'Hugh MacNaughton'
Sent: 17 July, 18h04
To: 'Jules'
Subject: Scorpion attack

Hey Jules,

Hard labour continued this week with the conservation crew. Although the work has been physically excruciating, Angus and I were separated for the second week, which came as a welcome relief. After my last email, his sarcastic commentary continued unabated until I cracked and there was a small brawl over a pick. The pick Angus had was desperately blunt and he was getting flack for slow work, so obviously he wanted to take mine. Of course, I was digging at a fearsome pace with my sharpened tool and the discovery of some padded gardening gloves that I found in the workshop. The more Angus was reprimanded by Jacob, the more jealous he became of my efficient digging.

"*Hantlisa, hantlisa, wa nuna angatsakangi,*" admonished Jacob. I found it amusing to hear that this meant "Hurry up, hurry up, the man who is never happy". I stifled a laugh when the meaning was explained to me by 1 of the men named Timot. This enraged Angus. He dropped his pick and tackled me into the trench we were digging.

I was only too happy to fight back.

This was too much for Jacob's patience. He leapt into the trench, grabbed us both by the collars, buried our faces in the mud and then hauled us out.

He bellowed at us in Shangane. Timot translated: "You 2 will work separately from now on. Hugh goes with Timot and Smile to the river and Angus stays here with Nhlanhla and Bertie."

Consequently, my week has been spent partially submerged in the river in front of the Lodge. Our task has involved filling sandbags and placing them strategically in order to redirect 1 of the channels to flow in front of the Lodge. This will bring birds, elephants and numerous other animals to the front of the camp decks. The task has not been a walk in the park because the channels are quite deep in places and midwinter has made the water temperature fjord-like. In addition, we have had to remove the thick vegetation surrounding the new channel. This activity has left me covered in little paper cuts and unspeakably itchy legs from the date palms.

I was also stung by a scorpion. Timot and I were moving a large log to cover a few exposed sandbags when I felt as though I had been stung by a bee. I peered down at my ankle to find a dark black scorpion attached to it. Mercifully its pincers were bigger than its tail so I realised death was not imminent. It stung like hell, though, and swelled up quite badly. I removed my boot and hobbled over the granite rocks towards the fastest-flowing channel in the river. There, I plunged my foot into the icy stream. The pain subsided a fraction.

I lay back on the rock and my mind drifted to Simone and what she was doing on her farm in the Waterberg. I smiled, but my trance was shattered by the spine-chilling snort of a hippo at close range. He surfaced in the middle of the channel and glared straight at me as if to ask what the hell I was doing on his property.

Timot helped me up and we made our way back to the trench. We arrived to find that a far worse event had taken place on their side – 1 member of the team had been rushed to hospital. He sadly seems to have injured one of his eyes very badly.

But on a positive note, I found the most amazing little spot in the river. Between the 2 middle channels there is a raised sandbar which is completely sheltered. It is quite close to the Lodge but you can't see it. I thought it would make such a nice picnic spot for breakfast in the winter and plan to test it with Simone when she gets back. Maybe a visit there will help her forgive me for buggering up her holiday.

I am seriously looking forward to getting back into Tamboti Camp.

Lots of love,

Your river-diverting brother,

Hugh

From: 'Angus MacNaughton'
Sent: 18 July, 18h28
To: 'Julia MacNaughton'
Subject: Tractors and hospitals

Dear Julia,

This has been a tumultuous week with the conservation team.

My personal highlight was learning to drive the four-wheel-drive tractor. Bertie taught me during one of the runs back to the lodge with firewood for the camps. There is something primal and empowering about driving a tractor. When we chugged into Main Camp to deliver the load, dressed in matching conservation overalls, Jenny looked me up and down with barely disguised lust – at least I think it was lust (disgust?). At Bush Camp, Anna just laughed although she made sure Bertie and I were well plied with homemade lemonade and cake by the time we headed back out into the bush.

Hugh and I were split up this week. Jacob lost his temper with us one day because we were fighting over a pick. SB likes that particular pick because it doesn't hurt his soft handies quite as much as the others.

SB was sent off to work in the freezing, crocodile-infested river and I continued work on the pipeline with Bertie and Nhlanhla (another young member of the team). We were in the process of clearing a path for the trench through some thick bush when the most distressing thing happened.

Nhlanhla bent over to pick up a stump but failed to notice a sharp twig extending up from another branch. He impaled his left eye straight onto the twig. The shock made him reel back which, of course, was the worst thing he could have done because he left half of his eye on the twig.

There was mayhem.

The poor guy started screaming. Bertie immediately went to Nhlanhla's assistance and I grabbed the radio to call Jacob – who was checking a pump somewhere. He arrived very quickly in the conservation Land Rover, walked over to Nhlanhla, pulled his hand from his eye, and let out a gasp.

By this stage I was already on the radio back to the lodge to tell them we had an emergency. Nhlanhla was going into shock. His screaming had subsided but he was starting to shake. Jacob led him to the Land Rover, put him into the back and held him still. He then instructed me to drive for the lodge as fast as possible. When we arrived at the offices PJ was there with Anton and a few others. Anton tried to take control of the situation in typically useless fashion.

'OK, everyone, don't panic, give this guy some space. Let's have a look.' He walked over to Nhlanhla and pried the hand covering his eye free. Anton, despite all the bluster, is not made of firm stuff. When he caught sight of Nhlanhla's bleeding, oozing, jellified eye, he went green and dropped like a stone.

At this point PJ declared, 'Right, Angus, go and fetch the double-cab, you're going to have to take him to hospital – the government hospital because he opted not to have medical aid.'

A little while later Nhlanhla and I were haring along the road to Tintswalo Government Hospital in Acornhoek. Nhlanhla had a patch on his eye and a Coke in his hand. I was driving at roughly 160 kph. Halfway there, a fat, smug and dull-looking policeman stepped out into the middle of the road. He was delighted to have caught me so far over the speed limit. I pulled up next to him, opened the window and before the lawman could speak a word, I leaned over and lifted Nhlanhla's patch.

'Yoh, yoh, yoh, yoh!' bleated the wide-eyed traffic cop, ticket book slapped over his mouth, 'carry on!'

'Thank you, occifer,' I replied, and sped off. We arrived at the hospital shortly thereafter.

My experience at this institution has convinced me that the national and provincial health departments are being run by a bunch of brainless pilfering cretins. The place is as organised as a three-year-old's birthday party and some of the equipment is so antiquated that I believe it was designed by the original Stone Age inhabitants of the Lowveld. The treatment to which Nhlanhla was subjected was surreal, to say the least.

We sped into the Emergency Trauma section of the hospital parking lot. As I screeched to a halt I expected a great bevy of pristine and concerned-looking medical staff to come charging out with a gurney. Instead, the dusty Arrivals area was occupied by a corpulent security guard sucking the last meat off a chicken bone. The rest of this bird's skeleton, and apparently its extended family, was scattered about the legs of the chair that was struggling to hold his immense mass.

I jumped out of the car.

'This guy's about to lose his eye, I need help!' I yelled at him. The obese cretin looked at me with contempt.

'You can't park here,' he said, tossing the bone over his shoulder and wiping his hands on his already grease-stained jacket.

'I'm not parking. I need to get this man to a doctor,' I replied. He pointed a fat finger at a crud-encrusted sign. The sign read 'BULANC NLY'. I assume it was supposed to read 'ambulance only'.

'You are not ambulance. You can't park here,' he said as though he'd just concluded a complex legal argument. Nhlanhla, who had been exceptionally brave until now, was starting to moan in the car. I became testy.

'I realise I'm not an ambulance any more than you're a four-minute miler. Just tell me how to get this man some medical help.'

'No, you must do the rules, then the help,' he replied.

'Piss off,' I said, running to Nhlanhla's door. I helped him out and made for the emergency entrance. The guard lumbered out of his chair and came forward.

'I am a security! You can't park here and swear at me, it is not my culture!'

By this stage, blood was seeping from below Nhlanhla's patch and the guard, who looked like he might try and get physical with us, recoiled when he saw the ooze. I took the gap.

'Bugger off out of my way,' I said, pushing him in the chest. I pulled Nhlanhla into the hospital.

Once inside, things didn't improve. There was pandemonium. The place was packed full of the sick, lame and infirm. The noise from the ailing and their families was deafening. Everyone seemed desperate for help. The queue for admissions consisted of about 50 buggered chairs arranged in rows. These were all full and, behind them, seated or prone on the floor, were at least another 50 would-be patients. Along the full length of the corridors there were beds on which people lay in various states of disrepair. One man, lying on a gurney, had a panga lodged in the back of his skull. It was unreal. A young, tired-looking intern was bandaging the head to stop the bleeding.

The admissions desk itself stood behind a thick wire mesh, probably because of the masses clamouring for attention. Behind the mesh sat three individuals. Between them was a plate filled with yet more fowl skeletons. The clerks' eyes were half shut and their dispositions completely disinterested.

I ran to the front of the desk, elbowing someone out of the way in the process.

'Help, now, please!' I said. 'This man is about to lose his eye.' The three sloths looked at me as though I'd stepped from a piece of cheese.

'Back of the queue,' said one, pointing. I could see his point – it's not like Nhlanhla was the worst injured or infirm. I looked over the queue and realised that some of its occupants would probably not make it to the front before they died.

I knew I would have to jump the queue if there was any chance of saving Nhlanhla's eye. I turned to the intern who was about to leave the man decorated with the panga.

'Excuse me,' I yelled, grabbing Nhlanhla by the arm. The intern turned around and looked at me. Despite the bags under her eyes and the paleness of her skin, I could see she was quite lovely. Her jaw clenched and she glared at me. I smiled the biggest smile I could muster, hoping that she'd respond positively.

'I'm sorry to bother you, I can see you're exhausted, but would you mind having a look at my friend's eye, I think he's going to lose it.'

She wiped a pretty blonde lock from her left eye and looked at the queue.

'Please, most of it's stuck on a stick somewhere in the Kruger National Park.'

This rather black joke brought a smile to her tired face.

'I'll buy you dinner at Hoedspruit's finest restaurant – god help us both,' I offered.

She smiled again and, without saying anything, waved us towards her. She turned on her heel and walked off down the corridor. I pulled Nhlanhla after her. A minute later we found ourselves out of the maelstrom and in the privacy of a consulting room.

'Thank you,' I said to her. 'This is Nhlanhla. I'm Angus.'

'I'm Cathy,' she replied, slipping on two latex gloves, 'and you're both lucky I didn't chase you to the back of that queue. I'll be holding you to that dinner.' She turned to Nhlanhla. 'Let's have a look,' she said.

An hour later I drove out on my own. Nhlanhla had to stay the night. Because of Cathy, he was seen by the resident ophthalmologist very quickly. Unfortunately, that's where his good fortune stopped. His eye was removed in an operation shortly thereafter. Poor chap had to spend three days in that hellhole. He's now at home recovering.

So that was my heavy week.

I'll be home in two days for my leave which I am very pleased about. Tell Trubshaw I'm coming and let's have lunch with The Major on Sunday.

See you soon,

Angus

P.S. I have Cathy's number – still deciding if I'm going to use it or not.

188

From: 'Hugh MacNaughton'
Sent: 24 July, 17h40
To: 'Jules'
Subject: Forgiven

Hey Jules,

This week, I am happy to report only excellent news.

To start with, I am back at Tamboti Camp and, despite the intermittent excitement that went with joining the conservation crew, I have to admit that I am far more content concerning myself with the demands of the rich and famous. Depositing sandbags into the Tsessebe River simply doesn't measure up to tasting fine South African reds with Bob and Maureen from Texas.

I suppose it took 2 weeks of hard labour to truly appreciate the benefits of my job. You can be sure that I will be doing everything in my power to prevent having to report to Jacob again. I do, however, have a new-found respect and insight for the work his crew does. Timot (who was with me during the scorpion incident) has also become a good friend of mine, so in return for a couple of cold Black Labels every now and then, he is assisting me with the presentation of the Tamboti Camp gardens. Not everyone in this Lodge has connections with the man who pretty much wrote the book on working a chainsaw.

PJ has also forgiven me.

Hallelujah.

He eventually replied to that letter I wrote to him which came as a great relief to me. Subsequently, we have met and had a very mature conversation, which I appreciated, but I have included his letter below for you to read:

Dear Hugh,

Thank you for your letter.

My apologies for the belated reply, but I wanted to consider my response thoroughly before answering.

I think you have great potential here and in this industry, but often you are your own worst enemy. Your enthusiasm rubs off on others and you clearly enjoy the company of guests and staff, but you need to slow down a bit and remind yourself that the lodge does not revolve solely around you and your camp.

Don't be afraid to ask for help: it is impossible to do everything yourself and trying to be the hero in every situation actually does you more harm than good. Start using the incredible human resources around you and commit your energy to the growth and development of all these people.

Don't burn yourself out, Hugh – I have seen too much potential fall victim to this in the past.

Feel free to come and chat at any point.

Sincerely,

PJ

Not all doom and gloom, I suppose, and I think he really wants me to succeed here, but I have to confess that I found the comment about me thinking the Lodge revolves around only me a fraction harsh. But we had a chat afterwards and he explained what he meant in more detail. I don't plan on letting him down again.

Simone's world does revolve around me, though, which is the best news.

She returned from her holiday and has found it in herself to forgive me. She came back with all manner of gifts and showered me with attention the moment she set foot in the camp. When she read the card in which I apologised for letting her down and reiterated how much I loved her, she flung her arms around me and gave me a significantly longer kiss than normal. It is so wonderful having her back but we have agreed that our next holiday has to be together at her farm with her parents. I think I'll be ready for a holiday by then as I will have worked for 14 weeks without a break. Things are really good between us at the moment. Ironically, I think the blow-up in the boma with Angus has actually helped. Funny, that.

The other piece of good news (well, sort of good news) is that a new Chef has arrived. His name is Ronald O'Reilly and, not surprisingly, he hails from Ireland. He ran a 2-star Michelin restaurant over there and seriously knows how to cook. Not sure why he chose the bush, but after the speedy departure of our last Chef, his arrival has been greatly welcomed. I suspect he is on a whopping salary.

He is very white and has a thick Irish accent. The local staff are having some difficulty understanding him as a result, but his food is so good that everybody seems to be overlooking this detail. Yesterday, he 'articulated' the Tamboti Camp breakfast special of soft-poached eggs, with spinach, tomato and crispy pancetta on toasted baguette with parsley hollandaise sauce, in just under 2 and a half seconds. Even the Guests looked a little mystified – and some of them were Europeans!

What is it like having Angus home? Tell him I say hi and that nobody is missing him here.

Your decidedly merry and most chipper brother,

Hugh

From: 'Angus MacNaughton'
Sent: 24 July, 18h28
To: 'Julia MacNaughton'
Subject: Stuffed car

Dear Julia,

Well, I'm home and rather sad that your firm has sent you off on a beastly training course or conference or whatever it is that you legal people do.

As you know, the fact that I share a car with SB irks me deeply. It is going to irk him even more, however, when he beholds the current state of the automobile. It no longer has a back windscreen and is adorned with a stuffed front-right panel. This is why…

I decided to make good on my offer to the not-unattractive doctor I met while Nhlanhla was losing the use of his left eye. To my satisfaction, she had the afternoon off and acquiesced to a meal in Hoedspruit.

Finding somewhere to go for lunch in the armpit of the Lowveld is not easy. As far as I was aware, my options extended to Steers, KFC and a street-side stall selling chicken feet fried in five-year-old oil. Thankfully, Cathy suggested we go to a restaurant just outside town that she knows quite well.

An hour after leaving the lodge, I pulled into the parking lot of a little centre called The Fort. I had no idea the place existed. There are roughly ten shops selling curios, local crafts and outdoor gear. It's nicely set in the trees just off the Balule River and is centred on a courtyard. The eating and drinking house there is called the Mimosa Cocktail Bar. I wondered who would frequent a cocktail bar in Hoedspruit. I couldn't imagine too many local Shanganes wandering in for strawberry daiquiris on a Friday evening.

By the end of the afternoon, the local patrons would have made themselves known – through the medium of a half-brick. But that is for later.

I headed into the restaurant where about six of the 20 or so tables were occupied. The manager, a large blond man with a haircut and jaw like Johnny Bravo, sauntered over.

'Do you want a table?' he asked breezily.

'No, I'd like some lunch,' I replied. He didn't get my joke and clicked his fingers.

'Custard!' he bellowed. A small, downtrodden-looking Shangane appeared hurriedly.

'Yes, sah,' he said, his eyes darting uneasily from me to Johnny.

'Take this customer to a table,' Johnny snapped, turning on his heel and returning to his newspaper at the bar.

Custard (I'm not joking) waved me obsequiously to a table on the terrace where I began to relax, watching a paradise flycatcher in the branches of an enormous mahogany tree. Ten minutes later, my absorption in the bird was arrested by the arrival of my date. She looked even better out of her scrubs, dressed in a pair of tightish jeans and a green shirt. I stood as she approached and we exchanged a friendly hug. Custard appeared.

'Hello, Custard,' she said. 'I'll have a gin and tonic.' I was pleased with this development. If she'd ordered a mineral water on a Friday afternoon, I'd have excused myself. (In hindsight, this would have been prudent.) I ordered the same and Custard headed off.

As you are aware, I am not easy to talk to. With this girl it was different. We instantly fell into animated conversation. Custard returned with the drinks and we ordered some food, I forget what, and continued chatting. Four G&Ts and three hours later, Cathy was laughing hysterically and I was getting funnier by the minute. We'd even shared a pudding – I've never shared a pudding before. At 17:00 I knew, pissed as I was, that driving home to Johannesburg was not an option. I suggested we go to the cocktail bar. This she thought was a marvellous idea.

I forget at what point of the afternoon I noticed Johnny looking over at us and then making what seemed like an urgent phone call, but the incident is somewhere in the recesses of my memory.

The Mimosa bar area was dimly lit and I ordered a mojito and Cathy a cosmo. There we stood, both fairly rat-arsed, chatting away amiably. My drink finished, I excused myself and headed into the gents.

As I was relieving myself, two enormous individuals walked in. I was standing at the middle of three urinals. The other guys stood on either side of me and the hair on the back of my neck began to tingle. One of them was wearing khaki shorts and a two-tone top which was untucked so that his fat belly could observe the world. There was so much facial hair on the other that he reminded me of the Wookie from *Star Wars*.

'Haven't seen you in vis place before,' said Fatty, trying to extricate his member from beneath his stomach.

'No,' said Wookie, already in full flow, 'I fink you is new.' His accent was marginally thicker than his trunk-like neck.

'No, I've not been here before,' I replied, finishing up and heading out quickly.

I returned to Cathy, who had ordered us two more drinks. I quickly forgot Fatty and Wookie but did notice Johnny sat in a booth not too far from us. Cathy seemed slightly on edge.

'Let's move over there,' she said, pointing to a sofa in a secluded part of the room.

We took our drinks and moved off. Some music started playing and the chemistry between Cathy and me fizzed as we sipped our drinks and then ordered two more. Halfway through these I stood, pulled Cathy up and we started to dance – a sort of slow rock 'n roll. I think Katie Melua was singing. It was not long before we dispensed with the arm's-length stuff and found our arms around each other in the quiet corner. A minute later, our heads parted and we looked into each other's eyes (hers are blue, by the way). The inescapable attraction welled, she closed her eyes and I moved in to capture the sweetest moment of this god-forsaken year.

As our lips were about to touch, the proverbial shit hit the fan.

More precisely, a full beer glass came flying past my head and smashed into the window behind us. Beer and glass filled the air. Cathy and I spun round to see Fatty, Wookie and Johnny looking at us (well, me) menacingly. The music stopped and a hush quickly enveloped the bar.

'What you doing with my girl, *boet?*' asked Wookie.

'Ja, what you doing wif his chick?' repeated Fatty. I turned to Cathy.

'Do you know these creatures?' The booze and the fact that I was attached to the best-looking girl in the Lowveld (except for Anna, perhaps) made me feel bullet-proof.

'I sort of know them ...' Before she could continue, the question came again.

'I asked you a fokken question. What you fokken doing with ... my ... girl ... *boet*?' asked Wookie.

They were standing behind the sofa, Wookie leaning with his hands on it and his goons backing him on either side. Fatty started to make his way left around the sofa and Johnny went right.

'You need to get out of here,' whispered Cathy as my mind raced boozily through the options.

I grabbed my mohito glass and flung it at Wookie's head. It cracked into his forehead and he bellowed and fell backwards. I jumped onto the couch, grabbed Cathy and we jumped over the back and were out of the door before Wookie and Fatty could react.

'Who the hell are they?' I asked as I pulled her across the car park.

'The hairy one has been bugging me for ages. I better go. They'll kill you.'

This I did not doubt for a second. She made for her car. I tried to stop her but she pulled away.

'I have to go and you must too, as fast as you can. I'll explain later.' I grabbed her wrist again. 'Come with me,' I said.

'I can't. Go, quickly, they're coming.' She ran to her car, started the engine and was gone.

I was in the shadows and saw the goons emerge at the door of the Mimosa, cursing. My car was close by so I slipped through the shadows, fumbling for my keys, shocked and irritated by the events that had conspired to ruin my evening.

I had reversed into the parking place so it should have been easy to make my escape. Unfortunately, I was drunk. I managed to start the car, which I knew would alert my enemies to my position, but I figured I could get out quickly. Unfortunately, in my inebriated state, I ground the gears in my efforts to find first and the goons came hurtling down the stairs from the Mimosa. I slammed the accelerator down and lurched out of the parking place – I was quite pleased with my efforts, so I wound down the window and shouted, 'Fuckerrrrrrrrrrrrrrs!' as I sped past my pursuers.

The next thing I knew, the back window of the car exploded. I didn't wait to find out what they'd thrown; they might well have been shooting for all I knew. I swerved in shock, and drove over a flower bed and out onto the road. Unfortunately, there was a fairly thick knobthorn in the flower bed and it dented – well, more tore – the right front panel of the car.

Anyway, that's why the car is mangled. The half-brick which they threw through the window is still on the back seat as Dad wants to have it finger-printed. I have given up trying to convince him that this is a stupid idea.

Pity you are not at home at the moment. Mum is still upset about the fight incident but Dad cracked a smile the other day when I told him about flying bits of ignited paraffin landing on the guests.

Enjoy your conference and see you in a few days.

Angus

Hey Jules,

Firstly, thanks for forwarding Angus's email about our car. It is very disappointing that he has done this to our vehicle but, luckily, I have experienced something truly wonderful in the last few days. Not even the destruction of the Tazz could knock me off my high.

I would like to inform you of some ecstatically good news.

No, I haven't received a second promotion and no, I haven't even received a tip so generous that I am able to pay off the damage to the car. I *have* done something else, though ... and something has happened to me.

It is something so wonderful that I feel the need to prance about with joy. It is so marvellous that my life could end today and I would be a happy man. It is so smashingly good that I am all abuzz and not even the darkest cloud could dampen my high-spirited mood.

Simone and I have experienced the ultimate in emotional and sensual bonding. We have, admittedly for only a short period, *made love*!

I took her out to that little island I described last week. There I opened a bottle of Veuve Clicquot (my final apology for ruining our holiday). We sipped the incredible champagne as the sun went down and, eventually, we were overcome with spontaneous passion. It was perfect – just the way I hoped it would be 1 day.

We are really completely in love.

By now, I'm sure that you have established that I have finally lost my virginity with Simone and it was, without doubt, the most wonderful experience of my life.

Given the circumstances, I couldn't give a damn about the car. Angus could have written it off and I would still be happy.

Your ecstatic brother,

Hugh

JAMES HENDRY

From: 'Angus MacNaughton'
Sent: 31 July, 18h28
To: 'Hugh MacNaughton'
CC: 'Julia MacNaughton'
Subject: Plucking and pregnancy

String Bean,

If what you have told Julia is true, then I offer the following list of possibilities to explain your breaching of the sacred hymen of Simone:

- You gave her Rohypnol – which rendered her unconscious;
- You gave her too much wine – which rendered her unconscious;
- You hit her over the head – which rendered her unconscious;
- She is delirious with malaria – almost unconscious;
- She is psychotic (a real possibility given the place at which she works) – unconscious of reality.

Your description of the place and time of the 'event' led me to the following conclusion: you did not have a gumboot with you. This is amusing. I can just imagine your current state of panic – not knowing how to broach the subject of imminent parenthood with Simone.

Perhaps there is no need to worry – the withdrawal method is about 60% effective.

The thought of String Bean Junior is vile.

Angus

From: 'Hugh MacNaughton'
Sent: 07 August, 18h00
To: 'Jules'
Subject: O'Reilly

Hey Jules,

O'Reilly is not going to last out here.

The man has the temper of a musth bull elephant!

Frivolous use of assorted swear words may have commanded the respect of some of Dublin's hard-working commis Chefs, but this sort of language simply doesn't fly with the senior citizens of the Shangane community. This truth came home to roost when the glorified Michelin Star Chef had his entire kitchen staff walk out on him.

It had been a bad morning for O'Reilly. Melissa reported negatively on the previous evening's food in her camp at the Morning Meeting. As I have explained in previous mailings, the Morning Meeting is a compulsory meeting for all staff except the Rangers who are driving. The day is discussed and feedback from the previous day is heard. PJ always begins the meeting with the arrivals and departures of the day but then each Camp Manager is afforded the opportunity to regale the assembly with a summarised account of the previous day's events. Melissa's summary went along the following lines:

"It was hectic at Kingfisher Camp. My Guests are not very friendly, you know, and dinner was a nightmare! The soup was cold, the Chefs didn't know the difference between well-done and rare beef and the veggies were floppy."

She sat down.

O'Reilly's complexion went from pale to pink as Melissa slobbered away. He was clearly not used to receiving feedback at all, let alone from the likes of Melissa. He glared at her for a moment after she had finished talking and then offered a retort lasting less than a second, which nobody understood. PJ asked if he could please address the feedback because, unfortunately for O'Reilly, reports from the other Camp Managers (except Main Camp) were also not ecstatic, mine included.

With 4 camps at the Lodge, it is impossible for O'Reilly to be everywhere so he relies heavily on the support and competence of the senior members of his kitchen. These senior members are all local Chefs who have learned their skills over a number of years and they have no formal training. They have learned from many different Head Chefs and have also seen many an overpaid Executive Chef come and go. They are all very competent and consistent, but they respond slowly to change and rely on positive reinforcement and training in order to broaden their horizons.

Within his first week, O'Reilly had turfed the previous Chef's entire menu and introduced ridiculously complex dishes such as fricassee of quail and pan-seared *foie gras*. Ignorantly, he expected the local guys to understand his complicated cuisine. He consulted none of them about the changes and took great offence when they were unable to produce his dishes. I happened to be in the kitchen when O'Reilly marched in and called a meeting straight after the Morning Meeting. The following paragraph would be best read at a fast pace and in an Irish accent (a bit like Brad Pitt's gypsy character in that movie *Snatch*):

"A'right, now, ya listen ta me ya bunch a stchoopit little feckers. I've just sat troo de most god-awful excuse for a meeting I've ever seen. Now, having to listen to some slapper who tinks she knows about my food is too mooch for me to bear, but de fact remains dat last night tree out a 4 camps served up a complete pile a shite. Now, I sure as hell haven't crossed the world to gain a reputation of serving piles a shite out here, have I? Hmm? Have I? De food at Main Camp where I was cooking last night was top-draw stuff and I refuse to be fecked around by de mediocre efforts of de rest of ya. I've given ya de recipes, now cook de feckin food and cook it feckin properly, ya bunch of useless feckers."

With the arrival of the first "F-word", cries of "haaaaiii, haaaaaaiiiii, haaaaiiii" echoed around the kitchen, but O'Reilly refused to relent. These words were probably standard practice back in Ireland, but this Lodge's kitchen brigade took great offence at his idea of a little morning "motivation". With much shaking of heads and more groaning, the Sous Chefs led the whole crew out of the kitchen and up to the village. O'Reilly screeched at them to turn around, but there was no stopping them and the prospect of a slick breakfast service suddenly dwindled.

PJ was not pleased.

His office is situated between the village and the main kitchen, where he is able to see everybody walking up and down. You can imagine his surprise when the entire kitchen personnel came shuffling past his window. It took him 40 minutes to persuade the staff to return to camp so that breakfast could be served. They agreed only on condition that O'Reilly stop his foul language immediately and change the recipes back to normal.

PJ agreed.

O'Reilly was then hauled into PJ's office, where I think he experienced a few swear words directed at him for a change. Rumour has it that unless he changes his approach immediately he will be thrown out of here.

Simone found the whole episode wildly amusing when I related it to her.

"You sound exactly like him when you do that Irish accent, Hugh," she said, chuckling away. "I really don't think he is cut out for Africa."

"Mmm, I'm not sure, you know," I said. "I think he may come around."

Things are still fantastic between us. Really fantastic...

Anyway, that just about wraps up this week at my place of "work".

Lots of love,

Hugh

P.S. I'm sure it's nothing, but Angus managed to freak me out about my wonderful experience with Simone in the riverbed last week. I really hate to burden you with the gory details but I did manage to "pull out", as they say. I'm still worried that this wonderful incident could result in pregnancy, however, despite knowing the chances are really tiny ... please send some advice.

From: 'Jules'
Sent: 07 August, 18h45
To: 'Brother H'
Subject: Fear not

Hey Hugh,

Just a quick one before I head out for one of the few perks of working for a commercial law firm – a celebratory dinner after we closed one of the Mergers and Acquisitions deals that has been pending for the last while.

I am sure there is nothing to worry about ... well, probably.

Jokes. Don't stress until you have confirmation of either potentiality. Nonetheless, I would have thought that private school education of yours would have included some sex ed – it really is quite easy to get a girl pregnant!

Try not to stress too much in the interim, though. It should be fine.

Chat soon,

Jules

From: 'Angus MacNaughton'
Sent: 08 August, 20h28
To: 'Julia MacNaughton'
Subject: Walk in the late winter dusk

Dear Julia,

I'm back.

The highlight of my arrival was SB's puce face when he beheld the mangled front panel of our car. It improved the deep sense of dread I felt as I drove into the lodge. He came out to see the Tazz as I arrived and made a vain attempt to start haranguing me. I raised my hand to shut him up and headed back to my room. It's hardly my bloody fault.

He's upset because he's taking Simone on a site inspection to a fancy country retreat some time soon. He thinks our Tazz is an embarrassment at the best of times and is mortified at the thought of arriving at a five-star establishment in a vehicle that looks like a piece of old tinfoil.

On return from leave, it is customary for returning staff to receive a letter signed by a number of other staff. It welcomes returnees with pukerous messages about how much they were missed – sentiments of goodwill for the coming work cycle. It is normally headed – *Welcome back, from your Sasekile family.* The thought of anyone here being my 'family' is too miserable for words.

The offending 'welcome back card' is penned on coloured paper with felt-tip pens, affixed to a beer of some description and left on the returnee's doorstep. The beer on my doorstep was empty. I suspect Petrus Mhlongo, my alcoholic neighbour. Petrus is an ancient Shangane who works in the kitchen. He is pleasant but has not been sober since the Rinderpest.

My note was sparse, to say the least. On one side it had three messages. They read:

- Welcome Back, PJ. (He has to sign them all.)
- Hey, Angus, so cool that you back, really missed you a lot bru!!!!! (Jeff remains unoffended by the fact that I continually compare his brain with that of a nematode. Probably because he doesn't know what a nematode is.)

- Welgum bek, lots of luv for you. (A genuine missive from Bertie who I shall have to aid with his spelling.)

I was about to toss it in the bin when I turned the orange piece of A4 over and saw another sentence which surprised me somewhat:

- Hello, Angus. Good to have you back. Anna.

Hmmm…

On my pillow was a letter – old-style, complete with postage stamp. It was addressed to 'Angus the ranger'. On the reverse side was the sender's name and, more disturbingly, her address: Catherine Jenson, C/O Edendale Hospital, Pietermaritzburg, KZN.

The reason for the letter's far-flung origin was contained in the note.

The contents went some way to explaining the events that transpired at the Mimosa Cocktail Bar.

It seems that Wookie began stalking Cathy as soon as she arrived to intern at Tintswalo Hospital. He had propositioned her endlessly and found, to his eternal mystification, that she found him more offensive than a pile of vomit. This did not sit well with him as he considers himself the Mafia Don of Hoedspruit (apparently he has an Italian great-great-grandmother). His goons used to follow Cathy all over the place, always lurking where she was and asking where she'd been or was going. Between Wookie, Johnny and Fatty, they made her life in the Lowveld very unpleasant.

On the verge of leaving, Cathy approached the police. An obliging officer named Oubaas Godi, whose brother had been assaulted by one of the gang at the Hoedspruit KFC, sent a contingent round to Wookie's place. History doesn't relate what happened but Cathy had no more trouble. Wookie went back to his job as the cashier at a local hardware store, Fatty returned to beating workers on the family banana farm and Johnny found employment at the restaurant where I met Cathy. Three months later, I took her to lunch. Apparently, Wookie had not found anyone else on whom to lather his odious affections.

Anyway, the incident at the Mimosa Cocktail Bar inspired her to take up an intern position offered at Edendale Hospital in KwaZulu-Natal.

I guess I won't be seeing her again.

I put her letter in my drawer and headed out of my room. I found Bertie in the village at about 16:00 and suggested we go for a short walk. On our way out of the camp, we came across Anna, who had just finished some admin in the office. She gave me a big squeeze, which improved my mood, and joined Bertie and me on our walk.

We chose a route along the river and trod carefully through the dense vegetation for about half an hour before coming across a huge mahogany tree that overlooks the river. We climbed its knobbly old trunk and peered out of the thick foliage. In the middle of a thick stand of reeds, a herd of about ten elephants fed slowly. We could hear their deep rumbling as they lazily tore up the reeds, shook them free of sand and chewed them. A young bull, glowing golden-grey in the setting sun, drank from a shallow pool – some of the only water left in the river.

We stayed in the tree until the sun dipped over the mountains in the west and then wandered slowly back in the gathering dusk.

Away from the river, the bush was very dry. It seems to be eagerly awaiting the first rains which I believe can arrive any time between early September and December.

Tomorrow I start driving some Spanish guests who speak no English. This is good because it means I will not have to converse with them.

Until next week ...

Angus

From: 'Hugh MacNaughton'
Sent: 14 August, 18h20
To: 'Jules'
Subject: Public displays of affection

Hey Jules,

O'Reilly came and spoke to me after he caused the kitchen walkout with his foul language.

"How de hell am I supposed to run a kitchen without de odd swear word?" he asked with hurried speech but genuine interest. His ego had taken a knock from PJ's bollocking. "Surely *you* know how de restaurant business works?" he followed.

"Yes," I said, "I *do* know how the restaurant business works, but this is *not* a restaurant, it's a game lodge. It works differently here."

I told him about the time I made the same mistake as he had.

We had a repeat Guest staying in Tamboti. He was fastidious about fast service at meal times. One morning, he ordered his usual cup of coffee at breakfast, but 5 minutes later it had not arrived. I got up from the staff breakfast table and stormed into the kitchen. There I found both Butlers huddled around the toaster. Incredible was peering into the cavity of the machine (it was still on, of course) while Difference was poised with a fork just beside him. There was smoke emanating from a trapped piece of crust. Neither of them was showing any signs of making coffee.

"For Christ's sake, guys, John has been waiting for his coffee for ages," I said. "He is about to go fucking berserk and you 2 are trying to electrocute each other with the toaster!"

They both glared at the floor and said nothing to me, which riled me even further.

"Alright, fine, then," I said. "Don't put yourselves out. I will make the coffee. After all, it really would be a crime to have to ask you to do your jobs correctly, but that's OK. Perhaps I'll also fill up this Guest's mini bar when I'm done or issue more tea for your tearoom."

With that I sped, irritated, out of the kitchen with a fresh pot of coffee.

Although I had not shouted any of my vulgar language at either of the 2 gents directly, there was still outrage. I was accused of being disrespectful and rude.

For a while after the incident, they would not speak to me. Eventually, they called a meeting and they explained that if I wanted things done quickly, then I needed to ask nicely and that no shouting or swearing was allowed. Given that they were doing precious little at the time of the incident, I completely disagreed with them, but decided that rationality was simply not going to win over ingrained culture. I have never sworn around any staff member since then and it has made all the difference.

O'Reilly nodded his head backwards and forwards and then from left to right as he tried to decide what he thought of all of this.

"Perhaps," he said. "Good lad you are, but I'll be going now to have a good tink about this lot."

With that he headed back to the main kitchen, muttering to himself.

Simone and I are as tight as ever, but she has become particularly affectionate lately. The whole "holding hands" and "I love you" thing is very new to me and I find it a little awkward, to be honest. I had lunch with her the other day at the Avusheni Eatery and it was verging on ridiculous. She clung onto my right hand throughout the meal – forcing me to eat with only my left. Fortunately, it was macaroni cheese so I managed with just my fork, albeit in the wrong hand.

She also drops the "Love Bomb" regularly which is weird for me. I definitely love her as well, but these public announcements embarrass me a bit. I suppose it just feels funny saying "I love you" to anyone other than you, Mum or Dad. I have never wanted to be the guy who is seen cooing and gazing into his lover's eyes. I'll have to get over it, though, because there is no stopping her.

JAMES HENDRY

I also had my introduction to malaria phobia this week. As spring approaches and the temperature begins to warm up, the mozzies become more prolific. There is always 1 Guest who is excessively anxious about being bitten. For me at Tamboti, this Guest came in the form of a woman named Felicity who arrived yesterday. She is a middle-aged lady from America (surprise, surprise) who is convinced that if she so much as hears the buzz of a mosquito she is guaranteed to contract cerebral malaria.

By the time I had finished tending to the requests concerning her room, the place looked like a Bedouin tent because she had made me hang mosquito nets in 3 different areas. She wanted 1 each over the bed, the dressing table and the bath. She is also never seen without a can of Peaceful Sleep mosquito repellent in her hand, which she sprays liberally at anything resembling a mozzie.

She has been a nightmare to manage on the deck during meal times in that she always sprays a perimeter ring around the table. Most of this wafts across to the other poor Guests sitting next to her and they end up with mouthfuls of mosquito poison. It is not a happy arrangement but Felicity is too petrified to reason with. I already can't wait for her to go, but she still has 3 nights left.

I haven't spoken to Angus for a while. I think he is driving a bunch of Spaniards out of Main Camp.

Hope you're well.

Love,

Hugh

P.S. All OK on the Simone front (I'm not going to be a dad just yet). Thanks so much for the advice. I shall, in future, be prepared in advance!

From: 'Angus MacNaughton'
Sent: 15 August, 19h35
To: 'Julia MacNaughton'
Subject: Death by secondary smoke

Dear Julia,

Five weeks till my next reprieve.

I've been driving guests solidly for the last week. I am currently working out of Main Camp where September and Jenny are 'in charge'. As mentioned, my first assignment this week was a Spanish family: Juan, Elena and their four offspring whose names I remembered for precisely four seconds after we were introduced. They ranged from early to late teens. From my point of view, the safari itself wasn't too bad because the family spoke no English at all. This meant that Elvis and I could converse at will and I spent their three-day stay learning the Shangane medicinal uses for various trees.

Elvis decided to impart this suite of lessons because he'd been dosing himself. He arrived for the first game drive looking like he'd been in a sauna for four days. Sweat was pouring down his face and the back of his shirt was wet. I introduced him to the Spaniards and they exchanged nonsensical greetings. Just before we headed out into the bush, I asked if he was feeling alright.

'Oh, yes!' he replied. 'I tell it in a bush.' (I'll explain while we're on the game drive.)

A little while later my illustrious friend explained that once a month he takes the leaves of a tamboti tree, soaks them in water and drinks the concoction. Apparently it takes roughly five minutes before he must avail himself of a loo. Here he sits with a bottle of water for the next 24 hours. I asked him why in god's name he felt the need to do this to himself and he explained that it purges his digestive tract of the impurities associated with the traditional diet – although he didn't use that exact expression.

I should state at this juncture that tamboti leaves contain a sap that has had fatal consequences on many occasions for those foolish enough even to cook on the wood. Black rhino eat it happily, however, and as Elvis is roughly the same size as a black rhino, this is probably how he survives the monthly purge of his bowels.

That afternoon, he had just completed his 24 hours on the john and was still feeling the effects. He kept spotting phantom tracks and had to 'follow' them to a secluded bush from which he emerged looking relieved.

Enough of the vagaries of Shangane traditional medicine and on to the guests.

They all smoked. Yes, all of them – from mid-teens up. So addicted to nicotine were they that I had to stop the Landy every half hour for one or the other to light up. Evidently, lung cancer is all the rage in Iberia this year.

It is lodge policy that the ranger sits with his guests for dinner. This apparently enhances the guest experience because we are supposed to play raconteur, recounting spellbinding yarns of our time in the bush. This might work for some but for me it is a pain in the arse. Normally guests ask the same interminable questions. Please read the following with an American accent for greatest effect:

'So, how does one train to be a driver?' (Some people think this is my job title.)

'Has any animal tried to kill you?'

'What's your favourite animal, Angus?'

'Have you ever been scared in the jungle?' (Quite how the semi-arid Lowveld qualifies as a jungle, I cannot fathom.)

And my personal favourite ...

'So, Angus, are you dating any of the camp managers? What about Jenny? She's cute!'

I have to fight back the overwhelming urge to answer the last one with,

'Yes, Jenny and I are having a meaningless physical affair. I shall shortly excuse myself but instead of going to the lavatory, I shall meet Jenny behind the kitchen where we will behave in a depraved manner up against the freezer compressor.'

Anyway, my dinners with the Spanish were something of a trial for different reasons. All four participated in completely unintelligible conversations at the same time. They displayed an incredible ability to multi-task, yelling at each other, eating, drinking and smoking all at the same time. The most remarkable thing about my dinners with this jovial family was the fact that they included me in every conversation – in Spanish.

During heated moments, Elena would turn to me and plead for my opinion, gesticulating with her fork in one hand and a cigarette in the other. I obviously had no idea what the hell she was on about so I'd shrug or nod. This she would take as my opinion on the matter and resume shouting at her family.

September and Jenny found their three-night stay most amusing. They stood at the bar and laughed as I suffered through each of the three dinners. The weirdest part of the last evening concerned Clifford, the waiter who nearly incinerated himself a while back, if you recall. He arrived to fetch the dessert plates and Elena, who was in the middle of an impassioned monologue about god knows what, asked Clifford for his opinion. Undaunted by his lack of Spanish – he probably thinks Spain is a village in KwaZulu-Natal – he weighed in with a treatise of his own ... in Shangane. Elena and Juan seemed completely happy with his response and slapped him heartily on the back as he left. Jenny and September were in hysterics at the bar and even I had a little laugh at the bizarre interaction.

Oh, yes, I phoned Cathy this week. We had a great chat – we find talking to each other so easy. Alas, she is not to return to this area. I have resolved to take revenge on Wookie, Fatty and Johnny for frightening this gem off. Not sure when or how, though.

Anna has been on leave and returns tomorrow, which will be good.

That's it for this week.

Angus

P.S. I'm sorry to hear that Trubshaw ate Dad's new leather briefcase – I'm sure Dad must have been in a fine rage.

From: 'Hugh MacNaughton'
Sent: 21 August, 18h15
To: 'Jules'
Subject: Melissa in trouble

Hey Jules,

Felicity has finally left (without malaria, we hope) and Simone still loves holding hands and saying "I love you". Otherwise, all is reasonably well at the Lodge. There was 1 incident during the week, though, which will probably be of interest to you.

The irritating Melissa finally got the reprimanding she deserves!

Although she is utterly incompetent, in my opinion, and a massive cringe around Guests with her silly jokes and incomprehensible speech, she never really steps out of line with the rules and consequently parades around like PJ's pet. Unfortunately for her, though, her last move was not so law abiding and PJ came down on her like a ton of bricks.

I was hosting a dinner for my Guests in the Tamboti Boma. I had the usual mix of a family and a few couples. When we have Guests staying for 3 or 4 nights I like to mix up the dinner venues a bit to add variety to their stay. Some of the venues I have used in the past include the outside deck, next to the fire inside, beside the pool with lots of lanterns, and the boma.

The boma at Tamboti Camp has been slightly modified from the traditional army style (there are no cows in ours, for example). It is enclosed by a split-pole fence and the floor is covered in river sand. Inside are tables for the Guests and a built-in gas braai for the Chefs to cook on. There is also a small bar. The boma is my favourite of all the venues so I try to serve dinner there as often as possible.

Kingfisher Camp doesn't have a boma so Melissa sometimes takes her Guests to 1 of the other camps for dinner. The other night she asked if she could join us for dinner. I agreed with trepidation.

Although I was not aware of it at first, it became evident that the dinner was quite an occasion for Melissa. She arrived spruced enough for a New York night club and smelling like the cosmetics department at Harrods. I realised eventually that she was attempting to impress Jonesy, who is her most recent flavour of the month. Jonesy has been driving out of Kingfisher Camp for a few weeks now and Melissa is quite obviously keen on him. She was definitely nervous and drank heavily of the house chardonnay during dinner (I think that excessive drinking on account of anxiousness before a big event is the only thing Melissa and I have in common). By dessert she had ceased any contribution to the dinner conversation. She rocked back and forth on her chair and gazed across the table at Jonesy as he regaled the company with stories from the bushveld. Then...

"Shiiiiiiiiiiiiiiiiiiiiiiittttt!!!!" broke the stillness of the night and grabbed the attention of the entire boma.

Melissa had rocked back a few too many degrees and went toppling over into the sand. Her head collided with a lantern that was positioned behind her so it was not a pretty sight.

Jonesy roared with laughter, which fortunately took a bit of the awkwardness out of it, but Melissa had to excuse herself as her hair was drenched in paraffin. The 2 Butlers also had to excuse themselves as they were hysterical, but PJ was not so amused. He had popped in to the boma to see some of the Tamboti Guests and witnessed her loud fall. He glared down at the ground and then shook his head before continuing his conversation.

She was called in the next day and has not been so chipper since. Ha, ha, ha.

I am really looking forward to coming home in a week or so. Simone wants me to visit her farm, but I'd like you and the folks to meet her before that. What do you think?

Lots of love,

Hugh

213

From: 'Angus MacNaughton'
Sent: 21 August, 19h28
To: 'Julia MacNaughton'
Subject: Anna

Dear Julia,

This week, like many in this place where the world's most bizarre occupants have gathered, has been interesting. The interest was not provided by the spluttering Melitha, the boorish Anton, a drunken security guard, the Irishman who now works in the kitchen or our fool brother.

This week it was Anna.

I have been driving out of Rhino Camp, where Anna is manager. One evening, we had a boozy dinner with some guests. (I normally have to drink heavily to tolerate an evening of small talk with over-moneyed strangers.) When the guests eventually buggered off to bed, Anna and I decided to finish the stunning bottle of Luddite shiraz that they'd bought.

We sat on a comfortable sofa on the deck looking out over the Tsessebe River. It was a moonless night lit by a billion pin-pricks in the black sky. As we sipped the wine and the candles burned quietly down, Anna told me her life story.

It's the most extraordinary yarn.

Anna is English. In her nearly 33 years of life, she has lived, laughed and cried more than anyone I've met. She was born in Ascot in 1976. Her father is an earl – apparently descended from Robin Hood. His inheritance included vast tracts of land and pots of money. Through business dealings that would make the bones of his illustrious ancestor rattle, Lord Robert of Huntington increased this booty exponentially. He appears to be a hard, unscrupulous man with a mean, abusive streak. The earl subjected Anna, her mother and younger brother William to a constant barrage of psychological abuse.

When Anna was just fifteen, her mother suffered a massive stroke. It left her paralysed and mute. They were desperately close. Anna watched as her mother wasted away, unable to communicate, in a home run by indifferent nurses with stiff, British upper lips.

Without the influence of his gentle mother, William developed into a cowardly version of their father. Anna found herself completely alone in the family.

On her mother's death, Anna was shipped off to a boarding school in the country. She was grieving and morose and so couldn't fit in with her peers. Eventually, she befriended the school groundsman, Arthur. He was 68 at the time. She used to join him in the afternoons at his small, neat house on the school estate where they'd drink tea and chat. Arthur's only surviving relative was his grandson, Richard, who was working on a farm nearby, trying to save money for his university education.

Richard came home one weekend about halfway through the year. Anna was having tea with Arthur when he arrived. Their chemistry was instant and the young man came home more often after that day. A romance blossomed. Over the next two years, they became very close. Anna didn't tell her brother or father about Richard until she absolutely had to ... It was a classic love tragedy.

Just after her final A-Level exams, she fell pregnant. Soon enough her father found out and predictably went off his rocker. He tried to convince her to abort the baby but she refused. The devious old bastard then conspired to have the infant removed and put up for adoption at birth.

Meanwhile, Richard pledged his complete support for Anna and, although Arthur was bitterly disappointed by his grandson's irresponsibility, he too was loyal. Richard continued his work on the farm.

Three months before the baby was due, Richard and another farm hand were driving back to the sheds on a tractor after the day's work. Richard was sitting on the arch of the wheel, facing inwards. The tractor hit a bump and Richard, who was not holding on, overbalanced and fell sideways towards the front of the tractor. As he did so, his foot stuck under the driver's seat. He might have recovered but the other chap made to grab his friend and in so doing let go of the steering wheel. The tractor lurched left. If his foot hadn't been caught, Richard probably would have fallen clear. Instead, his body swung under the heavy machine. As his head hit the ground, the huge back wheel went straight over it. He was killed instantly.

Anna had to deal with the loss of her soulmate while experiencing a very difficult pregnancy at home with her cowardly brother and malevolent father. She was forbidden from attending Richard's funeral.

A few months later she gave birth to a little boy. It was an emergency caesarean.

They put him in her arms briefly and she drifted off into exhausted sleep. When she woke, the baby was gone. She never held him again. It devastated her and she swore never to speak to her father again.

As soon as she was strong enough, she packed a backpack and bought a ticket for Marrakesh. For the next ten years she travelled the world. She rode horses across the Sahara, camels across the Empty Quarter, backpacked through south-east Asia, caught the trans-Siberian express, crewed on a sailing yacht across the Pacific and bussed her way from Tierra del Fuego to Panama. Some time during her travels in the Amazon, she met a doctor who was researching traditional medicine in rural Brazil. She became his assistant and spent six months precisely recording various herbal remedies that the local people use. This is where her impressive apothecary skills, of which I have personal knowledge, developed. She worked when she needed cash and then moved on to the next place. Three years ago, while she was working in a hotel in Cape Town, she answered an advert for a camp manager position at Sasekile – where I met her nine months ago.

By the time she'd finished telling me this story, it was well after midnight and we had consumed another bottle of Luddite. I'm not sure how or when it occurred – I think somewhere between Riyadh and St Petersburg – but she leaned back and rested on my chest. For the remainder of the tale, that is how we remained. I had my back resting in the corner of the sofa and she reclined with her head and shoulders on my chest as we drank our wine and the story unfolded.

The epic saga complete, we headed back to the staff village, arm in arm. When we reached her house (the site of my concussion some months back), she turned to me.

'Angus, thanks for listening to me. I haven't talked all the way through my life like that before ... I found it really cathartic.' I was a bit pissed so I didn't say anything to her. I just looked at the black dress hugging her figure in the August breeze. She leaned forward to kiss my cheek goodnight. Acting entirely on instinct and booze, I put my right hand gently round the back of her neck. I locked on her dark eyes and our lips touched softly once, then again, a bit harder. Ten minutes later we released each other, smiled wordlessly, and I left.

Wow ...

Other than that, the weather is warming up again. The air is hazy with smoke from fires set by local people burning their grazing lands outside the reserve in anticipation of the coming rains. Fire takes off all the dead winter grass and makes the ground sprout green at the first sign of moisture. The dust and smoke make for spectacular sunsets over the mountains.

Out on game drive, I always make sure that we stop for drinks where I can see the sun go down over the mountains. Elvis and I give the guests their drinks and then withdraw from the group, he with a Coke and me with an Appletiser, to watch the end of the day. Sometimes we say nothing; we just listen to the last calls of the white-browed scrub robin or the first hoots of the white-faced owl – 'do-koo-do-koo-dooooo'.

As the first stars emerge, we sometimes chat about the wonders of the universe. Explaining astrophysics to someone with no English and only basic primary schooling is not easy but we make a valiant attempt to understand each other.

Glad to hear that you managed to patch Dad's briefcase, although I imagine Trubshaw is still *persona non grata* (like my legal term?).

Angus

JAMES HENDRY

From: 'Julia MacNaughton'
Sent: 22 August, 13h45
To: 'Brother A'
Subject: Bush romance - wonders never cease!

Angus, you old romantic – don't worry, I won't tell anyone!

I think it is so marvellous that you have had a genuine romantic interaction with another human being. I have to say, I did think it was coming, given how you have written about Anna through the course of the year. A partner older than you is probably exactly what you need – someone with a mature and less complicated take on the world.

I had to tell Mum and Dad, of course. Dad, as usual, didn't look up from his newspaper but I did see the corners of his mouth turn up and he gave one of those approving grunts. Mum, of course, wanted to know all the details and got quite panicked until I let her read bits of your email.

I look forward to meeting her one day – she must be quite a woman to put up with you! (Jokes.)

Lots of love,

Jules

A YEAR IN THE WILD

From: 'Hugh MacNaughton'
Sent: 28 August 18h00
To: 'Jules'
Subject: Bush fire

Hey Jules,

It's all been happening this week!

When I started here as an assistant Camp Manager, not once did I think that my duties would include fighting fires. But as with so many things out here, expectation and reality rarely coincide.

A few days back, I was up in the village enjoying a late afternoon beer with the other Camp Managers. The camp was quiet with all the Guests out on drive. For Camp Managers, this is the 1 part of the day when we can switch off a bit: have a sleep, join our Guests on game drive, catch up on emails or have drinks in the village. On this particular afternoon, all of the Camp Managers were there (Anna, Melissa, Jenny, September, etc.). Simone was sitting next to me and the stories were flying as they always do after a long day in camp. Conversation is almost always dominated by 3 topics: Guest interaction, Lodge skinder or plans for the next leave.

Jenny was in the middle of telling us how she had accidently locked 1 of her Guests in their room, when everyone's radios exploded to life with Candice's voice.

"Fire, fire, fire!" she screamed. The radio was quickly blocked with people trying to find out where the fire was. We all ran down to the reception office and found Candice prancing about like a recently beheaded chicken, arms flailing and mouth squawking in an incoherent panic. She kept pointing to the radio but it was impossible to decipher what she was saying.

Eventually, I recognised Angus's voice from the mayhem. I grabbed the receiver and told him to go ahead. He explained that there was a fire in the northern part of the property and that they had been trying to get through to the Lodge for ages.

I turned to Candice.

"Christ, Candice," I said. "They've been calling for ages. What have you been doing?"

She just stared back at all of us, her bottom jaw quivering.

"I needed something from my room," she mumbled.

Angus's voice came through on the radio again.

"Contact our neighbours all over the reserve and tell them to get out here and help us with the fire. Also, get hold of our idiot northern friends from Elephant Lodge and find out if they know about the fire. Come back to me on channel 2."

Jacob speaks very little English so Angus was relaying his instructions through the radio.

I did as I had been asked. I established that the lodge next door had been burning a fire break earlier that day. Clearly they hadn't extinguished it properly and when the wind got up, an ember must have set our northern section alight.

By this stage channel 2 was being used exclusively for the fire fight and an instruction had gone out that no Rangers on game drive were to use it. Unfortunately for Angus, he had accidentally activated the roaming function on his radio. This meant that he picked up on all 4 channels (the Lodge, game drive, channel 2 and the neighbouring lodge's channel). As he was unaware of his error, he assumed that everybody was blatantly ignoring his request to keep channel 2 clear. Eventually, he exploded down the radio at 1 of the neighbour's Rangers.

"I have clearly said that channel 2 has been blocked for game drive use because we are fighting a fire. What part of fighting a fucking fire don't you understand?" his angry voice bellowed down the radio.

"That guy was talking on channel 4, Angus," said Jamie, who was still out on drive. He too was using the scan function on his radio so he knew what was going on. "Turn off the scan function and you won't hear anyone else except the people on channel 2," he followed.

There was a pause...

"Copy that, thanks," said Angus.

I stayed at my post for a while, listening to the goings on and more particularly to Angus. He actually did quite well, even though he was relaying commands from Jacob. Just as I thought they had things under control, Angus came back onto the radio. He told me that they needed as many people as possible to help with the fire. I dashed out of the office and ran straight into Simone, who was on her way to see how I was doing.

"You feel like fighting a fire?" I asked.

"Sure!" she replied.

It took me a while, but I managed to gather about 30 staff outside the office. At this point the Rangers, who had cut their game drives short in order to help with saving the Lodge, arrived. We piled into their Land Rovers and headed for the red glow in the not-too-distant north.

The scene that greeted us was not for the faint-hearted. Flames and smoke were about all we could see. Eventually, we found Jacob and Angus, who were both yelling commands at an assortment of vehicles and people from a number of the surrounding lodges. A small group pitched up in a vehicle which looked like a cross between a buffalo and an old police casspir, while another lodge's Rangers arrived with fire-fighting backpacks containing something called "fire sludge". I had to chuckle when Angus asked 1 of them if he was serving hot chocolate.

About 2 hours after my arrival and about 4 hours after the beginning of the episode, the fire had been reduced to a large smouldering expanse of bushveld. After exchanging thanks, everyone headed back to their respective camps, except for Jacob's crew, who rotated watch all through the night.

Angus caught a ride back with Simone and me and things were astonishingly jovial. He even stifled a laugh when I brought up his confusion about channel 2.

I am looking forward to seeing you in a couple of days, Jules, and introducing you to Simone.

Lots of love,

Your fire-beating brother,

Hugh

From: 'Angus MacNaughton'
Sent: 28 August, 18h45
To: 'Julia MacNaughton'
Subject: Emergency procedures

Dear Julia,

The bush here in August makes a tinder-box look like a wet sponge. For 25 years, Sasekile has operated in an area that, at this time of year, ignites at the slightest provocation. Because of this, you'd be forgiven for assuming that this 'five-star' establishment would have sophisticated protocols in place to deal with potentially catastrophic bush fires. It would be logical to suppose that as soon as smoke was smelled or seen, staff would scramble for predetermined posts with the efficiency of a fighter squadron.

Not so at beloved Sasekile.

I was not driving on the afternoon in question and all the other rangers were out on drive. At about 16:30, I was in the rangers' room identifying a tree sample and Jeff was at the computer stalking women on Facebook, dribbling slightly. The radio crackled to life on Anton's desk. This radio is supposed to be on the head ranger's person at all times in case of emergency. Anton had left it behind before going to have his four-hour midday sleep. The voice on the radio belonged to Timot, one of the conservation crew. He was calling frantically for Jacob (head of conservation) or Anton (head of not-very-much).

Jacob answered and they had an animated conversation in Shangane. The gist of it: there was a huge fire just to the north and it was heading towards the lodge. Jacob now called for Anton, who obviously didn't answer. Jeff went for the radio but I kicked his chair out from under him before he could reach it and confuse matters more. I explained to Jacob that Anton was nowhere to be seen and then asked what I could do.

The calls from Timot were becoming more strident.

As I came out of the office, Bertie came rushing by, heading for the workshop. I grabbed Jeff and followed. A few moments later Jeff, the conservation crew and I departed. There were two tractors with water bowsers and two Land

Rovers, one of which carried a large water tank. The other was filled with conservation crew who were in various states of undress – they had all been hauled away from showers and cooking by Jacob. Each of them was armed with a fire beater – a thick broomstick with a heavy piece of rubber attached to it.

Jacob told me to sit next to him. On the way out to the fire, he explained that he would coordinate the fire fight but that I would have to relay his instructions on the radio because of his scanty English.

The first thing Jacob told me to do as we hared out into the bush was radio the office. Apparently the person in the office is supposed to phone all lodges in the area and alert all of Sasekile's management. Candice, of course, was more useless than a brick. It took me ten minutes to get hold of her. Instead of following a well-ingrained protocol when I told her there was a bush fire, she panicked.

'Oh, maa Gaaaaard!' she squealed down the radio. 'Fire, fire, fire, help, there's a fire, HEEELP!'

In order for you to understand the next bit I must explain a bit about the radios. There are four channels. No. 1 is for game drive only, No. 2 is for everything else, No. 3 is for use if you have something lengthy to say and don't want to block traffic on 1 or 2, and No. 4 is the neighbouring reserve's game drive channel. All the camp mangers, Anton, PJ, Arno, the head chef – all management staff and the office live on channel 2. Thus, if some blithering fool yells 'fire fire fire' down the mouthpiece and fails to say *where* the fire is, about 25 people start haring around in blind terror looking for smoke.

Candice's outburst completely blocked up the channel. Everyone in the lodge tried to radio the office to find out where the fire was. Eventually, there was just a loud squelching noise.

Ten minutes later we arrived at the point where Timot was watching the blaze. The conservation team immediately set about fighting it. Four women and six men wielded their beaters at the flames while Bertie, Timot and two others drove the tractors along the fire line, spraying water onto the flames. They were highly effective but the front was too long to contain – we needed more people.

I sat next to Jacob in the Land Rover as he drove up and down the fire line bellowing instructions. Every so often, we'd jump out of the car, beat some of the flames out and then carry on.

Eventually the squelching noise on channel 2 ceased. I quickly leapt onto the radio. For some reason, SB had displaced Candice in the office. I can safely say this is the only time in my life I've been happy to hear his voice. I explained the situation to him and he began relaying messages to the camp management. Again, there was no following of a predetermined plan.

The fire was moving from north to south down a wide front of about two kilometres. It was being fanned by a strong northerly and, although some way from the lodge, if left alone, it would reach the Tsessebe River (by this stage dry but for a few pools), catch the dry winter reeds and leap into the lodge in a few seconds.

'We need more people!' Jacob said to me urgently.

Normally, when a fire is spotted, the person in the office is supposed to alert the other lodges on the reserve. There's a gentlemen's agreement that when a fire occurs on someone else's property, you gather your fire-fighting team and head over to help. Because Candice has the temperament of a colobus monkey, no such call went out. Eventually, our neighbours saw the smoke and, at about 18:00, radioed in.

'Any station on Sasekile come in,' came the worried call. Jacob and I had just climbed out of the vehicle to sack a particularly virulent tongue of fire.

'Go ahead!' I yelled, holding the radio in one hand while frantically beating at the flames using a guarri branch with the other. The heat was searing.

'Confirm you're aware of a runaway fire on Sasekile?' said the twit on the other end.

'No, we had no idea it was a runaway fire, we're all just out here cooking marshmallows on what we thought was the world's most enthusiastic braai,' I bellowed down the radio as the hair on my beating arm singed. 'Of course we know there's a bloody fire. Where are you guys?'

There was no answer for a second.

'No one informed us of the emergency. We'll send a team at once.'

'Angus, come in!' It was Bertie's panicked voice.

'Go!'

'Our pump is finished petrol – bring more!'

Jacob and I were carrying the spare fuel for the bowser pumps. We leapt back in the car and drove for the east end of the inferno. All the way along, the conservation team was valiantly attacking the flames. Off to the west, the sun was setting bright red through the smoke. We were winning the battle where we had people but the fire front was simply too long. Jacob told me to get every able-bodied person at the lodge out to help. I relayed the message. SB was still manning the office.

As the sun set, the neighbours started arriving. I directed the first of them to the western end of the fire line and they sped off. Next came a fire-fighting vehicle that looked powerful enough to douse the sulphurous fires of hell. It had a huge water cannon on the front and a massive tank at the back. Guthro, the vast and enthusiastic driver, stuck his head out of the cockpit.

'Ja, howzit, guys!' he said. 'Big fire! Where shall me and The Buffel begin?' I thought we were saved. Jacob pointed at the middle of the fire line. Guthro sunk back into his seat. The Buffel's mighty engine roared, its great wheels spun and it sped off. Ten metres later there was a loud backfire and the Buffel ceased its forward momentum. It began belching acrid smoke. Guthro and his assistant climbed out yelling 'fok' loudly.

Jacob and I left.

The fire was now an arc – the sides being pushed back but the middle section was still steaming towards the river. It only had 50 metres to go when, finally, the lodge staff arrived. The rangers and trackers had dropped their guests off and picked up the camp managers and anyone else they could find.

With the flanks under control, we concentrated efforts on the middle section. Jacob and I left our car and joined the fray. It was a tremendous fight. Anna, Jenny, Melitha, Elvis, One-eyed Joe, SB and any number of others set to the task. Even PJ was there beating the flames. (Hilda was notably absent but she is not really able-bodied for anything but pie eating.)

By this stage it was dark and I could see the red glow of the fire line stretching from east to west.

Two hours later, blackened, singed and exhausted, we stopped the last flames in the forward arc. There were still various small areas burning to the east and west but the battle was won. Jacob patted me on the back – high praise indeed.

I walked back east along the line to check on the state of things. Halfway along, I found Guthro sitting on a rock looking distraught. At first I thought he must be injured.

'What's up, Guthro?' I asked.

'My Buffel, my byootiful Buffel.' The huge man seemed close to tears. 'I couldn't make her start and now she is burned in that fire.' He pointed out onto the blackened earth. There, in the light of the rising moon, I saw the burnt-out shell of The Buffel. I started to laugh and I laughed until I found Bertie, and then we laughed together.

On the way back to the lodge, I sat in the back seat of a Land Rover with Anna. It was freezing after the heat of the fire. SB was driving. He and the other five people in the car were all pumped full of adrenalin and they chattered excitedly all the way back, reliving the fight. Anna and I sat close and quiet. I slipped my hand into hers and squeezed it. She smiled and then kissed me, just under my ear. She smelled so perfect. She laughed softly.

What a day.

Angus

From: 'Hugh MacNaughton'
Sent: 04 September 15h00
To: 'Jules'
Subject: Meet the Robertsons

Hey Jules,

This is a quick note from the lounge of Simone's parents' place in the Waterberg. The area is really stunning and the little camp they have is beautifully decorated. Mrs Robertson is a warm and sweet person who welcomed me just as generously as you, Mum and Dad welcomed Simone. Meeting her father, however, was like meeting a cranky version of Trubshaw. He is ex-Special Forces and treated me like an invading enemy.

The worst thing I was subjected to was a "man's" walk on my second morning here. I woke some time before first light (in a room on my own, of course) to find Mr Robertson staring at me. He tossed an apple at me and said, "Come on, sonny, time for a little walk, just the men."

We returned to the camp 8 hours later in time for lunch! It was the closest I've ever come to dehydration. We took no water and Mr Robertson told me to suck on a stone when I plucked up the courage to ask him if he had brought any sustenance.

I think this might turn into the most life-threatening holiday of my life.

Lots of love,

Hugh

From: 'Angus MacNaughton'
Sent: 05 September, 19h30
To: 'Julia MacNaughton'
Subject: Talisker at dusk

Dear Julia,

This week I went to visit Elvis's home outside the reserve. He lives in a village called Boxa Huku (pronounced *Borsha Hookoo*). This means 'Stab the Chicken'.

I'm not joking. My illustrious tracker friend lives in a place called Stab the Chicken. He too started giggling when I nearly fell out of the car laughing.

Boxa Huku is a dusty village about ten kilometres from the reserve gate. There are a number of other similar villages dotted around the Bushbuck Ridge region of the Lowveld. Most of the houses are made of homemade cement and sand bricks and average between one and three rooms. The roofs are generally corrugated iron and there is very little shade. This means that, for at least six months of the year, most dwellings are hot enough to smelt ore in. Every house is in a permanent phase of construction. I don't think there was one stand where there wasn't a pile of bricks, a mound of sand or the shell of an unfinished room.

One common feature of each homestead is the outhouse. The government, with its eternal failure to provide basic services, has not brought water to the people of Gazankulu during two decades or so that it's been dicking around in power. The latrine is a deep hole around which a ramshackle shelter, made of leftover building materials, is erected.

Paint is not a priority in these villages. About one in ten houses had a coat of paint. The rest were a dull cement grey which made the place slightly depressing in the midday sun.

There are many things about the Shangane people I admire but they have some strange fetishes. The most bizarre of these is probably their fanatical need to sweep the dirt. Every morning, a Shangane woman will emerge from her home armed with a bunch of twigs tied together with twine. She will then sweep the vegetation-free soil in front of her house for half an hour or so, creating an extraordinary cloud of dust which then settles on her furniture, windows and children. The lack of water and the obsession with sweeping means that not even the hardiest pioneer grass has the remotest chance in hell of growing around the houses. There are, however, enormous marula trees in abundance.

Elvis lives in a modest four-room domicile with his wife, two kids and both parents. There is a kitchen, sitting room and two bedrooms. The obligatory outhouse is, in this case, made of corrugated iron, branches and wire. The gasses in there on a mid-January day must be caustic enough to dissolve Teflon. There is also a small wattle-and-daub traditional hut where his folks choose to reside.

Elvis's father looks like something out of a story book. When we arrived he was sitting on a stump in the shade outside the hut. He was leaning on a stick, staring into the distance, stroking his white beard. He is completely blind and spends most of his days on this stump, staring at nothing much. Elvis says he is thinking about becoming an ancestor which basically means he is waiting to die. When we were introduced, Matimba Sithole harangued me in Shangane so deep that I caught only one in every ten words. Elvis eventually dragged me away, while the old boy carried on his monologue.

The family provided me with lunch. This consisted of pap, tomato and onion sauce, traditional spinach and chicken. I found the chicken difficult to eat because I had met it in the yard half an hour before we ate. While Elvis and I sat drinking Fanta Grape on his doorstep, the bird and its four clucking friends were pecking about in the dust. His wife emerged from the house, caught the wretched fowl and sawed its head off with a blunt bread knife. It was a great sacrifice for them to murder it in my honour but I can still taste its gamey flesh.

Around the lunch table, we chatted about the Boxa Huku community and the various problems they experience. Can you believe that people, children mainly, still die of malaria out here? It is unforgivable that in South Africa – the largest economy on the continent – people still regularly die of a curable disease.

I returned to the lodge in the late afternoon and went in search of Anna.

We drove out to a stunning little glade on the river with a bottle of Talisker ten-year-old. There we sat on a blanket and talked while the day faded into night. The sky changed colour a hundred times as the diurnal birds quietened. For a moment, the only sound was the trickle of the Tsessebe River. Then the fiery-necked nightjars began to call and a scops owl started its 'prrrrrp' in a sycamore fig tree next to us. We lay there for hours, sipping the fine malt and watching the stars pop into the sky. Anna rested her head on my stomach and told me star legends she'd learned from the Aborigines.

Anna is an incredible woman.

Angus

From: 'Hugh MacNaughton'
Sent: 11 September, 17h59
To: 'Jules'
Subject: Relations improve

Hey Jules,

Another quick one from the Waterberg.

Simone and I are heading back to Sasekile tomorrow and I'm happy to report that things have improved a lot since the walk with Mr Robertson. My survival seemed to give me some credit with the guy and he has been much friendlier since then.

We've actually had the most amazing holiday after my initial scare. The animals are very different to those we see in the Lowveld – particularly the antelope species. I saw eland (which are the biggest of all the antelope species), hartebeest and loads of springbok.

I learned to ride a motorbike and a horse (not sure which I prefer) and Simone's elder brothers took me fly fishing in the river which runs along the outskirts of the farm. I drank tea with her mum, had a few beers with her dad and brothers in the evenings and played some of the most competitive games of Scrabble in history with all of them. They are a really nice family and seem to have accepted me as 1 of their own. Simone seemed proud to introduce me to all of them. Funnily, however, the "I love yous" dried up a bit when her father was in the room.

Obviously, the holiday was completely celibate. I'm quite looking forward to getting back to work so that Simone and I can resume our exploration of the Kamasutra.

Because we spent an extra day here, we're going to have to drive straight back to Sasekile tomorrow. I'll see you on my next leave.

Lots of love,

Hugh

From: 'Angus MacNaughton'
Sent: 11 September, 18h28
To: 'Julia MacNaughton'
Subject: 11:00 nature trail

Dear Julia,

One of the activities that this lodge and most others offer is the eleven o'clock nature trail. This jaunt, of dubious entertainment value, is right up there with the torture of sitting with my guests at dinner (although nothing is that challenging). Once a week or so, I have to conduct the walk, the purpose of which, we are told, is to show guests the 'little things' like birds (active at dusk and dawn), tracks (obliterated by mid-morning), trees (they are present at all times of the day) and insects (all guests *hate* insects).

As you know, I enjoy exercise a lot. I also enjoy walking in the bush in the cool morning when the day is new, the tracks are fresh and the birds are calling. At 11:00, any sensible animal is dozing in the shade, as is any guest with a modicum of sanity. There are always, however, the few who feel the need to 'do something'. They refuse to give in to the fatigue induced by a 05:00 wake-up, a four-hour game drive and a breakfast large enough for the Seventh Army.

The 11:00 walker comes in one of four general guises.

- **Guise 1:** The Empire Builder. This is a Brit, red-faced and horribly out of shape. He has a pair of ancient binoculars and a stuffed panama hat. By the time he arrives for the walk, he has consumed his first G&T and eaten two full-house breakfasts. Despite his corpulence, this is a human of remarkable toughness and he can withstand sweltering heat and no water. Men of this ilk conquered the tropical world in the nineteenth century.

- **Guise 2:** The German Health Fanatic. While his wife is reserving pool loungers, this Aryan is heading into ze jungle. He is dressed impeccably in the latest sweat-absorbent khaki bush gear. He gyms at least eight times a week and does not eat any trans-fatty acids or refined carbohydrates. He carries a bottle of mineral water at all times.

- **Guise 3:** The Timid Naturalist. This is a person of varying nationality and indeterminate sex. It is a gentle sort with thick round glasses, a bag of field guides, a notebook, and a waistcoat with endless pockets for collecting samples. This person is shy and initially inoffensive but by the time it has stopped to identify its 80th grass species, I want to kill it.

- **Guise 4:** The Walking Dale Carnegie American/South African. This creature is forcibly friendly in his quest to make everyone think that he lives life to the full. He arrives in bright clothing with brand-new sneakers, and shakes everyone's hand vigorously while looking into their eyes and saying his name. God, I can't stand this one.

My last walk was quite exciting, however. Three days ago it was my turn. I dragged myself to the front of Main Camp where four idiotic guests were waiting to be entertained for the next hour. I shook their hands with a forced smile, gave them a brief safety talk and we headed out into the midday lull. One of them (Guise 4) thought it was an exercise walk and sighed audibly every time another (Guise 3) stopped us to ask about a tree. About 45 minutes later, we had moved just 200 metres and I had explained 900 plants, 100 birds and innumerable scuff marks on the path. The mood of the walk was hypnotic.

At plant number 901, I thought Guise 4 was going to crack. It was a huge red spike-thorn tree on the banks of a thin, shady drainage line. I was about to explain the bush to Guise 3 when the biggest buffalo in the Lowveld stood up behind the bush and belched. Guise 4 reacted first.

'Oh, my Gaad, man, there's a fucken bison!' he shouted.

'Sshhh,' I hissed. 'All of you back up slowly – don't run!'

The buffalo did not take kindly to being mistaken for his New World cousin. He snorted and took two steps forward.

'Fucken A dude, that bison's crazy, ya better shoot it!'

'It's not a bison, and I'm not going to shoot it. Now, back out slowly!'

The old bull relaxed gradually as we retreated. I lowered my rifle and we made our way back to camp unharmed. Mercifully, Guise 3 was too terrified to ask any more questions. Alas, very few of these interminable 11:00 walks are as much fun.

Things between Anna and I are extremely fun, however.

Our bond is firming at quite a speed. I'm not sure how to define what there is between us but we increasingly cannot be apart to the point where we now seek each other out whenever we aren't busy.

I can't believe I'm sharing this much detail with you, Jules, but the connection is quite unlike anything I've experienced and there is an electric buzz when we are in the same place. There is none of the irritating game-playing that mandatorily goes on when two people hook up. There is only an insatiable hunger for one another.

This is all becoming increasingly obvious to the rest of the staff but because they are in awe of Anna, and wary of me, no one says anything.

This week saw the coming of spring. On the first warm night of the year Anna came to my room. I had just finished a deathly dinner with an American family. She was dressed in a cream linen dress and carried a lantern. Her thick, dark hair was loose; a piece of it fell across her eye. She looked otherworldly.

She lifted her eyes to mine, smiled and turned.

I threw on a shirt and followed. Just outside the staff village, she'd parked a Land Rover. In it was a mattress, a duvet and a few lanterns. We drove in silence to a platform set in a huge mahogany tree overlooking the river. I carried the mattress up into the tree while she lit the lanterns and placed them all round. There, surrounded by the subtle sweet smells and sounds of the first night of spring, we became as close as two people can be.

Angus

From: 'Hugh MacNaughton'
Sent: 12 September, 18h05
To: 'Jules'
Subject: Angus on a DW!

Hey Jules,

Our brother's relationship with Anna seems to be progressing at an incredible pace! I arrived back at Sasekile to find them gone away on a dirty weekend. Miraculously, he actually found someone to take to Quintessential House after all.

I knew there was something going on but had no idea it was anything serious. I wonder how on Earth she tolerates his surly manner . . .

I'll send you a proper email in a few days when I'm back in the swing of things.

I just had to tell you this.

I'm amazed!

Love,

Hugh

From: 'Angus MacNaughton'
Sent: 13 September, 17h59
To: 'Julia MacNaughton'
Subject: Alpine bliss

Dear Julia,

I am writing this short message to you from Quintessential House where I'm spending two nights with Anna. I was supposed to be driving out of Rhino Camp but the guests cancelled, which freed us both up for two nights. I thought about telling SB to make good on the deal I'd made with him before we were nearly fired but I figured the chances of success were slim, given the ultimate result of our bargain.

Anna asked PJ if we could go and he sorted the whole thing out, which was good of him. No doubt a favour to Anna, not me.

Anyway, this is the second of our two nights and it has been just spectacular here. We sat up till very late last night, drinking whisky (me) and wine (her) by the fire in our room. This morning was freezing and misty so we just lay in bed for hours until it cleared. Then we went for a spectacular walk in the mountains before a late lunch which was followed by a snooze.

Anna is in the shower as I write this and we are about to go and have a drink before dinner. The bar is in a very old stone cottage, has a huge roaring fire and is wood-panelled.

I think you'll really like Anna. Mum might even approve.

Right, well, I'm off to polish my shoes for dinner.

Angus

From: 'Hugh MacNaughton'
Sent: 18 September, 18h15
To: 'Jules'
Subject: Responsibility and redemption

Dear Jules,

Life at the Lodge has begun again for me at its normal hectic pace. After catching up with PJ over a beer in the village, he informed me that there would be an enormous group arriving at the end of the year. The group is called the Young Millionaires' Society (YMS) and comprises a few thousand members from various corners of the globe. The members have to be under 50 years of age and their businesses need to turn over a minimum of 80 million rand a year in order to qualify. The society was established many years ago for the purposes of networking and linking up like-minded business brains. PJ told me that a YMS group often books out the entire Lodge (not just a single camp) at the end of each year. They bring their spouses and kids. He explained that the booking brings in a huge amount of money for the Lodge, that the group is immensely demanding and that it is extremely hard work hosting them.

"They are staying for 7 nights this year," PJ told me.

"Wow," I replied. "What are the dates?"

"Right over Christmas," said PJ with a grimace. He lifted his beer. "Here's to hoping this group will go better than your last 1, hey Hugh?" he said, laughing.

Not surprisingly, Angus was in trouble again this week, but fortunately PJ didn't find out about this 1. He and Jonesy got into a fist fight on the touch field due to Angus's outrageous temper. Jonesy was defending on the team against Angus when the incident occurred. Angus got through a gap and Jonesy gave chase from the other side of the field. About 10 metres before the try line, Jonesy dived in a final attempt to touch Angus and prevent a certain try. Entirely by accident, Jonesy's fingertips nicked Angus's foot, causing him to trip, lose the ball and land in the dirt. The following sequence of events occurred:

Angus went a shade of purple.

Jonesy remained calm.

Angus went completely overboard and swore brutally at Jonesy.

Jonesy apologised, saying it was a mistake.

Angus picked up the ball and threw it at Jonesy's face.

The ball hit Jonesy on the nose.

Jonesy retaliated and stormed towards Angus.

Angus punched Jonesy in the chest and winded him.

Jonesy recovered and managed to put Angus in a head lock.

They both ended up on the ground.

I got involved and split them up with the help of a few other Rangers.

Jonesy and Angus left the field in different directions.

The game ended.

I must say that it really is marvellous to be back. O'Reilly seems to have rallied a bit and the Chefs are actually talking to him now. He is far more talented than the last guy so I hope he stays. His menu is now a lot simpler, with a focus on local and fresh ingredients, as opposed to the latest European delicacies. His cold gazpacho soup, made from locally grown tomatoes and basil planted in his garden, is absolutely incredible!

Lots of love,

Your brawl-intervening brother,

Hugh

From: 'Angus MacNaughton'
Sent: 18 September 19h28
To: 'Julia MacNaughton'
Subject: The Legend

Dear Julia,

I develop an instant dislike for any living human given the label 'Legend'. These days, when someone is described as a legend, it does not mean he has changed the course of history against impossible odds through immense sacrifice and courage. No, the Earth-shattering individual given the moniker of 'Legend' these days is someone who can drink twelve beers in an hour, puke, drink another dozen and then bed a particularly stupid woman. The 'Legend' calls his friends 'bru' and he refers to waiters or barmen as 'chief'. Jonesy, one of the rangers, is a 'Legend'.

Just behind the Sasekile staff village there is an old soccer field. It slopes heavily from south to north and at this time of the year, the grass is sparser than the hair on Dad's head. The staff (girls and boys) play touch rugby on this goat track. The games are tremendously competitive, although most players have distressingly little skill. This does not daunt some.

A number of the rangers play like they are expecting to be called up to Super Rugby franchise in the near future. Anton, for example, harbours the fathomless delusion that he is blessed with cheetah-like speed and footwork. He never passes the ball and, without fail, tries to side-step whoever is defending him. Unless the defender is the gargantuan Hilda from finance, he is always touched. He then loses his temper and accuses the defender of being 'fokken offside'.

I make sure not to play on the same side as Anton or SB.

While I am not really built for the great game of rugby union, I am no mean exponent of the touch version. At the beginning of the week we played an epic game. Right at the end of the match, I received the ball in the fly-half position. I dummied a long pass to the left and stepped right. This wrong-footed Jamie, who was defending against me. I sped through the gap and made for the try line. From the corner of my eye, I saw Jonesy, 'the Legend', sprinting across the field in cover defence. He had the angle on me so I decided to step inside him. Alas, my ancient running shoes lost traction on the slippery gravel and I began to slide. I would have recovered my balance but for Jonesy. He made no attempt

JAMES HENDRY

to slow down as it became clear we were going to collide. He just kept coming. He is not a small 'Legend' so as his body rammed into mine and I fell onto the stony ground, Jonesy's momentum carried him onto my back. The result was that he ended up riding me like a boogie board as I slid, chest first, along the gravel.

I was not wearing a shirt.

When I stood up, my chest was covered in grit-filled cuts and grazes. Jonesy stood up, shrugged and then said a perfunctory sorry as he winked at Jamie as if to say, 'Got him good, didn't I?'

I lost my temper at this point and a brawl ensued. We were dragged apart before I could make him swallow a mouthful of gravel. At least I managed to cover his white shirt with the blood from my wounds. What a 'Legend'.

Anna spent much of lunchtime cleaning my wounds with disinfectant. She just laughed when I told her the story.

'Do the words "just a game" mean anything to you?' she asked, pulling a stone from a cut on my flank. I winced.

'Not where a "Legend" is concerned, no,' I replied.

By the way, it is a thing of beauty to watch Anna play. She wears a pair of knee-length khaki ski-pants which show the idyllic shape of her legs and a black T-shirt which hugs her figure just enough. She ties her hair up in her careless, sexy way. She is very quick and runs with long, graceful strides with a constant smile on her face. She finds it hilarious when the men start posturing at each other. I suppose she has seen far too much in her life to be concerned about a silly game of touch rugby at a game reserve.

I haven't spent a single night in my room this week. I hate it when I have to wake up early and leave Anna's sleeping form. If I'm not driving, she has to leave before me, which is equally unpleasant. We have made each other late just about every day this week. I can't wait till we can go on leave together and just lie in bed till we are ready to move.

Well, that's it for the week. Please send news of The Major and Trubshaw.

Cheers,

Angus

From: 'Julia MacNaughton'
Sent: 19 September, 19h28
To: 'Brother A'; 'Brother H'
Subject: Trubby and The Major

Hi guys,

A little message to tell you about the Sunday lunch last weekend. The whole family came around – Great Aunt Jill (the stalwart of Roedean elegance), Al, Andy, Uncle Ant, Mandy, Richard, Nicky, etc. Of course, The Major came too. Al also brought her new boyfriend Barry to meet the family.

Meeting the MacNaughton clan is not easy at the best of times but The Major and Trubshaw made this spectacularly difficult for poor Barry.

Dad forgot to lock Trubby in the laundry for the arrival and, predictably, he went ballistic. As everyone arrived, the slobbering hound emerged from behind a lavender hedge at the speed of a cruise missile. Nicky started screaming, Great Aunt Jill said the F-word and side-stepped with amazing agility for her 82 years, and The Major bellowed,

'That bloody dog!'

Wide-eyed Barry was first in the firing line and his courage failed him. He flew back into his black BMW and slammed the door. Unfortunately, before the electric window had reached halfway, the dog was through the gap and covering the dapperly dressed investment banker with saliva and mud.

Trubshaw emerged shortly after that and went to greet The Major. Our grandfather was leaning heavily on his stick which the over-excited mutt knocked out from under him. The octogenarian found himself on his back in the pansies and it was only after Trubshaw had licked his face all over that Dad, swearing like a Hell's Angel, managed to haul him off.

Mum then helped her father up and dried him off. She handed him his stick as Barry emerged from his car. The Major then lost his temper.

'Why didn't you stop that bloody dog?' he shouted at Barry. 'What the hell is the matter with you? I could have been killed!' He had Al's beau pinned against the car, the walking stick thrust at his throat.

It was hilarious.

Love to you both,

Jules xx

From: 'Angus MacNaughton'
Sent: 25 September, 19h47
To: 'Julia MacNaughton'
Subject: Cobra

Dear Julia,

Anna was bitten by a Mozambique spitting cobra this morning.

On return from a walk, I went to her room to see her. Just as I was about to knock, I heard her scream from inside. I wrenched the door open and saw her reeling back from the cupboard clutching her right wrist. A huge cobra came off the third shelf. It flopped onto the floor and made for the door where I was standing. It reared up and spat when it saw me but I managed to jump back and turn. The venom hit the back of my head and the snake sped past me and out into the bush.

I rushed back into the room to where Anna was breathing heavily on her bed. Her big eyes looked up at me in fright.

'Just relax and wait here,' I said with my hand on her cheek. 'I'll be back now.'

I ran out of the room to the office and told PJ what had happened. He sent me to the workshop to fetch a car.

When I got to the workshop, I found the lodge double-cab had no fuel in it. I yelled for the mechanic, a corpulent and bad-tempered fool called Jackson. Jackson did not take kindly to being yelled at and attempted to begin a lesson on Shangane etiquette. I grabbed him by the throat and told him to give me the keys to the petrol pump. He obliged and about five minutes later I was parked outside Anna's room.

When I arrived, Jenny was helping PJ to put a few of Anna's things in a bag. Anna's arm was swelling and her breathing was becoming laboured. I helped her gently into the car and flung the bag in the back. As I was about to climb into the driver's seat, PJ stopped me. He put a hand on my shoulder.

'Angus, you must stay calm. Drive with care. I'll phone ahead to the hospital.'

I drove like a man possessed. As much as I tried to heed PJ's advice, I was completely consumed by a throat-closing worry for Anna. I completed a trip that normally takes two hours in an hour and ten minutes.

When we arrived at the hospital, I almost drove into the emergency room. Unlike at the government hospital I visited with Nhlanhla, the doors opened and three medical staff came running out. They were expecting me and knew exactly what to do. Within seconds, Anna was on a gurney being wheeled into the hospital. I ran after them with her bag. They took her straight into a private ward where a doctor was waiting. They wouldn't let me in.

It was the worst feeling in the world.

Never have I experienced a slowing of time like I did during the half an hour they were examining her, taking her blood and hitching up a drip with a cocktail of powerful antivenom. It was truly excruciating. I was nauseous and light-headed with fear and worry. Eventually the doctor, an old and kindly Afrikaans man, came out of the ward.

'Are you her family?' he asked.

'No, she doesn't have a family she talks to,' I replied. 'I'm what she has at the moment.' He smiled at me warmly.

'This is serious,' he said. 'Normally with a cobra bite like this, the snake has spat at its victim first so the venom is much less. Unfortunately, the snake gave her a full bite. We have given her all the antivenom we can but, much like with bees, reactions to snake venom vary between people. This patient has reacted particularly badly to the venom but she should respond to the treatment.'

'What do you mean "should respond"?' I asked.

'Well, we just don't know with a bite like this.' He paused. 'I know this must be hard but we are doing all we can. You can go and see her now.'

I headed into the ward where the sister was fiddling with the drip. They had hooked Anna up to one of those heart monitors. It was beeping reassuringly in the corner of the room. Her arm had swelled all the way up to the shoulder. Her breathing was laboured but she managed a weak smile as I walked in. I sat next to her and held her clammy hand. She fell asleep soon after that. Throughout the afternoon, she would wake suddenly and struggle to breathe. Each time, a nurse would come in quickly to check if they needed to intubate her.

At 19:00 the night sister came in and replaced one of the bags on the drip. She told me that visiting hours were over.

It killed me to leave Anna lying like that. I felt such a sense of helplessness. At least she is in good hands.

I am writing this from an Internet café near the hospital and I'm staying at the Road Lodge round the corner. The room is about the same size as the bat cave but it's clean and close to the hospital.

Please tell Mum and Dad where I am.

Will keep you posted ...

Angus

P.S. In case you are wondering, the Mozambique spitting cobra delivers both cytotoxic and neurotoxic venom. This is why there was such bad swelling combined with breathing difficulty. It's the neurotoxic effects that are the most worrying because they could paralyse Anna's respiratory system.

From: 'Angus MacNaughton'
Sent: 26 September, 17h13
To: 'Julia MacNaughton'; 'Mum'; 'Dad'
Subject:

Dear Mum, Dad and Julia,

Anna died today at half past two in the afternoon.

It was a week before her 33rd birthday.

She died in the Hoedspruit Military Hospital.

She died while I was holding her hand although I don't know if she was conscious of it. At about 14:00 she looked up at me. I was sitting at her bedside, still holding onto the vain hope that the doctors were wrong – that her body would process the venom that was shutting down her organs. She, on the other hand, had no doubt that her time was up. She told me so.

Just before she slipped away, she looked up at me. The colour was gone from her smooth skin and her normally bright eyes were dull in her beautiful, perfectly formed face.

'Angus, I can't hold on much more,' she wheezed. 'I need you to know something.'

I tried to tell her to save her strength, that she could tell me later when she was better.

'I'm not going to get better, Angus.' She smiled lovingly up at me. 'I'm ready and I need you to listen to me now, for the last time.' I could taste blood as my teeth bit into the inside of my bottom lip.

'Okay,' I croaked.

'Angus, I didn't think that I would ever love another man. After Richard died, I told myself it would never happen – that it was simply not worth it.' She swallowed hard, her face contorting with the effort. 'I was wrong. The connection we had at the beginning of the year has grown so strong that I really can't think of being at the lodge without you.'

246

I opened my mouth to reply.

'Please, just listen,' she continued. 'I love you because you have a real strength and integrity, because I can see – you have let me see – that you have such a big heart.'

'Is that all?' I made a poor attempt at humour. She smiled weakly and shuddered.

'Angus, I'm the only one you've shown this to and I want you to promise me something.'

'I'll do my best,' I replied, as a tear escaped my eye.

'That's not going to be good enough. Promise me,' she said, frowning.

'I promise,' I replied.

'Angus, you have to let go of your anger or it will make you a bitter and lonely man. You need to make a conscious decision to stop being an arse because of what you perceive as the world's great injustices. You have to get over it. The world is not against you, it is the other way round. You're wasting yourself.'

Well, how the hell was I supposed to keep it together after that?

'Do you promise?' she said as the tears began to flow freely from both our eyes.

'I promise,' I whispered, leaning over to kiss her. I slipped my hand under her neck and lifted her gently into a sitting position. She wrapped her weak uninjured arm round me and I buried my face and tears in her long, thick, dark hair for the last time.

'I love you,' I said.

This is the first time I've ever said these words.

'I love you, too,' she whispered.

'I miss you, Anna,' I said, my voice cracking.

'I know you do, but I'm happy.'

I let her down gently onto the bed and we looked into each other's eyes for a final time. She smiled and then gently slipped away, her hand going limp in mine as the coma took her. The tears streamed down my face uncontrollably.

Suddenly, the ward filled with nurses and a doctor frantically running round to check various things, but Anna was gone. I stared at her lovely face until a nurse covered it with a sheet. I wanted to tell them all to fuck off and leave Anna be, but I was too dazed with shock and grief.

Eventually PJ's wife, Amy, who had been waiting outside the whole morning, came into the room. She put her arm round me and gently told me we had to go.

Today is the worst day of my life.

I don't know what to do with the little wooden giraffe I had bought for Anna's birthday.

Anna loved giraffes.

Angus

From: 'Hugh MacNaughton'
Sent: 26 September, 17h40
To: 'Jules'; 'Mum'; 'Dad'
Subject: Tragedy

Hi Dad, Mum and Jules,

I'm not sure if Angus has told you yet, but the most awful thing has happened.

Anna was rushed to hospital yesterday and died this afternoon from the effects of a huge spitting cobra bite. Everybody is in shock.

Angus got back around tea time, having been with her at the hospital until she died. He is a mess. He arrived back at the lodge looking withered and lifeless, his complexion void of any colour. His eyes were red and his cheeks caked in salt from what must have been an endless stream of tears. When he got out of the car he looked at me wide eyed, but was not able to articulate much. All he could muster was,

"I can't believe she's gone, Hugh, I can't believe she's gone."

I hadn't a clue what to say at first.

"But why couldn't they help her, Angus? Surely, there must have been something …" I started.

"It doesn't matter," he interrupted. "It's over, isn't it?" He sniffed and walked past me towards his room.

I watched him walk slowly all the way down to his front door.

"Fuuuuuuuuuck!" he screamed as he punched the middle of his wooden door hard 3 times. The full gravity of what had happened had hit him again. But he was so drained that soon his enraged strikes turned to pitiful thumps and his tears welled up again into sobs of despair. All I wanted to do was try to console him, but I knew that he wanted to be alone so I let him be.

I haven't seen him since.

We are all so sad.

Love,

Hugh

From: 'Dad'
Sent: 27 September, 09h00
To: 'Angus'
Subject:

My dear son,

I am so very sorry to hear about the death of your friend Anna. While there is no advice I can give you that will make any difference to the tremendous pain you must be feeling, I do want you to know that you are in our thoughts and prayers.

If you would permit, I would like to say a few things that may, in time, help you to cope with your loss.

I think it is important for you to embrace how you are feeling right now. The pain will eventually subside when you have processed the loss. Embracing how you feel right now will be cathartic and help you to deal with it. Go and find a quiet spot and cry your eyes out for as long as you like.

It is also very important that you love yourself through this. You are very bad at this generally. Please take some time to do things you love doing and spend some quality time on your own. This brings me to my last point.

From your letter, it would seem that Anna really understood you and gave you some wonderful advice. An experience like this can make a man tremendously bitter but I truly hope that you will do as you promised Anna and be more open to the world.

Your Mum and I are available to talk at any stage if you feel like it. We are thinking of you and love you very much.

Keep strong, my boy,

Dad

From: 'Hugh MacNaughton'
Sent: 02 October, 18h00
To: 'Jules'
Subject: Memorial

Hey Jules,

We had Anna's memorial service yesterday. It was held at her favourite spot, a little upstream of the Lodge, on the banks of the Tsessebe River. This part of the river narrows slightly to form a small set of rapids over a few exposed granite boulders. The rapids are overhung with shade cast by what must be at least a hundred-year-old schotia tree, and though the bank which supports its vast trunk is dry from the long winter, it is all still remarkably beautiful.

Having recovered fractionally from the initial shock of her death, Angus managed to make contact with Anna's surrogate father, an old man named Arthur. I am not entirely sure of the background to their relationship, but Angus insisted that he be informed and invited to the memorial service. In an immense show of generosity, PJ covered the cost of Arthur's airfare from England on behalf of the lodge while Angus handled the logistics.

The service was held at 16:30 during the quietest part of the day. The Guests staying in camp were all out on game drive which allowed the majority of the Lodge to attend. PJ ran proceedings, while Angus and Arthur stood together to 1 side, both clearly emotional as they held the little calabash containing Anna's ashes. The members of staff who form the Sasekile Ladies Choir were dressed traditionally and they too stood solemnly together. The rest of us stood to the other side of PJ and did our best to be strong.

PJ began by welcoming everybody and thanking Arthur for making such a long journey. Arthur reciprocated by raising 1 of his old hands and nodding.

PJ then expressed his deep regret over the circumstances, before extolling the virtues of Anna and her immense contribution to the Lodge. He ended by saying,

"She was arguably the most respected member of this community. Not only did she delight the hearts of many guests, but was a tower of strength to so many of us standing here, an inspiration to young, new staff and a source of guidance to even the most experienced. Unfortunately, she is irreplaceable here, not only for her talent, but also for her spirit. She will be deeply missed by us all."

Even PJ was a bit choky as he handed over to Arthur and Angus after that.

Both Arthur and Angus spoke with similar poignancy before navigating their way down to where the river meets the bank. Angus assisted the old man and they scrambled down to the water's edge. They stood for a moment together, before casting Anna's spirit and her ashes into the gentle breeze which carried them into a shimmering pool welling from the dry riverbed.

At that point members of the choir began to sing – their voices loud and moving. They started with some traditional songs in Shangane, but they added a beautiful English 1 as well. I can't remember all the words but the last verse went along the lines of:

Remember the people,

Remember the river,

Remember the bushveld,

While you are in heaven.

Can you imagine how Angus must have felt when they sang that in their beautiful voices? He just stood back, unblinking, his jaw clamped shut.

When the choir had finished, we moved back up to the road where we had parked the Land Rovers. Apart from the odd snivel and the sound of shuffling footsteps, there was quiet. It was as though the bushveld was paying its respects.

Angus is due to leave for home in the morning. This is probably best.

Love,

Hugh

From: 'Angus MacNaughton'
Sent: 02 October, 18h28
To: 'Julia MacNaughton'; 'Dad'; 'Mum'
Subject: Final rest

Dear Dad, Mum and Julia,

It was Anna's memorial yesterday.

After the initial shock of her death, I've felt numb. Thankfully, I have not been required to drive as the lodge has been quiet.

A few weeks back, I told you about the old boy who was like a father to Anna – Arthur. He was the only person from her old life who came out for the service. He is a wonderful old man. I picked him up from the airstrip two days back. There were a number of cheerfully ignorant guests who climbed out of the plane before Arthur. Eventually he tottered out of the plane, leaning heavily on a stick. He looked proud so I thought better of offering to help him down the stairs. I waited for him at the bottom.

He was dressed in an old, fraying tweed suit with a bright red tie. On his head sat an old weather-beaten deerstalker.

'You must be Angus,' he said, shaking my hand warmly, a life of tragedy behind his eyes.

'Arthur,' I said.

'I'm so sorry we are meeting under these circumstances. Anna mentioned you often in her letters. I wish she could have made the introductions.' He put his hand on my shoulder and I led him to the Land Rover.

'Me too,' I replied pathetically.

I drove him back to the lodge. PJ, who had made sure all of Arthur's expenses were paid, put him in a Tamboti Camp suite. It was a tremendously generous gesture and not lost on the old man.

In my room I had Anna's ashes. They arrived in an incredibly impersonal cardboard box. I felt sick thinking that the woman I had fallen so hopelessly in love with could have been reduced to a box of grey powder. I stared at it for ages, not knowing what to do. I asked Elvis what he thought. He was scandalised that anyone should not be buried whole – the idea of cremation was utterly appalling to him. Once he'd recovered from the shock of Western post-mortem etiquette, however, he provided me with an old calabash – it was perfect. I very carefully emptied the ashes into it.

The memorial was held in the glade next to the river where, only three weeks ago, Anna and I had lain, watching the sky change colour. All the staff except the rangers and trackers who were driving were there. PJ officiated. No priests for Anna – she'd have liked that. Then Arthur and I offered our eulogies.

PJ was brief but brilliant. He stood on the banks of the river and spoke without notes, his eyes staring into the setting spring sun. By the time he had finished, everyone had wet cheeks. Then Arthur spoke. In his gravelly old voice and in beautiful English, he told everyone about meeting Anna and all that she had meant to him and why.

Then it was my turn. My eulogy went as follows:

I did not know Anna for long but I wish I'd known her forever. Despite the incredible tragedies she faced in her life, she was inescapably positive. She filled my constantly half-empty glass until it overflowed. Until I met Anna, I believed that love was a construct of the human psyche – a biological trick our genes play on us to make us breed. I thought I was too clever to miss someone so much that I couldn't eat. I was convinced that anyone who felt weak at the knees because of someone else was being duped by their biology.

Yet Anna made me feel all these things and more.

To my consternation, I hated saying goodbye to her in the mornings. Perhaps something in my subconscious knew that I had to savour every last moment with this astonishing woman because, despite my best efforts, I was never going to be able to satiate my desire for her.

What was it about Anna that I, and perhaps all of us, found so attractive? Well, she was inescapably beautiful in a classical yet mysterious way, with her chocolate-brown hair, dark eyes and impish mouth. The ethereal way she moved on her long, perfect legs turned all heads. Her warm, deep laugh and her wicked sense of humour lit everything around her. The fierce way she argued so cleverly about her beliefs motivated us all.

I think above all these things, however, Anna was just Anna. She knew exactly who she was all the time. She felt no need to try to be anyone else. She was completely comfortable with herself and that made her completely accepting of everyone around her. For this reason, people just felt good around Anna. They never felt the need to try to be someone they were not. Anna refused to believe that anyone did anything out of spite or malice – for her there was always a reason that someone behaved in a certain way. She had an inescapable faith in the goodness of humanity – including me, believe it or not.'

There was a bit of a laugh. I paused and bit my lip.

Anna turned my world around. I started to see things in a positive light and then, just as I was getting comfortable, she threw the ultimate test at me. She left me, with no hope of ever seeing her again, with a final task – to see good in the world and enjoy it. I'm really not sure I'll ever be able to do that but she made me promise to try, and try I will.

Anna, I know that wherever you are, your smile is still filling the space around you with radiance and laughter.

I will miss you, always.

Then, while the choir sang, Arthur and I made our way down to the river to scatter the ashes in a little pool that wells up through the sand in the dry season.

I'm going on leave tomorrow but I've decided to drive straight to Kenton. I need some time alone to think about things.

Angus

P.S. As I made my way back towards the waiting Land Rovers, Elvis put his arm around me. 'Come, we walk home,' he said. So the two of us wandered slowly back to the lodge along the river bank. Elvis didn't say a word the whole way but it was great having his companionship in the aftermath of the miserable occasion.

From: 'Hugh MacNaughton'
Sent: 10 October, 18h15
To: 'Jules'
Subject: Big-time planning

Hey Jules,

We are now well into spring, but the atmosphere about the Lodge is still unmistakably dull following Anna's death. The usual laughter and social banter is not the same and smiles have been reserved for Guests only.

It is all still so sad.

How do you think Angus is doing? I haven't heard from him since he went to Kenton. I don't think I have ever seen him as upset as I did at the funeral. Thank goodness he is on leave and not at the Lodge. Please send him my regards. Jeez, I really feel for him.

But life must carry on, I suppose, and October is busy in the Lodge. So despite the difficult situation, the rest of the Camp Managers and I are trying to pick ourselves up and carry on with life. Being busy does make it easier, I must say.

PJ called the first meeting about the YMS group this week and Jenny and I have been put in charge. Because the group is so large, PJ has broken the 4 camps up into 2 sections – west and east. I am in charge of the east, comprising Tamboti and Kingfisher Camps, while Jenny is in charge of the west, which includes Main and Rhino Camps. As Melissa manages Kingfisher Camp, I will have the dubious pleasure of working with her again, while Jenny will be working with September and whoever replaces Anna in the future (apparently interviews start this week). For the moment, though, Candice from reception is covering Rhino Camp and PJ is down there a lot as well.

The YMS group will be arriving during the week leading up to Christmas, with Christmas Eve and Christmas night both celebrated at the Lodge. They leave for Mozambique on Boxing Day after 5 nights. They have requested bush breakfasts, bush dinners, special game drive drinks and that the entire group eats together on the last 2 nights. This is going to be challenging as there are 64 people in total and the camps do not usually join up for dinners.

Simone is going to have her hands full with all the kids (about 20 of them, apparently). O'Reilly will also need to be on top of his game with the incredible variety of dietary needs. When they started requesting specific animal sightings, though, PJ put his foot down, so the Rangers don't have quite the same pressure as the rest of us.

Although the group arrival is still about 2 months away, PJ has insisted that we have regular weekly meetings to monitor progress.

"I want us to plan for this thing like Christmas is at the end of November," he said. "Hugh and Jenny, good luck," he concluded with a wry smile and a wink at both of us.

I'm looking forward to it already – determined to redeem myself after the disaster in the middle of the year.

I haven't seen much of Simone this week. I think there is a holiday in the States at the moment as the Lodge is full of American families. Tamboti Camp doesn't normally accommodate anyone under 16 so I have been OK, but Simone and Jenny have been going flat out at the Main Camp. The little creatures have been tearing around for days now. One child managed to staple his sister's skirt to the seat of the game drive vehicle which provided the only amusement of the week.

Please don't forget to say hello to Angus if you speak to him.

Love,

Hugh

From: 'Angus MacNaughton'
Sent: 10 October, 05h32
To: 'Julia MacNaughton'
Subject: Trying to find peace

Dear Julia,

I'm writing this to you from our deck at Kenton, overlooking the beautiful Kariega River. It is dawn and the sun is about to peep up over the dunes on the eastern bank. I come down here every morning at around this time with my coffee and a rusk.

There is activity in the old farmhouse across from our place. The ancient farmer and his wife come and sit on their veranda to greet the day in the same way I do. I watch them through my binoculars – two people grown old together, completely comfortable in each other's presence. When they've finished their coffee, he stands up first and, without fail, kisses his ageing wife on her head before heading out to work his land.

It is a source of some wonder to me.

The water below me is like glass and the tide is moving gently out. There is a southern boubou pair calling in the bush behind me and a thousand other birds are singing in the spring morning. A tern is trying to catch breakfast off towards the sea. There is no human sound.

I've been writing a journal of my memories of Anna, desperate that I should not forget anything that we shared. I'm not sure if it is cathartic or just plain morbid. Anyway, it's been good to have some alone time to think about her, what she meant to me and the things she said to me before she died.

God, I miss her.

I feel sick at the thought of going back to Sasekile. Anna would be so disappointed to hear me speak like that. At least I have another week here.

Hope things are all OK your side.

Angus

From: 'Hugh MacNaughton'
Sent: 16 October, 17h32
To: 'Jules'
Subject: Amber

Hey Jules,

Anna's replacement arrived this week.

After numerous interviews, the position was eventually given to Amber Thompson from Cape Town. She arrives with very little experience, but looks to kill and a 22-year-old body like something out of the *Sports Illustrated* Swimwear Calendar. She finished a BA degree at UCT at the end of last year and spent the first 3-quarters of this year travelling around Europe and South America. She is very engaging, full of energy and seems like lots of fun so I think she will fit in nicely here – although some disagree...

The entire Rangers team is obviously in a complete flutter about the arrival of "New Meat" and a number of bets have already been placed around who will be the first to "bed" her. Jonesy is currently the favourite (Ashleigh, the Student Chef with whom he has been having sex for the last few months, is leaving at the end of the year so we all know what he is thinking), but Jamie is a hot 2nd. The girls of the Lodge have also been talking to each other in hushed tones since Amber's arrival. They are all massively threatened by the arrival of this young cracker. None more so than Simone because Amber has literally not left my side since the day she started.

In addition to assisting with the planning of the YMS group, PJ has tasked me with training Amber. Anna used to do all of the Camp Manager training but with her tragic passing, PJ has handed this task to me. He asked me to draw up an induction programme for Amber in which she will visit all the Lodge departments, like I did. When this is over, she will shadow me for 2 weeks in Tamboti Camp. After that she will move to Kingfisher Camp as the assistant Camp Manager. I suppose Melissa will undo all of my good work.

As I explained in my last email, Simone and I have both been going pretty flat out since Anna's funeral so I haven't seen much of her. You can therefore just imagine how the advent of my new shadow has added to her brewing frustration.

"How can you justify spending so much time with her when we haven't even talked properly together in weeks?" she asked me angrily.

"What?" I replied with deep confusion.

"You stare into those big blue eyes of hers all day," she followed illogically – as if I have a choice. "You never look at me that way!"

I was astonished.

"I am spending time with her because I have been instructed to train her, Simone," I replied with irritation. "And I 'stare into her big blue eyes all day' because normally I look at people when I am talking to them. As I am doing most of the talking and she is the 1 being trained, I think it only reasonable that I face her on these occasions. However, if you would prefer me to talk to her pink-coloured toes or the bushveld behind her, I will gladly indulge you."

Simone looked back at me for a while – motionless. Then she cocked her head, sighed and rolled her eyes towards the ceiling.

"You know I'm right, Hugh," she said and brushed past me.

Please explain this logic to me, Jules. How in the hell can she possibly think that she is right? For the moment, though, I am ignoring her ridiculous comments, consoled by the suspicion that she is as intimidated as Jenny and the rest of them. Whatever!

I also had to deal with a couple who had ants in their room. All of the rooms are thatched which, of course, is wonderfully aesthetic, but they are havens for insects. Every year, when the temperatures rise, it is a certainty that a nest of ants – adults, eggs and larvae – will plummet onto the white duvets. These current Guests phoned reception and Candice alerted me over the radio. I rushed down to the room as soon as I heard. I was expecting a tirade of abuse, but I could not have been more wrong.

In a gentle Scottish accent, Barbara MacMurray (around 60 years of age) said almost apologetically,

"So sorry to bother you, Hugh, but we're having a spot of bother with some insects. A few of them seem to have fallen onto our bed. Bob is just trying to identify them now with his field guide." I apologised and went through to her room to have a look.

The "few ants" turned out to be an enormous understatement – there must have been 4 million ants on her bed! They were everywhere, most of them carrying the eggs off to the next nesting site. Bob MacMurray was kneeling next to the bed, a magnifying glass in 1 hand and a field guide in the other.

It astounds me how differently Guests behave at this Lodge. Barbara was perfectly entitled to have gone absolutely wild, but she didn't. In the same situation, another person may have slated the Lodge over the Internet before the day was out or demanded a free night for the "incomparable inconvenience" of it all. Barbara simply understood that out in the sticks sometimes things go wrong. I am now determined to make it up to Barbara and Bob during the remainder of their stay.

Please send advice on how to handle Simone's petulant behaviour. I'm completely in the dark here!

Lots of love,

Your brother (with the best-looking shadow in the Lowveld),

Hugh

From: 'Angus MacNaughton'
Sent: 16 October, 18h28
To: 'Julia MacNaughton'
Subject: Elgar's storm

Dear Julia,

My days have swung from miserable, to pensive, to OK. I almost feel guilty when I'm not miserable although I know Anna would hate me to be dwelling on her passing. I really can't help it, though.

Today I sat up on that huge dune above the main beach. I watched a storm come barrelling in over the slaty ocean from the south-west. I had my iPod on and Elgar's *Nimrod* was playing at full volume as the clouds billowed overhead and began to empty themselves. I just sat there while the storm raged all around me and the music built to its exquisite crescendo.

I cried and cried and cried.

The storm eased after a while and it seemed to pull my tears away with it. As I walked home, the sun broke through the clouds and I felt like I was over the worst.

In two days I must return to Sasekile.

I think I'll be OK.

Angus

From: 'Angus MacNaughton'
Sent: 19 October, 11h43
To: 'Hugh MacNaughton'
Subject: My room

String Bean,

I am returning to Sasekile tomorrow. Please can you ask Queenie to clean my room and leave the key under the pot plant next to my doorstep? Threaten her with violence if necessary. The last time I returned my room had been neglected so badly that there was a family of woodland dormice nesting in my bookshelf. This, in itself, would not have been a disaster but the bloody things had torn up my priceless first edition of Van Wyk's *Trees of the Kruger National Park*.

Angus

P.S. Incidentally, the female dormouse gave birth on Faidherbia albida – *page 68 of the Van Wyk's.*

From: 'Hugh MacNaughton'
Sent: 19 October, 16h03
To: 'Angus'
Subject: Your room

Hey Angus,

I will have your room cleaned up, with pleasure.

I imagine the thought of coming back here must be very hard for you. I hope Kenton was good and that the time alone has helped you deal with the terrible loss of Anna. Let me know if there is anything else I can do before you come back.

Despite our difficulties, I feel really bad for you and I hope you are OK.

Hugh

JAMES HENDRY

From: 'Hugh MacNaughton'
Sent: 22 October, 18h00
To: 'Jules'
Subject: Action – real action!

Hey Jules,

Jeez, what a week!

Before I get onto the real excitement, a report on our brother. Angus
and I have been working together this week at Tamboti Camp. His mood
seems to have improved since I last saw him, but he still experiences the
odd bout of sadness. He did have 2 altercations this week so he must be
feeling a bit better.

The first was with Amber, the new Camp Manager I mentioned last
week – the 1 I've been training. Short of going to bed with me at night,
Amber has not left my side (this has obviously delighted Simone no
end). We begin the day at the 07:30 Morning Meeting with the other
Managers. We then head to camp to meet with the staff – Butlers,
Gardener, Housekeepers and the Maintenance Man. The noticeboard
gets written up, departing Guests' bills are revised, welcome notes for
arriving Guests are written and the breakfast buffet is checked. All of
this, as well as any problems from the day before, needs to be dealt with
before the Rangers arrive back from their morning drive.

Angus, while driving out of Tamboti, has spent some time with the young
Amber. He, astonishingly, is the only person not completely mesmerised
by her. Perhaps he is just angry with her because she is here to replace
Anna, but who knows? Angus greeted her the other morning upon
returning from his morning drive.

"Morning, Amber," he said acerbically.

"Good morning, Angus, how are you?" she replied brightly.

"You seem to have missed a spot with your eye shadow this morning," he
said, frowning at her.

"Oh!" Her hand went up to her eye and she turned away.

"Wait, wait, wait ..." he continued as she turned to leave, "before you attend to your panel-beating, I'd like some scrambled eggs and a cup of tea. That would be marvellous."

Upset, Amber walked away towards the kitchen.

"What is your problem with her?" I asked.

"There's something inherently irritating about someone with the name and looks of a soap character," he replied.

Angus's other altercation this week was with 1 of our Guests. He arrived back from another morning drive absolutely seething (mercifully, I had asked Amber to collect some laundry from a Guest's room so she was out of the firing line). He harangued me for 20 minutes about how his "god-forsaken" Guest was slimier than Russell the Love Muscle. Apparently, the Guest only wanted to see rhino, despite the property being awash with leopards. Eventually, for the sake of the other Guests, Angus told the guy that they were now done with rhino viewing and that they would be looking for something else. He said that this infuriated the "rhino-loving" Guest.

"I didn't give a shit, though, String Bean," he said to me. "We must have seen 20 different rhino by that stage."

I have to admit I thought the Guest in question was a bit shady. He looked like a dodgy sort from the south of Johannesburg. But he was well-dressed and decent enough to deal with around camp. He had introduced himself as Frank when he arrived the day before and asked how long I'd been working here. I told him about 9 months, to which he began a string of questions about rhino sightings, rhino population numbers and poaching prevention in the area. I did not know the answers to all these questions so I suggested he ask Angus in the morning.

Frank sat at a table on his own for breakfast, glued to his BlackBerry, which irritated the hell out of me. I chatted to the other Guests for a while before finding Amber to discuss the check-out process with her. She asked lots of questions while the Guests finished their breakfast and headed back to their rooms. We then did some role-play. I pretended to be a Guest and she, the Camp Manager. Amber did not master the check-out process immediately. She kept getting flustered when I (the Guest) asked about how gratuities work. During 1 of the role-plays she answered,

"Well, it's completely up to you and your discretion as to how much you'd like to tip me! Aaahh," she screeched immediately, putting her hand to her mouth upon realising her error. "I didn't mean me ..." she began, but I was laughing like mad by this stage. She began giggling as well.

Of course, it was at this precise moment that Simone walked in to find us rolling around with laughter.

"Mmmm, this looks like fun," she said. "I'm sorry I disturbed you 2." With that, she glared at me with unadulterated rage, turned and stormed out.

"Oh, Christ," I said to Amber. "I'm sorry but I'm going to need to deal with this."

I gave chase but paused when I noticed somebody in the Tamboti Camp car park. I dashed into the boma (which is adjacent to the car park) and peeked through a gap in the split-pole fence. It was Frank on his BlackBerry. He had obviously been battling with the signal in his room. He was not looking comfortable, though, as he kept glancing around as if he was doing something illegal. He was right in the corner of the car park underneath a big sausage tree which is situated just beside the boma wall. Something made me stay and listen for a few moments longer. My blood ran cold when I heard the contents of his conversation.

"Listen carefully, Andre," he whispered. "I have the coordinates of 3 different bulls from this morning's drive. You'll need to move fast because they will be mobile so get that bird in the sky, chop chop." He then rattled off a string of coordinates and finished with, "Remember, keep the bird running after you've shot them and make sure that Gary has primed the chainsaw before you land. Any questions? Good. Call me when it's done and I'll get the hell out of here."

I started shaking but didn't make a sound. As Frank left the car park, I sprinted to Angus's room.

"Angus!" I yelled as I burst into his room.

"What the hell is the matter with you?" he asked.

"It's Frank ..." I began.

"If he wants a bush walk, you can forget it," said Angus, without letting me finish.

"No, you idiot," I replied. "He is a poacher. Frank is a poacher. I've just overheard him talking to his chopper pilot on the phone. He said something about the GPS coordinates of 3 bulls."

"Shit," said Angus. "It makes sense. We saw 3 big bull rhinos at Jeffrey's Pan in the south this morning. It was the only time the prick looked even remotely happy with life."

"We'd better tell PJ," I said hurriedly.

"No, he is out for the day," replied Angus. "Went to watch his boy play cricket in town. I saw him leaving on my way back from Tamboti."

"Well then, what do you suggest?" I asked. "The guy was talking about a chainsaw and everything."

Angus began biting the nail on his thumb as he always does when he's put under pressure.

"Get Jacob and Elvis," he yelled suddenly. "Don't try to explain anything to them. Just point south and say *poacher* and then look worried – a bit like you are now should do it. Then meet me at the top gate of the village on the southern side. I'll get a rifle and a vehicle and meet you all there."

"What about telling Anton?" I asked.

"That's the stupidest thing you've said all week, String Bean," replied Angus. "Just find Jacob and Elvis, quickly!"

We both rushed off.

I found Jacob and Elvis at the canteen and did what Angus said. It worked like a charm. Jacob rallied 2 of his guys and we all met Angus at the gate and sped off towards Jeffrey's Pan, but not before Jacob had retrieved a flare from the conservation storeroom. Angus began explaining the situation to Jacob and Elvis in Shangane, while Nhlanhla and Bertie listened from the back seat with me. As Angus sped along the bumpy roads, Jacob looked up towards the sky and pointed to a blue chopper in the distance. Jacob also told Angus to get hold of reception and tell them to contact the Hoedspruit Airbase to explain the situation.

"*Hantlisa, hantlisa,*" shouted Jacob. This meant hurry.

When we arrived at the pan there was no sign of the 3 bulls. The blue chopper was now circling to the east of the pan.

The poacher's sniper, sitting in the open door of the aircraft, jolted as he fired his weapon.

We drove even faster in that direction, through the thick bush. We arrived on the fringes of the clearing over which the chopper was hovering. One bull was on the ground and the other 2 were galloping around in distress. There was dust and grass flying everywhere. Jacob shouted at Angus to shoot at the helicopter.

A bullet collided with the tail of the blue chopper and knocked it slightly off its path and in so doing stopped the shooter from killing the other 2. Angus then chased the other bulls out of the clearing by firing over their heads.

We huddled together in the thick bush as the chopper landed. Then we heard the voices of the poachers. They did not sound happy – 1 of them was shouting at the pilot for ruining his second shot. The pilot shouted back at him that something had hit the back of the chopper. Then we heard the sound of a chainsaw start but Jacob kept us together and still we waited.

Eventually, we heard the sound of a second chopper. It was much louder than the blue 1. Jacob told us that he was going to have to give up our position and fired the red flare. There was mayhem as the large War Bird cut towards our position and fired on the poachers. Two of them ran.

We all gave chase. Being pretty quick myself, I caught the first 1. He managed to punch me once before Nhlanhla and Bertie arrived to nail him. We tied him properly as Elvis and Angus caught the other 1. We dragged them back into the clearing where Jacob was helping the Air Force guys tie up the others.

The sight was bitter-sweet. The 4 men from the blue chopper were lying face down on the ground with their hands cuffed behind their backs. There was a pool of blood below the rhino bull we had seen earlier and a jagged horn lying beside him. It was an awful sight.

When I explained to the Air Force pilot what I had overheard, he decided to accompany us back to camp. Frank was arrested with little trouble. Imagine his surprise when he was greeted at his door by an officer of the law and not a housekeeper to remove his laundry. The officers thanked us before heading back to Hoedspruit with the 5 criminals.

There are already a number of versions of the story circulating around the Lodge. It is amazing how these sorts of things are spiced up so fast. In 1 version, I think Jacob was hanging from the blue chopper with 1 hand and wrestling the poachers with the other. Amazing.

Simone couldn't believe it when I told her. Now that I was a hero, sporting a swollen jaw from the punch I received, she was happy to talk to me again.

"I'm so proud of you, Hugh," she said.

PJ was equally astounded by the news upon his return and invited Jacob, Angus and me round to his house to hear the story.

Angus and I walked back home together, reminiscing about the day's events.

"Hell, that was fun," we agreed. Petrifying, but fun.

What a great week!

Hope you're well, Jules.

Lots of love,

Your poacher-arresting brother,

Hugh

From: 'Angus MacNaughton'
Sent: 22 October 19h15
To: 'Julia MacNaughton'
Subject: Anti-poaching

Dear Julia,

Action from the word go here at Sasekile Private Lunatic Asylum.

It's been good to be busy again – takes my mind off the blackness that threatens to envelop me every so often.

My arrival back was awful. I had a lump stuck in my throat as I drove through the reserve in the mid-morning. I sat for a long while in the car park, collecting myself, before taking my bag out of the boot and heading numbly for my room.

The normal welcome note was there and it had been signed by more people than the usual three. I hate it when people feel sorry for me. There was obviously no special note – beautifully written on fine paper. But there was no time to mope because I had to pick up guests from the airstrip almost immediately.

My guests consisted of two couples and a strange, oafish human from somewhere deep in the middle of Limpopo Province. I should have been suspicious from the outset because the average Limpopo farmer cannot afford the obscene rates charged to stay in this place. The name he gave us was Frank Botha – more than likely not real.

Frank was a bear of a man – the kind of person who likes to crush your hand into a fine powder while shaking it. I think there is permanent damage to the cartilage of the baby finger on my right hand. Frank and the other guests were staying in Tamboti Camp. This meant that I had the pleasure of driving out of SB's camp.

Normally, this would have been torturous. In this instance, however, it was a blessing because String Bean knows better than to ask me how I am feeling all the time – something Jenny and Melitha insist on doing whenever they see me. In Jenny's case it is well-meaning but I really don't want to talk about it. I think Melitha still thinks I wrote that letter all those months back and harbours a hope now that Anna is no more.

I suppose I had my mind on Anna when Frank said all he wanted to see was rhino. I thought nothing of it and the other guests were first timers so they didn't mind seeing rhino. After the fourth sighting of the morning, it was becoming a bit ridiculous and I told him we were going to find some other animals. He was deeply put out and paid no attention to a leopardess and cubs that delighted the two couples.

'I didn't come yaah for stchoopit pussy kets,' he muttered on the back seat in a deep Musina drawl.

The reasons for his fascination with horned pachyderms revealed itself in spectacular fashion during the course of an extremely exciting mid-morning.

I was in my room doing some press-ups after breakfast when SB flung the door open in a typical Hugh-like panic.

I asked what the hell was wrong with him, initially thinking that bloody Frank wanted to go on a bush walk. He blubbered on about Frank being a rhino poacher. His voice faded into the distance as all the pieces of the puzzle fell into place – his home in Limpopo, travelling alone, the GPS he carried on the game drive and, of course, his fascination with rhino. SB explained that an attack was about to take place.

I knew there were only two people for this job – Jacob 'Spear of the Lowveld' Mkhonto and Elvis Sithole. I dispatched SB to fetch them while I went for a rifle and Land Rover.

About half an hour later we arrived at Jeffrey's Pan where we'd seen three rhino on the drive earlier. On the way there, Jacob instructed me to tell the lodge to phone the airbase in Hoedspruit and explain the predicament. Candice reported back that the Air Force had scrambled a gunship immediately.

The poachers were already overhead in their chopper, hovering off to the east of the pan – they had found the rhino. We could see someone hanging out of the door aiming a high-calibre rifle.

'*Famba, famba!*' said the fearless Spear of the Lowveld. I geared down and we sped off-road to where the chopper was hovering. The occupants of the helicopter did not see us – they were too focused on the rhino and we were hidden by a thick acacia canopy overhead. As we drove, I saw the rifleman fire.

We couldn't hear the sound above the roar of the chopper blades but we saw the muzzle flash and the rifleman jolt with the recoil.

'*Yima!*' said Jacob. I stopped the car behind a thicket.

In the clearing beyond we could see two young bulls running in terrified circles. They were being skilfully herded by the pilot – clearly a highly experienced game pilot. The biggest animal lay slumped in the middle of the clearing, blood pumping from a wound in his head.

'*Dubula!*' (Shoot!) said Jacob to me, pointing at the rifle. I leapt out of the driver's seat, chambered a round and, using the tracker's seat as a dead rest, took aim at the chopper's fuel tank.

By this stage, their rifleman had reloaded and was taking aim at his second mark.

I fired.

A spark flew off the tail of the light chopper. I reloaded and fired again. The heavy .458 slugs threw the chopper off course and the rifleman fell back into the doorway.

Elvis directed me to the remaining rhino. He told me to shoot over their heads and frighten them out of the clearing. This had the desired effect. They scarpered off south into a thicket. The chopper, still unaware of our presence, landed.

We heard a chainsaw start.

We peered out from our secluded position and watched as one of four men began to cut off the priceless horn. The rest of the men were armed with automatic weapons. It would have been suicidal to expose ourselves – I had one round left in my slow-firing, bolt-action hunting rifle.

As the sawing began, we heard the low, heavy thud of a huge helicopter engine. It was the Air Force. We had no choice but to fire the flare Jacob had brought and give away our position – hoping that the Air Force pilots would arrive before we were mowed down by automatic rifle fire.

We crouched behind the Land Rover, keeping an eye on the poachers – all dressed in matching military fatigues. Jacob gritted his teeth and fired the bright red flare. The poachers saw it immediately and realised they were in trouble because the gunship changed course and belted down towards us. Two of them turned their attention to the enormous attack helicopter and started firing wildly. The pilot unleashed a short burst of heavy-calibre machine-gun fire which shredded the poachers' light chopper. They dropped their rifles – two of them froze and two ran.

Hugh, Nhlanhla, Bertie, Elvis and I gave chase. Hugh is not slow and caught up to the fleeing criminals with relative ease. He is, however, not a fighter. One of them turned and clocked him one in the jaw. He fell back but the poacher's hesitation allowed the rest of us to catch up. Nhlanhla and Bertie piled into him and in a short time he was trussed up like a gammon. Elvis and I continued after the other one. He was in poor shape and slowed fast. I went low and Elvis high. He probably hardly felt me grabbing at his knees but when Elvis's huge frame clattered into him there was a sickening thud and he went down.

A while later the bastards were all immobile and lying on the floor of Flight Lieutenant George Ndlovu's Rooivalk attack helicopter.

Frank was arrested shortly thereafter. We arrived at the lodge and I personally escorted the police to his room. It gave me huge satisfaction. I knocked on the door and walked straight in. Frank was smoking a cigar on his deck, dressed in nothing but a bathrobe.

'Oh, Frankie,' I said. 'Frankie, these men have come all the way from Hoedspruit to see you. They'd like a word, if you don't mind.' Frank stood up and turned around. When he saw the uniformed officers, the cigar fell from his mouth. He thought about leaping off the deck and making a run for it but he was barefoot and virtually naked. He was bundled off shortly thereafter.

Quite exciting, really.

The other thing to report is the arrival of Anna's replacement. She is the quintessential bimbette – platinum blonde, blue-eyed and big-boobed. I get the distinct impression she was hired for her Barbie-esque physique and not much else. Her name, predictably, is Amber – like a character from a soap opera. She is always in such a smiley good mood. It makes me sick.

I like her as much as I would a rabid mamba. Perhaps this is because she is not Anna.

JAMES HENDRY

All the rangers, Carrie included, think she is wonderful and the amount of testosterone-driven showing-off is incredible to behold. Suddenly, my quiet sessions in the staff gym (where I am normally the only visitor) have become like a Planet Fitness. The rangers are now trying to lose the extra covering gained from too much lodge food.

That's it for this week. Chat soon.

Angus

276

From: 'Julia MacNaughton'
Sent: 23 October, 08h50
To: 'Brother H'; 'Brother A'
Subject: Happy Birthday!

Hi guys,

First of all, Happy Birthday, Angus! I hope your day was an epic day out there and that you don't have to work too hard. I also hope that everyone is being super nice to you – Hugh especially.

Secondly, what brave and skilful big brothers I have!? So glad that you guys emerged from your gallant anti-poaching efforts with no more than a bruised jaw. The parentals are quite proud of their boys. Well, once Mum had stopped hyperventilating at the thought of her babies being shot, that is. The Major approved with comments of 'jolly good show' and 'bloody Germans'. Dad explained calmly that poachers were in no way connected to the Third Reich.

Right, well, though I am not saving the world from the evils of poaching, I do have to get back to work in order to ensure that another fat cat profits off this dire market ... not sure the firm would let me handle these derivative calculations if they knew anything of my horrendous maths.

Have popped something in the post for your birthday, Angus – hope you like.

Lots of love,

Jules

From: 'Hugh MacNaughton'
Sent: 30 October, 18h09
To: 'Jules'
Subject: More planning for YMS

Dear Jules,

After last week's action a degree of normality has returned to the Lodge. I have been busy working with Jenny on the YMS group and Amber is almost ready to move into Kingfisher Camp.

It is incredibly hot and the insects are out in force. Eating dinner out on the deck above the river is simply not an option at the moment as the new season's population of stink bugs swarm towards the candlelight. We have had to move dinner inside 2 nights in a row – I have had enough of fighting with stink bugs. They get into everything: the food, the wine, down ladies' shirts and all over the tables. If 1 is murdered, the smell is enough to make you retch so it is easier to be inside where they are not as prevalent.

The planning for the YMS group is going well. In our spare time, Jenny and I have been meeting to discuss dinner venues, daily programmes, Christmas day, staffing, kids, etc. I really like working with her, I must say. She is methodical and very precise. If she says she's going to do something, she does it by the following week, which is great. Consequently, she has made us both look good in our weekly meetings with PJ.

I have also got to know her a bit better on a personal level. She comes from a pretty similar background to us and grew up going to the Kruger with her folks from a young age. She eventually wants to run her own travel business specialising in game reserves so she thought it a good start to work at 1 first. She asked me a bit about my life and what I wanted to do eventually, but strangely seemed most intrigued by my relationship (or lack thereof) with Angus.

One of my main responsibilities for the group has been food and beverages so I have had a few independent meetings with O'Reilly about the menu.

We discussed options for the traditional dinner and what would work best on open fires. O'Reilly asked if a spit had ever been done. I wasn't sure, but thought it a brilliant idea to have an impala or a lamb roasting away during the traditional supper. We also discussed pairing food and wine in the individual camps on 1 of the nights as O'Reilly has worked extensively with wine and food in Ireland. His knowledge of local wine is limited, however, so we have agreed to try something together at Tamboti Camp this week.

Fortunately, Simone has found it within herself to view my working relationship with Amber through an adult set of eyes, which has improved our own relationship remarkably. She and I are talking regularly again, which is nice. I took your advice on how to deal with her jealousy and it worked a treat. I swear you have to be a woman to understand 1. I have also become a lot more comfortable with her public displays of affection having read your last email. Again, I am grateful for the local knowledge you impart so effortlessly. If you ever need me to reciprocate, I will be more than happy to oblige, but given that you enjoyed your first sexual encounter long before I did, I suppose you won't need my advice on the opposite sex. I'll have to pay you back in bed nights at the Lodge.

Oh, I nearly forgot. I am due to go on leave again next week, but unfortunately I won't be seeing you until the end of it. Simone has planned the most amazing trip for us. We are borrowing her father's Land Rover (which is kitted out something cruel) and are heading for the Central Kalahari Game Reserve in Botswana. It's just going to be the 2 of us so it should be awesome. We are visiting 2 camps up there for 4 nights each, but it is a long way there so we will take at least 2 days from Johannesburg to get there and back.

"It's going to be proper camping," she says.

Should be interesting. I don't think I've camped since that school hike we did in the Drakensberg.

She'll have her phone, so hopefully I'll be able to send you the odd mail. I will definitely be in touch before we cross the border, though.

Lots of love,

Hugh

JAMES HENDRY

From: 'Angus MacNaughton'
Sent: 31 October, 18h50
To: 'Julia MacNaughton'
Subject: Cicadas (Christmas beetles to you and other non-biologists)

Dear Julia,

The summer is upon us in many ways. There has been little rain – frontal drizzle mainly – that has moved into the Lowveld from the south-east, just enough to tinge the grass green. Most of the trees have produced good crops of new leaves, however, because the ground water is relatively high after the last rainy season.

It has also been hot – lava hot or 'blerrie fokken hortt' in Anton-speak. By 11:00 it hits about 38 degrees Celsius. Often there is a dry wind that goes with the searing heat. Still, there are idiots who pitch up for the 11:00 nature walk – the guiding of which takes monumental self-discipline in these conditions. Who the hell wants to look at tracks in the scorching midday when they could be lolling in the pool?

The cicada population is the one part of the reserve's ecology that appreciates the heat. They are on a massive sex drive, having recently emerged from the ground after a year of enforced celibacy. The males, as you may know, make a high-pitched buzzing sound. Their call is very pleasant in the distance on a lazy summer's day when one is drinking G&Ts. Driving through the mopane woodland on a hot November evening when these things are trying to attract mates is quite different.

The cicada's method of seduction involves the complicated use of a membrane and sound-reflective chambers somewhere on the abdomen. Each day, about 6 billion of them enthusiastically vibrate their membranes at each other. If you stop next to a well-populated tree, it feels like your skull is being penetrated by a thousand small but powerful drills. How the hell the females choose a mate from this numbing clamour, only they know.

As the cicadas emerged, I was landed with a family of American guests from Florida – typical nuclear family affair with mother and father in early forties and kids mid-teens. On arrival, they were astounded to find a small beetle in their room and complained loudly. Their matching safari suits bore testament to their profound terror of all things with an exoskeleton and jointed legs. The outfits, despite the volcanic heat, were always buttoned and zipped to the limb ends. The most amusing part of the family getup, however, were the hats that emerged after our sundowner drinks stop. As Elvis and I were packing up the cooler box and he was setting up the spotlight, Mrs Florida unpacked four hats from the recesses of her enormous 'Safari Equipment Bag'.

'OK, guys, let's put on our critter visors.' The family dutifully gathered around and Mrs Florida handed them each a bizarre headpiece. Wide-brimmed like cricket hats and hard as pith helmets, the hats had special fold-down nets that could be fastened neatly onto the collar line of the matching safari shirts – the idea being to make the wearer impermeable to invertebrate life forms.

Elvis pissed himself. He had to walk off into the bush for five minutes.

On the way home, I stopped in the middle of a little grove of mopane trees. I did this to demonstrate the awesome noise that the sex-crazed cicadas are able to generate.

'Oh, Gaad, what is that?' asked Miss Florida – for the first time she was paying attention because she could not use her iPod with the net fastened.

'The noise is that of hundreds of cicada males trying to attract mates,' I yelled above the din. There were blank looks – accent issues. 'Si-kay-dahs,' I shouted again. Realisation dawned. As this happened, Mr Florida retrieved his field guide and switched on a headlamp – specially fastened to the pith/cricket/bee-keeping helmet.

The effect of this was startling. Within seconds, he and his family were beset by a great swarm of cicadas, attracted irresistibly to the light. All four of them began screaming, contorting and slapping. In order to see their attackers, the rest of the family switched on their headlights. This had the effect of quadrupling the attack. The noise emanating from the Floridas was almost as deafening as the cicada buzz.

For the second time that night, Elvis became hysterical.

When I had watched sufficient comedy for the night, I drove on.

The new girl – Amber – continues to create ructions amongst the male staff. She was spotted emerging from 'the Legend' Jonesy's house two nights ago. This means that Ashleigh, the trainee chef he has been bonking for the last few months, is incandescent.

That's about it for this week. How are things with you?

Angus

P.S. I still keep being reminded about Anna. It is amazing how many things remind me of her. I guess that's an indication of how big a part of my life she was here. Half of me wants to forget these things and the other half is terrified that I will forget them and in so doing sully my memories of her.

From: 'Hugh MacNaughton'
Sent: 06 November, 16h00
To: 'Jules'
Subject: Kalahari adventure

Hey Jules,

This is tremendously exciting stuff!

Simone's dad's Land Rover is the most incredible machine I have ever seen. It has more drawers than you have in your bedroom. In these are all manner of tins, pots, pans and gas burners. It also has a roof-top tent with a built-in mattress which is where we are going to be sleeping. Mrs Robertson is not entirely pleased about sleeping arrangements but I think she'll get over it. The Landy roars like a rogue male lion and has the strength of an elephant. I think that I am going to get used to this whole camping vibe quicker than I expected.

We are due to cross the border at 06:00 tomorrow and I don't suspect that we will have signal after that.

If we never return, please tell the folks that I love them and that it was only a pleasure being a better son than Angus.

I hope that we have brought enough water!

Lots of love,

Your Camel Man brother,

Hugh

From: 'Jules'
Sent: 07 November, 05h00
To: 'Brother H'
Subject: Happy birthday

Good morning, dearest brother,

Happy happy birthday!

So glad that you are spending the day in what must be a beautiful place but very sad that you aren't around to share it here with the family. The Major phoned about half an hour ago (can you believe it?) to wish 'his favourite' grandchild a happy birthday. He still can't get it straight that you are living away from home.

Hope you get this before you cross the border.

Lots of love,

Jules

From: 'Angus MacNaughton'
Sent: 08 November, 19h34
To: 'Julia MacNaughton'
Subject: Advanced rifle handling

Dear Julia,

I have settled into the rhythm of driving. The lodge has been full so I've been going pretty much flat out. I'm glad not to have driven out of Rhino Camp so I'm not reminded of Anna every time I walk onto the deck – the result of which would be a deeply morose safari for my guests paying in excess of R10 000 a night for the pleasure of my company.

I have been driving out of beastly Melitha's camp, however. This has not been marvellous as she has appointed herself my personal psychologist and counsellor. She is too thick to understand that I would sooner seek advice from the resident baboon troop.

'Oh, Anguth,' she said to me as I arrived for tea yesterday afternoon, 'how are you feeling today, my friend? Come here and unload your troubleth. We have a bit of time before the guethtth arrive.' She sat on a sofa and patted the cushion next to her.

'Melitha, the chances of my disgorging the machinations of my soul to your self-designed techniques of psychoanalysis are negligible.' I walked over to the tea table and cut a huge slice of chocolate cake for myself.

The one afternoon I had off this week, I sat on a crate outside my room as the sun went down. I had a book to read but my attention was arrested by the nesting and courtship activities of a woodland kingfisher pair that has taken up residence in the huge mopane tree outside my room. They like these trees because of the natural holes that occur in the heart wood.

'Chip prrrrrrrrrrrrrrrrrrrrrrrrrrrrrrrrrrrrrrrrrrr,' the male screams in early October. He does not shut up for the next five months. Despite his irritatingly incessant call, the breeding dance I watched on the branches as I sipped milk stout, the setting sun silhouetting the performers, was most entertaining. Both male and female hold their wings out and churrrrrr wildly at each other while performing

180-degree pirouettes on the branch outside the nest. It's a sort of 'check this out, no, you check this out, OK, well, how about this then' event. Very funny, especially after three milk stouts.

The greatest entertainment of the week, however, came from my old favourite: Anton. Some background first.

One of the infinitely efficient government departments of our beloved country has decided that everyone guiding tourists must have official qualifications. The actual information a guide is expected to assimilate for these qualifications could be learned by a senile stone. That's the easy bit. Wading through the bureaucracy and red tape, however, requires a law degree and about three hectares of paper per application. In an effort to comply with legal regulations, all the Sasekile rangers have to pass the Advanced Rifle Handling course or 'ARH *boet*' in Anton-speak.

We all went through the ARH course this week – in the heat of the day, between drives. There was much back-slapping and joking as the course began. Behind some of the jokes, there was a huge amount of anxiety for some. The thought of shooting poorly in front of the team made palms clammy.

The test was on the last day – when the actual shooting took place. There were three major exercises focused on speed and accuracy. For the first test, we set up targets at fifteen, ten and five metres. We had to fire a round into each of them, reload two rounds and then fire into the ten and five again. This had to be done in 20 seconds. Given the fact that even a guinea fowl can cover fifteen metres in less than three seconds, I consider the exercise to be of limited value.

Anton, as our fearless leader, should have gone first. Instead he stood back, the fear obvious in his eyes.

'Ladies first,' he said, trying to sound amusing. He pointed at Carrie, our lady ranger. This was a gargantuan mistake on his part. Carrie may look like the back end of a Soweto taxi but it turns out she can shoot like an SAS sniper. It took her eleven seconds to complete the exercise. The trainer, a retired army sharp shooter, was agog – as were the rest of us. Spontaneous applause rose from the group. Anton had created a situation where failure would be all the more embarrassing. He pointed at me. 'Your turn.' He was getting sweaty.

I shrugged and moved up to the firing line while Carrie reset the targets. I am OK with a rifle. Not sure I'd back myself against a pissed-off charging male lion, but a stationary box is not too much trouble. I was calm and took a bit more time – 19.8 seconds – but I managed to send bullets through all the right targets. I smiled at Anton as I ejected the last cartridge, catching it coolly with my free hand.

One by one, the rest went. You are allowed two attempts at the exercise – some did it in one attempt and others in two. The Legend took two attempts and nearly missed the fifteen metre, which gave me great satisfaction. He looked profoundly relieved.

Eventually, Anton had to step up to the mark. His hands were shaking.

And he couldn't cope.

He finished the exercise in nine seconds. Unfortunately, he only hit two out of five targets. He went pale as the smoke from his last round dissipated. There was silence. Jamie coughed, fighting back a chuckle.

'Fokken rifle!' he shouted. 'It's not shooting straight – my rifle is buggered, someone has bashed it in the safe. Fok it!' He spun round. 'Carrie, give me yours.' He stormed over to her and grabbed her immaculately cleaned weapon. He stepped up to the firing line again. By this stage his back was wet with sweat and he dropped two rounds in the dust as he loaded.

'Three, two, one, GO!' said the trainer. Anton tried to take his time over it but the adrenalin was coursing through his huge frame far too fast.

He didn't even complete the exercise. He loosed off the first three rounds and missed three times. He knew that there were no excuses and no amount of bluster was going to save him. He just put the rifle back onto the vehicle and climbed into the passenger seat, silent and utterly defeated. I'm not sure he'll recover from this – perhaps he'll go through another Buddhist phase.

Hope things are cool that end,

Angus

Hello Angus,

I have never sent you a post-card. Don't know what I'm thinking as it will no doubt end up in the bin on receipt.

Anyway we are having such fun up here and I know that you would love the peace and quiet of this incredible wilderness area. On that basis I thought of you.

I hope you are well and in strong spirits – genuinely.

Hope you like the picture.

Hugh & Simone.

BOTSWANA P4.90

Angus MacNaughton

P BAG X 7

HOEDSPRUIT, 1380

RSA

13/07

From: 'Angus MacNaughton'
Sent: 14 November, 18h55
To: 'Julia MacNaughton'
Subject: Rhino walk

Dear Julia,

This week the quest for a legally qualified ranging team continued – this time with walking evaluations. Each ranger had to guide a walk to view a big game species with a number of other rangers and the evaluator acting as a guest. Interestingly, Anton developed a bad case of diarrhoea that only cleared up ten minutes after the evaluator left. He has thus not been evaluated. He has been very *sotto voce* since his disastrous shooting test the other day.

Allow me to digress for a brief description of the evaluator, who I shall refer to as Lizard from now on. Lizard is a large, unattractive, reptilian creature with a burgeoning paunch and an immaculately shaped goatee. He thinks he is a genius in the bush and spent the evenings telling us about the learners he has bedded at the various training institutions at which he has worked. I can only think that these women agreed to giving Lizard carnal knowledge of themselves in order to pass their exams. Perhaps Anton should offer the same service.

My walk started out well enough. We tracked a rhino bull into a clearing dotted with small clumps of trees and a few large termite mounds. I spotted him at some distance and then led my 'guests' a bit closer, using the trees as cover. The wind was perfectly in our favour so we approached to within about 40 metres. He was feeding calmly in the cooling afternoon, blissfully unaware that we were watching him.

During these evaluations, it is best not to push the boundaries. The idea is to move in, have a look, and then get out before the animal ever becomes aware of your presence. I was about to suggest a retreat when the bull moved off and we lost sight of him behind a termite mound. The mound was about 20 metres in front of us and I guessed the rhino was the same distance behind the mound. I decided on one more approach – termite mounds provide ideal cover in these situations.

I beckoned to the 'guests' and told them to be quiet. Then I checked the wind again with my ash bag and we crept silently towards the mound. The mound was about ten metres wide at the base and about three metres high. There was a thicket of false marula trees on top of the mound so the view on the other side was obscured – it was impossible to see what was going on until right on top.

The 'guests' and I snuck slowly up the side of the mound and peered over the top. There was nothing where I expected the rhino to be. We were all lying quietly on our bellies, me just above the others. I looked down at Lizard and he raised his eyebrows as if to say 'Where is it, buddy?'

We lay in silence for a few minutes. I was deeply confused.

Suddenly, a slapping sound, like two great pieces of leather being hit together, came from only a few metres away – just over the lip of the mound: the unmistakable sound of a rhino's lips smacking together as he grazes. I leopard-crawled to the top and looked over the lip. There I beheld the bull grazing gently, still blissfully unaware, around the base of the mound. I beckoned and my 'guests' came very slowly to the top and peered over the edge.

They all grinned widely – being in such close proximity to a rhino is marvellous. Because rhinos can barely see anything, you can get pretty close without putting your life in grave danger. Being that close to an elephant would be perilous, to say the least, and I would not have enjoyed the predicament with real guests.

For the next 20 minutes, we moved silently around the top of the mound on our bellies as the rhino grazed around the base and we made sure we were always 180 degrees away from his immense horn.

When he eventually grazed off towards the next mound, I turned to address my 'guests'. They all had the hugest smiles on their faces. Even Jonesy nodded approvingly. We made our way slowly back to the car without incident. I was worried that Lizard would take a dim view of my approach, which landed us so near, but in the end he passed me on condition I promised never to take real guests on foot so close to rhino.

It is still very dry in this part of the world. The small amount of drizzle that we have had has long evaporated and the last of the pools in the river have dried up. The pregnant impala ewes are looking a bit haggard and they will really struggle to feed their lambs if the rain doesn't come pretty soon.

That's it for this week…

Angus

From: 'Angus MacNaughton'
Sent: 16 November, 15h28
To: 'Julia MacNaughton'
Subject: My nemesis moves on

Dear Julia,

Glory be, hallelujah, joy, rapture and unforeseen happiness.

Anton has resigned!

At the rangers' meeting this morning PJ came in to make the announcement. All the rangers and trackers were there and, in the embarrassing silence that followed, Elvis started to giggle, which set me off. Before we had to excuse ourselves, Anton rose to speak.

'Ja, it is time to move on for this wild man. I got this fokken incredible, amazing land management offer there by Musina that I couldn't refuse and Sasekile couldn't match it.'

Translation: 'I can't handle the fact that I failed the shooting exam and I will never be able to deal with the blow to my ego so I am going to mend fences on a farm in Musina.'

The goon leaves in a week.

The lodge is thus full of rumours about who the new head ranger is to be. The front-running candidate at this stage is Jonesy 'the Legend'. If he accedes to the throne I'll have to go on strike. Quite from left field, the dark horse candidate is Carrie. PJ will make an announcement some time in the future. Jonesy thinks he is a shoo-in and I heard him talking about how he is going to re-decorate the head ranger's palace when he is installed. He's such an arrogant prick.

Time will tell.

Cheers,

Angus

From: 'Hugh MacNaughton'
Sent: 20 November 17h00
To: 'Jules'
Subject: Teamwork!

Hey Jules,

Well, I'm back from leave and it's been all action since I arrived!

The big news, although I'm sure Angus will have told you, is that Anton, the esteemed Head Ranger who nearly got me killed in my first week, has resigned. Jonesy is in line to replace him. I think he'll be good although he is quite full of himself. No doubt, Angus will be mortified when it is announced.

PJ took me up to the Staff Shop for a beer yesterday afternoon. We had a good catch-up about things. After a few quarts, he confessed that he was greatly relieved about Anton's imminent departure. Apparently, the owners insisted on his employment as Head Ranger about 2 years ago. He used to work on another 1 of their properties as a camp hand. One afternoon, he caught Dennis in a clinch with a young, nubile receptionist. The exposure of Dennis's infidelity and penchant for younger women would have looked very bad for Nicolette, Dennis and their business empire. To keep Anton quiet, they posted him to Sasekile with a promotion well beyond his capabilities.

Jenny has been working tirelessly on the finer details of the YMS group visit and O'Reilly is still around, so that is a positive. We had a beer in the staff village the other day and he seems to be settling in and beginning to enjoy working with the staff in the kitchen.

"Hugh, dose fellas in de kitchen are actually a good bunch." He said this halfway through his fourth quart of Castle Milk Stout which he refers to as the African Guinness.

The major YMS group update concerns Simone rather than me. There will be about 20 kids in the camp and they will be accompanied by a number of "counsellors" who are apparently professional American child minders. I imagine that corporal punishment will be out of the question so Angus is going to struggle.

My holiday in the Kalahari was truly spectacular. Simone and I really bonded. We have similar interests and she is such fun. We seem to have developed an excellent understanding of each other.

Angus seems better and some of his humour has returned. We had a great chat about my trip and he seemed genuinely interested in some of the animals and birds we had seen. He obviously didn't believe that I hadn't got the vehicle stuck. I really hadn't – well, only once, but that was before we crossed the border, so it doesn't count.

On the subject of our surly brother, we collaborated successfully this week for the first time ever. Quite unbelievable.

The first proper rains of the year arrived a few nights back. There was an immense storm over the Lowveld and, as apparently happens every year, some of the roofs leaked quite badly. Tamboti Room 4 was 1 of them.

The standby maintenance was all tied up fixing another roof when I called them to fix the leak over Angela and Tony's bed. Angus was the only 1 on air during my frantic calls and, quite astoundingly, he agreed to help me fix the roof with a huge plastic sheet. Angela and Tony were dining privately in their suite during the event and were not nearly as sympathetic as the Scottish family who were attacked by ants a few weeks ago. The leak was dripping straight onto their bed.

Angus nearly fell off the slippery thatch a number of times and the language that came out of his mouth was incredible. He was really very funny. It just seemed like he wasn't genuinely angry, and was quite enjoying the absurdity of our position. He got all sarcastic about his degree, complaining that his Animal Behaviour professor hadn't prepared him for fixing thatch in the rain.

I took the Guests a complimentary bottle of vino, but before I could give it to them, Angus marched into their room wearing his ghastly yellow raincoat and announced,

"You will be pleased to know that the leak over your bed chamber that was revealed by the inclement conditions has been repaired by the tireless efforts of my good self and your Camp Manager. It should inconvenience you no further. I trust that you will sleep soundly and dryly. Good night."

Could it be that our brother is starting to see that the whole world is not against him? I know it's unlikely but miracles do happen.

Lots of love,

Your roof-repairing brother,

Hugh

From: 'Angus MacNaughton'
Sent: 20 November, 18h28
To: 'Julia MacNaughton'
Subject: First rains

Dear Julia,

This week saw the one and only Twin Palms event that I have voluntarily attended – Anton's farewell (good-riddance) party. I made a special effort with the theme because I was so excited at the thought of my tormentor's departure. The theme was 'Pirates and Prostitutes'. My pirate costume consisted of some shredded shorts, a head scarf and a half-eaten chicken carcass from the Main Camp boma. The bird was tied to my right shoulder and proved popular with the other revellers. Jenny and Jeff thought it was hilarious but Amber thought it disgusting.

The highlight of the party was the obligatory farewell speech that PJ had to make. He tried to look genuinely sad that Anton was leaving but no one is sad that he is buggering off. There was muted applause after the speech and just as Anton looked like he was going to stand up and say something, someone killed the lights and the music started. He is leaving in a fortnight.

The other notable piece of information was that String Bean and I managed to do something together for the first time since he became an idiot (at conception). Our team effort occurred on the night that we had the first storm of the summer. I was on game drive as the storm built and churned up the western sky. Previously this year, the clouds have built up over the northern Drakensberg and we've looked on as the thick grey tongues of water have fallen far off to the west of us. This time, the clouds swept north and then spun east over the Lowveld.

I was driving some Germans and stopped the Land Rover on a high point so that we could watch the cumulonimbus clouds rolling in.

'Vat are vee doing here?' asked Hans or Gunter or Wilhelm (I forget which).

'We are watching the first storm of the season – is it not incredible to see it build like that?' I replied enthusiastically.

'Vee haf rain in Chermany,' he said, 'vee do not vish to be struck by ze lightening.'

At this point the heavens opened and we were all drenched within a few seconds. The rain ponchos that Elvis and I handed out looked great but may as well have been made of tissue paper for all the use they were.

Back at camp there was predictable chaos. Apparently, Arno van der Vyfer – our exceptionally talented maintenance man – and his team had failed dismally to prepare the camp for the eventuality of rain. There were people haring about the place trying to patch roofs with huge bits of plastic. Guests kept up a steady flow of complaints to the reception about their rooms being in various states of flooding.

After supper at the Avusheni Eatery, I headed for my room, radio in hand. I was looking forward to reading my book, sipping on some Talisker and listening to the rain. On my way, the radio crackled to life.

'Any station maintenance, come in,' said the voice of String Bean. There was no answer. 'Any station maintenance, come in, I have a leak in Room 4 and need it fixed ASAP!' came the strident plea for help. Still no answer from the fully occupied maintenance crew. He called a few more times unsuccessfully and then pitifully said, 'Does anyone copy me? Is there anyone on air?' Still his cries went unanswered.

I swore loudly, grabbed my radio, re-zipped my rain coat, and headed back out into the rain.

'String Bean, apparently I am the only one with a brain on air right now. What do you need?' I said into my radio. There was a pause and then SB answered, clearly surprised, that he would meet me in the maintenance shed. There, we exchanged short greetings and retrieved a huge piece of plastic and some wire.

Ten minutes later SB and I were on top of the slippery thatch roof of Tamboti Room 4 in the pelting rain, trying to spread the plastic sail over as much of the porous shelter as possible. SB nearly fell off at least ten times. It was actually a very amusing experience, and he laughed a lot at my running commentary of our predicament, which, in turn, increased the precariousness of his position. Eventually, we finished sewing the sail down with the wire and slid recklessly off the roof.

A while later, I poured myself the scotch I'd been waiting for and sat down on my bed with a sense of satisfaction.

Well, that's it from the thankfully wet Lowveld.

Angus

From: 'Hugh MacNaughton'
Sent: 28 November, 18h02
To: 'Jules'
Subject: Christmas party

Dear Jules,

This week saw the celebration of the staff Christmas party. Melissa and Amber were put in charge of the event because Jenny and I were deemed too busy planning for the important YMS group. Melissa, rightly, saw this job as something of an insult. Despite this, she actually did a good job of the party and it was a great occasion. It is the only night of the year when the whole Lodge is closed for the night – it means that everyone can attend.

Everybody from the gardener to PJ gathered in the village for the party, and for 1 night, no one had to worry about Guests. This year, the party theme was "What you wanted to be when you grew up".

Jerry, 1 of the maintenance guys, came dressed as Anton. He wore the shortest pair of shorts I have ever seen. Anton didn't see the humour, declaring that the young man's spindly Shangane legs looked nothing like his beautifully sculpted trunks (Anton left forever the next day). Jerry won best-dressed anyway, much to the delight of everyone.

A DJ was brought in and the staff partied long into the night. Everyone did their bit: Chefs cooked, Maintenance helped set up and Jacob and his men acted as bouncers – i.e., controlled hard-drinking staff. It was brilliant fun.

Angus and I collaborated successfully for the second time in history by putting on a play – this 1 was significantly better than our last performance, but there was less pressure this time round. We decided on a game lodge version of *Jack and the Bean Stalk* where I played the giant and Angus played Jack. It was called *Jack and the Mealie Stalk*. The staff loved it and we received major high 5s. Even Arno gave me a pat on the back.

Angus initially huffed and sighed when I volunteered his writing services for the event. Secretly I think he really enjoyed being involved with something creative. He actually turned out to be the star of the show as he divided his words between English and Shangane so that all the staff understood. At 1 point I thought Mavis from the laundry was going to pass out she was laughing so much at Angus's ridiculous half-Shangane Jack character.

In usual style, a few staff got carried away and made some regrettable decisions – Candice took the DJ to bed, Ashleigh (the Chef spurned by Jonesy) kissed 2 Rangers on the dance floor in an attempt to make Jonesy jealous, Arno tried some dirty dancing with Jenny but she poured beer on his head, and Jonesy had his way with Amber in the back of the Staff Shop on a sack of fortified porridge. The greatest highlight of all is that Jeff and Melissa have finally found each other. Part of me is genuinely chuffed for them. Even Angus smiled when he saw them groping in the shadows of a large marula tree next to the Staff Shop.

The party was a short break from the tension of planning for the YMS group. Their arrival is getting very close and Jenny and I are getting more and more nervous as the big day approaches. I must have sent 1 000 emails out to various food and drink suppliers and another 5 000 to the YMS organisers who are unbelievably pedantic. I've been dealing with the American end and their requests range from reasonable to completely ridiculous. The latest have included demands for the final evening Christmas dinner:

A black-tie/*Out of Africa* dinner

A string quartet to play the *Out of Africa* music throughout the evening

Sugar- and alcohol-free cocktails for the kids

African Christmas music sung by a local choir (I tried to explain that Christmas is not part of Shangane tradition but Martha, the YMS co-ordinator, just didn't believe me. I have included her response below.)

Dear Hugh,

I am unsatisfied with your response to my very reasonable request for an African Christmas choir. I feel you are being unhelpful in this regard. Next, you'll be telling me Shanganini people don't celebrate Thanksgiving Holidays either! Make sure the choir is at the Christmas dinner.

Kind Regards,

Martha van Dyk

Senior Liaison Officer, YMS New York.

I've had good meetings with Jenny, O'Reilly and PJ, so things seem to be on track, but I know how quickly they can all fall apart so I'm keeping focused.

Lots of love,

Hugh

From: 'Angus MacNaughton'
Sent: 28 November, 18h28
To: 'Julia MacNaughton'
Subject: Three-legged race

Dear Julia,

The highlight of this week was the lodge Christmas Party. The behaviour this year ranged from mild to completely bizarre, but what else is to be expected here? It was, on the whole, quite entertaining, however. String Bean even managed to convince me to pen a pantomime which was more successful than the last piece I wrote.

The party began in the afternoon with a sports day of sorts. At this time of the year, the schools of the local area close, so many of the younger kids come to visit their parents who live in the staff village. Consequently, the sports day consists of events geared towards the kids, e.g., sack, and egg and spoon races, etc. The culmination of this athletic spectacle is the traditional three-legged race. All of the staff and their children have to take part in this. The prize is R500 so competition is vicious. The pairings are drawn randomly from a hat. So it was that I was paired with Gladys Khoza, one of the village cleaners.

Gladys has been working at Sasekile since dinosaurs roamed the Earth. She has skin the texture of shale and a single tooth in her mouth. She has also never won the three-legged race and this is a source of some frustration for her. She shook a bony finger at me and told me in no uncertain terms that she would feed me to a hyena if we didn't win and that she wouldn't be sharing the winnings.

About 80 pairs of people lined up at the bottom end of the soccer field for the start so space was extremely limited. PJ was the starter. His partner was Elvis's eight-year-old daughter, Zodwa. His method for starting the race was simply to start limping towards the other side of the field. This set in motion scenes of chaos not seen since Johnny Gordon shouted 'scrambles' and threw a bag of Jelly Tots onto the nursery-school playground 22 years ago. Most of the pairs just fell over each other in their efforts to get through the scrum of people. The noise was deafening. My partner began screaming all manner of Shangane obscenities in my ear and at everyone else as soon as PJ set off.

About 60 metres down the 100-metre track there were only about ten pairs left in contention. The rest were either too slow or too badly injured to carry on. PJ and Zodwa were still clear after their head-start; Jonesy and Fortunate from the laundry were hot on their heels. I and the bellowing Gladys were gaining fast from tenth place. Gladys wasn't really playing fair. In the pockets of her green overalls she had packed stones. These she began flinging at our competitors. Her throwing was wildly inaccurate but the raining missiles had the effect of distracting five of the pairs in front of us, including SB and Queenie, who lurched to the side and took cover behind a leadwood stump.

With only 20 metres to go, Gladys let go her one and only well-aimed stone. This collected Jonesy upside the head. He howled loudly, lost his rhythm and he and Fortunate fell in a heap. We were gaining on the field with relative ease by this stage, but the sight of Gladys's missile hitting Jonesy was too much for me and I began laughing. This made my partner increase her yelling, which made me laugh even more. Eventually, we too lost the rhythm and tumbled to the floor. Jacob and Carrie just pipped the false-starting general manager to the finish line. The tirade I was subjected to while trying to detach my right leg from Gladys's left was wild and full of spittle.

When the competitors were all patched up, we moved to the Staff Shop where the real party began. There was a huge amount of drinking and frivolity as spit-roasted impala was served. All were fairly well on their way by the time *Jack and the Mealie Stalk* was performed. I have to say that SB was very good at playing the giant. He made all the kids laugh hysterically.

After that, the music began and there was a lot more drinking. Melitha and Jeff hooked up around midnight. I can only think that this is because Jeff can no longer stand living in the bat cave and is now trying to sleep his way out. There were a number of other public displays of affection during the course of the evening. These ranged from innocuous to pornographic.

I am coming home on leave in a few days' time so I'll see you then. When are you and the folks going to Kenton?

See you soon,

Angus

A YEAR IN THE WILD

From: 'Julia MacNaughton'
Sent: 29 November, 18h46
To: 'Brother A'; 'Brother H'
Subject: Trip to the Eastern Cape

Hi boys,

Sounds like the two of you had a marvellous time at the Christmas Party ... and a play together? Without violence? Well, it has the MacNaughton household somewhat surprised! That pensive frown that usually divides Dad's brow when I relate stories of your bush adventures softened noticeably when I described your combined Shakespearean efforts. Mum raised her eyes from her embroidery and commented,

'Oh, I hope Angus wasn't too vulgar.'

The great migration to Kenton is set for the 20th, though how it will all happen remains to be seen. Of course, how we are getting there has yet to be decided. The Major has decided that he is up to coming along this year. He has, however, refused point blank to go in the car with Trubshaw.

'I'm not getting into an automobile with that bloody hell hound! I'd rather be knee-high in a muddy trench than be forced to endure ten hours in an automobile with that beast!'

He looked loathingly at the hound, who was illegally spread-eagled upside-down on the sofa, gently sucking on a corner of one of Mum's hand-embroidered silk cushions.

Dad left the room at this point, biting his lip.

So it looks like Mum will fly with The Major, and Dad and I will drive with the heavily tranquillised Trubshaw. Mum won't let The Major fly alone since he called that air steward 'a sexual deviant with roaring homosexual tendencies'. He was nearly arrested.

Love to you both,

Jules

JAMES HENDRY

From: 'Hugh MacNaughton'
Sent: 04 December, 16h45
To: 'Jules'
Subject: Fek

Hey Jules,

I'm having all-too-familiar, frightening flashbacks from the Travel Luxury Group 6 months ago, as various parts of Jenny's and my well-laid plans hit snags. Fortunately, the problems are not insurmountable and this time I had the sense to speak to PJ.

The first issue was with O'Reilly. I have really grown to enjoy him but he is an extremely emotional guy. He lost his cool with 1 of our suppliers this week. Since he is not allowed to shout at staff, he tends to take his frustrations out on the Lowveld suppliers of fresh produce. He was dissatisfied with the quality of their latest fruit delivery and stormed into the office where I was sending an email to Martha of the YMS group. He grabbed the phone and dialled furiously.

"Yes ... hello. Who is that? Hmm? Who is it? Give me de fekken manager. I don't care who de fek you are, just fetch dat useless urrshorl you've got playin de fool dere orderin your fruits!"

There was a pause as whoever answered the phone went to fetch his superior. The tirade continued when the manager of Miombo Fresh Produce picked up the phone.

"Now, look here, you fekken pathetic excuse for a greengrocer. I ... don't ... know what kind of clown show you fekkers are runnin over dere but I can't deal with bruised peaches and half-rotten fekken ploms with less flavour dan an Irish potato. Can you tell me how I'm supposed to make world-beating puddins with you urrshorls sendin me de Lowveld's rotten garbage? Hmm? Can you tell me dat? Hmm? *Can you*?"

The person at the other end tried to answer but O'Reilly cut him off.

"I'm not interested in your fekken nonsense excuses. You fekkers sort it out or I'll take my business elsewhere!"

He slammed the phone down so hard that the mouthpiece fell apart.

As a consequence, Miombo refused to deliver the whole lamb which we need for the spit at the traditional evening on the penultimate YMS night. Thankfully, PJ got on the phone and sorted the problem out. He knew someone higher up the chain than the man who had received all the "feks" on the phone.

The other problem is that the bloody ice machines have gone on the fritz again. The December heat is simply too much for them to cope with. One of the Rangers suggested moving them into air-conditioned rooms, which seems like a good idea, so we will try that later today when Arno has fixed (or should I say tried to fix) them.

Yesterday, monkeys invaded Simone's stationery cupboard full of paints, crayons and all things fun for kids. With the YMS children descending on the place soon, this discovery is something of a disaster. I'm going to have to ask Angus to pick up replacements at Waltons on his way back from leave – he'll be really charmed. This incident did end amusingly, however, as a troop of multi-coloured vervet monkeys arrived at Tamboti Camp during tea yesterday afternoon.

Otherwise, all is on track. Ranger allocations have been done. Menus are ready. Daily programmes have been set. All animals are in position – lions, leopards, elephants, etc. (only joking – we're not *that* prepared).

What are the family's plans for Christmas Eve? This will be the first ever year that I have not spent Christmas with the family. I am really excited about things here but I feel a bit hollow that I won't be with you, Mum and Dad. Pity we can't all be together.

I am going to get Jenny to write and ask Angus to bring the stationery replacements. I may be wrong but there seems to be something brewing between the 2 of them.

Love, your organised-ish and nervous brother,

Hugh

From: 'Jenny Sutherland'
Sent: 04 December, 18h06
To: 'Angus M'
Subject: Help!!

Howzit Angus,

How's your leave going?

Things here are pretty hot here at the moment (weather-wise, that is) and hectic with the planning for YMS – something I'm sure you're not that interested in!

You might be interested, however, to know that Jacob saw a black rhino in the south yesterday. The rangers rushed out to see it but it had disappeared. Anyway, I'm sure Jacob will tell you about it when you get back as you are about the only ranger who can speak to him.

My mail to you is not purely social – I actually need your help with something. I hope you don't mind. The sad story of why I need your help is: the monkeys managed to break into the stationery store a few days ago and they destroyed all the paints, crayons and other stuff that we were keeping for the YMS kids.

I hate to ask you this – especially given how much you love children! – but would you mind fetching some replacements for us at Waltons? We'll send them the order and pay; if you could just pick it up, that would be amazing. Hugh says that there's a branch right near where you live.

Please would you write back and let me know if you can pick the stuff up before you come back from JHB?

What's happening on your leave? What have you got up to?

See you soon,

Jen x

From: 'Angus MacNaughton'
Sent: 05 December, 19h15
To: 'JennyS@Sasekile.co.za'
Subject: Vic Falls

Dear Jennifer,

My leave is good fun.

I found a special in the travel section of the *Sunday Times*. As a consequence, I am writing this from the Victoria Falls Hotel in Zimbabwe. It is a grand old building – one of the oldest in the town. The waiters are all dressed as they have been since the late 1800s and some of them are so old I suspect they served cocktails to Cecil John Rhodes. My flight and stay were on special, but nothing else about this place is cheap. The lamentable collapse of the Zimbabwean dollar means that everything is paid for in very expensive United States dollars. This makes eating extortionate. Still, the falls are spectacular despite the US$20 I had to pay to see them, and the people are cool (even the myriad pedlars trying to sell me carvings of varying quality).

I have just returned from a sunset cruise on the Zambezi so I'm quite pissed. This is lucky for you as I am inclined to acquiesce to your request. I will pick up the kids' kit on my way back to Sasekile Loony-Bin – that is, of course, unless I'm drowned on my white-water rafting expedition tomorrow.

Right, I must sign off, I'm meeting two dubious Swedish UN aid workers for dinner in a few minutes.

Cheers,

Angus

P.S. Jennifer, tell my errant brother he can ask me himself next time – did he really think I wouldn't guess he'd put you up to this?

P.P.S. That doesn't mean I object to hearing from you.

From: 'Hugh MacNaughton'
Sent: 11 December, 20h00
To: 'Jules'
Subject: Filthy Maintenance Man

Hey Jules,

Another really exciting week out here.

I'm pleased to report that the ice machines are working again – we have installed them in the air-conditioned Avusheni Eatery, which has necessitated the removal of the ping-pong table. There are many grumblings from the Rangers.

The big news of the week, however, is that Arno has been fired! When you hear what for, you'll be utterly astounded. I feel very little for him, both because of what he said about Simone that 1 time (when I struck him with the hammer), and because of the vile circumstances surrounding his departure. We have not been friends at all – despite the high 5 at the Christmas Party.

I was doing a room check a few days ago when I found Arno in Tamboti Room 3. There was a last-minute booking so he wasn't expecting anyone to come in that day. I found him halfway up a ladder in the bathroom. The look of guilt on his face made me ask him what he was doing. He looked at me through his slitty eyes and said he was replacing a light bulb. This was clearly not true as the ladder wasn't positioned anywhere near the light and he didn't seem to be carrying a bulb.

I went back into the room later on to have a look and there I found a tiny camera pointing at the shower. It was very cleverly hidden in the thatch – it simply looked like a blemish in the roofing. He is quite a technical sort so knows about these things. I then headed to all the other rooms in Tamboti to check them and I discovered that there were cameras in 4 of the 6 rooms! The cameras were linked to recording boxes set up under the deck, hidden next to the geysers.

Who knows how long the cameras have been up there and what sort of bathroom scenes Arno has recorded? Some, I imagine, must be quite saucy – what with the honeymoon couples we have through here regularly. Others must be downright disgusting, given the fat rolls and south-swinging boobs attached to some of our other Guests. What a sick bastard he is. It makes me really angry to think of him invading the privacy of my more treasured Guests.

My dislike of Arno made it easy for me to report my find to PJ. That evening I brought him down to Tamboti while the Guests were having dinner. He was completely flabbergasted.

The next morning Arno was called into the office for a disciplinary hearing. I had to be a witness in the case. Arno stared at me with malice throughout the hearing. It is amazing to me that anyone could be bitter about being fired for something so obviously wrong and vile. I hate him. He was escorted off the reserve before lunchtime.

I am trying to think of a suitable Christmas present for Simone – thought I'd try without your help initially but I'm too scared in case I buy her something stupid. Any ideas? Perhaps you could pick something out for me and ask Angus to bring it back when he returns from leave.

Right, I must run – I have lots of planning to do for the YMS group.

Lots of love,

Your instrumental-in-the-firing-of-Arno brother!

Hugh

From: 'Julia MacNaughton'
Sent: 10 December, 19h50
To: 'Brother H'
Subject: Christmas

Hey Hugh,

Hmmm. Present for Simone ... I'll think of something and send it down with Angus.

It is a great pity you chaps aren't going to be in Kenton for Christmas. All the cousins, uncles and aunts, etc., are coming this year. Dad has already taken delivery of a huge ham which will be travelling down next to Trubshaw (in a cooler box, of course).

The funniest part is that Al is bringing Barry down. I don't suppose The Major will be giving him much of a present. Trubshaw might, though!

Lots of love,

Jules

From: 'Angus MacNaughton'
Sent: 11 December, 20h28
To: 'Jenny Sutherland'
Subject: Crayons crayons crayons

Dear Jennifer,

I have returned from our northern neighbours unscathed by the crocodiles, UN aid workers or the Zambezi. I believe that Arno has been fired in my absence. What very good news – I think I may even prefer Hugh to Arno, although it's a close call.

I have collected the stationery as requested. There are enough crayons here to colour in the Great Wall of China. I cannot imagine what in the blazes the YMS children are going to do with them all but I guess that is up to Hugh's lover.

See you in a few days.

Angus

From: 'Hugh MacNaughton'
Sent: 18 December, 19h00
To: 'Jules'
Subject: Baboons wreak havoc

Hey Jules,

The YMS group has arrived and it is seriously intense.

I have never dealt with a check-in like this before. Behind the scenes it was complete chaos but as far as the Guests were concerned, everything ran like clockwork. Jenny and I were the "go to" people so the adrenalin pumped. Luckily, I had Simone at Tamboti and she was just fantastic.

Some of the Rangers told me that the airstrip arrival was very difficult. This delayed arrival in camp, which was a very good thing. While the Rangers were dealing with the mess at the strip, a baboon troop broke into Rhino Camp – into the suite reserved for Martha van Dyk and her husband!

On our final check of the camps, Jenny and I discovered the suite door slightly ajar. When I pushed it gingerly open, a truly horrific scene was revealed. The place looked like a smashed-up night club, smelled like a sewer and the baboons were still inside. They had done what baboons do best – completely destroyed the place, drunk the booze, eaten all the snacks, chewed the soap, and shat *everywhere*. One of them must have tried to punch and then bite his reflection in the mirror. He cut himself severely in the process and left a trail of blood all over the room. There was even a small 1 hanging from the circling ceiling fan. He let go when he saw us and flew, screaming, across the room into the bathroom. Our arrival sparked panic in the troop as we were blocking the only exit. As 1, they charged at us. We jumped back out and the beastly animals scampered past and out into the bush.

As we stood up to dust ourselves off – the plane carrying the YMS Guests flew over the top of the Lodge! We were up shit creek – literally and figuratively. Jenny reacted first. She picked her radio up out of the dust and began shouting instructions into it. She basically asked everyone in the lodge to help us clean up. The staff responded superbly and in a few minutes there were people all over the room, cleaning, fixing and replacing. Even PJ was on his hands and knees in the bathroom, cleaning baboon crap out of the shower.

When the Rangers radioed that they were on final approach, the room was beginning to look OK but the smell was staggeringly awful and no amount of air freshener would hide the foul stench of baboon shit. Then Jacob had an inspired idea. He flung open the sliding door at the front of the room and disappeared into the bush. He emerged a few seconds later with an arm full of dry elephant dung. This he placed at the entrance to the room. He shouted something at 1 of the housekeeping ladies. She took her bucket, filled it with pool water and poured it over the dung. This, to the untrained eye, gave the impression that an elephant had just deposited it. It was Jacob's idea that this be used to explain the stench. "Wow, an elephant has just been at your room! Isn't that exciting?" PJ was primed to con the Guests.

We all hurtled out of the room and up to our respective camp car parks to check in the most important group of the year. When the Guests arrived, they thought everything was peachy.

The next challenge for us came with the luggage, which was all mixed up. We had to have it in the correct rooms by the time the Guests had finished their welcome drinks. There was more panicked activity behind the scenes as the Camp Managers blamed the Rangers for not placing the correct Guests on their vehicles. Jamie and Melissa almost came to blows when she accused him of deliberately trying to make her look bad. Carrie, the new Head Ranger, managed to devise a brilliant system and, miraculously, all the luggage arrived in the right places just in time. The Van Dyks were highly impressed that elephants come into the camp – so close that they drink from the pools! Things have been much smoother since then.

Everyone has just returned from game drive and they are dressing for dinner. Angus, naturally, has managed to piss off 1 of the South Africans. She complained to me that he was rude and surly on the game drive. I said I would reprimand him severely but obviously that would be ridiculous. I shall simply make sure that they are not on the same vehicle again. To be fair to him, she is very painful but Angus should surely be able to control himself by now – he is 27!

Anyway, the first few days should be smooth. After that we have the bush dinner with a traditional South African menu for the whole group. I hope it doesn't rain. All the prep has been done, though, and O'Reilly has put together a real feast. The night after that we have the whole group in the Main Camp boma for Christmas Eve – this is going to be tricky.

We have put together a programme for each day which should keep the group busy (bush walks, tracking adventures, cooking for the kids, fishing in the river, mini Game Rangers' courses, orienteering exercises, etc.). I think they are all going to be completely exhausted by the time they finish their holiday.

Not much more has been said about Arno. I think we are all simply too busy. After the hearing he said to me that I and everybody else at the Lodge would regret messing with him. Sounds like a silly threat to me. I told him to do his best.

It is Christmas next week! Thanks for sending the *eau de parfum* down with Angus. It is wonderful. I'm sad not to be with the family this year but I am really enjoying things here, so it is not too bad.

Lots of love,

Hugh

P.S. I must say that, although I thought Jonesy would make a good Head Ranger, Carrie has so far been incredibly effective and efficient. She has implemented some great systems, and relations between the hospitality and field staff are at an all-time high.

From: 'Angus MacNaughton'
Sent: 18 December, 18h28
To: 'Julia MacNaughton'
Subject: My new boss and arrival of the money-club

Dear Julia,

My arrival back from leave this time wasn't as bad as usual. This was mainly due to the news that the new head ranger is not Jonesy 'the Legend' but Carrie 'the Lesbian'. I am profoundly pleased with this development. While Carrie is further from an oil painting than Trubshaw is from a mathematics professor, she is mature, tough, makes an effort to understand the local people and is seemingly free of ego. I am looking forward to less tumultuous relations than I had with her predecessor.

Jonesy is trying not to let this development affect him by pretending he didn't really want the job – but it is cutting him up. He was the only ranger who didn't show up to move Carrie's stuff into Anton's old schloss. Good. Serves the jock right for assuming he'd be the chosen one – like he has been his whole life. A clever decision by PJ.

The first five days back were calm and I drove a bit out of Main Camp. The guests were forgettable (as they normally are) but I slipped into an easy rhythm with September, Jenny and Clifford – the mentally defective butler. Jenny seems to have forgiven me for the altercation we had early this year (the one that resulted in my first disciplinary). I think she has also eaten a few more muffins and her fuller figure is quite fetching. I have decided that she has rather a good, dry sense of humour.

My sense of peace was rudely destroyed by the arrival of the YMS group. I wasn't keen on them before they arrived. Now I detest them.

They arrived in an old Dakota DC3 – apparently travel on historical planes is the exotic thing to do these days. The old bird disgorged 70 people of assorted ages, nationalities and sizes into the Lowveld afternoon. I think a collie dog would have proved the most effective means of organising them as they immediately split up in a hundred directions.

The summer midday had made the low-flying DC3 buck and shake like a rodeo bull. This had had a predictably disgusting effect on the YMS group, particularly the children – all stuffed full of sweets and Coke. At least half of the group carried paper bags full of puke. I spotted these early and stood far back as the first over-eager rangers made their way to welcome the guests. The sick bags – not always intact – were handed to them.

The unsick children behaved like hyperactive samango monkeys – some ran off down the airstrip, others hared into the bush to pee. I watched as their 'highly qualified' counsellors tried in vain to coax the most spoilt children on god's Earth back with 'rewards'. The kids took absolutely no notice. The parents were either too sick or too busy comparing share portfolios to notice their offspring hurtling off to certain death by lion, leopard, buffalo or snake.

One, a snotty, fat ten-year-old, came running past me, so I grabbed his collar.

'Hey man, lemme go, lemme go!' he bleated.

'Shut up,' I said dragging him back towards the flustered counsellors.

'I said, let go of me, asshole!' Lucifer's offspring shouted.

'If you don't shut up, I'm going to put a scorpion in your bed. It will bite you and you will bleed from your ears, eyes and mouth. I have killed many children before you.' He went pale and quiet. Tears welled up in his eyes, so I quickly let him go and he ran for the safety of the counsellors.

I took no part in the herding operations, choosing rather to help with the mountains of luggage which were infinitely better behaved.

There were signs with names attached to the front of each Land Rover. These were specifically placed there to attract the right guests to the right rangers so that they could be taken to the right camps. This did not happen. YMS members climbed onto the vehicles willy-nilly, which made for complete entropy when we arrived at the lodge and had no idea where to take everyone or their bags.

So far, my initial fears about this group have been borne out. The women are mostly so botoxed that their faces are only able to display one expression. The men talk about business and money. The kids, I have mentioned. The counsellors are all American, which means they are terrified of litigation and will therefore not deliver beatings. Their ridiculous attempts to reason with their charges are hilarious to watch. The kids take full advantage, happy in the knowledge there are no consequences.

I'm driving out of Tamboti Camp. One of my guests is a South African woman. She has a completely square figure and has tried to hide her numerous chins with frequent surgery – to little effect. She has been to the bush a few times and thus thinks she's a world authority on wildlife and guiding. I gave up trying to tell anyone anything after a few minutes because she took it upon herself to explain the biota of the greater Kruger National Park to her foreign pals. She spoke without pause from the moment we were on the Land Rover.

About two hours into the drive, we happened upon a giraffe with her foal. I switched off the engine and sat in silence. Margo's giraffe knowledge is apparently poor, so she said,

'Angus, tell our friends about giraffes.'

'Sometimes,' I replied, 'it's best to let sightings talk for themselves.' Elvis giggled and Margo shut up, mercifully. She did, however, go puce and I shan't be surprised if there is a complaint.

No doubt, there'll be much ridiculous YMS behaviour to report in the next edition.

I'm very sad not to be travelling to the coast with you all this week.

Angus

From: 'Hugh MacNaughton'
Sent: 25 December, 18h00
To: 'Jules'
Subject: Heroic Happy Christmas!

Hey Jules,

First of all, Happy Christmas. I hope Dad filled your stocking with lots of cool things last night.

Secondly...

Angus and I are heroes!

You will not believe what went down in Tamboti last night. It makes the tale of old man Thesiger pale into insignificance. What a conclusion to our wonderful, humorous and absolutely absurd year in the wild.

Things had gone really well with the group – PJ was well impressed with Jenny and me. The Cultural Dinner went off like a dream. We had it in a clearing on the Tsessebe River floodplain. There were 100s of lanterns hanging in all the trees surrounding the area; it really looked like some sort of fairyland. The round tables were covered in locally made cloth and decked with beautiful centrepieces designed by me and Jenny. There was a delicious roasted lamb on the spit and the Guests could not believe they were eating out in the middle of nowhere.

After dinner, the choir sang, the Shangane dancers flung themselves around and even the Guests joined in the dancing – although not very well. In the end, the evening turned into a sort of rock 'n roll/Shangane dance party that raised huge clouds of dust. I think Fortunate's hands must have been on fire when she finally stopped pounding her drum and the last Guest sat down. The whole Lodge team came together and pulled off the most sensational evening.

All the daytime activities we had planned for the group went extremely well and the kids loved their programme. They were surprisingly taken with Angus, much to his apparent disgust, but I suspect he was secretly quite pleased. I think they appreciated not being molly-coddled. When he pushed a particularly obnoxious child into a muddy pan on the second day, I thought there was going to be real trouble, but all the kids just leapt in after their friend and dragged Angus in after them. The counsellors all stood on the side wailing about health, safety and disease but the kids seem to be fine despite wallowing where the buffalo normally do.

The game drives were exceptional – there were mating lions, leopard kills and wild dogs hunting all over the place. The Guests were in serious awe. Despite what Angus thinks, some of them are actually very pleasant people.

Then came the final Christmas Eve dinner.

I thought, given that relations between Angus and me seemed to be warming, that we should toast the family just before dinner with some special whisky I had found in the storeroom. Halfway through our drink, Efficient, the useless Security Guard, came running onto the deck shouting, "Fire, fire, fire!"

I immediately went to the storeroom to fetch the fire pump and hose, and Angus ran for the blaze.

A few moments later we were outside number 6, where we faced a frightening sight – it was not an insubstantial fire.

"There's someone in there," said Angus.

I went at the flames with the hose in order to prevent them jumping to the next room while Angus grabbed 1 of the huge towels next to the pool and told me he was going in. He smashed the glass sliding door and, between us, we found a space for him to get into the room. Bits of the roof kept coming down inside and I realised that I didn't really care if the Guests emerged or not – I was terrified for Angus. I kept spraying like my life depended on it. After what felt like an age, I glimpsed him through the flames of the collapsed roof. He yelled and pointed,

"The bathroom window!"

By this stage Jacob had arrived – it was a real comfort to have the big man with me. I saw that Angus was not going to escape without help so

I pointed Jacob at the window just as his fire extinguisher ran out. He attacked the frame with the extinguisher and destroyed it just in time for the family of 4 and Angus to escape. There was a very funny moment during the escape when the mother of the family got stuck in the window frame – Jacob and I had to pull her out. She was very unimpressed but if we hadn't she'd have been burned by the collapsing ceiling and Angus would have been incinerated.

By this stage, a lot of staff had arrived on the scene, each 1 as gobsmacked as the next. The Guests were mercifully unharmed – they just coughed a lot. We led them back to the deck where I took it upon myself to calm them down with hot chocolate and cookies, while Angus calmed himself with more of the whisky I had brought out for our little Christmas toast.

Just as things were beginning to calm down, who should walk straight onto the deck but Arno! He was dressed in his old Defence Force uniform with a low peaked cap over his blackened face. He glared at me and at the Guests.

He was carrying a blazing stick, covered with a huge flaming cloth.

"I told you not to mess with me, you fokken little snitch," he yelled.

With that, he hurled the flaming stick at me. I ducked and it went past my head towards the couch on which the Guests were sitting. The Americans resumed their hysterics. Arno rushed at me and, before I could react, punched me hard in the face. I was stunned by the blow.

Angus then lost his temper like I have never seen before. He rushed at Arno. Our brother is not a large man but he hit Arno under the ribs with his shoulder, lifted him and then drove him hard into the wall behind us. I heard the wind being knocked out of the former Maintenance Manager. Arno tried to retaliate but the fury in Angus was too great. He set to Arno with his fists. I think all the frustration and sadness he has experienced this year came out in those furious blows. PJ stepped in between them when it became clear that Angus was not going to stop any time soon. Jenny pulled him gently away and managed to calm him down.

It was then that I realised the couch behind us was on fire. I tore a curtain off the rails and managed to smother the flames before they could spread. I received a nasty burn to my arm as a result, but it is not too bad now.

PJ tied Arno up with a curtain rope and he was locked in the Security Office for the night before being carted off to Hoedspruit by the police this morning.

The General Manager then did an amazing damage control job with the group leader. YMS, except for the woman who had had to be levered out of her room, were thankfully very understanding. The Christmas Eve dinner then proceeded without further incident and also proved a roaring success.

I have been granted an extra day's leave for my heroics, so Simone and I are coming down to Kenton tomorrow! We'll leave very early but the trip will take about 16 hours, so we'll see you in time for supper. I can't wait to get there and relax after the tension of the YMS group. I'm utterly exhausted.

Also looking forward to a good New Year's Eve thrash. For the first time ever, I actually feel sad that Angus is not going to be with us.

Lots of love and see you tomorrow!

Your heroic brother,

Hugh

From: 'Angus MacNaughton'
Sent: 25 December, 18h28
To: 'Julia MacNaughton'
Subject: Fire in the lodge and Christmas greetings

Dear Julia,

Happy Christmas, sister – I trust the mince pies are good this year and that Mum has refrained from putting onions in them again.

News from here...

The YMS group has finally buggered off ... but not without incident.

Your brothers were required to save the lodge and some of its guests last night. I'm not sure we are quite the heroes that SB seems to think we are, but we put on a damn good show.

It all started after game drive last night. I dropped off my deeply painful YMS guests after an arduous drive. SB was in the car park to greet his returning charges. They headed off to their rooms to dress for the Christmas festivities. I was about to leave to freshen myself up when SB suggested that we have a Christmas whisky and toast the family in Kenton. A year ago I would have told him I'd sooner have a drink with a putrid buffalo carcass, but feeling somewhat better disposed to him in recent times, I acquiesced and we headed down to the Tamboti deck. There were no staff around – they were all preparing the enormous dinner at Main Camp.

SB poured us generous measures of Laphroaig and we headed onto the deck overlooking the river. There, with the waning moon rising off to the east, we toasted you, Mum, Dad, The Major and, of course, Trubshaw. We supped on the marvellous elixir and chatted – surprisingly easily for the two of us – for about ten minutes. As our glasses drained, Efficient came hurtling down onto the deck, blethering,

'Nzilo! Nzilo! Nzilo!'

Of course, a security guard is supposed to be trained to deal with emergencies in a calm and professional manner. He is supposed to notify the relevant help and then make sure everyone is safe. Unsurprisingly for this madhouse, Efficient chose blind panic as his method of crisis management.

'Where?' I asked him.

'*Nzilo! Nzilo! Nzilo!*' he yelled again.

'Where, you idiot?' I shouted.

'*Nzilo! Nzilo! Nzilo!*'

I grabbed him by the shoulders and shook him. 'WHERE IS THE FIRE?' I shouted. The shaking brought him round.

'Numba siggis!' he said.

I shoved him out of the way as SB and I hurtled off the deck. Off to the east we could see there was a blaze coming from the roof of Room 6.

'I'll get the pump,' said SB. He ran for the tool shed and I sprinted for the room. When I arrived, the residents of Room 5 were emerging, drawn by the shouts, which were emanating from their neighbours' room. The reason the occupants of number 6 hadn't self-evacuated became quickly apparent – there was a huge flaming leadwood log blocking the door.

SB arrived and we hurried around the side of the room. SB put the pump in the pool and I started the engine. The glass sliding door at the front of the room was blocked by a flaming section of collapsed roof. Beyond this, I could see a family huddled in the corner – my snot-nosed friend from the airstrip, his sister and their parents. They were making no attempt to save themselves. In fact, Mrs Snot Nose was frantically packing up her jewellery.

SB yelled, 'The table – use the table to break the glass!' I grabbed the iron table next to the pool and flung it with all my strength at the sliding door. The thick glass shattered. Next, I took one of the pool towels, soaked it in the water and covered myself in it.

I just couldn't see a way in.

'There!' yelled SB as the water revealed a small gap in the burning timber and thatch. 'I'll spray you as you go!' I gritted my teeth and dived at the gap. I felt the hair on my legs and arms singe as I went through but I landed inside the room, mercifully not on fire. As I stood up, another piece of the roof collapsed, completely blocking the access I had just used.

'Into the bathroom!' I yelled at the four Americans. There was no door to the outside there but I figured we might all be able to escape out of the window before the whole roof collapsed.

'I'm not leavin' my stuff!' shouted Mrs Snot Nose, continuing to stuff handfuls of makeup and jewellery into her bag.

'Go, NOW!' I yelled at them. 'Take the boy!' I shoved Mrs Snot Nose towards the bathroom entrance, and picked up the daughter while Mr Snot Nose grabbed his other vile offspring. We made it through to the bathroom just as the rest of the roof over the bedroom gave way. The children were crying by this stage.

I looked out of the bathroom window above the loo. There were more people outside, including Jacob. SB was marshalling a second pump into place to aid our escape.

The smoke was becoming fairly unbearable inside. The window I planned to escape through was small – large enough for me but I doubted whether Mr and Mrs Snot Nose would make it through. It was a cottage pane with a wooden frame that had to be knocked out. I took the lid off the cistern and began beating at the criss-crossed window structure. I managed to break some of the latticework before my tool cracked in half. Jacob then set to it from the other side with an empty fire extinguisher and in a few seconds the window was obliterated.

I sent the kids out first and their father followed quickly, leaving me and his fat wife in the inferno (she was still clutching her jewellery bag).

'Out!' I said.

'I won't fit!' she bleated. I grabbed the bag from her and tossed it out of the window.

'Fetch!' I shouted. She lunged at the window. My initial estimation of her proportions turned out to be correct. She stepped up onto the loo seat and then sort of flopped into the open window – her midriff sticking fast, the fat rolls wedging her in.

She started bellowing like a distressed buffalo but there was no time to ask her if she was OK – I could see flames licking through the bathroom roof. Our only protection came from the ceiling above the loo, which wasn't going to last long. I stood up on the toilet and looked over the stricken hippo.

'We're going to have to pull her out!' I shouted. With that, SB handed his hose to a guest and grabbed Mrs Snot Nose's left arm. Jacob took her right. I returned to the floor to push. Jacob and SB started hauling and I lifted her huge, dimpled thighs and pushed. There was renewed bellowing. Eventually her great mass shifted, along with a brick in the wall, and she fell out. I followed, just as the ceiling in the loo collapsed.

'You hurt me!' she yelled as I landed next her prone figure.

'I'm so sorry,' I replied. 'I'll make sure to have the windows enlarged and gallons of lube on standby for the next muffin-topped, jewellery-crazed Yank who gets stuck in her toilet.'

At this point SB arrived to drag me away before I said something offensive.

The whole conservation team and a lot of the staff had arrived some time during the evacuation and the fire was extinguished before it could spread to the other rooms.

A few minutes later the guests, SB, PJ, Jenny and I were on the Tamboti deck. The guests had all been plied with warm (spiked) drinks to make them feel better. I was a bit shaken and drinking Laphroig liberally.

Then, from the darkness, the cause of the fire emerged ...

Arno van der Vyfer.

The idiot was dressed in camouflage fatigues and his face was covered in black polish. He was holding a huge, flaming torch.

He pointed a calloused and skinny finger at SB, uttered something threatening and flung the torch at him. SB ducked but the torch hit the sofa behind him – scattering the Snot Noses, who threw their drinks and screamed. Flames exploded from the cushions. Arno kept coming. He swung a fist at SB, who was distracted by his guests. It connected with his jaw and sent him reeling.

I saw red – more like crimson. It was the strangest sensation. I can't ever remember feeling angry *for* SB before. Without thinking, I launched at Arno. My attack was ended by PJ and Jenny a bit later and it took me a long time to calm down.

So, this Christmas Eve was not quite like the usual trudge off to Midnight Mass after a huge, delicious meal, but it was memorable nonetheless.

Well, Happy Christmas, Julia. I hope you, Mum and Dad are having a great time in Kenton. I'm sorry not to be there with you but SB is heading down tomorrow and I'm sure it will be nice to see him. I'll send a present for you with him.

Angus

A YEAR IN THE WILD

From: 'Hugh MacNaughton'
Sent: 31 December, 14h12
To: 'Angus'
Subject: Happy New Year and request

Hey Angus,

I trust your recent heroics will stand you in good stead for the New Year's Eve party at the Lodge this evening. Surely the women of Sasekile Private Game Reserve will not be able to resist the fire-fighting, Guest-rescuing, Arno-tackling hero called Angus? No doubt you will be beating them off like flies.

Prior to the end of this year, it would have given me great pleasure to have drafted you a letter, driving home the fact that while you were toiling away at the Lodge, I was sunning myself on the white sandy beaches of the Eastern Cape. It would have been only too wonderful to know that while you were rising before dawn, the hardest part of my day would be deciding on how many bitterly cold beers to enjoy with lunch. Ironically (and quite amazingly), that is not the case any more.

My first year in the wilds of Africa has been a transforming experience. I have learned, laughed and loved more than ever. I have gathered an insight into human nature I never thought possible and have found an industry in which all of my passions are ignited. I have formed relationships with people from entirely different backgrounds and met incredible human beings hailing from all corners of the globe. I have found a mentor in PJ, who I feel so privileged to have worked for. I even stumbled upon love for the woman I thought was out there, but never believed I would find. I truly have so much for which to be grateful.

With this in mind, it will probably come as no surprise to you that when PJ asked me to stay on for another year or so, I was only too happy to accept. The purpose of this email, however, is to ask that you do the same.

327

We have had our differences – of that there is no question – and for a long time I truly felt that our relationship was irreparable. As you've always said, "Some siblings are just never going to get along".

However, towards the latter part of our year together, I felt a change. Your intolerable anger with life, me, other human beings and the world in general seems to have softened somewhat and, although you are never going to be "Mr Bubbly", you have become a far more pleasant person to be around.

Believe it or not, Angus, I actually have a great deal of respect for you. I admire the way you are true to yourself and that you never try to be someone who you "ought" to be. Pessimistic? Yes. Sarcastic? Definitely. But also genuine, authentic and possibly misunderstood. After our year together I have come to the conclusion that I finally "get who you actually are".

I have had some pretty amazing experiences this year, but the prospect of a vaguely decent relationship with my brother has unquestionably been the most significant. It would be really fantastic if you would extend your stay at Sasekile for a few more months. I'm not asking for a lifetime commitment, just a few months to see how it goes.

At least think about it.

Happy New Year, Angus.

Your brother,

Hugh

P.S. Anton has left, so you can't use that as an excuse.

P.P.S. Melissa is shacked up with Jeff, so you can't use that either.

From: 'Angus MacNaughton'
Sent: 01 January, 19h28
To: 'Hugh MacNaughton'
Subject: Another Year in the Wild

Dear String Bean,

Thank you for your email.

Yes, it was quite a year – a real watershed for me and for you too. I didn't hold out much hope for our parents' plan but, against all odds, I think they will be pleased with how things have turned out.

It does come as something of a surprise to read that you have a great deal of respect for me. I always thought you saw me as an unpleasant blight on the MacNaughton landscape – although that may have been me projecting.

Through the course of the year, mainly during and after the short, magical time I had with Anna, I gradually came to see things differently. I reassessed my view of the world and myself. While I suppose I will always remain cynical and a little sarcastic, my views of life have indeed mellowed somewhat.

I suppose one of the most important realisations I came to during the last few months was that I have been unnecessarily harsh to you (and many others – although Melitha deserves it). I have not been fair to you or given you the credit you deserve. I looked back through our childhood and realised that, despite our conflict, I have watched your many successes in life with a certain element of brotherly pride – pride that someone was doing something for the family name and not just burning bridges at every turn. I have always been amazed at how positively you are able to see the world and I hope you will never lose your cheery outlook.

It is quite remarkable that we come from the same DNA.

I am extremely pleased that we have managed to forge some kind of a bond. After that fight in the boma, I thought my views of you had finally been vindicated. But then there was Anna – beautiful Anna. When she died, pieces of me started to change. I think things probably turned a corner on the night you and I had to fix the roof in the rain. What a laugh that was.

I have considered your request for me to stay on at Sasekile. It did not take me long to realise that I really enjoy the bush out here and, despite the fact that I dislike most guests, I would like to be here for a while longer. I spoke to Carrie and PJ last night and they actually looked quite pleased (Carrie slapped me on the back which knocked the wind out of me), so I will be here when you get back. PJ smiled in his knowing manner as if to say,

'We knew we'd get through to you eventually.'

On the subject of last night, we had a huge New Year's Eve thrash in the Main Camp boma. Some of the guests were up for a party but most went to bed before midnight. The staff, however, were in the mood for a big one after a heavy year. They dragged the remaining guests off to the Twin Palms.

Someone put on some really cool house tunes and the lights were turned down low. The atmosphere was marvellously relaxed and, as the countdown to the New Year began, I found myself standing next to Jenny – to be honest, I think we'd been looking for each other.

The whole place erupted as New Year struck. The champagne bottles popped and as 'Human' by the Killers started to pound from the stuffed old speakers, Jenny and I turned to face each other.

'Happy New Year, Angus,' she said, looking into my eyes and smiling. 'I hope it's a really good one for you.' I smiled back at her, put my arm round her slim waist and pulled her closer as the crowd was going mental all around us. I looked into her pretty brown eyes and then kissed her rather fetching mouth. Perhaps it was the hero status we gained last week or perhaps some genuine feeling but she responded immediately and we didn't let go of each other for a long time.

When I woke up this morning, I felt a pang of guilt for kissing Jenny – like I'd somehow betrayed Anna's memory and our time together. Then I realised how silly that is because the last thing Anna would want is for me to live my life in mourning. I still miss her so much sometimes.

I'm very jealous not to be in Kenton at the moment. It would be good to paddle across the river and play cricket on the island with you and Julia. Please send my love to everyone there. I hope Trubshaw has not pulled Dad into the sea too many times.

Thanks again for the sentiments expressed in your email. I appreciate them. I look forward to your return next week for the start of our next spell in the wild.

Your brother,

Angus

ACKNOWLEDGEMENTS

So many people have contributed to this book through my conversations and experiences with them over the last decade or so. Their companionship served to make my time in ecotourism inspirational enough for my ADD brain to complete this book. Special mention must go to Chris Roche, Elvis Kubayi, the late Johnson Mkansi, Mike and Jessica Fender, Yvonne Short, Ian Thomas, Cry Mkansi, Lucky Mkansi, Robert Sithole, Isaac Mkonto, the late David Rattray, Fanni Mathonsi and the Double Os of 2009.

The ultra-efficient team at Pan Macmillan has been incredible to me as they guided me through the process of creating something readable. I hope it rewards their faith. Thank you to Andrea Nattrass for her, without exception, excellent guidance. Thanks also to Wesley Thompson, Terry Morris, Tarryn Talbot, Laura Hammond, Kelly Ansara, Tracey Hawthorne, Sharon Dell, Manoj Sookai and Michiel Botha for their roles in producing the final book.

I am extremely grateful to all the patient people who read through various drafts of the book as it went from a simple idea to what it has become. Special thanks to Mum and Dad Hendry, Ian and Karin.

Thanks to my sister, Kathryn, who put a woman's touch to Julia's letters in the midst of trying to write her final exams.

To my brother, Douglas, for the unstinting faith he has shown in his older and somewhat less stable brother.

Special thanks to my long-standing business partner and friend, Alex, who has put up with a lot of nonsense over the course of this project's completion. For his patience and compassion I am very grateful.

Most importantly, many of the ideas in this book came from a great friend of mine. We spent many evenings under the starry skies of the Lowveld sipping fine malt whisky and rare bottles of wine while laughing about the ideas in the pages that follow. Without his input *A Year in the Wild* would not have been remotely possible. For his help I am profoundly grateful and his influence in this story should not be underestimated.

9 781770 108271